BOOK 3
THE HUNTRESS

A NOVEL BY
RINA S. MAMOON

ISBN: 978-1-7771315-1-7

Author Website: rinasmamoon.ca

Acknowledgements

Thank you, Michael, Mom and Dad, for your love and support. I also express my gratitude to other relatives and friends for taking an interest in my book series.

And thank you, dear reader, for taking the time to read *The Huntress*. I hope you enjoyed reading it as much as I enjoyed writing it.

Table of Contents

Chapter One

The Week After

It was a cold morning as Mara Ashwood wandered across a snowy field. She held a funeral urn close to her chest. Her tattered black cape fluttered in the frigid air. Mara never liked the cold, but she kept going until she spotted a mound. A fresh layer of snow almost hid the grave.

"Hi Allen," Mara began. She reached for her mask and pulled it down. Despite her human appearance, she kept the habit of hiding her face. Her light brown eyes drifted to the right, where the ruins of Golden Mountain stood.

Today was the second of January, 1000ED, the one-week anniversary of the deadly incident. Mara switched her attention back onto the grave. She glanced down at the funeral urn in her hands.

"James is here with me," Mara spoke, cradling the urn close to her bosom. She closed her eyes. "I'm sorry I couldn't save him."

She could still see James' face twisted in pain as Commander White took his life. "His body was taken to the hospital. The doctors had already burned it. At least they were kind enough to let me bury his remains."

After placing the urn on the ground, Mara crouched down and pulled the earth away using her hands. She kept going until Allen's remains became visible. Mara carefully placed the funeral urn beside the box, reuniting the two brothers. A bell tolled while she refilled the grave. The City of Mirahyll was mourning the guardsmen who lost their lives last week. Upon finishing, Mara heard the galloping of horses.

She rose to her feet and looked back. A wooden carriage pulled by two brown horses drew closer. Within ten feet, the carriage stopped. Three guardsmen poured out. The fourth was a woman with pale skin and short black hair. Her greyish-blue coat decorated in silver plating was familiar. The female guardsman faced Mara with steel green eyes.

"Mara Ashwood, I presume," the female guardsman spoke, holding her hands behind her back.

"Yes," Mara answered. "Is there a problem?"

"Chancellor Davis requests your presence."

Mara tilted her head to the right. "For a monster contract?"

"It's nothing like that. Both chancellors are meeting in Mirahyll to discuss the Faith."

"Oh, yeah," Mara murmured. "The referendum was cast a few days ago."

"Correct," the woman said. "I'm sure you are pleased with the results."

Mara furrowed her eyebrows. "And you're not?"

The black-haired woman shook her head. "Don't get me wrong—I'm just as relieved to see them gone." Then, "Allow me to introduce myself." She held out her hand. "My name is Beatrice, Captain of the Guardsmen. We've met before."

Mara studied her face. "You led the attack on the Temple of Kallisto. If not for the Guardsmen, Mr. White and I wouldn't be here." She shook the captain's hand. "My name's Mara Ashwood, the Huntress."

"I know who you are," Beatrice said flatly, "and I know what you are."

Mara paused. "You know I'm not human?"

"I know about the undying. I was a Silver Thorn before Master Harold dismantled the guild." Then she asked, "Do you remember that day?"

"Commander White invited the men to join the Holy Blades," Mara replied. "Were you one of the women he insulted?"

"Jen and I. Not that it matters anymore…"

Mara grew silent as a grim look decorated her face.

Beatrice kept watching her. "To think a woman bested Commander White."

"It wasn't my proudest moment," Mara grumbled.

"The right choice is never easy." Beatrice glanced back at the carriage. "We should return to the city. The chancellors are waiting for us."

"Do I have to?" Mara questioned. "The referendum had passed. The people have spoken."

"I insist." The captain gestured to the coach. "There is plenty to discuss."

Mara wondered what was going on. She gazed at the grave and sighed. Then she accompanied the guardsmen. Once everyone was inside, the transport began to move. Mara suspected this would be a very long day.

* * *

Mara sat beside Beatrice during the ride. The other three guardsmen were across from them. The huntress gazed down at Nightingale, which rested on her lap.

"Those who fled to Corlin have returned," Beatrice began.

"You mean those who conspired to awaken the Dark One?" Mara questioned.

"We don't know how many were involved, but they remain a problem."

"How?"

"They claim their religion is under attack due to the referendum."

Mara raised an eyebrow. "Yet they worship false gods."

Beatrice sighed, "Very few witnesses remain."

"Meaning Mr. White and me?" Mara inquired.

The captain nodded. "Those in a coma died as if they had lost the will to live. And Kallikratés remains prevalent in Corlin and Loris."

Mara gazed out the window. "How many returned?"

"Six hundred in the last four days. They tried to flood the ballots in favour of the Faith. But the people have spoken."

Mara gave a wry smile underneath her mask. "As it should."

The captain kept her arms folded while looking out the window on her side. "They'll fight to keep Kallikratés here, and they have the support of Corlin and Loris."

"I thought Corlin wanted nothing to do with Ardana," Mara said.

"The events of last week has drawn their attention. And they're likely aware of Ardana seeking an alliance with Thoron."

"An envoy was sent?" Mara asked.

"Yes, after repairing Har' Yhan's port. We'll find out in a few weeks if Thoron accepts."

"Could've sent me." Mara planned on travelling to Thoron because the eastern land possessed the one thing that could lift her curse. And she had something they wanted—the soul of Aazalith.

* * *

Despite the solemn occasion, there was the odd ruckus upon the snowy streets of Mirahyll. While entering the city, Mara spotted a group of nobles being harassed by those from the lower-class.

"Away! Away!" A lower-class man threw rotten food at the nobles.

The upper-class cried out in distress as they took cover.

Another lower-class man shouted, "We don't want your kind here!"

Beatrice could have stepped out and stopped this, yet she did not budge, nor did she order the guardsmen to intervene. "Such squabbles are the norm, considering these people abandoned everyone else to die."

"Thought the guardsmen bring law and order?" Mara asked.

"We've much more to focus on, such as dealing with the Blackthorns." Beatrice gazed at Mara. "I heard you've done a number on them."

"I did. But what about Theo?"

"He can't hide forever." The captain looked out the window. "We're almost here."

Gazing out the window, Mara saw two people mugging a noblewoman. The thieves had their faces covered with cloths. The middle-aged woman cried for help, but no one came. The two boors fled with her jewellery and coin purse. The incident made Mara think of Mr. White, hoping he was okay.

Once the carriage stopped, Beatrice opened the door. "We're here."

The captain was the first to leave, followed by Mara and the guardsmen. As Mara followed Beatrice to the Council Hall, she noticed a familiar old blacksmith. The burly man owned long grey hair, which was tied back. A stringy beard descended to his upper chest while a thick moustache adorned his wrinkled face. He wore a thick cloak over his attire, though she could see the apron he always wore.

"Talon," Mara called. "What are you doing here?"

The blacksmith saw her and waved. "Ah, fancy meeting you here," Talon greeted gruffly. He glanced at Beatrice. "And with the Captain of the Guardsmen."

Beatrice held her hands behind her back. "Hello, Talon."

"Greetings to you as well." He returned his attention to Mara. "I see my services helped you survive."

"True," Mara said, "or I wouldn't be standing here."

The blacksmith's dark eyes fell onto her sword. "How's the beauty?"

Mara unsheathed the sabre from its black and gold sheath, revealing the dark gold and silver blade. "Nightingale has been through a lot, but seems okay."

Talon studied the sword. "Hmm, the pommel looks a little warped."

"Is it?" Mara took a closer look. She never noticed the flaw, but Talon was right. Aazalith's essence took a toll on her sword, yet it was the only known flaw.

"At least I can fix it," Talon said. "Come by my workshop later."

Mara changed the topic while sheathing Nightingale. "Did you find Dad's diagrams useful?"

"Been through half the book. If Bear were alive, he would've been the only one worthy of being a master blacksmith."

"Speaking of which, I hope you took the offer," Beatrice addressed him.

Talon frowned at the captain and folded his arms. He grew silent.

Beatrice took notice and sighed, "Talon..."

Mara switched her gaze from the blacksmith to the captain. "What's going on?"

"The chancellor promised to name me a master blacksmith, if I return," Talon revealed.

"You belong here," Beatrice said. "We need you."

"Do you?" Talon questioned. "The city did nothing when those damned Holy Blades destroyed my last workshop. What's worse? You went back to that crook!"

Beatrice frowned at him. Mara figured Talon remained sour, although she was surprised to see him here. Talon avoided Mirahyll like the plague since losing his last forge. Now Davis wanted him back because there was no one else in Ardana to forge weapons.

"They haven't found Edwin yet?" Mara asked.

Talon and Beatrice shook their heads in unison.

"No one has found the weasel yet," Talon replied, looking at Beatrice.

The captain held her ground. "If sighted, he'll be arrested without question."

The old blacksmith gazed at Beatrice. "Very well. Find him, and I may change my mind."

"You have my word," the captain reassured.

Talon nodded, then left the Council Hall. Beatrice remained still for a moment. As soon as the tension lifted, she moved forward while Mara followed.

"Talon is passionate about his craft," Beatrice said. "He's the only blacksmith who gives a damn."

"Why didn't you help him?" Mara asked.

"We couldn't." Beatrice stopped and looked at her sharply. "Keep this between us," she said quietly. "Davis was a puppet whose strings were pulled by Commander White."

"And Kallisto controlled the commander," Mara added.

The captain sighed, "We had no power until Kallikratés fell."

Mara knew all along. Lady Isabella, the former ruler of Hema, had said similar things about Davis.

"The chancellor finally stood up to the Faith," Mara said.

"He did." Beatrice turned around. "Come, they're waiting for us."

The captain escorted Mara into the chancellor's office.

Walking through the doors, Mara saw a large crowd gathered before her. She recognized Davis, Evan, and some of the aldermen. Davis looked less stressful, having fewer wrinkles on his face. The dark circles underneath his eyes had nearly faded. Fewer grey strands sat in his hair and his beard. He wore a clean black suit.

Very little had changed with Evan, though he seemed to have more colour than before. The young dark-haired man's attire consisted of a black suit with some golden trimmings.

Mara gazed at the aldermen, recognizing Nigel of Ozin and Jonathan of Har'Yhan. Nigel had been scowling at her since she entered the office. Mara figured the older man remained sour over Ozin's destruction, but the circumstances were out of hand. She turned her gaze onto another middle-aged man and recognized his dark skin and long greying hair. Elder Ravenclaw was also present. What was he doing here?

Several people in fancy attire also attended the meeting. They were nobles and members of the Faith. Many of them watched Mara with apprehension.

"The slayer of gods," a male follower called her.

Several guardsmen were at the scene to keep the peace.

Davis rose to his feet and gazed at Mara. "Greetings, Miss Ashwood."

"Likewise, Chancellor Davis." Mara looked at Evan. "And Interim Chancellor Evan as well."

The interim chancellor rose to his feet and gave a bow. Accompanying him were four knights. The huntress returned a similar gesture before switching her attention to Ravenclaw.

"I didn't expect to see you here," Mara addressed the elder.

"The Stone Mages shall become citizens," Davis explained, "as part of our integration and reconciliation pact. They'll be relocated to Haranta Village, to have better access to services. Elder Ravenclaw shall be its alderman."

Kallikratés' followers grumbled to each other.

"Savages in Ardana?"

"Unthinkable!"

Mara wasn't surprised by their racism. For many years, the followers had thought the Stone Mages as savages and heathens. She also recalled that the Faith had pushed them to the Outer Frontier. To her, it was another reason to banish Kallikratés.

"Great idea," she said, "considering they helped save this land."

Ravenclaw smiled in response.

Ozin's alderman stormed over to them. "What about Ozin Village?"

Everyone looked at him.

"We haven't forgotten the people of Ozin," Davis addressed him. "Once the area is declared safe, we'll start rebuilding."

"With all due respect, that could take months!" Nigel glared at Mara and Ravenclaw. "Since the Stone Mages have Andel, Haranta should be ours!"

"The Stone Mages deserve Haranta Village," Mara said flatly. "Your people are fine where they are."

Davis nodded. "Mirahyll has plenty of amenities to accommodate the displaced villagers."

Ignoring the chancellor, Nigel glared at Mara through his round glasses. "How dare you?" He pointed at her. "You caused Ozin's destruction!"

"I saved your people!" Mara argued. "You executed me for a crime I didn't commit! And I slew the White Lady for you!"

Everyone gawked at her, and then Ozin's alderman.

"What?" Jonathan questioned. "This is the same woman who saved Har' Yhan from the Siren. And if not for her, the town would've been destroyed by the Dark One!"

"She also saved my people from the wendigo," Ravenclaw added.

Har' Yhan's alderman folded his arms. "What about Cerebell?"

Mara pondered Jonathan's words. "It's possible." She gazed at Ravenclaw. "Cerebell might be more accommodating, and migration would be easier."

"What about the darkling sealed within the Black Tower?" Davis questioned.

"Anna is dead," Mara answered. "I had to save Commander White after he tampered with the seal."

The disciples appeared unhappy with her comments about the late commander.

"So, the city is safe?" Davis asked.

"Yes," Mara replied.

The elder rubbed his chin. "I see," he said calmly. Ravenclaw gazed at Nigel. "Very well, we shall take Cerebell. The people of Ozin can have Haranta Village."

Nigel gawked at Ravenclaw. He should have been thrilled about obtaining Haranta, but he looked unsatisfied. Mara wondered what was going through his head. Glancing at Ravenclaw, she saw how composed and calm he was in comparison. Stone Mages were supposed to be savages and heretics, as well as being uneducated and inferior. However, Ravenclaw's presence seemed to shatter some of their views.

Davis gazed at Nigel. "Is this okay with you?"

Ozin's alderman snapped out of it, then broke eye contact with Ravenclaw.

"Yes, it's fine," Nigel replied. The frown remained on his face as he returned to his seat.

Davis cleared his throat. "Onto the next item—the complete dismantling of Kallikratés."

Most of the followers shot up to their feet.

"This is an attack on religion!" shouted one of them.

Mara rolled her eyes. "The Faith cared only for power. Everyone knows this."

The followers glared at her, but she didn't care.

Beatrice stepped forward. "We obtained a confession from Vernon. There was no prophecy of the Cursed Herald. Kallikratés plotted to awaken the Dark One, due to their waning status in Ardana."

Some gasped as others murmured. Some of the followers, however, were unmoved by the claims.

"These are lies," said a nobleman. "Lies spread by the Cursed Herald!"

Mara remained silent, yet her anger began to build. These people worshipped one of her murderers.

"Miss Ashwood," Evan addressed her.

Mara snapped out of her thoughts and gazed back at him. "Yes?"

"If Kallikratés conspired to break the seven seals, then Lady Isabella…"

Mara frowned. "Commander White used me to kill her, just like he did to Heru."

Evan took a deep breath. "I see," he said. "Thank you for being honest. I wish things could've been different as well, but at least we can move forward." He picked up a document to show everyone. "This is the treaty between the Faith of Kallikratés and the Kingdom of Hema. Lady Isabella opposed this document, believing it would oppress her people once again." He furrowed his eyebrows. "Thanks to the truth shared by Miss Ashwood, I've reached a solution."

He tore the treaty in half. The disciples looked horrified.

One of them shouted, "You can't do that!"

"I already have," Evan replied coldly. "All projects Kallikratés had requested to my office will be cancelled." He closed his eyes. "I'm sure Lady Isabella's spirit is resting easier now."

Davis nodded approvingly. "I will also follow suit." He looked at the worshippers. "However, I'll give a few weeks, as I'm sure it will take a while to make the transition. The Grand Cathedral and other facilities will remain open until the end of the month."

"Wait till the Goddess finds out!" shouted a male disciple. "Kallisto will strike you all down!"

Mara gave a deadpanned look. "Kallisto is in no condition to be smiting anyone." The followers gazed at her in bewilderment. She noted their facial expressions. "Oh, I guess you didn't know…"

Some of the followers gasped in distress.

"The Cursed Herald slew the Goddess and Commander White?" one of them asked.

"Yes, I killed Commander White." Mara paused. "Kallisto was unable to contain Aazalith's soul, and caused a magical explosion which destroyed her and brought down the mountain."

The huntress looked at Nigel, who was gaping at her. Mara looked away, feeling elated. This day had finally arrived.

"Then we shall conclude this meeting," Davis announced. "I look forward to seeing what this new year will bring."

"Same here," Mara replied as she headed for the exit.

While leaving, the huntress heard the grumblings from some of the followers.

"Unthinkable! Kallikratés has fallen in Ardana!"

"We're certainly entering a darker age!"

"It was a mistake coming back."

"This land was better off destroyed!"

Mara was disgusted by their attitude. If they knew what happened, why return? Many of these nobles likely had a property in Corlin. They could have stayed in the neighbouring nation, and none would miss them. Even the Whites owned property in Corlin.

It was time to head home. It was getting dark as Mara left the Council Hall.

* * *

Mara spotted the middle-aged woman from earlier. She remained paralyzed, appearing very distraught from the mugging. No guardsmen were present to assist her. Mara grew concerned, so she decided to help her. It seemed like the right thing to do.

"Excuse me," Mara began. "Are you okay?"

She offered her hand to the noblewoman. The woman glanced at her. All of a sudden, she smacked Mara's hand away.

"Get away from me!"

Mara yanked her hand back, stunned by the cold response. Her eyes drifted to the woman's face, now twisted in rage. It reminded Mara of Kallisto after being reduced to an old crone.

The woman continued to rage. "Our land is ruined! It's all your fault!"

Mara remained astonished, and then a range of emotions washed over her. Sadness and anger were the most prevalent. She frowned at the older woman, then walked away.

'What a bitch!'

Mara froze, shocked by the words that surfaced in her mind. The undying was not entirely wrong feeling this way. Mara was better off not helping her, for kindness did not always reward those willing to offer a helping hand.

Mara sauntered off, ignoring any other words the noblewoman had to say.

Chapter Two

Lady of the Manor

The White Manor had been Mara's home for the past week. The large and luxurious-looking mansion had several rooms and could house an extended family with ease. Before ascending the steps, Mara spotted an unfamiliar carriage. Someone was visiting. As she took a few more steps, the door opened as if anticipating her arrival. On the other side was a man in his forties. He owned a head of black hair with some grey. His skin was pale with some wrinkles. Mara recognized him as the butler by the black suit he wore.

"Good evening, Miss Ashwood," the butler greeted, watching Mara with dark green eyes. "I trust you had a good day?"

"Hello André," Mara responded, stopping before the butler. "I did, though it was long."

"I see." He gestured to the space behind him. "Please, come inside," he beckoned. "This is your home."

Mara entered the manor. As soon as she got inside, she looked back at him. "I saw a carriage in front. Is someone visiting?"

"Mr. White has invited the barrister to change his will."

Mara knew about the inheritance. She looked to the living room. "I'll go see them."

"Of course, Miss Ashwood," André said, "but perhaps you should look a little more presentable for guests."

Mara glanced down at her black Silver Thorn armour before lifting her gaze to him. "What's wrong with this?"

"Miss Ashwood, you are to become the Lady of the Manor."

Mara raised an eyebrow. "But I'm not human."

"I'm aware." Then he said, "Mr. White will do everything in his power to aid you."

"I don't need his money," Mara argued. "He could've given me a small amount, enough to hire a ship to Thoron. I'll figure out how to get back."

"Very well, but what about the rest of your human life?"

"I'll probably remain a hunter. That's what Dad trained me to do."

"I see. I cannot tell you what to do, but please consider this—Mr. White has given you a grand opportunity. And the life of a hunter is often short, especially as a human."

Mara took a deep breath. "I will."

"Good." André headed upstairs. "Please follow me. We shall have you prepared for the evening."

"Lead the way," Mara responded.

The butler led her into a hallway with three doors. The door on the left went to her room. The room was a massive improvement over the spare bedroom Allen and James had once prepared for her. The large bed was adorned with soft sheets, while the mahogany frame had an elegant design. The dressers shared a similar design and colour. They were all filled with a variety of clothing. Also present in the room was a large matching wardrobe. Despite having better accommodations, it was the smallest room on this floor.

André approached the wardrobe and opened its doors. "This shall do," he said, grabbing the first thing he saw. "First, we shall have you cleaned up."

Two maids entered the room.

André glanced at them. "Prepare a bath for Miss Ashwood."

The maids nodded.

"This way," one of them beckoned.

Mara followed them to the washing area. The maids ran a hot bath while the huntress undressed. After Mara removed her hood and mask, she undid the messy braid that fell past her shoulder blades. Then she began to remove the layers of her black Silver Thorn armour. Mara undid the open-bust corset, which held much of her attire together. She took off her gloves and boots before the matching shirt and pants. Once naked, she noticed the maids gawking at her. They took in every detail of her features, including the faded blots on her tanned skin and the scar on her lower abdomen. Gazing at Mara's face, they saw her doll-like eyes and full lips. Her nose was not as pronounced as a Stone Mage's because it was something inherited from Mom. The maids kept staring at her like she was some animal at a zoo. Mara heard of such places in Corlin, where living animals were locked in cages. Many people visited them for entertainment. It sounded interesting, for none of these places existed in Ardana.

Upon entering the bathtub, the warm water took the chill out of Mara's body. But there was one thing preventing this moment from being perfect or relaxing. The maids remained in the room, staring at her while holding some towels.

Mara frowned at them. "You can go."

The two maids exchanged glances.

"Just leave the stuff here," Mara said.

The maids looked uncertain as they lowered the towels and left her alone. Once they were gone, she proceeded to clean herself.

After cleaning herself, Mara rose out of the bathtub. She grabbed a towel and dried herself. A brush was also present, which she used to comb her dark hair. Returning to her room, Mara discovered the black and white bustle dress on the bed. Her black Silver Thorn armour was missing. The maids probably took it away to be cleaned, or at least Mara hoped. She grew very fond of the attire, for it fitted well and was comfortable. The huntress sighed and got dressed.

* * *

Mara emerged from her room wearing the bustle dress. A braid of dark brown hair sat over her left shoulder. Before heading downstairs, Mara's eyes fell onto the closed door before her.

"Miss Ashwood."

Mara snapped her gaze onto André, who stood before her.

The butler studied her appearance. "I see you are ready, though I can tell you did these things by yourself."

"Is that a problem?" Mara asked.

"You could have asked the maids for assistance," André explained. "That is what they are here for."

"You mean they're supposed to be there when I bathe or put on my clothes?"

"Yes, Miss Ashwood," he answered. "I heard you sent them away."

"I didn't exactly feel comfortable with them gawking at me."

"My apologies, but it is rare to serve someone such as you, who will become the new heir." The butler gazed at the closed door before them. "Master White was the original heir, and Lord of the Manor."

Mara gave a solemn look. "Sorry for what happened to him."

André changed the topic. "I shall see to dinner. You may join Mr. White in the living room."

The butler left Mara to her own devices.

Mara headed to the living room. The first thing she always saw upon entering was the large portrait of the former lord, hanging above the fireplace. His green eyes watched all who entered the living room. He was adorned in his commander's garb, looking dignified. Despite everything, Commander White remained with them in some form.

"Ah, there you are," called an elderly man.

Mara broke her gaze with the portrait and spotted Mr. White sitting in his favourite chair. He looked better compared to last week, though the rapid ageing took its toll. His pure white hair, bushy beard, and moustache hid much of his wrinkles away. His blue eyes seemed brighter than usual, and he appeared to be in higher spirits. The short and round man wore a clean dark suit. Mara also noticed another man beside him and assumed he was the barrister Mr. White had invited. The barrister appeared to be at least sixty years old with semi-long greying hair. He was a little plump with pale skin. Like Mr. White, he also wore a black suit. Thick glasses adorned his face. The barrister gazed at her with a questioning glint in his eyes.

"I see André has found some proper clothes for you," Mr. White said in a cheerful tone.

Mara looked down at her dress. "Not exactly used to dresses, but I guess it'll take a while."

Mr. White glanced to the barrister. "I've added the final changes to my will."

The barrister frowned. "Are you sure you want this?"

Mr. White gave a stern look. "Yes, I intend to make her the heir."

"I see," the barrister said. "In addition to the changing of heirs, all funeral expenses will be paid by the estate." He took the will and handed it over to Mr. White. He also offered a quill filled with ink. "Sign here."

Mr. White took the quill and signed on the dotted line. Then he handed the papers over to the barrister, who inspected everything.

"Everything is in order." The barrister took a copy for himself, then gazed at Mara. "To begin the process of inheritance, I must be notified of his passing."

"André will assist you," Mr. White added.

The barrister walked past Mara and left the manor. The two were now free to talk.

"How was your day?" Mr. White inquired. "I don't think I heard you come in."

"I arrived a while ago." Mara gestured to her dress. "André insisted I clean myself up."

He gave a small smile. "So, he's teaching you everything you need to know?"

"You mean how to be civilized?" Mara questioned dryly.

"André doesn't mean to offend. He wishes to help in any way, and to the best of his abilities." Then, "So, how was your day? It took you a long time to bury James."

"Davis requested my presence for a meeting," Mara explained, "though I don't know why. I'm not one for politics."

"Your actions have changed the fate of this land. Ardana is free from Kallisto's control."

"I guess you're right." Mara held her hands over her lap. "It was quite a spectacle. Evan ripped up the treaty, and Davis declared Kallikratés banished from Terra. The followers weren't pleased."

"It's no surprise," he said. "They're only upset because they lost."

"They'd rather see this land destroyed."

Mr. White grew silent for a moment. "They likely remain poisoned by the magic. Hopefully, it will fade. But there's one thing I do regret..." Mr. White gazed up at the portrait. "Karl," he murmured.

Mara also looked up at the painting. Her eyes remained locked with the cold gaze of the commander. "Do you have any regrets?"

"Had I done more for Karl, he would still be here."

André arrived before the two.

"We shall be serving dinner soon," said the butler.

Mr. White rose from his chair. "Good, I'm hungry."

Mara watched as he hobbled past her. His walking seemed worse. She remained curious about the effects of removing the spell. Instead of being in his sixties, Mr. White now appeared to be either in his late eighties or nineties. Yet, he remained happy.

* * *

They arrived at a grand long table with several candles sitting on top. Flames flickered and danced, offering the only source of light. Mara sat at one end while Mr. White sat opposite of her. The servants arrived with dinner. Cooked slices of beef and vegetables were on the menu tonight. One of the servants placed a plate before Mara. The meal looked very delicious. Then she noticed the array of knives and forks. There were at least three different forks and two knives. One appeared to be a butter knife while the other had a serrated edge.

André poured her a glass of red wine. He was also watching to make sure she used the right utensils. Before deciding what to use, Mara took the napkin and placed it on her lap. The undying remembered to do this, thanks to the friendly lecture yesterday. The butler remained silent, indicating that she did the correct thing. Then she reached for the knife with the serrated edge. André stayed silent. Mara turned her gaze onto the forks. The small one was for desserts, or at least she was told. That left the other two. Mara reached for the middle one, only to hear the butler clearing his throat. It was the wrong choice! She immediately grabbed the larger one on the outside. The butler went silent.

After serving her wine, André supervised her etiquette to make sure she made no mistakes. He then moved towards Mr. White to pour his glass. Another servant arrived with Mr. White's meal. She was a young woman with tanned skin, dark hair and brown eyes. Seeing her reminded Mara of the many tales about Karl and how he ran the manor.

"What is the matter?" Mr. White asked.

Mara looked back at him, realizing that he was watching her. "Oh, it's just... You once mentioned hiring a servant before, but Karl fired her. I thought she was..."

"Lea from Loris," Mr. White said. "I believe she returned to her homeland."

"Oh," Mara murmured, gazing down at her plate. "I would've rehired her."

"So would I," Mr. White added. "She was hard-working and kind. She reminded me of you."

"Is that why Karl fired her? Or was it because of her skin colour?"

The older man gazed at his plate. "I believe it was the former. He thought I was trying to make him feel guilty."

"I see," Mara responded.

"Is there something else on your mind?" Mr. White asked.

Mara lifted her gaze to him. "I was thinking about your meeting with the barrister."

He frowned at her. "If this is about the inheritance, I'm not changing my mind."

"I know. But you made it sound like you weren't going to live for much longer."

Mr. White gave a sympathetic look. "I'm not going to live forever."

"Please, be honest," Mara pleaded. "Have things grown worse?"

"I think this was all expected for betraying Kallisto," he replied. "I'll admit growing old is not fun."

"Neither is immortality. What good is outliving all your loved ones and ending up alone?"

"We'll find a solution," Mr. White assured her. "Everything will be fine."

"I hope so." With her knife and fork, Mara sliced into her meal. Taking a bite, she found dinner to be delicious.

* * *

After a very long day, Mara sauntered up the stairs. Before entering her room, she glanced at the closed door behind her. She sensed someone was on the other side. Mara kept staring at the door, then moved towards it. No one should be in the room, but she wanted to make sure. Mara lifted her right hand and reached for the doorknob.

"Miss Ashwood," called the butler.

Mara snatched her hand away and gawked at André, who stood before her. How long was he standing there?

"Yes? What is it?" Mara asked.

"Your nightwear has been laid out for you."

Mara began to relax. "Oh, thank you."

André nodded, then disappeared around the corner. Mara took a deep breath before looking at the closed door. Her curiosity faded away, but there would be other opportunities. And hopefully without the prying eyes of others.

Upon retiring to her room, Mara spotted the silk gown on the bed. The undying took off the bustle dress, then slipped into her nightwear. Never wearing thin silk before, she was unsure if she liked it. It felt like she was wearing nothing. It clung to her body, hugging every curve. Lace straps decorated her shoulders while the silk gown covered everything to just above the knees.

Mara climbed onto the large bed. She would find no problem falling asleep with soft sheets and pillows. Mara pulled the sheets over her body and fell asleep.

* * *

Mara woke up in the middle of the night. Unable to go back to sleep, she rose out of bed. Mara gazed at the door and approached it. She entered the dark hallway. Everyone else remained asleep.

Her eyes fell onto the door on the opposite side. Mara exited her room and took a few steps closer to the door.

She opened the door to reveal a large bedroom with fancy furniture and a king-sized bed. Included was a study area with a desk and three book-shelves filled with literature. Mara stood at the doorway, unsure about entering the room. Then her eyes fell onto a headless mannequin donning the commander's garb. It stood near the bed. Mara reckoned Karl kept an extra just in case. It looked identical to the one he always wore.

Mara approached the mannequin to get a closer look. Lifting her right hand, she placed it on the chest. The material for the dark grey long coat felt like leather, yet it was softer. Every part of the commander's garb looked very expensive. The plates on the left shoulder, arm, and knees looked like real gold. Even the pendant that was part of the neck guard had a ruby in it. The only thing missing was his sword, the Hand of Kratés. Gazing back at the dark grey coat, Mara found a red spot on the chest, which was never there before. It began to spread, slowly turning the coat red. It was blood. The chest rose up and down, making her realize that it was moving. Mara lifted her gaze and saw pale green eyes staring back at her. Karl stood before her! His skin was ghostly pale while his brown hair was darker.

Mara was speechless. The commander remained silent while watching her with lifeless eyes upon his frozen face. She backed away, but he took a step towards her. Spinning around, Mara dashed out of the room and slammed the door shut.

Chapter Three

New Beginnings

Mara's eyes flew open as she gasped in fright. She shot up to a seated position and found herself back in her room. The morning sun crept through the drawn curtains. Mara remained in her bed, trying to understand what she witnessed last night.

A gentle knock on the door drew her attention.

"Miss Ashwood?" André called from the other side.

Mara gazed at the door. "Yes? What is it?"

The door opened, revealing the butler and some maids. They entered the room.

"Good, you're awake," André said. "It seems you are adapting to life in the manor."

One of the maids approached the wardrobe and opened it. Two others began to clean the room, even though Mara had yet to get out of bed. She eventually got up, and a maid helped remove her nightwear.

Another presented her with a white blouse and a long skirt. "Will this be fine, miss?"

Mara nodded. "It's fine."

The maid also provided her with a brassiere and fresh underwear. Mara took them and got dressed. Even though she preferred trousers, Mara had no desire to receive another lecture from André about female etiquette. At least the attire was lighter compared to the bustle dress from last night.

"I shall oversee the meals," the butler said, then he gazed at the maids. "Once you finish with Miss Ashwood, please assist Mr. White." He returned his attention to Mara. "I thought it would be easier to address you first. Getting Mr. White out of bed has proven to be more difficult than before."

"Figured as much," Mara said, knowing the consequences of removing the spell.

"We can handle him for now, but I suggest we get someone who is best suited to handle a person of his age."

With that, André left the room.

Mara was almost ready, so she allowed the maids to assist Mr. White. She was buttoning her blouse when a terrified shriek emitted from the end of the hallway. Mara responded by dashing out the door. She saw the other servants and André rushing into the room at the end of the hall. A sense of dread washed over Mara as she followed them. At least ten people were obstructing the doorway. She sifted through the crowd to get inside. Mr. White looked like he was sleeping, but his chest was not rising or falling. Mara watched him as she drew closer.

André saw this. "Miss Ashwood," he addressed her.

Ignoring the butler, Mara began to inspect the body. She reached over with her left hand and rested two fingers under the ear. His pulse was absent, and he was as cold as ice. Mara heard the maid crying while gazing at his lifeless face. Everyone knew this day would come, but none had expected him to go last night. It was unfortunate the day had to begin like this. Mara then noticed a black mark on the chest. It looked like a bruise. She was unaware of such a mark, nor did Mr. White ever bring it up. She reached over and pulled at the sheets and his shirt. Mara's eyes widened upon seeing blackened veins.

"Miss Ashwood," André addressed her again.

Mara snapped her gaze onto the butler. Everyone watched her as she focused on André.

"I shall notify the barrister, as well as contact the funeral home to retrieve the body," the butler spoke.

Mara nodded. "Yes, go do that."

After André left, Mara glanced at the maid who discovered the body.

"Let her rest for a while," she ordered. "She can use my room."

The maids obeyed and helped the poor woman to her feet. While everyone left the room, Mara looked back at Mr. White's body. Despite feeling sad for the former college professor's passing, she could not help but feel something was amiss.

* * *

The unfortunate discovery had ruined Mara's morning. The servants had prepared a plate full of scrambled eggs, golden toast, fruit and cheese. Everything was fresh and made to perfection. Even though Mara had little appetite, she forced herself to eat.

After finishing, she wandered into the living room. The morning light filled the room, yet it remained gloomy. Mara gazed at Mr. White's chair. It would not be the same without him. Then her eyes drifted up to the portrait of Commander White. Seeing his visage reminded her of the nightmare. Mara sighed as she gazed out the window, doing her best to ignore the commander's glare.

She waited until André returned. When he finally appeared, she spotted a frown on his face. The butler looked very disturbed while approaching the manor. Rather than waiting for him to come to her, Mara rose from her seat to greet him personally. No longer did she wish to stay in the living room for another moment.

By the time she approached the foyer, the butler was already inside. The frown on his face remained. Mara and a few servants approached him.

"André," Mara addressed him. "What's wrong?"

The butler gazed at her. "I'm afraid I have run into some problems. The barrister is away at the moment."

Mara shrugged. "You can try again later. What about the funeral home?"

"Regrettably, they cannot pick up the body."

She furrowed her brow. "Why?"

"The funeral home has been infested."

"Infested by what?"

"Ghouls, Miss Ashwood," André answered.

"Ghouls?" Mara questioned. "The result of a vampire draining a human of all their blood. As long as the body is intact, it'll rise as a corpse-eating ghoul. They're usually exclusive to Hema, unless..." She paused. "There's a vampire in this city."

The servants gawked at her. They were either stunned by her knowledge or the fact that a vampire was lurking in Mirahyll.

"Dad told me about them," Mara explained. "And I've personally met Lady Isabella. She used a blood-draining machine to curb ghoul populations." She gazed at André. "Is the Council Hall aware of this?"

"There is a bounty," André replied.

"Okay, I'm off." Mara headed upstairs.

"Miss Ashwood," André called. "Are you sure you wish to do this?"

Mara looked back at him. "I may be the Lady of the Manor. But I am the Huntress." Then she said, "I didn't forget our talk yesterday."

Returning to her room, Mara approached the wardrobe. Her Silver Thorn armour had to be on the other side. She opened the doors to find it shoved in the back. She shook her head. If André thought she would change overnight, he was mistaken. She got out of her morning attire and equipped her armour. While getting dressed, Mara could smell spring flowers emanating from it. She reckoned the maids had cleaned it. The keepsakes of the undying remained. A few days ago, the servants could not see the significance of the tarnished comb, the faded letter, or the withered flower, and threw them out. Mara had to dig through the garbage to retrieve them much to André's dismay. No one else understood their value. Once Mara was fully dressed, she approached Nightingale on the dresser. She grabbed the sword and headed out.

* * *

Walking down the streets of Mirahyll, Mara spotted the information board. Among the many postings, she found the one regarding ghouls. Anyone interested was to meet with the owner of the funeral home for details and the reward.

On the way to the funeral home, she spotted some people watching her with contempt. Their fancy attire hinted to their noble status.

"The Cursed Herald..."

"Why is she here?"

"It's her fault Ardana's in this mess!"

Mara ignored them the best she could. She finally encountered the large brick building with a sign over the front entrance.

"Funeral Home," Mara read the sign before inviting herself in.

The owner of the funeral home was a middle-aged man with a slim build and grey hair. He also sported a thin moustache and a small beard on his pale face. He wore a monocle over his left eye, as well as a black suit with matching shoes and silver buttons. Mara assumed he was also a noble, not just by his attire or the fact he was a wealthy business owner, but by his scowl.

"What are you doing here?" asked the owner.

Mara kept her composure. She had a task to do and refused to let Mr. White down. "I'm here about the notice," she replied. "Heard you have a ghoul problem."

He folded his arms. "Another hunter came by and accepted the job."

"Another hunter?" Mara questioned.

"Yes," he replied coldly. "You can leave."

"How long were they gone for?"

"A couple of hours, but I'm sure he'll return. So there's no need for your help."

Mara raised an eyebrow. "Okay, fine." She faced the door. "Hope your hunter knows what he's doing. When there are ghouls, there are usually vampires involved."

"A... a vampire?"

She looked back to see him gaping at her in surprise. Mara shrugged. "Guess I'll go back home. I'll wait until all operations are running again." She headed towards the door.

"Wait," the owner called out to her.

Mara paused and gazed back at him. The business owner had a hand raised to her.

He lowered his hand and said, "Maybe it's a good thing you're here. You seem to know more about the monsters plaguing my business." Then, "A few days ago, I lost one of my morticians. The beasts are terrible, like an overgrown bat. We managed to retrieve the body, or what remained of it. We found several bite marks on the neck and shoulder."

"Your mortician likely encountered the vampire first," Mara said. "After draining the victim's blood, it probably tossed the remains to the ghouls. The vampire has personal servants to clean up after it." She noted the urgency in his eyes. It became clear that he wanted her to deal with this threat. "The vampire must be dealt with if you want to get rid of the ghouls."

"I'll readjust the reward," he said. "Kill the ghouls and the vampire. Return with the vampire's head, and I'll pay you one thousand five hundred gold. Do we have an agreement?"

Mara nodded. "I accept."

"So, where to start? Do you want to see the body for any more clues?"

"I have enough information to know what I'm dealing with, but I need to know where the attack occurred. How did the ghouls get in?"

"We discovered a hole in the storeroom where we keep the deceased. That's when the attack happened. Since then, we locked the room. Talk to the other mortician in the crematorium. He has a key."

Mara went into the crematorium to meet the mortician. She glanced at all the bodies fated for incineration. They were all wrapped in a white sheet. Then she saw the mortician and the heavy leather attire he wore. It covered his whole body to protect him from the searing heat. Some blood stained his attire as well, but that was normal. The morticians also acted as coroners, determining how the person met their end. A mask with a long beak covered his face. She assumed the beak was filled with spices to help mask the smell. Being a mortician was anything but glamorous.

The mortician spotted her approaching him. "Who might you be?"

"I'm here to deal with your problem," Mara answered.

"Are you? Even after the boss sent another?"

"You might be dealing with a vampire."

The mortician gawked at her through the goggles on his mask. "I guess it's no surprise. I examined the body of my colleague." He glanced away. "It's been hours since I last saw the other hunter. Chances are, he's already dead."

Mara gave a peculiar look. "Who's this other hunter?"

"Ah, I can't remember his name."

"Do you know what he looks like?"

"A young man with short black hair and dark eyes. He wore leather armour. Wielded a spear and a great shield."

Mara gaped at him. "Him? He's back?"

It was unbelievable, but she knew no other with such traits.

The mortician questioned, "I suppose you wish to enter the storeroom?" He reached into his pocket and retrieved a key. "Here, take this. And don't die. If you do, we might be unable to retrieve your body."

Mara took the key. "Thanks, but I've no intention of dying."

Upon entering the storeroom, a gaping hole in the corner drew her attention.

"Large enough for a fully grown man to get into," Mara murmured to herself. She took notice of the corpses scattered around. Some were half-eaten. The stench of death seeped through her mask and invaded her nostrils. As soon as Mara got used to the smell, she spotted more bloodstains on the floor. "Must've belonged to the mortician."

She returned her attention to the hole. Upon further observation, Mara reckoned it led into the sewers. A trail of body parts led the way. Following the trail, the huntress found herself wandering into familiar territory. She stood before another large hole, leading into the Dark Labyrinth. Mara never imagined returning to this place.

"The creatures dug their way out," Mara observed. "I wonder where this goes."

* * *

Entering the Dark Labyrinth, Mara heard the snarls of ghouls and the sound of metal. She followed the sounds where she found the creatures and the other hunter. Five ghouls swarmed him as he cowered behind his great shield and poked at them with his spear. The ghouls were displeased. One of them latched onto the spear and almost yanked it out of his hand. He dropped his shield, thus placing himself in danger.

Mara began to transform. Her eyes glowed yellow as the markings on her face grew darker. The huntress unsheathed Nightingale and dashed at the ghouls. The corpse-eaters had no time to react while the huntress sliced through the neck of one of the creatures. Ambushing them was an effective strategy. Mara slew the first three ghouls in ten seconds. The last two turned on her and attacked, but they were no match. As Mara killed them, she realized it had been almost two months since venturing into Misty Valley to slay the White Lady. The Forgotten Ones were more difficult. Then again, she had lost her memories, including Dad's training. With all her memories restored, Mara became a different person.

After the danger had subsided, the huntress reverted to normal. Mara's attention was now on the so-called hunter. The coward hid behind his great shield. He eventually opened his eyes and saw Mara staring at him.

Boyd's jaw dropped, revealing the gap in his front teeth. "You!"

"What are you doing here?" Mara asked.

He regained his composure. "Well, I've turned a new leaf. Finally cleaned up my act, and now I'm a hunter, just like you."

Mara grew skeptical. "Weren't the Holy Blades searching for you?"

"They were, but that's no longer the case. I can start over without Kallikratés breathing down my neck."

She kept watching him with a questioning glint in her eyes.

Boyd took notice. "Don't give me that look! I've changed, I have."

"Go home."

"What?"

"This isn't some pest control job," Mara claimed. "It involves a vampire."

Boyd froze upon hearing those words. Mara figured he was unaware. In reality, he only took the job just to be paid.

A frown formed on his face. "I'm coming with you."

"Excuse me?"

"Come on! Two hunters are always better than one."

"You said that before, and look what happened," Mara retorted.

Boyd sulked. "Oh, come on! You still can't be mad at me over that incident. I've changed, I have. I promise no funny business."

Mara sighed, "Fine. But if you do that again, I will end you."

The two travelled deep into the Dark Labyrinth, following the trail of body parts. They encountered more ghouls along the way, but they were easy to kill. Even Boyd slew some on his own. Much to Mara's surprise, he didn't try anything funny. Maybe he did change, but it was too early to tell. If faced with real danger, Boyd would likely run away. They soon came across an open door. Mara recognized its design; they were about to head into another part of the Dark Labyrinth.

She gazed at Boyd. "This is about to get dangerous."

"I'm not turning back." He stormed past her.

Passing through the door, they encountered a horde. Several ghouls gathered around a stockpile of corpses, devouring the rotten flesh.

Mara was stunned. "I've never seen anything like this," she murmured. "This must've been caused by the cataclysm." She drew her blade. "The vampire must be close by."

The two began to slaughter the ghouls congregating around the corpse pile.

"So, you managed to slay the Goddess?" Boyd questioned while stabbing a monster. "Can't imagine her followers being pleased with you."

"Kallisto was never a goddess." Mara sliced through the neck of a ghoul. "Her followers knew all along." She gazed back at him and saw his frozen expression. "I suppose you knew about it as well."

"I did," he admitted. "They got their comeuppance."

After dealing with the last of the ghouls, Mara looked around. "Where's the vampire?"

She heard something falling to the ground behind her. The huntress looked over her shoulder and found a severed arm. As Mara inspected it, she heard a low growl from above. The two lifted their gaze to the ceiling.

A large bat-like creature hung above them. Leathery wings wrapped around its body. After a few seconds, the creature looked down at them and gave another growl. Spreading its bat-like wings, it flew down to greet them. The vampire resembled the beastly form of Lady Isabella, but with masculine features. He was at least ten feet tall, though his wings seemed smaller. The monster eyed Mara, then Boyd, and then back onto Mara while he continued to growl. The two hunters watched as the vampire moved towards them. The monster opened his mouth, revealing large fangs stained in blood. One bite could prove fatal.

The beast gave a screeching roar before launching into the air. He went straight for Mara. She dodged his attack. When he landed, she ran up to the creature and slashed at him. The beast screeched and retaliated, but the huntress stepped back. Boyd came in and gave a few stabs with his spear. The vampire glared at Boyd. He intended to kill the new hunter, but Mara slashed at the creature. Nightingale sliced through muscles and bones, taking off one of his wings. The vampire released a loud screech before falling to the ground and writhing in pain. He tried to crawl away, but the huntress stabbed Nightingale into his heart, then sliced his head off.

The huntress bagged the severed head as proof. She also found a healing stone, which was useful. Since becoming the last undying, Mara had only one way to restore her human form. As soon as the huntress was ready to leave, she noticed Boyd slumping to the ground and panting in exhaustion. She also took note of his pale face and figured he had never faced a real vampire before.

"Jeez, no wonder why they call you the slayer of gods!" Boyd exclaimed.

Mara raised an eyebrow. "Kallisto destroyed herself."

Boyd rose to his feet. "Well, it seems I missed out while in hiding."

"You want to hear about it?"

"Sure, why not? It could help pass the time."

As Mara told him everything that happened in the previous month, they traced their footsteps back to whence they came.

* * *

While drawing closer to the funeral home, the two encountered three men. Mara thought the funeral home sent them, but then recognized the black and brown leather armour and their rough appearance. They were Blackthorns! What were they doing here? They brandished their weapons, making their intentions clear. Unwilling to put up with this nonsense, the huntress approached them with a bloody Nightingale and glowing yellow eyes. One dashed at her, but Nightingale sliced through his neck, lopping off his head. The bandits took a step back while Boyd froze.

"I just slew a vampire." Mara gazed at the other two Blackthorns. "And you have the nerve to attack me?" The huntress glared at them. "Perhaps I didn't send a clearer message."

The second Blackthorn gathered enough courage to challenge her, but Mara stabbed him in the heart before he could lift his blade. The remaining bandit ran away in terror. Mara chose not to pursue him.

"Shouldn't we go after him?" Boyd questioned.

"I've dealt with them before," Mara replied, sheathing her sword. "If they know what's best for them, they'll finally get the message."

Taking the bag, Mara and Boyd returned to the sewer.

The two arrived at the storeroom within the funeral home. As they emerged from the hole, Mara saw the owner and the mortician waiting for them.

The business owner appeared surprised to see them both alive. "Is it done? Have the monsters been dealt with?"

"You shouldn't have any problems now," Mara replied.

The owner eyed the bloody bag. "Is that...?"

The huntress gazed at the bag as well. "It's the severed head of the vampire. The same creature who killed one of your morticians."

"May I see?"

She handed the bag to him.

He opened it and looked inside. "Oh my!" His face twisted with disgust. "What a dreadful creature!" The business owner looked up at her. "Are you sure it's dead?"

"I destroyed the heart and severed the head. According to my father, it's the best way to slay them," Mara explained.

"Was this the only one?"

"As far as I'm concerned," Mara answered. "But if you encounter another, let me know."

The owner nodded. "Very well." He glanced at Boyd. "I see you're still alive. I suppose you'll want a reward as well?"

"We can split it." Mara glanced back at Boyd, who looked astonished. "He did help." The huntress gazed back at the business owner. "There is one thing. Mr. Arthur White passed away last night. I need someone to pick up the body so we can move forward with the funeral arrangements."

The owner nodded. "I'll send someone immediately."

"Thank you," Mara responded.

Mara and Boyd were each awarded with seven hundred fifty gold. It was a little low for killing such a creature. But with the rise in monster activity, Mara would gain more opportunities. After being paid, it was time to part ways.

"I must get back," Boyd told Mara. "I'm sure the missus is missing me."

"Missus?" Mara was surprised to know Boyd managed to get himself a significant other.

"She's the reason why I changed," Boyd claimed.

Mara gawked at him. She got over her brief shock and said, "Okay, stay out of trouble."

Boyd nodded, then walked away. While gazing at him, the huntress began to notice a change within the former thief. He did seem like a much different person. Mara then headed back to the White Manor.

Chapter Four

A Great Inheritance

As soon as Mara returned home, the door opened to reveal the butler.

"Miss Ashwood," André greeted, "you have returned safely."

"The funeral home should be arriving soon to pick up the body," said the huntress.

"I see," he responded. "While you were gone, I was able to contact the barrister. He shall arrive very soon."

Mara glanced at her attire. "I'll clean myself up."

"A hot bath has been drawn for you. I have already arranged your attire for tonight."

"Thanks," Mara said.

"My pleasure, Miss Ashwood."

Mara headed upstairs to the washing area. The maids helped her out of her clothes and took them away. While the huntress entered the bath, she spotted the maids sifting through her satchels. They were making sure to remove all items before cleaning her armour, yet Mara grew wary at how they handled the keepsakes.

"Please don't throw them away," Mara ordered.

The maids obeyed, though remained curious.

"Miss Ashwood," one of the maids addressed her. "Why do you keep these?"

Mara watched them for a while before tending to her cleaning. "They belonged to my predecessors, to warn me."

"Warn you of what?"

"How they met their fate and the one who caused their misery." The huntress looked back and spotted the tarnished comb in one of the maids' possession. "That comb once belonged to Karl's wife."

The maids looked astonished.

The one who had the memento gazed down at the comb in her hand. "I've heard Master White was once married to a commoner."

Mara nodded. "Her name was Evelyn."

The maids gazed at Mara for a while before removing everything from her armour.

"Miss Ashwood, I will store the seven hundred fifty gold in your deposit box," said one of the maids.

"Thank you." Mara returned to washing herself.

* * *

Once Mara was cleaned up and fully dressed, she headed to the living room. She emerged in a dark blue bustle dress. Upon entering the living room, Mara did her best to ignore the commander's cold gaze. The barrister had yet to arrive, so she sat down and waited. Now and then, she found herself staring up at the painting. The commander's face reminded her of the time he stabbed her with a basilisk blade.

"Miss Ashwood," André called.

Mara broke her gaze with the painting and noticed the barrister beside André.

"The barrister is here," said the butler.

Mara nodded. "Thanks, André."

The butler nodded in return, then left the two alone.

Gazing at the barrister, Mara could sense he was uncomfortable being in the same room with her. She stood before him and bowed her head.

"Thank you for coming," Mara began.

"I've received word of Mr. Arthur White's passing," the barrister said.

"He died last night. One of the maids found him this morning." Mara gestured to a chair. "Would you like a seat? Anything to eat or drink?"

The barrister shook his head. "I only need you to sign some papers, and you'll officially own this manor, along with the family fortune." He opened his briefcase to retrieve the documents he needed her to sign.

"Here, sign these." He handed over the papers and a quill.

Mara used a side table to sign the papers. Once finished, she handed the documents back to the barrister to inspect.

"Everything looks correct," said the barrister. Then he handed over some papers to her. "This is the newly updated deed, as well as a copy of the paperwork. These are for your records."

"Thank you," Mara said, nodding to him.

"That will be all," he said. "I will take my leave."

The barrister left Mara alone in the living room. She gazed at the paperwork in her hands.

"Remarkable," spoke an unfamiliar male voice. "You should throw a gala in celebration of your newfound wealth."

Mara lifted her head. "André? Is that you?"

"Miss Ashwood, I'm right here," André said, appearing by her side.

She gazed at him in confusion.

"I'm afraid you're incorrect," said the mysterious man.

Both Mara and André grew apprehensive.

"Show yourself!" Mara shouted.

A tall and slender man entered the living room. He had both his hands up while giving a relaxed smile. He wore a green overcoat adorned with leather armour and metal. A dirty white shirt was visible underneath the coat. Brown gloves covered his hands. Black slacks adorned his legs while muddy boots covered his feet. The rugged man appeared to be in his thirties. He owned short, messy black hair and a five o'clock shadow around his mouth.

Mara watched him with curiosity. "Who are you?" Judging by his tanned skin, she assumed he was a Stone Mage.

André looked horrified. "Theo Blackthorn, the most wanted man in all of Ardana!"

Mara gaped at the butler before turning her bewildered gaze onto the intruder. The man, now identified as Theo, smiled.

"At your service." He took a bow.

Both Mara and André watched him warily.

"What do you want?" Mara demanded.

Theo stood up straight and gazed at the huntress. His amber eyes remained stuck on her.

"I never expected such beauty." Placing his hands behind his back, Theo took a few steps forward to get a closer look. "Yet behind that face lies a creature who slaughtered more than half of my men five years ago."

Mara glowered at him. "You're either brave or stupid, breaking into my home."

"I am not your enemy. I'm only here because we need to talk. I think it's time we were acquainted." Theo looked at Mr. White's chair. "May I?"

No one permitted Theo to sit in the chair, but he did so anyway. He acted as if he owned the place. He gazed at Mara, studying her features.

"Mara Ashwood," Theo said. "To others, the Cursed Herald. And to my men, the Black Smoke."

Mara frowned. "I wasn't myself back then."

"Yes, and I'm merely an honest man trying to run my business. A business you nearly destroyed in recent times."

"No one knew of Kallikratés' deception." Then she said, "If not for the raid at one of your hideouts, the truth would remain hidden."

The Blackthorns' leader shrugged. "I do agree they had set us up against each other. For that, I'm glad Kallikratés was exposed. Maybe you can be of further use to me."

"What are you talking about?" Mara asked.

"I'm looking for someone," Theo explained. "After deserting the Holy Blades, he came to me for protection."

The huntress tilted her head to the left. "You mean Boyd?"

Theo nodded. "After the Faith fell, he decided to leave with a large sum of my gold."

Mara gave a wry smile. "Interesting... a thief stole from another thief."

"I don't think so. I want my gold back."

Mara grew perplexed. "You're asking me to help you find him?"

"Tell me where he is, and I'll reward you."

The huntress kept her eyes on him. "I'm afraid I don't know where he is."

"Are you sure? I heard that you met him not more than a day ago."

"I assume you sent those men after us?" Mara asked. "I'll have you know I could finish what I started five years ago."

Theo frowned. "I'm not your enemy." He rose from his seat. "I want you to reconsider our deal. We're so much alike than you realize."

Then he left the manor. Mara and the butler watched the space with apprehension. André moved forward.

"I will speak with the servants," he said. "That scoundrel must've found a way to get in."

Mara was left alone in the living room. Her eyes drifted over to the painting of Commander White. Not wanting to stay any longer, she rose to her feet and went to her room.

* * *

It was late in the night. Everyone was fast asleep, except for Mara, who tossed and turned in her bed. It felt like someone was watching her. Upon opening her eyes, Mara rose out of her bed and headed towards the door. Poking her head out into the hallway, Mara stared at the closed door before her. Something about Karl's room drew her attention.

Mara opened the door, only to see a large bloodstain on the floor. The large red spot reminded her of the commander in his last moments. The blood looked fresh as it slowly spread towards her.

Mara stared at the blood-soaked carpet before noticing the central area. It grew darker, taking the shape of a man. She stood frozen. Her heart was pounding in her chest. Several images of Commander White's death flashed in her mind. She closed her eyes for a moment. When Mara opened them, she saw his body lying before her. Blood thoroughly stained his garb. His lifeless face stared up at the ceiling. Mara approached him to get a closer look.

Crouching down, she reached towards his face. All of a sudden, the commander's hand grabbed her wrist. Mara was startled by the sight as his lifeless eyes glared at her.

* * *

Mara jolted awake. She was back in her room. It was only a dream. The huntress looked around in confusion, unable to explain the nightmare she had. She turned her gaze onto the door and got out of bed. A nagging voice in the back of her mind told her to investigate Karl's room. Mara entered the hallway and discovered she was the only one awake. She approached the door and opened it.

Time stood still for Karl's room. Since the commander's passing, no one had entered this place. Much of his belongings remained here, including his clothing, bedding, and books. Even a spare commander's garb adorned a mannequin, like the one in her dream. Mara eyed the attire while approaching it. She carefully inspected the dark grey coat, looking for any traces of blood. The whole garb was flawless, save for a thin layer of dust.

Her eyes drifted over to a journal. Wondering what sort of things Karl wrote, Mara approached the desk and picked up the journal. Before opening it, she grew hesitant about reading the thoughts of the late Commander White. Then again, it could not be any worse than discovering the whole truth about him. Opening the journal, she noticed several missing pages. Someone had torn them out. So she began with the first entry she could find.

"The Goddess showed me the truth," Mara read. "I am the reincarnation and descendant of the Great Lord Kratés, whose return the Goddess had been awaiting. She warned me of an evil woman who sought to keep us apart."

Mara gazed at the entry before turning the page.

"Evelyn is evil. Not only does she seek to come in between our love, but she also seeks to halt the Golden Age. There is no choice. The Goddess has spoken."

Mara felt a cold chill running up her spine. She reckoned that he wrote this before murdering his wife. Mara turned the page again.

"It is done. But the Goddess has warned me of an evil entity, the Cursed Herald. She shall return. As heir to Kratés' legacy, I must stop the Cursed Herald. I must serve my Goddess."

Mara could no longer read the rest of his delusions. She reckoned the torn pages were from a time when he was happily married to Evelyn. Now they were all gone, like his memories of his former wife. Mara closed the journal and left it on the desk. She could hear the servants stirring. André and the maids would arrive at any moment, ready to dress her for the day. Mara left the room and returned to her own.

* * *

The whole morning routine of getting dressed and being served breakfast became natural to Mara. Every morning was the same, except for the breakfasts. Today, she had something called pancakes, served with butter and maple syrup. Mara assumed it was something nobles ate; she never heard of such a thing before. Despite the delicious breakfast, Mara's mind was on other things.

"I've been putting off Nightingale's repair," she told the butler.

"Very well," André spoke. "I will take the sword to the blacksmith."

Mara shook her head. "No, I'll go myself."

"Miss Ashwood, with all due respect, you are the Lady of the Manor."

"Yes, André, I haven't forgotten," Mara sighed. "But maintaining Nightingale is a personal matter between Talon and me."

The butler stood his ground while Mara watched him defiantly. Neither one was backing down. After a moment, the butler sighed.

"Very well. I'll arrange the transport to the blacksmith's shop. And I shall accompany you." He turned around. "I am your butler. It is my job."

Mara's face softened. "Thanks, André."

The butler glanced back at her and nodded. Then he departed to arrange the transportation. While he did this, Mara headed upstairs to retrieve Nightingale. She entered her room and saw the sword resting on the dresser. Once she retrieved the sword and some money from her deposit box, she headed downstairs.

By the time Mara was ready, the carriage was waiting outside. A maid was nearby, holding a thick shawl for her to wear. She placed it on Mara's shoulders. Mara and the butler ventured out into the cold. They approached the familiar wooden carriage once used by Mr. White and Karl. The transport was decorated in golden accents and pulled by two brown horses. André opened the door. Entering the coach, Mara took a seat. While the butler got onto the driver's seat and took the reins, Mara observed the interior. Everything remained the same since the last time she rode in it.

André directed the horses to move, and soon they left Mirahyll.

* * *

Almost a full day had passed since their departure. Mara gazed out the window while holding Nightingale on her lap. Heavy snowfall made the roads more difficult for the horses to traverse, let alone pull the carriage. Mara knew she should have gone sooner to see Talon, but the last few days kept her busy.

Once they reached Talon's workshop, Mara spotted another carriage. Someone else was visiting. The old house, once dilapidated, now looked new. It was much different with plumes of smoke rising out of the chimney. Another location Mara had not been to in a while; this was once the herbalist's house. The original owner was named Madeline, and she was one of Thalia's reincarnations and a victim of Kallikratés. Thanks to both Harold and Aspen, Mara learned the terrible truth behind the herbalist's transformation into the Marionette. Approaching the workshop, the huntress noticed a grave near the edge of the woods. She reckoned Talon gave Madeline a proper burial.

Speaking of which, Mara was expecting the sound of a blacksmith's hammer forging a new weapon. Instead, she heard Talon bickering with another.

"When will you stop pestering me? The answer is no!"

"Please, Talon," a woman spoke in a low tone. "Take the offer."

Mara recognized Beatrice. As she drew closer, the huntress could hear their conversation much clearer.

"I'm sorry," the blacksmith grumbled. "No offer or proposal will change my mind."

Mara invited herself while André followed. Talon did a fantastic job of transforming the home into a workshop. Half of the living room became a forge, while the other end was for weapons on display. A couple of weapons drew Mara's attention, reminding her of the ones Dad used to make. Near the forge, she could see the blacksmith with the captain. The two were glaring at each other until Talon noticed Mara. He gazed at her in confusion, as if he didn't recognize her. Mara could not blame him, considering she was not wearing her usual attire. And the fact that she had a butler beside her likely threw him off.

The old blacksmith's eyes widened. "Mara, is that you?"

The huntress nodded. Beatrice also gazed at her. Unlike the slack jaw Talon gained, the captain remained nonchalant. Mara took a step forward.

"Yes," the huntress answered. She gazed down at her attire. "Since I inherited Mr. White's fortune, I have to look the part."

"I see." Talon glanced at André. "Did he come with the inheritance?"

Mara gazed at the butler. "André used to serve Mr. White. He works for me now."

André stepped forward and bowed. "My pleasure to meet your acquaintance."

"Sounds like you're moving up in the world." Then his eyes were drawn to Nightingale. "Ah, you've brought the beauty!"

Mara approached the blacksmith. "I wanted to see you sooner. A lot of things happened, like clearing the funeral home of its ghoul and vampire problem."

"Ghouls and vampires?" Beatrice questioned.

The huntress gazed at her. "They wanted the creatures dealt with after losing one of their morticians."

The captain gave a questioning glance. "Why weren't the guardsmen notified?"

Mara shrugged. "I assume it's because you're focusing all of your attention on the Blackthorns. With no more Silver Thorns or Holy Blades, it's now up to independent hunters to deal with actual monsters."

Beatrice glared at her in silence.

Talon folded his arms. "Aye, that is true. We don't know how many monsters remain, but hunters are dwindling. I hope your new status doesn't mean you're retiring from the business."

Mara shook her head. "As long as I'm cursed, I've no intention of quitting." She glanced at André. "However, I would have to consider once I become human. I won't have the benefits of this curse forever." Mara looked back at Talon. "Besides, it's the reason why I'm here."

She handed Nightingale over to the blacksmith. An excited glint formed in Talon's eyes as he took the sword out of its sheath.

The captain frowned. "With all due respect, you're willing to offer your services to her, a citizen of Mirahyll?" Beatrice questioned. "I thought you'd never offer your services to anyone from the city."

"She's an exception," Talon explained as he repaired Nightingale. "Thanks to her, I was able to rebuild my business in Mirahyll."

"And because of her, you lost your business," Beatrice argued.

"I'd blame Edwin for that." Talon waved to his forge. "A monster once inhabited this house. I have Mara to thank for making this place available."

Beatrice gazed at Mara in disbelief. "You slew the undying?"

"Harold sent me to kill her," Mara said, "and the Siren in Har' Yhan."

Shock faded from Beatrice's face, to be replaced by stoicism. "You certainly live up to your reputation," the captain murmured. "A slayer of monsters and gods."

"I much prefer the Huntress," Mara said.

"I see. Very well." Beatrice turned around. "I'll take my leave." She took a few steps, then scowled at Talon. "I wish you would take the offer."

Mara and Talon watched as Beatrice walked out the door. As soon as she was gone, the old blacksmith took a deep breath and gazed at Mara. The huntress looked back at him as he turned to his forge in silence. Talon continued to repair her blade.

"This sword has been through a lot," he broke the silence. "Yet it lasted as long as it did. Your father was a great blacksmith." He gestured to the weapons on display. "These were made after studying those diagrams."

Mara observed the weapons on display. "Your skills have improved."

A composite longbow drew her attention. The wood was black while the metal was silver. Mara remembered using a bow long ago, in which Dad made practice dummies for shooting.

Once Nightingale's repair was complete, Talon approached Mara and returned her sword. "Here you go. Good as new."

Mara looked at Nightingale, then sheathed her sword. "Thank you."

"No, thank you." The blacksmith glanced at the weapons on display. "How about I offer you a weapon for free? One of these on display can be yours."

Mara was quite surprised. "Are you sure? You don't have to…"

"Please, I insist."

Mara looked back at the weapons.

"I think I'll have this one." She pointed to the bow from earlier. Having a ranged weapon would be a great idea. Mara used to own a crossbow before being captured by the Holy Blades.

"Okay then," Talon said, handing the bow over to her.

After taking the bow and finishing any business with Talon, both Mara and André left the workshop. The two returned to the coach and headed back home to Mirahyll.

* * *

Mara gazed out the window while the carriage headed home. The horses snorted while traversing the deep snow. The carriage moved slowly, yet remained in motion. Another day had passed as the sun descended behind the horizon.

"Miss Ashwood," André began.

"Yes, André?"

"I wish to thank you."

"For what?"

"For listening to me earlier—about considering your future."

Mara gazed at her sword. "One thing at a time."

They returned to the manor by sundown. Mara felt relieved to be home, for it had been a very long day.

"Miss Ashwood," André called. "According to the maids, the funeral home has picked up Mr. White's body while we were away. His funeral will take place by the end of the week."

"Okay," Mara said. "Is there anything I need to do?"

"No, Miss Ashwood," André said. "Now, I will oversee the dinner. I'll let you know when it is ready."

Mara nodded as she allowed him to perform his duties. Entering the living room, Mara found herself gazing at the painting. She glared back at the commander as an unfamiliar sensation washed over her. It was the realization that this was now her home. No longer did this manor belong to Mr. White or Karl.

Chapter Five

Come Crashing Down

It was January 8, the day of Mr. White's funeral. Mara had a rough start due to a lack of sleep last night. To make matters worse, she needed to get up earlier to prepare for the funeral. It remained dark outside as the servants served breakfast. As soon as Mara finished, André escorted her back to her room.

"This is perfect," the butler said as one of the maids retrieved a black bustle dress from the wardrobe.

The dress reminded Mara of the one Thalia always wore. The maids helped her into it. Then they fixed her hair, smoothing out any frizzles.

Mara wore a mourning veil and hood, similar to what Thalia had. If Thalia was alive, none could tell them apart.

Mara headed to the foyer. Another servant placed a black shawl over her shoulders. Ready to leave, Mara followed André to the carriage waiting outside. The butler opened the door to the transport. After Mara went inside, he got into the driver's seat and took the reins. The two horses pulled the coach away from the mansion.

"We'll be heading to the Grand Cathedral, Miss Ashwood," André announced.

Mara gave a strange look. "Wasn't Mr. White considered a traitor?"

"It could be due to his servitude to Master White."

"You mean he was essentially a servant as well?"

"Not quite, Miss Ashwood, though you are not wrong. His family did have an obligation to Master White and the Faith, starting with his great grandfather."

"He was a prisoner and an unwilling pawn," Mara stated.

André changed the subject. "If you don't mind, I've noticed quite a peculiar behaviour from you ever since you came to live in the manor."

"What kind of behaviour?" Mara inquired.

"I've noticed you secretly entering the former quarters of Master White. And pardon me for saying this, but I often hear you cry out in the middle of the night. Are you sleeping well?"

Mara froze. How obvious was it?

"Ever since I came to live in the manor, I've been experiencing unusual dreams."

"You mean nightmares?"

"I guess you can say that."

"Do you mind if I ask what these nightmares include?"

Mara took a deep breath. "I find myself entering Karl's room, and he's there."

"Master White?"

Mara nodded. "I see him emerging from a large puddle of blood. Or the mannequin, wearing the commander's garb, comes to life."

André remained silent for a brief moment. "I see," he responded. "Perhaps you feel guilt over the death of Master White?"

"I had no choice," Mara said.

"I understand, Miss Ashwood," André spoke. "Living in the home of the ones who played a role in your predicament must be very difficult. May I suggest we remove all the belongings of the former lord? It might make things easier. We can do this after the funeral."

"Okay," Mara agreed.

* * *

The coach halted upon their arrival. André left the driver's seat and opened the door. Exiting the carriage, Mara was astounded by the sheer number of people. It seemed like all of Mirahyll was invited. Then again, Mr. White was a well-known professor at the College of Ardana. Many of his former students might have come to pay their respects. Mara didn't recognize anyone from her school year, for thirty years had passed. And she doubted anyone remembered her because she looked not a day over twenty-five.

Mara spotted a man dressed in black among the crowd. He held his hands behind his back while speaking with some nobles. Even though his back was facing her, his hair drew her attention. The lustre of his brown locks was familiar. His build looked similar to the late Commander White. She kept staring at the back of his head.

"Greetings," called another man.

Mara spun around and saw Theo standing before her. The Blackthorns' leader wore a clean black suit. She reckoned he stole the outfit, though he made an effort to look presentable. He had his hair neatly combed. He even shaved. Theo's transformation left none the wiser of his presence.

Mara gaped at him. "What are you doing here?"

Theo frowned. "I thought dressing up for the occasion would impress you."

"I asked you a question," Mara said flatly. "What are you doing here?"

"I was invited to this event."

She raised an eyebrow. "This is a funeral. It's open to anyone who wishes to pay their respects, yet you never knew Mr. White. So, what are your true intentions?"

"Perhaps you'd like to join me?" Theo offered his hand to her.

Mara was apprehensive about taking his hand. Theo then focused his gaze onto an approaching couple. Mara glimpsed in the direction he was looking at and spotted Boyd with his partner. The young woman had pale skin, blonde hair, and blue eyes. She wore a similar dress to Mara's, but with a wide-brimmed hat on her head. She also wore a mesh veil over her eyes. The undying assumed the woman was Boyd's betrothed. Both showed up at the funeral service.

When Boyd spotted Mara and Theo, his expression turned grim. Taking his betrothed by the hand, he attempted to guide them away. But Theo pounced on him.

"Hello, Boyd," Theo began, wrapping his arm around Boyd's shoulder. "Long time, no see. How are you?"

Boyd remained silent, but the look on his face was very telling. He never expected to see the leader of the Blackthorn Guild.

His betrothed looked confused. "Who are these people?"

Theo took a bow. "You may call me Theo." Standing up straight, he gestured to Mara. "And this is Miss Mara Ashwood. The three of us are well-acquainted. Boyd and I had worked together in the past." He turned his attention onto Boyd. "There's something we need to discuss." Theo glanced at Mara. "Would you please stay with the lady while I speak to him?"

Mara folded her arms and sighed, "Fine."

The thief smiled. "Thank you."

Theo took Boyd to another area while Mara stood next to a stranger. The undying felt very awkward because she had nothing in common with this woman. Boyd's betrothed might have sensed the awkwardness as well, but tried to lighten up the atmosphere.

"My name is Claire Lilystone," the woman introduced herself, "heiress to my family legacy. The Lilystone Family owns much of the general stores in Mirahyll, Désir, and Har' Yhan. We just started a new shop in Hemal."

While Mara was impressed, she wondered what this woman saw in Boyd. Claire stared at Mara, hinting for her to add something to their conversation or at least introduce herself, even though Theo already did that.

"I'm Mara," the undying introduced. "I'm the daughter of Daniella and Mathias "Bear" Ashwood."

Claire just stared at her as if those words meant nothing. Then again, Mara doubted that anyone knew her parents. Dad died three decades ago, while Mom rotted in a hospital.

"My father was one of the best blacksmiths until his untimely death," Mara explained. "Talon continues his legacy."

"Ah, yes, Talon," Claire spoke. "I've heard that Chancellor Davis had little success in persuading him to return. So he has invited another blacksmith to forge weapons for the guild."

Mara narrowed her eyes. "Who?"

"Raymon of Corlin," Claire explained. "He's said to be from a line of reputable blacksmiths. He is considered an artist and is much younger. We won't need to rely on that geriatric."

Mara sulked. "Talon cares about his craft. When his workshop burned to the ground, the Council Hall and the Guardsmen did nothing."

"He should get over it," Claire said nonchalantly. "With Raymon supplying weapons for this city, that old blacksmith will regret rejecting the chancellor's offer."

Mara gave a deadpanned look. *'She's so arrogant.'*

The huntress changed the topic. "So, how did you meet Boyd?"

"Boyd Masterson is a very wealthy bachelor whose family deals in trading various goods," Claire claimed.

Mara could not help but be surprised at the noblewoman's ignorance. Claire was unaware of Boyd's past as a thief, yet the undying chose not to tell her. She would let the poor fool find out on her own.

Eventually, Theo returned with Boyd. The Blackthorns' leader appeared to be in a pleasant mood while Boyd looked sour.

Claire took notice of her betrothed. "What's wrong?"

"Just some business we needed to resolve," Theo told her, then he bowed. "I bid you farewell."

Boyd remained unhappy, while Claire was clueless. The two lovers eventually walked away.

Mara gazed at Theo. "What are you planning? You didn't come here to pay respects."

He glanced back at her and smiled. "You're right. I managed to track him here through my spies. I've given Boyd one week to return my gold."

Mara folded her arms. "You're quite generous, giving Boyd enough time to flee Ardana."

"He's in no position to run or hide. If he does, my men will hunt him down."

"I hope you're not thinking of harming anyone innocent."

"I've no intention," Theo said. "Besides, this matter is none of your concern."

With that, he left the cathedral.

The funeral service was about to begin. Mara and André sat near Mr. White's coffin. After everyone was seated, a priest took to the podium. Mara wondered where this priest came from, considering that most of them died in the incident. He was not Father Petyr Vernon, who remained imprisoned. The older priest had several wrinkles decorating his face.

"We have gathered here today to say farewell to Arthur White and commit him to rest for all eternity," the priest began. "Let us pray."

Everyone bowed their heads and began to pray. Mara followed suit. She was unfamiliar with the proper etiquette at a funeral.

"Praise Kallikratés," the priest continued. "We thank the Goddess, Kallisto, who gave us life and purpose. The Great Lord Kratés, who defended us from our sworn enemies. May our gods guide us into eternity and safeguard us from all evil."

Mara resisted the urge to roll her eyes. The undying glanced around. She stuck out like a sore thumb, being in a place dedicated to false gods, and surrounded by their worshippers. She remembered her friend, Allen, calling this place an eyesore, while Dad described it as an insult to regular Ardanians. Hopefully, the transition would be smooth, though she heeded Beatrice's words. The Faith of Kallikratés would not give up without a fight. At least the funeral service was impressive. Mara was astounded to know the Grand Cathedral was willing to host Mr. White's funeral. Even the priest spoke favourably of him.

The priest looked over the crowd. "I hear someone wishes to share some final words."

Mara looked confused, then glanced at André. They never planned a eulogy, but someone did. A young man approached the podium. His brown hair was familiar to Mara, for she had seen him earlier. The man turned to reveal a face only seen in her dreams. His flawless pale skin and bright green eyes triggered alarm bells in her mind.

'It can't be!'

Mara couldn't believe her eyes, but no other man possessed such a hairstyle. The young man's hair was semi-long in the front and short in the back. He even had the stubble on his chin and a tuft of hair under his bottom lip.

"Thank you for coming," Karl began. He reached into his pocket and pulled out a piece of paper. "I have a few words for the man I once saw as my father."

Mara froze. How could this be? She saw him die! The funeral was not even over when she shot up to her feet. Her actions drew everyone's attention.

André looked concerned. "Miss Ashwood?"

She ignored the butler while her eyes remained locked on the man at the podium. Karl glared back at her. Her actions also drew his attention. She wanted to flee. Mara headed for the exit, ignoring the stares of onlookers. Some of the nobles whispered among each other. She didn't understand their whispers, nor did she care. Mara ran out into the snowy streets.

"Miss Ashwood," André called as he followed her outside. "Please, stop."

Mara stopped and looked at him. "Am I dreaming?"

The butler frowned at her. "No, Miss Ashwood. I saw him as well."

"What's going on?" Mara asked. "He's supposed to be dead!"

"Perhaps we should speak to him? Figure out what's going on."

Mara shook her head. "I want to go home."

André watched her for a moment, then he nodded. "Very well," he said. "Right this way, Miss Ashwood."

She followed the butler to the coach. André opened the door, allowing her entry into the transport. As soon as Mara got inside, he took the reins and guided the horses to take them home.

* * *

Mara sat in the living room by early afternoon, trying to figure out how Karl was still alive. She remembered mounting Nightingale with the moonstone from her necklace. She vividly saw the blade plunging into his chest, undoing his immortality and ending his life.

Her thoughts were interrupted by three loud knocks on the door. André decided to answer.

"Where is she?" Karl raged from the foyer.

Before Mara could move, he stormed into the living room. A group of nobles also followed him into the manor. They stood behind him to give support. Karl glared at Mara while holding his hands behind his back.

"Hello, Ashwood," he greeted with contempt. "I see you're doing well, living in my manor!"

Mara spotted the barrister among the angry crowd of nobles. Rising from her seat, she scowled at Karl. "I saw you die!"

Karl took a few steps forward. "Yes, I did die thanks to you, but Kallisto resurrected me. Before you ended her life, she used the last of her magic to bring me back to save this land."

The nobles stood in awe.

"Praise Kallikratés," said one of the disciples.

The commander folded his arms as he bristled with anger. "I never believed you could sink any lower."

"What are you talking about?" Mara questioned.

Karl gestured to the barrister, who was now beside him. "You manipulated Arthur into changing his will. You stole what is rightfully mine!"

"This is quite the predicament," the barrister added.

"Can you make a draft for her to sign everything back to me?" Karl asked him.

"Yes, as long as she's willing," said the barrister.

Karl nodded. "She will since she obtained this wealth illegitimately." Then, "I've spoken with the funeral home. It turns out my guardian died of supernatural causes!"

Mara gaped at him in shock. "What?"

"A black substance filled his heart, causing cardiac arrest." Karl sneered at her. "As far as I'm concerned, you are inhuman."

The crowd behind him gasped while others glared at her.

"I didn't kill him!" Mara cried.

"I beg to differ." Karl turned to the barrister, who had the document ready for signing. The commander took the paper and held it up. "We can do this the easy way or the hard way." Then he beckoned a disciple to him. A priest came forward with a golden box. He stopped before Karl and opened it, revealing a familiar green blade.

Mara's heart began to pound. Her body trembled, for she remembered the dagger.

Karl reached into the box and retrieved the basilisk blade. He gazed back at Mara while holding the dagger up to his face. "I will give you one chance. If you refuse, I'll finish what I started."

The followers appeared confused.

The priest holding the box gave a curious look. "Commander White, you're going to let the Cursed Herald go? After all the things she's done?"

Karl gave a stoic look. "The Faith of Kallikratés has been significantly weakened. We lost our Goddess. We are without a leader. The Holy Blades are no more yet I, Commander White, live." He looked at the priest. "According to our code, the Commander of the Holy Blades shall inherit the powers of the High Priestess or Archdeacon, am I not correct?"

"Yes, Commander White," the priest replied. "But wouldn't both roles be too much?"

"I'll eventually find a new commander while we regain our strength," Karl replied.

"And we'll offer our sons," spoke a nobleman, "to help you rebuild the Holy Blades!"

"Thank you," Karl said. "I'm sure Kallisto shall recognize your good deeds." Then he looked back at Mara. "But first..." He handed her the paper and quill. "Will you sign, or will you make things difficult? Though I do have specific terms. After you sign, you must vacate Mirahyll immediately. Once I regain my full strength, I will hunt you down like the lowly creature you are."

Mara figured no one would defend her. Even the servants and the butler remained silent. The barrister had no problem helping Karl reverse the will. He never approved of Mr. White's plan to give everything to her. In the end, she had no choice. Mara took the quill and signed the paper. Once finished, Karl snatched the document away. He returned it to the barrister to inspect it.

"Everything is in order," said the barrister. "Congratulations, Master White. Both the house and Mr. Arthur White's fortune now belongs to you, as it should."

"Thank you," Karl said. "That will be all."

The barrister left, though the nobles remained.

Karl kept his scowl on Mara. "André," he addressed his butler.

"Yes, Master White," André responded.

"Get her out of this dress. And get me the inventory. I want to know how much Arthur spent on her."

"Yes, sir," André said as he went to get the inventory. Never once did he look at Mara.

The maids escorted Mara to her former room. They offered no help with removing her attire. Karl watched as she undressed before the wardrobe, making sure she stole nothing. It was humiliating for Mara; she never expected gawkers. They likely made snide remarks about her appearance, possibly comparing her to a zoo exhibit. She found her Silver Thorn armour, shoved in the back of the wardrobe. Mara equipped it while ignoring everyone. Back in her old attire, she approached her sword. However, Karl stepped in her way.

Mara scowled at him. "What are you doing? That's my sword!"

"Is it?" Karl took Nightingale. "André," he called.

The butler appeared beside him with an inventory ledger.

"How much was spent on her?" Karl inquired.

"Around ten thousand gold," the butler spoke.

"Ten thousand?" Karl glared at Mara. "He spent that much on you?"

"I never asked for this," Mara hissed.

Karl kept his eyes on her. "Return the gold you stole. Then I'll let you go."

"I didn't steal from you! You already got your money and house back!"

"I want it all back." He glanced at Nightingale. "You have things of value. Who knows? Maybe this sword is worth something."

Mara's heart pounded in her chest. Her blood began to boil. Nightingale was one of the last connections to Dad, and this man threatened to take it away. Tears formed in her eyes. The thought of losing this one connection drove her over the edge.

"No!" Mara snatched Nightingale out of his hands. She clutched it against her chest while seething with anger. "I won't let you take Nightingale!"

Karl was stunned until he noticed the shocked expressions on his servants' faces. "So, this is the true face of the undying."

Mara was confused, yet a nearby mirror revealed her reflection. She had transformed before everyone. They saw her glowing yellow eyes, the dark markings on her face, and the elongated canines.

"Good gracious," André spoke.

"She's not human," said one of the maids.

"Of course not," Karl said. "I assume Mr. White left out this detail, which was a mistake on his part."

Mara glowered at him. "I didn't kill him. I signed your damn paper!"

"You thought everyone would believe you just because you signed?" Karl asked. "You're more pathetic than I thought." He looked to his butler. "André, escort her out."

"As you wish, sir." The butler began to approach her.

However, Mara had other plans. Karl's return could spell trouble, reviving the Faith of Kallikratés. She wrapped her right hand around the grip of Nightingale. Everyone froze while she began to unsheathe her sword.

Karl looked very displeased. "What do you think you're doing?"

Mara remained silent as she drew Nightingale from its sheath and held it out before her.

The commander gave a stern look, despite being unnerved by the undying's actions. "You intend to fight me in my home?"

"You threatened to hunt me down," Mara replied as her glowing eyes locked on him. Black smoke billowed from her body as she bared her fangs. "But not if I kill you first!"

Karl glared back at her. "Everyone out!"

Many nobles fled, although a few remained.

"Master White," André addressed him, "what about you?"

"You mustn't fight her alone, Commander White," warned one of the noblemen. "We outnumber her!"

"No!" Karl shouted. "I will deal with her myself!" Then he got into a fighting stance while gripping the basilisk blade in his right hand.

Staring down her prey, Mara dashed at him with Nightingale in hand. Karl dodged to her right. Mara swung her blade at him, but he stepped back. He drove the dagger forward. Mara vanished in a wisp of black smoke. She reappeared behind him, poised to attack. However, Karl caught on to her tactic. He spun around and slashed at her. Mara had very little time to react. She tried to block with Nightingale, but the basilisk blade cut her left arm. An intense pain shot up into her arm, causing her to stagger backwards. Mara checked her wound and saw it promptly heal. The injury wasn't serious. Unfortunately, while Mara was distracted, Karl stabbed her. The intense pain returned as she looked down at the dagger embedded in her abdomen. The undying could feel the poison coursing her veins as her skin began to decay. She lifted her gaze to the cold commander. His face brought back all those painful memories she held. Anger began to build, fuelling her strength.

All of a sudden, Mara pushed Karl away. The commander was caught off guard by her reacquired strength. The undying ignored everyone as she stared at the dagger. With her left hand, Mara grabbed the basilisk blade and pulled it out. She groaned in pain as it sliced through flesh and muscle. After the dagger's removal, only a blackened wound remained. Sparks of magic floated from the cut. The basilisk blade had cut through muscles, allowing a tiny glimpse of her insides. Then the wound healed, thanks to Mara's regenerative abilities.

"So, the rumours are true," said the priest. "She has stolen the gods' power!"

Mara looked up at Karl, who glared at her in shock.

"How dare you steal the very essence of the gods?" Karl raged.

Mara glowered back at him. Blue sparks appeared along with the black fumes billowing out of her body. "You will pay for what you've done!"

She gripped the basilisk blade. Blue flames engulfed the dagger, melting it into an unrecognizable shape. Mara, however, did not feel the scorching heat. She focused her gaze on Karl.

The commander took notice and began to back away.

"She's using the power!" cried the priest.

Mara glanced over her shoulder to look back at the astonished followers and servants. While doing so, she saw her reflection in the mirror. Her eyes were now glowing blue. The huntress understood that the soul of Aazalith was behind her heightened state. So Mara used this to her advantage. She turned on Karl, who had just realized that he was no match. Mara lifted Nightingale once more, intending to end this once and for all.

She dashed at him and drove Nightingale forward. The commander's face was the intended target.

"Commander White, look out!" shouted a follower.

Before the tip of Nightingale could make contact, Karl slammed his hands together, catching the blade in between his palms. He stopped her attack, although the force pushed him against the wall. Still, he was able to keep her from stabbing him through the face. Mara tried to push the blade forward, but it would not budge. She could not understand what was happening. She was a supernatural creature who had Aazalith's soul, yet he was able to block her attack. What was going on? Did he still possess some of his powers?

Karl suddenly deflected the attack to his left as he attempted to duck out of the way. But Nightingale managed to graze him on his left shoulder and tore his sleeve. The skirmish loosened his collar. Then she saw the tattoos on the left side of his neck and shoulder. Mara looked back at him, noticing his glare. He had realized that she was staring at his tattoos. He reached over and held his wounded shoulder.

"Remove her from my home," Karl ordered. "I never want to see her face in this city again!"

The nobles grabbed Mara and pulled her away from Karl. She kept a grip on Nightingale, which came out of the wall.

"Let me go!" Mara cried as she struggled against their hold. Not only was she outnumbered, but the power from the divine's soul had been exhausted. She was powerless.

Karl leaned against the wall while holding his injured shoulder. His eyes began to glow blue. A similar light emanated from both his right hand and the tattoos underneath his clothing. His injury healed. His eyes returned to normal as he gave a smug look.

Only Mara noticed. Everyone was busy gawking at her for the stunt she pulled.

The nobles pushed her out the door. All Mara had left were her clothes, the keepsakes, some healing stones, and Nightingale.

Mara walked past the front window, seeing all the nobles gathered around the commander. Karl spoke to them until he noticed her. His frozen face watched her. Something was not adding up. Despite the commander's resurrection, Mara sensed something was amiss. She looked away as she walked past the manor.

Bereft of gold or home, there was only one place Mara could go.

* * *

Mara traversed the snowy fields outside of Mirahyll. She headed west in the dark. It was cold, but she kept moving. The undying saw a faint light from a house outside of Haranta Village. She approached the doorstep, although her legs protested against another move. Mara knocked on the door. An old muscular man answered.

"You better have a reason to be pestering me in the middle of the night!" He looked at Mara, and the anger melted from his face. "Mara? What are you doing here this late?"

Mara shuddered from the cold. "Can I please stay?"

The old blacksmith gazed at her face. "Yes, of course. Come in!" He could tell that she was in distress. "What happened?"

"It's a long story," Mara said.

Talon folded his arms and shrugged. "Well, I'm wide awake."

She told him everything. Naturally, he grew furious.

"And the city did nothing?" Talon shook his head. "I swear, no person from Mirahyll will ever touch my weapons ever again, as long as I draw breath!"

Chapter Six

Starting Over

Talon was kind enough to lend Mara the spare bedroom upstairs. As Mara drifted off to sleep, her mind continued to reel.

'How could Karl still be alive?' Mara wondered as she closed her eyes.

When she opened them again, she found herself standing before the burnt remains of a manor. The snow silently fell around Thalia's former home. The faint smell of smoke remained in the air. Mara stepped forward, then spotted some footprints in the snow. Her eyes followed the trail until she saw a man in the distance. He was too far away for her to see any features, yet she saw a blue blanket wrapped around his shivering form.

Mara lifted her right hand to her mouth and shouted, "Hey!"

The sound of her shouting woke her up. Mara opened her eyes to the morning light. She felt well-rested despite the strange dream, the events of last night, and only having a few hours of sleep. The undying rose out of bed and headed downstairs.

* * *

"Ah, good morning," Talon greeted.

He already had breakfast ready. Mara sat at the kitchen table and saw a variety of dried fruit, cheese, and bread. It was unlike the breakfasts served at the manor, but it was better than nothing. She took a few pieces of each and began to eat.

Talon sat on the other side. "Can't believe what happened last night."

Mara glanced up at him. "It was like a nightmare."

"What will you do next?" Talon asked.

"Well, I could wait for the Great Commander White to come after me again," Mara sighed. "I'll gladly finish what he started last night. Otherwise, I'm seeking a chance to board a ship to Thoron. The envoy should have reached them by now."

"You can stay here for now," Talon told her, "but I'd like you to do some work for me."

"Of course," Mara said. "What do you need me to do?"

"Gather some items for me. In exchange, I'll either pay gold or give discounts on my services." He handed her a piece of paper. "Here's a list of items I need."

Mara gazed at the list. "Monster hide, bones, and tissue." She looked up at Talon. "Any specific creature?"

The old blacksmith shrugged. "Any creature will do."

"Okay," Mara said.

She gathered her things and left. Mirahyll could offer some leads. Mara hoped to avoid Karl White.

* * *

As Mara travelled to Mirahyll, she spotted a group of horsemen coming her way. She thought of ignoring them until they stopped before her.

"Mara? What are you doing here?"

Mara glanced up at the masked riders. She recognized a male voice among them. The lead horseman unveiled his face, revealing himself as Elder Ravenclaw.

"How have you been?" asked the elder.

Mara was relieved to see familiar and friendly faces. "Hello, Elder Ravenclaw," she began in a low tone.

The elder frowned at her. "I sense you are not well."

"Had better days," Mara admitted. "I lost almost everything."

The riders glanced at each other and murmured among themselves.

"What happened?" Ravenclaw questioned.

"Mr. White removed Karl from his will and added my name. After he died, I inherited his fortune and his mansion. But Karl is alive. He contacted the barrister and forced me to sign everything back to him. We fought last night. I was lucky enough to walk away with my life."

Ravenclaw gave a sympathetic look. "I'm sorry this happened, but money can never buy you happiness."

"I know," Mara murmured. "It's just... He accused me of killing Mr. White, but I did not. No one came to my defence." She shook her head. "How is Karl alive? I saw him die!"

Ravenclaw looked puzzled. "He returned to life?"

Mara nodded. "Claimed Kallisto resurrected him."

"Is that so?" Ravenclaw pondered her words. "I will ask Alkina to perform a seance. She can commune with the spirits of the dead, and may get you the answers you're looking for."

"Thanks," Mara said, gazing down the road. "I have to get some materials for Talon. I need monster hide, bones, and tissue."

"You should head to the ruins of Golden Mountain," Ravenclaw suggested. "I hear a creature is terrorizing a group of surveyors."

"Thanks for the tip," Mara said. "I'll check it out."

She headed for Golden Mountain Ruins.

* * *

Arriving at the ruins, Mara saw many tents and wagons. A group of men sat around a campfire. The huntress approached them. They noticed her as well.

"I'm here about the monster," Mara began.

One of the men stood up and watched her warily. "Aye, I put up a notice." He looked her up and down. "Think you can take on the creature? Another hunter arrived before you but hasn't returned. I fear this monster is very formidable."

"I've dealt with many beasts," Mara responded, "but any information is helpful."

"I'm afraid we know little," the contractor admitted. "We were sent to survey this land. As soon as we began work, three of my men died, as well as two of our horses."

"Sorry about your loss," Mara said. "If you still have the bodies, I wish to examine them. Their wounds could help me identify the creature."

The leader of the survey team pointed to where the bodies were. "They're just over there."

Mara spotted the cadavers and approached them. The stench of death invaded her nostrils within ten feet. Drawing closer, Mara spotted the deep gashes riddling their bodies. The horses were torn apart with their stomachs ripped open by teeth and claws. One had their head torn off.

"Could be a werewolf, but they mainly reside in the Old Hunting Grounds unless it's a rogue." Mara noticed a clump of hair. "What's this?" The huntress examined the fur. "Black as night. A shadow beast, but they live in the deepest depths of the Dark Labyrinth." Mara sighed, "Hope it's the former, not the latter."

She then spotted bloody footprints leading away from the bodies. The creature could stand on two feet. Both alpha werewolves and shadow beasts were bipedal. It did not look good. Following the trail, she found the previous hunter, or what remained of him.

"Similar scars on the face and flesh," Mara murmured to herself. "Several bite marks on the neck. A torn jugular." The huntress glanced down to see the stomach torn open. Some of his organs were missing. Whatever did this had to be huge. "What a waste."

The nameless hunter might have thought he could take on the monster, but was no match for it. Lifting her gaze, Mara spotted a large hole in the ground.

"Came from the Dark Labyrinth. Must've dug its way out."

Before Mara entered the monster den, she unsheathed Nightingale.

A low growl echoed from the darkness. Glowing yellow eyes pierced the shadows. The beast's razor-sharp fangs seemed to glow. A pair of horns protruded from its wolf-like head. It was a shadow beast. The monster stood taller than Mara.

The shadow beast growled again as it stalked towards her. Mara responded with her own glowing eyes. She removed her mask and bared her elongating canines. Gripping Nightingale tightly, the huntress engaged the creature in battle. Shadow beasts were very dangerous by being able to adapt. They were also capable of evolving into a more efficient hunter through the blood they imbibed. They can disorient prey through teleportation. This particular creature might have acquired the taste for human flesh and blood. Mara had no choice but to slay the beast.

However, something was odd about this creature. Mara had fought shadow beasts before, but this one appeared more intelligent. It watched her, studying her attack pattern! The monster evaded many of her attacks. She would have to wait until the shadow beast attacked. It took a swing at her, and she dodged. A window of opportunity opened, and she took advantage of it. Realizing the huntress had caught on, the shadow beast changed its pattern. It began to teleport around, trying to confuse her. Unfortunately for the creature, Mara knew the tactic quite well. If the beast fought like a human, then it would think to attack from behind. It was a common strategy for both monsters and humans. The huntress spun around and parried the shadow beast's attack. The creature was stunned, leaving it wide open.

Mara plunged Nightingale into the creature's heart, sealing its fate. The shadow beast slumped to the ground. The glow in its eyes faded away as the monster succumbed to its injuries. While Mara observed the beast's corpse, glowing orbs floated out of it. The huntress watched with curiosity. The peculiar globes of light vanished into the darkness. Not wanting to stay too long, Mara reverted to her human self and pulled her mask up. Taking her sword, the huntress severed the shadow beast's head and harvested some parts for Talon. While removing the beast's hide, she spotted a shining stone within its flesh. It was a healing stone. She claimed the gem and put it away.

Once finished, Mara returned to whence she came.

* * *

Mara received many stares as she approached the contractor with the shadow beast's head.

The man looked at the head with apprehension. "What the hell is that thing?"

"A shadow beast," Mara answered. "This was responsible for killing your men and horses."

The surveyor leader shook his head. "I've never heard of them."

"They are uncommon," Mara responded, gazing at the head. "They reside in the deepest depths of the Dark Labyrinth, and rarely come to the surface."

The surveyor reached into his pockets and handed over two hundred gold. "Here, as agreed on the contract. If I had more money, I would've paid more."

Mara accepted the payment. "It's fine, but I'd suggest you deal with the hole, in case any more creatures come out."

"I'll take your advice to heart. I will have my men seal the hole immediately."

Before leaving, Mara looked at the ruins of the mountain. Ever since seeing those strange orbs, an uneasy feeling began to grow within.

"Have you ever experienced anything else unusual?" Mara asked. "See any other creatures?"

"Hmm? Well, my crew had claimed to see some ghosts," the surveyor told her.

The huntress looked back at him with a questioning glint in her eyes. "Ghosts?"

"Maybe you've noticed these glowing orbs during your hunt. My men claim these are the souls of those who lost their lives when the mountain collapsed."

Mara watched him for a while before turning her gaze back onto the mountain. Her eyes fell onto the destroyed entrance to the Dark Labyrinth. The huntress remembered seeing a ghostly figure standing near it while riding back to Mirahyll with Mr. White.

"Are you not concerned about more ghost encounters?" Mara asked.

"It won't be a problem anymore," the contractor answered.

"Why is that?"

"Surely, you've heard of Commander White's resurrection. It's quite a miracle. Kallikratés' disciples are supporting him. Many of them are having their sons join the Holy Blades, reviving the faction. We'll have a guild to protect us from the monsters. And I hear the commander will become the archdeacon in Ardana."

Mara frowned upon hearing this. Was the referendum all for naught?

"The Faith in Corlin and Loris wish to investigate the incident at Golden Mountain, and offer support for Commander White," the surveyor added. "They may perform a cleansing of the mountain, and the ghost problem will be no more."

While unsure about this particular news, Mara returned to Talon's workshop.

Chapter Seven

A Slow Recovery

Mara returned by late afternoon on January 11, only to discover the old blacksmith in a foul mood. He was grumbling to himself while striking a piece of metal with his hammer.

"That bastard," Talon growled underneath his breath.

Mara took a few more steps towards him, wondering what was bothering him. The blacksmith took notice and looked at her. The rage painting his face remained for a few more seconds before melting into a curious expression.

"Ah, I didn't hear you come in." He eyed the bag in her possession. "You got the stuff I asked for?"

The huntress held the bag out before her. "Got them from a shadow beast. I hope it's okay for what you need."

Talon took the bag and inspected the contents. "Hmm, this should do." He reached for his coin purse. "Here, take this. It's not much, but I do appreciate your efforts."

Mara accepted the payment, which was worth three hundred gold. "It's better than nothing." After putting away the gold, the huntress gave a concerned look. "Are you okay?"

The old blacksmith stared at her in confusion. "Hmm?" Then his facial expression fell to a frown. "Ah, yes, I'm fine," he murmured.

"Are you sure?" Mara questioned. "Haven't seen that look since losing your last forge. Thought maybe you had a bad customer."

"You could say that," he muttered. "That ass showed up at my workshop!"

Mara gave a strange look. "Who?"

"Commander White."

Her face twisted in rage. "What?"

Talon saw the anger in her eyes. "That was my exact reaction." Then, "He showed up here with a group of Holy Blades, asking if I could reforge his sword. Even offered a hefty sum."

She kept watching him. "Did you take the offer?"

"Not after what he did to my last workshop." He shrugged. "Hell, I even brought it up, and the fool just looked at me as if he had no idea what I was talking about!"

Mara gave a peculiar look. "He forgot?" Another thought crossed her mind. "Doesn't he go to Corlin to see a blacksmith? Why did he see you?"

"I don't know," Talon said. "The roads to Corlin might be in poor condition. Still, the nerve of that bastard!"

It was then the huntress remembered what she and her friends did to the commander. Aspen had erased his memories of his time serving Kallisto. That was at least two and a half centuries of memories gone.

"Well, I'm glad I missed him." She glanced at the forge. "Guess I can use the gold to upgrade and repair my stuff."

Talon took Nightingale in for repair and any possible upgrades. Once finished, he handed the sword back to Mara.

"There's nothing more I need from you at the moment," he said. "You can have the evening off."

The huntress nodded, then left the workshop.

* * *

The sun was setting as Mara ventured outside. She figured she could have the time and place to herself, watching the setting sun. As Mara stood alone in the clearing, she heard a horse neighing. The huntress looked to her left and saw a black mare, with a white diamond shape on her forehead, galloping towards her. The little lady, who the huntress had not seen for a while, stopped and looked at Mara with caution.

Mara attempted to get near, but the horse ran away. The undying sighed while the mare kept her distance. The animal remained uncooperative as usual.

"Ah, hello again," greeted a familiar man.

Mara looked behind to see Elder Ravenclaw mounted on a horse. A few riders accompanied him. The elder dismounted from his steed before approaching Mara.

"Likewise," Mara said. "What brings you out here?"

"Aye, great to see you!" Talon shouted while running to them. "Thank you for coming!"

Mara watched as the old blacksmith reached them. She grew confused. "What's going on?"

Talon grinned at her. "The Stone Mages have hired me to forge their weapons. In exchange, they'll trade knowledge on their forging techniques."

Ravenclaw nodded. "Yes, our youth are growing restless. They express a desire to become hunters. Alkina has foreseen the rise in monster activity, so the need for hunters is urgent."

"Good idea," Mara said. "Speaking of Alkina, did she do the seance yet?"

"She is seeking the proper spirits. I recommend you visit her tomorrow."

A young female rider dismounted from her horse and approached the huntress. She smiled while taking Mara's hands. "It is nice to meet you," she began. "My name is Shenoah."

Mara gazed at her in confusion. This woman seemed nice, yet a little too happy.

"Uh, likewise," the huntress responded. "The name's Mara."

"My daughter shall work with Talon as his apprentice," Ravenclaw said. "She mainly specializes in armour."

Mara gave the elder a questioning glance. "Your daughter?" She never knew Ravenclaw had a daughter or any children for that matter.

"Yes," Shenoah said. "I'll take care of the armour while he deals with the weapons." She looked at Talon. "I'd like to see the workshop."

"Sure," Talon responded, gesturing to the workshop. "It's this way."

The armourer walked past the blacksmith. She appeared very excited to see the workshop. Mara was left alone with Ravenclaw and his riders.

"Mara," the elder addressed her.

Mara gazed back at him. "Yes?"

Ravenclaw pointed to the little lady. "Is this your horse?"

She gazed at the mare, who stood a fair distance away.

"Yes," Mara sighed. "More or less. I don't think she likes me much."

Ravenclaw gazed at the horse in confusion. "Why do you say this?"

"I think she knows I'm not human. Ever since the day we met, she's been afraid of me. She often runs away when I come near."

"She appears improperly trained," he suspected. "She remains wild at heart." Ravenclaw looked back at Mara. "For many years, the Stone Mages have always kept a strong bond with horses. Horses are loyal creatures, always willing to please us."

Mara placed her hands on her hips. "I don't exactly have a strong bond with her." She shrugged. "Although she does come through if I help her. I did save her once during a werewolf contract."

"That may be the key." Ravenclaw reached into his bag and retrieved an apple. "Here, take this." He handed it to Mara. "Offer it to her. Show her kindness, and she'll come to you."

The huntress gazed down at the apple in her hands. She lifted her gaze to the little lady, who had spotted the fruit in her possession. The mare approached with a glint of intent in her dark eyes. Mara turned to face her, then took a few steps forward. The mare paused upon seeing the approaching huntress. Sensing the horse's uneasiness, Mara stopped and held out the apple before her. The horse moved again. The huntress remained still, making sure not to move a muscle. The horse came close enough to reach the apple, though she never took her eyes off of Mara. The mare remained wary.

"Show her your face," Ravenclaw suggested.

Mara took her free hand and reached for her mask. After pulling it down, she reached for her hood and pushed it back to reveal her face. The horse appeared stunned by Mara's appearance. The huntress could see her reflection in the eyes of the mare. As far as Mara could recall, the mare had never seen her human face before.

When the horse realized there was no danger, she focused all of her attention on the apple. She took a large bite from the fruit and chewed up the piece. The horse snorted and whinnied as she ate the apple. After consuming the fruit, she remained still.

"Okay, try to mount her," Ravenclaw instructed Mara. "She seems more comfortable now."

Taking the reins, Mara attempted to mount the mare. The horse watched but did not seem to object. Once settled in, Mara looked down at Ravenclaw.

"Now, direct the horse," the elder said. "Show her where you want to go."

Mara followed his instructions and managed to get the horse to move. Much to the huntress' surprise, the little lady obeyed her every order. Once she had a better understanding of handling the horse, Mara grabbed the reins and shouted, "Yah!"

The horse neighed loudly, then took off in a dash. The huntress almost fell off. Forgetting how fast the lady could be, she clutched the reins. Within a few minutes, she grew more comfortable riding the horse. In the past, she used the animal for some tasks but never rode for leisure. Mara began to smile as she grew confident. She displayed more control over the lady and rode around the Stone Mages.

Elder Ravenclaw folded his arms and laughed out of joy.

She gazed back at him and noticed someone beside him. It looked like Dad, who was a strong and burly man. Mara had to take her eyes off for a brief moment to see where she was going, but when she glanced back again, the image of her father had vanished. The huntress looked around while stopping her horse. A frown formed on her face as she dismounted from the lady.

Ravenclaw approached her. "You've done well!" His smile faded as soon as he saw the look on Mara's face. "What's wrong?"

"I thought I saw Dad," Mara murmured.

The elder and his riders appeared stunned to hear this.

"Did you?" Ravenclaw checked his surroundings.

"He was beside you," the huntress explained.

A small smile reformed on the elder's face. "He was a good person in life with a true heart of gold. The same heart of gold you inherited."

Mara gazed at the ground. She missed Mom and Dad so much and sometimes wished they were here.

Ravenclaw approached his horse. "It's getting late. We should be heading home." After he mounted his ride, he looked back at Mara. "Be sure to visit Cerebell tomorrow. Alkina will have the answers you seek."

Mara nodded as she watched them leave. She mounted the little lady once again and rode back to Talon's workshop. Mara gazed at the vast snowy field during her return, hoping to see Dad once more.

Within minutes, she arrived at the workshop. As Mara went inside, she spotted Shenoah looking around as Talon explained all the tools at the forge.

Shenoah looked very excited. "It's wonderful!" She then spotted the monster hide. "Is that…?"

Mara folded her arms and nodded. "It's from a shadow beast I slew earlier."

The armourer gazed at her in astonishment before returning her attention onto the hide. She studied it for a moment. "Hmm…"

"Is it usable?" Mara asked.

"Should be," Talon answered. "I've used hides like this before."

"A shadow beast's hide is stronger than cowhide." Shenoah looked at Mara. "It's sufficient."

Talon nodded. "But first, we should have dinner. I'm hungry."

Both Mara and Shenoah agreed.

In the kitchen, Talon began to cook a large slab of meat, while Shenoah prepared the vegetables. Mara glanced over at them. For one moment, she saw Mom and Dad. It was something she used to do with her family.

Once the dinner was ready, they sat around the table. While eating, the three talked about various things.

"I've never mentioned this," Talon addressed Mara. "I've got a new contract to forge weapons for Hema's knights."

"Sounds great," Mara said.

Talon glanced outside. "With your horse, delivering weapons will be easy. All I need is a wagon."

"Sure, as long as I get to help with some of the deliveries," Mara said. "I don't know how the horse will respond to being strapped to a wagon."

"Shouldn't be a problem," Shenoah told her. "I've dealt with many horses in the past. Training her to pull a wagon should be fine."

"Okay," Mara responded. She changed the subject. "So, Shenoah," the huntress began, "sorry if I cause offence, but Elder Ravenclaw never mentioned having any children."

Shenoah looked a little sad. "Father and I don't have a strong relationship, with him often away on hunts. I spent much of my childhood with my mother until she died." Then she asked, "What about your parents?"

Mara began to sulk. "Dad was murdered by Kallisto. Mom spent three decades rotting in a hospital." She sighed, "At least I saw her before she died. And sometimes I see Dad's ghost."

"They must've loved you," Shenoah murmured. "Sorry for what happened to your parents. It's similar to another story I heard."

Mara grew intrigued. "Really?"

The armourer nodded. "Over thirty years ago, a Stone Mage married a woman from Mirahyll, and they made a family. But he was killed one day. We believe the Faith was behind it."

"What was his name?" Mara asked.

"Blackthorn," Shenoah answered.

Talon gaped at Shenoah. "Theodore Blackthorn? Now that's a name I haven't heard in a while."

Mara gave him a questioning look. "You knew him?"

"Aye, he was a Silver Thorn. During my time in the guild, I've seen quite a few Stone Mages join. Theodore was a great hunter." Talon glanced at Shenoah. "The incident happened around twenty years ago. I heard he left behind a wife and son."

A thought crossed Mara's mind. "Wait a minute. Theo is his son?"

Talon sighed, "Desperate for a better life, the widow sought the heart of a noble and abandoned her son. She lived in luxury while the young one lived on the streets. He struggled to get by, and ultimately resorted to thieving. He took in others who had unfortunate circumstances or with a similar mindset, and thus the Blackthorn Guild was born."

The huntress cut into the meat with her knife and fork. Taking a bite, she found the meat chewy. Mara hated to admit this, but she missed the cooks from the manor. Yet she remained silent, for she did not want to provoke Talon's ire.

Mara lifted her gaze from her plate. "Still waiting on a reply from Thoron."

Talon and Shenoah gazed at her.

"How's that going?" Talon questioned.

"Mirahyll sent the envoy over a week ago," the huntress replied. "It'll take another week or two for Thoron's response. I hope Karl doesn't interfere."

"With the commander's return, things might be problematic," Talon said.

"According to father, the commander has become an archdeacon," Shenoah added. "He threw the referendum out at the behest of Kallikratés' followers."

"He also forced Evan to resume previously cancelled projects," Talon said. "Heard it from Hema's knights when they came to me for the contract."

Shenoah frowned. "It'll be a matter of time before he forces the Stone Mages back to the Outer Frontier."

Mara furrowed her eyebrows. "I'll find a way to stop him." She gazed at her plate. "I'm going to see Alkina tomorrow morning."

After finishing their dinner, the three cleaned up. Both Mara and Talon headed for bed, while Shenoah returned to Cerebell. Before turning in, Mara placed Nightingale on the dresser. As she began to relax in her bed, her gaze lingered on the weapon until she fell asleep.

* * *

On the next day, Mara mounted her horse and headed to Cerebell. It was a quiet morning as she travelled alone.

Entering Cerebell, Mara saw quite the transformation of the once-abandoned city. The Stone Mages were out and about on their daily business.

From what she could tell, they were settling in quite nicely. She hoped it would last, but had her doubts with Commander White's return. As she rode through the city, the Stone Mages paid no mind to her. After all, she was more or less family. She saw Elder Ravenclaw with some of his riders.

The elder took notice and looked at her.

"Ah, you are here," he greeted.

Mara stopped, then dismounted from her ride. When she looked at him again, Mara saw a smile forming on his face.

"I see you're getting better with your horse," he added.

"Yes, I am." She gazed at the mare briefly before looking back at him. "Where's Alkina?"

"This way," Ravenclaw said.

Mara followed him to his home, which was the largest house in the city.

"We were able to salvage these homes," Ravenclaw said. "In time, they will all be inhabitable."

"That's good," Mara said. "I hope Karl hasn't given you any problems."

"He acts as though I'm not an alderman. I suppose it's better this way. He stays out of my way, and I stay out of his."

"What about the other aldermen or the chancellors?"

"Davis, Evan, and Jonathan are fine. Nigel, on the other hand, has never spoken to me, nor will he look at me."

"He was a bit of a jerk," Mara admitted.

"I see," Ravenclaw said.

He led her to his home, where the shaman had also been living. When Mara entered the room, a strong scent of incense invaded her nostrils. The overpowering smell made her eyes water. Ravenclaw remained unfazed.

"She uses the incense to communicate with the spirits," the elder explained.

After growing accustomed to the smell, Mara gazed at Alkina. The white-haired shaman remained still as the smoke surrounded her. Her old eyes appeared more glazed than usual, indicating a deep trance. After a moment, some colour returned to her eyes. Alkina snapped out of the trance and almost collapsed.

Ravenclaw approached the shaman out of concern. "Are you okay?"

Alkina gazed at him before noticing the huntress. At first, she looked confused. Then her eyes lit up. The old shaman seemed happy to see Mara.

"Ah, our liberator has come," she began.

Mara gave a strange look, in which the shaman took notice.

"Don't give me that look. It's true."

Mara shrugged. "Guess it's better than whatever the others call me."

The shaman snorted. "They're just mad that you disrupted their way of life."

"You mean saving this land from their schemes and killing their so-called goddess?"

"The oppression of our people could no longer continue," Alkina said sternly.

"I agree. Kallisto was a threat to everyone."

"I know," said the old shaman. "I sensed a powerful wave of magic spreading throughout the land. I suspect you had something to do with it."

"Kallisto consumed the rest of Aazalith's soul," Mara revealed. "She transformed into a monster. I destroyed her core, and it created a magical explosion. Thanks to my curse, I came back, but I can't say the same about Kallisto."

"That foolish woman paid a very terrible price."

"The Faith remains, and Commander White is somehow alive, which is why I came to see you."

"Yes," Alkina responded, "and I agreed to perform this seance for you. To communicate with the spirits and find the answers you're looking for."

"What did you find?" Mara asked.

"Please, give me a moment." Alkina reached for a cup of tea. She took a sip while watching Mara. Then she lowered the cup. "You young people are so impulsive."

"I'm sorry. It's just…" Mara shook her head. "The last few days have been so confusing."

"You mean him?"

Mara nodded. "I want to know if it's true."

The shaman placed the cup on the ground before her. Alkina stared at it before lifting her gaze to Mara.

"The man who calls himself Karl White returned from the dead," Alkina said.

The huntress took note of her words. "Calls himself Karl White? Are you saying he's an imposter?"

Alkina nodded.

Mara gaped at her. Deep down, she knew it was true, for Karl never possessed any tattoos. She thought about the dream where she stood before the remains of Thalia's manor and saw a man disappearing into the cold winter night.

"I knew something wasn't right." The huntress looked back at Alkina. "But why is he pretending to be Karl White?"

"He lost the very power that made him a god," Alkina replied.

"He's human?" Mara questioned.

"Yes, but he can fool others," the shaman said. "He even fooled you."

Mara folded her arms. "At least he's human." Then she asked, "How is he alive?"

"Two vessels existed in this world," Alkina answered. "One dead and one alive. When one died, the other returned to the world of the living."

Mara looked baffled. "One dead and one alive?" Then she recalled, "Thalia's spell. Did it work?"

The shaman nodded slowly. "Yes, and we have you to thank."

"What do you mean?"

"You are the reason why he's alive."

The huntress grew confused. "I brought him back to life?" She remembered stabbing the commander with a moonstone-enchanted Nightingale. "Thalia wanted to stop Karl's heart temporarily to resurrect Kratés. But I slew Karl."

"He returned under the right conditions."

"What about Kallisto?" Mara asked. "He claimed she resurrected him."

Alkina shook her head. "Kallisto's soul was destroyed. She no longer exists."

Mara was stunned, though she had seen what became of Kallisto. Now she had another problem in the form of the false goddess' former husband. Kratés had returned and was pretending to be Karl White. The huntress was unsure what to do with this new information.

Mara looked at Alkina and nodded. "Thanks for your help." She rose to her feet. "I have to figure out what to do about him. Who knows what he'll do…"

Before Mara could leave, she felt a frail hand wrap around her wrist. The huntress looked back at the shaman, who gazed up at her with a solemn look.

"Beware of this man," Alkina warned. "He already suspects you of knowing his secret."

Mara stared at her for a while and then nodded. She knew well to heed the shaman's warning. Once Alkina released her arm, the huntress left the house. She mounted her horse and returned to Talon's workshop.

Chapter Eight

A Rescue Mission

By noon on January 15, Mara had planned to travel to Mirahyll and ask Beatrice about the envoy. First, she needed to return to Talon's workshop and drop off the various parts harvested from the monsters she hunted. The pay was not much, but at least she had claimed another healing stone. Mara grew more comfortable riding the little lady, which made fulfilling monster contracts easier.

However, her plan was put on hold once she returned to the workshop.

The old blacksmith waved to Mara. "Ah, here you are," Talon greeted. He spotted the full bag in her hand. "You've been busy."

Shenoah gleefully approached Mara and took the bag. She kept a grin on her face as she looked inside. "This is wonderful!"

Mara placed her hands on her hips. "Hope you like them."

It was then the huntress spotted a man near Talon. She assumed he was a customer until he turned around. She recognized the short black hair. The smug look he often possessed, however, was missing.

"Boyd? What are you doing here?" Mara questioned.

Boyd stormed up to her. "You have to help me!"

"With what?"

"Claire has been abducted!"

Shenoah and Talon looked surprised, while Mara was unmoved by his plight.

"Let me guess," said the huntress. "Theo wants his gold back."

Boyd's jaw dropped. "How did you know?"

"He told me," Mara recalled. "He gave you a week, but you didn't heed his warning."

Boyd sulked. "Well, you could be a little more sympathetic. I have three days, or I'll never see her again!"

"Then return his gold," Mara said flatly. "Why are you even asking for my help?"

"I can't get to the gold," Boyd admitted.

"Why not?"

"There's a ghost, and it won't let me near it."

Mara looked at him with a deadpanned expression. "What's in it for me?"

"Fine, I'll pay you two thousand gold." Boyd glared at her. "Jeez, you hunters have become so damn finicky!"

"Sorry, I've come under hard times," Mara said. "So, where's the stash? If you're talking about monsters, I'd assume it's near the Dark Labyrinth or within it."

"It's just outside of Har' Yhan," Boyd explained.

"Very well," the huntress said. "I assume you have a horse?"

Boyd nodded. "I do. We can go there together."

Mara followed him outside. They mounted their horses and rode to Har' Yhan.

* * *

As the two rode towards the northern tip of the port town, Boyd glanced over at Mara.

"I heard what happened," he began. "I'm just as surprised to see him alive. Commander White authorized my capture after I deserted the Holy Blades."

Mara stared ahead, wondering if she should tell Boyd about the imposter. She was one of the few who knew the truth. Then again, she was never on friendly terms with the former rogue. Instead, she asked, "Are you leaving again?"

"I don't know," Boyd answered.

"What do you mean you don't know?"

"Well, I encountered Commander White at a banquet the other day."

"What did he do?"

"Nothing," he said. "He just glanced at me and walked past."

"Maybe he decided to forgive you," Mara suggested.

"This is Commander White we're talking about," Boyd argued. "After that incident in Har' Yhan, he suspended me from active duty for a while. And I'd like to think my recent actions had me hunted. Thanks to me, you brought down the Faith."

"I'd like to think it was because I sought revenge against the one who murdered me. You only said those words to save yourself."

"But I shared that revelation with you," Boyd said. "He should've arrested me on the spot. And you—I was expecting worse."

Mara glanced back at him. "You think I got off easy?"

"False goddess or not, the man is very devoted. You caused her demise, yet all he cared about was getting his fortune back."

Boyd was right. Even though the imposter's disguise was imperfect, she remained unsure about revealing the truth.

"He promised he'll come for me," Mara said. "We'll finish what we started."

"Yes," Boyd said. "Commander White will be hailed as a hero while painting you as the bad guy."

"Why?"

"You are the Cursed Herald, and you slew their goddess."

"She wasn't a goddess," Mara said. "Or are they going to keep denying it?"

"Whatever the case, you got the attention of the Faith in Corlin and Loris," Boyd revealed. "I hear they might come to Ardana within a week."

The huntress sighed. She hoped to reach Thoron before encountering any more trouble.

They headed north towards Ghost Mountain, which had the second entrance to the Dark Labyrinth.

* * *

Two days had passed since Mara decided to accompany Boyd into the Dark Labyrinth.

"This is the place," he told her.

"Why would you keep the gold here?" Mara questioned.

"To deter thieves," Boyd replied. "Only the foolish or brave would so brazenly roam."

They soon encountered the alleged spirit. A skeletal woman stood before a coffin laden with gold. Her attire looked familiar yet tattered and torn. She held a bell in a frail and bony hand.

"Is this the ghost?" Mara inquired.

Boyd took a big gulp. "It appeared as soon as I used this coffin for the stash."

Mara snapped her gaze onto him. "You're kidding, right?" She glanced back at the coffin. "You used this to hide the gold?"

"I thought it would be a great place to hide it," Boyd admitted.

"Yes, and disturbed the ghost in the process." The huntress switched her attention back onto the ghost.

The ghost released a loud shriek, causing a pair of large black dogs with glowing red eyes to appear.

"What the hell are these?" Boyd cried.

Mara shook her head. "Probably the result of someone dumping dead canines rather than burning them."

The undead dogs dashed at them. Mara gripped Nightingale and slashed at her aggressor. After slaying the hound, she noticed the other one bashing its head against Boyd's great shield. Boyd became overwhelmed, ready to drop his guard. The huntress dashed at them. With a single thrust of her blade, she dispatched the beast. He glanced up at Mara to reveal a look of dread.

"Look out!" Boyd shouted.

Mara looked behind to see an undead being lunging at her with a pair of axes. She dodged out of the way. The huntress looked at the male creature and recognized the grey skin, white hair, and glowing blue eyes. The rusted armour he wore seemed to imply that he was a warrior in life. Mara glanced at the familiar tattoos on his left arm.

"A Labyrinth Guardian?"

"You know what this thing is?" Boyd asked.

"They're not easy to deal with." Mara looked at Boyd. "Stay back."

Boyd stood beside Mara. He readied his spear and great shield.

The huntress was baffled by his actions. "What are you doing? I told you to stay back!"

"I'm helping," he said. "I won't let anything come between me and that gold!"

Mara shook her head, thinking Boyd could be a detriment. He might get in the way or worse. The labyrinth guardian was a deadly foe, but Boyd refused to stand back. The huntress wondered if it was due to ego and pride, or maybe something else.

Despite them outnumbering their foe, the guardian proved to be a challenge. The huntress' eyes began to glow while the blots on her face grew darker. She transformed, hoping her supernatural powers were enough. If anything, she drew the guardian's attention onto her. Sensing she was inhuman, he focused on her. Boyd had been useful by giving a few stabs to draw the creature's attention, though it was brief. The undead creature knew Boyd was human and chose to ignore him.

After a while, the markings on the creature's arm began to glow, and red fumes billowed from his body. The huntress had seen this before during her battle with the twisted divine. A spell was strengthening the guardian! Mara needed to think fast or else. She then noticed the ghost exuding the same red aura.

"Is that…?"

While speculating the entity's nature, Mara had to stop her spell. Despite having little experience with ghosts, the huntress assumed silver was effective.

"Distract him," Mara ordered Boyd.

Boyd kept fighting the guardian while Mara dashed at the ghost and swung her blade. Nightingale connected, and the huntress managed to inflict damage. The spectre shrieked as she flinched. After a few hits, the ghost dissipated. Mara looked back at Boyd and the guardian. If her calculations were correct, the guardian should be weaker.

However, the red aura did not dissipate, and the guardian showed no signs of weakening. Mara had no idea what was going on, but she had to think fast. Boyd could not hold him off forever. She sensed a presence behind her. Mara turned to see the spirit reappear. It seemed her attacks were ineffective. She was running out of time.

All of a sudden, the ghost burst into flames. Mara was puzzled. What just happened? The ghost wailed in agony while she dissipated into the air. Then a bright flash drew Mara's attention. She looked behind and saw the guardian staggering. Without the ghost's powers, he was now vulnerable.

Mara dashed at the creature and assisted Boyd with defeating him. Their attacks overwhelmed him, and he succumbed to his injuries. Mara and Boyd panted as they watched the guardian's corpse.

"Never thought we get out of that one alive," Boyd said.

Mara gazed back at the spot where the ghost stood. "I think that was a purifier."

"A what?" Boyd asked.

"Harold told me about them," Mara said. "Purifiers who once served the Order of Aazalith in life were entombed down here. I've never seen one in person." She gazed at Boyd. "You disturbed her slumber by desecrating her grave."

Boyd gave a sheepish grin and scratched the back of his head. "Oh well... Tough luck with the ghost, but we managed to survive."

His eyes drifted past Mara, and the smile melted from his face. Before Mara could question what was wrong, she heard someone clapping as if to give applause.

"Bravo, bravo," a familiar male voice began. "You defeated the monsters and survived, but you forgot one detail. It could've been costly to you both."

Mara looked behind to see Theo Blackthorn and his thugs. Also next to him was a charred corpse of a woman. The burnt remains looked familiar. The huntress began to speculate what happened. Boyd removed the purifier from her grave, then used her coffin to store the gold.

Theo glanced at the body. "To remove a spirit, one must destroy the object that binds them to this world." He gazed back at them and smiled. "My father once told me."

The huntress was impressed by his knowledge, even though she knew he was Theodore's son.

Theo approached them. He noticed Mara and frowned. "I'm surprised you attacked the ghost. Didn't you train with the Silver Thorns?"

"Didn't stay more than a few weeks," Mara admitted. "This was the first hostile ghost I encountered."

"I see," Theo said. "At least you learned something, and lived to tell about it." He switched his attention onto Boyd. "Now, back to business. You have something of mine, and I have something of yours."

Boyd gestured to the coffin. "Every piece is there."

"Open it," Theo ordered.

Boyd opened the coffin, which was laden with gold and jewels. Theo's gaze was fixated onto the treasure as he approached it. He stood before the coffin and inspected his missing gold.

"Remarkable," Theo murmured. "It's all here."

"Of course," Boyd said. "What about Claire?"

"Yes, she is safe. I'm a man of my word." Theo looked at his men and nodded.

The men parted, allowing a single woman to walk through. Her clothes were dirty, and her hair was messy. Claire looked small and frail compared to the larger men beside her. The young noblewoman saw Boyd.

"Boyd?" Claire asked. Tears filled her eyes as she lifted an arm to reach for him. The noblewoman dashed into Boyd's arms. Even though she appeared unharmed, Claire did not hesitate to let her emotions out. She burst into tears as she clutched onto Boyd. The young man tried to comfort her, although he was also unnerved by the ordeal.

While watching the two, Mara could tell much had changed within Boyd. Once, he was a rogue and a scoundrel who almost got her killed. Now he became a different man who would do anything for the one he loved.

The huntress then noticed Theo approaching her. The brigands grabbed the coffin and lifted it off the ground. The Blackthorns' leader watched as they took it away. He placed his hands on his hips while looking back at her.

"I suppose I should thank you as well," Theo said. "Thanks to you, I got my gold back."

Mara folded her arms. "I only agreed to help because Boyd offered to pay me." She turned her gaze onto the couple.

Boyd and Claire looked back at her. He pulled away from Claire and approached Mara.

"Yes, I haven't forgotten." Boyd reached for his coin purse and pulled out two thousand gold.

Claire also approached her. "I'll tell my father of your deeds. We won't forget what you've done."

Mara looked back at her and nodded. Boyd and Claire left for Mirahyll. Theo watched as they walked away before turning his attention back onto Mara.

"Such great rewards," Theo said, "but I have something of greater value."

Mara gave a strange look. "What do you have?"

"A tip."

"A tip?" Mara asked.

"Go to Har' Yhan and find Lady Lorelei." He smiled at her. "Ask how her business is going."

Then Theo left with his men and gold, while Mara looked on in confusion.

* * *

The huntress decided to follow Theo's advice and rode to Har' Yhan, which was near. The sun was setting by the time she reached the harbour town. Har' Yhan was busy, so she dismounted from her horse and guided the mare on foot. While heading to the Black Smoke Inn, she briefly glanced at a man in his forties. He was overlooking the transport of goods while other folk pulled the wagons. Mara assumed the pale-skinned man was a noble entering Ardana. His attire looked fancy, but he also wore an apron.

"Careful with those," he ordered his men. "I don't want my tools damaged on my first day."

As the huntress passed him, the man looked back at her with pale green eyes. His dull brown hair had receded. Mara never saw him before, but she did notice his eyes drifting onto Nightingale. The stranger gawked at the sheathed blade. He then approached her.

"Interesting sword you have there," he said. "I doubt any boor forged your blade."

Mara glanced down at Nightingale. "My father forged this for me."

He looked somewhat interested. "Your father?"

"Mathias "Bear" Ashwood," Mara revealed.

"Never heard of him," said the man.

"Of course," she responded, "not many acknowledged his skills when he was alive."

"I am sorry," he said. "I would've liked to meet your father." He gazed at Nightingale. "He seemed to be a competent blacksmith, unlike the others I've seen in this land."

Mara's eyes narrowed. "What do you mean?"

He lifted his gaze to her. "Where are my manners?" He held out his hand. "I am Raymon of Corlin, invited to Mirahyll to smith weapons. It's my understanding that I am to replace a certain geriatric who refused to forge weapons for the city."

Mara frowned. "You mean Talon?"

"Yes, and I hope you're not using his services, especially with a remark-able blade like that."

She shook her head. "I've never had a problem with him."

Raymon looked at her in disbelief. "You allow that man to touch this blade? Then it's a good thing I am here. You'll get the utmost quality with my services."

Mara rolled her eyes. "Thanks, but I'll stick with Talon. He's been decent for the price. Besides, I don't even know you."

He scowled at her. "You should never be a slave to a brand."

"What?"

"You do realize there are many blacksmiths out there. Some of which could offer better services than the one you frequent."

"And you're one of them?"

"Precisely," Raymon replied. "It'll be a wondrous opportunity to use the services from one of Corlin's best."

"Why come here and start over? It seems you had it great back in Corlin."

"Who says I'm starting over?"

Mara realized some things. This man was full of himself. He came to Ardana because he thought there was no competition. He would likely demand high prices for his services, just like Edwin. And Edwin was a crook. The huntress took a few steps back.

"Thanks, but like I said before—Talon has never let me down."

Mara stormed away, still sensing Raymon's eyes on her. She reckoned she had offended him, but didn't care. His attitude towards her friend was just as offensive.

* * *

Mara headed to the Black Smoke Inn, where she would find the inn owner. She left the little lady outside and entered the inn.

It had been a while since Mara visited this place. The huntress scanned her surroundings until she saw a woman in a red and black dress. She recognized the long black hair, pale skin, and steel blue eyes. Lady Lorelei remained unchanged since Mara's last interaction with her.

Lorelei looked back at her and smiled. "Mara, what a surprise!" She wrapped her arms around Mara in a loving hug. "I haven't seen you in a while. What brings you here?"

"I was just in the area." The huntress looked at the patrons. Holy Blades mingled with some courtesans. Some looked as if they had a little too much to drink.

She looked back at Lady Lorelei. "So, how's your business?"

Lorelei placed her hands on her hips. "It's been good."

"Some of your patrons are Holy Blades?" Mara inquired.

The inn owner gave a wry smile. "How about dinner?" She gestured to a corner table. "There's something I need to share with you."

Lady Lorelei guided Mara to the table. As the two ladies sat down, an innkeeper arrived to take their order.

"We'll have the house special for tonight," Lorelei instructed.

The innkeeper nodded and left to get their order. Lady Lorelei then gazed back at Mara.

Mara gave a questioning glance. "Why are the Holy Blades here? I'm sure Commander White wouldn't approve."

"That's just the thing," Lorelei responded. "He doesn't seem to care."

"He doesn't?"

Lorelei shrugged. "He's changed."

"How so?"

"I heard the commander returned from the dead," Lorelei said. "The same man, who once denounced the brothels and lashed out at one of my girls, is now embracing them."

Mara gawked at the inn owner. "What?"

"He's a high-paying customer."

The huntress was stunned, yet a part of her was not surprised. According to Thalia, Kratés had an addiction to sex. His disguise showed more cracks, but very few had noticed or cared. Now this man was spending Mr. White's fortune on courtesans. The thought had crossed Mara's mind, making her realize what this man had stolen from her. If Mr. White remained alive, he would be as livid as she was at this moment. Her anger began to build, but she had to be calm. Mara needed to find some way to deal with the imposter.

The innkeeper arrived with their meals. A slab of steak was placed before Mara, snapping her out of her thoughts. It looked delicious.

"It's on me," the inn owner said.

"Thanks," Mara replied. Taking her knife and fork, she cut into the meat and took a bite. The medium-rare meat melted in her mouth. It was delicious as usual, taking her mind off of her troubles. While she ate, Lady Lorelei gazed at her.

"You should come back another night," Lorelei spoke. "Chances are, he'll return. You can catch him in the act."

Mara lifted her gaze to Lorelei. "You think so?"

Lorelei nodded. "They always do. He's no different."

"Okay," Mara said. "I think I'll stay the night. It's getting late."

"Very well," Lady Lorelei spoke. "I'll have a room arranged."

Chapter Nine

Blind Rage

At sunrise, Mara rose out of bed and got dressed. She headed outside and found her horse. A good night's rest was helpful to both ladies since it would take at least a day to return to the workshop. Har' Yhan was pretty silent, for most of the townsfolk had yet to get out of bed. Mara wanted to thank Lady Lorelei for the room, but she couldn't find the inn owner. The huntress did not wish to disturb her, so she mounted the little lady and headed home.

On the way, Mara spotted the town of Désir and stopped. Her eyes drifted to the black patch of forest where the manor stood. While gazing at the area, Mara thought about the vivid dream she had the other night. A spark of curiosity came to her mind. Visiting the charred remains was not out of the way, nor would it take long to check.

Mara pulled on the reins, changing the lady's direction. After wandering into the burnt forest, the huntress dismounted from the mare and surveyed her surroundings. The blood of Thalia's servants permeated the ground. An elegant-looking tombstone stood before the burnt ruins. It was missing a name, though the huntress sensed this was Thalia's grave. She assumed Kai had ordered its construction. He was the only survivor, yet Mara had not seen him since the tragedy.

As Mara stood in the burnt mansion, she noticed a corridor. It remained intact. While drawing near, she recalled Thalia bringing her here. At the end of the hall, the huntress spotted a light fixture. Upon pulling it, the passage opened to reveal a new hallway. The door at the end looked familiar.

"This was untouched by the fire," she observed. "But how?"

Glowing blue runes decorated the walls and floor. Mara could sense the magical energy from them, and it grew stronger the further she went. Nearing the end, she reached for the doorknob and opened the way.

The huntress entered a circular room, which was also intact. More glowing runes decorated the walls. Mara reckoned they were part of a protection spell. The reason for protecting this room sat in the centre.

Mara's eyes fell onto the gold and glass casket, filled with a glowing blue fluid. She approached it and looked down. Only the liquid remained in the coffin. It was not surprising to see the body missing. The huntress spotted some footprints leading out the doorway. They belonged to Kratés.

She followed them outside. Mara found herself standing in the same place as her dream. Snow began to fall as her eyes followed the trail to the road between Mirahyll and Har' Yhan. She mounted her horse and continued on her journey to the workshop.

* * *

It was the morning of January 19 by the time Mara returned. As she drew near, the huntress spotted Talon standing outside. He appeared to be searching for someone.

The old blacksmith noticed Mara and waved to her. "Ah, at least you've shown up."

"Just came back from Har' Yhan," the huntress explained as she came closer. She noticed his frown and stopped. "What's wrong?"

Talon scratched the back of his head. "Shenoah hasn't shown up."

"Maybe she's running late?"

"It's not like her," he insisted. "She always arrives early."

Mara studied the concerned look on his face. "Maybe she ran into some trouble?"

"I hope not," Talon grumbled. "Can you find out what's keeping her?"

The huntress nodded. She remained on the lady while returning to the main road. Mara continued south until she reached the crossroads.

As soon as she turned west, Mara spotted the armourer with four Holy Blades. Something was wrong, judging by the dismayed look on Shenoah's face. One of the Holy Blades had her bag.

"That's mine!" Shenoah cried as she tried to grab it, only to be held back by two Holy Blades.

"Well, well, what do we have here?" A Holy Blade rummaged through her bag and took out some items. "Stolen items?"

"Those are my tools," Shenoah said as calmly as possible. "I'm an armourer."

"Likely story," another Holy Blade spoke. "Seems we'll have to confiscate these."

They stopped upon seeing Mara's approach. The huntress watched them while stopping the lady and dismounting from her. The young men appeared apprehensive.

Mara then looked at Shenoah. "Is there a problem?"

Before the armourer could respond, one of the Holy Blades approached her.

"Who the fuck are you?"

He tried to make himself intimidating, as the other Holy Blades gave a light laugh.

However, Mara was not impressed. "Wasn't talking to you." She kept her gaze on Shenoah. "Are you okay?"

The armourer shook her head. "I was walking to work when they stopped me."

Mara snapped her gaze onto the nearest Holy Blade. "Why did you stop her?"

He sneered at her. "Who the hell do you think you are?"

"I asked you a question," the huntress responded.

The Holy Blade kept scowling at her. "We have reason to believe she has stolen property."

The huntress raised an eyebrow. "What proof do you have?"

"Well…" the Holy Blade paused. He was unable to come up with an excuse.

Mara folded her arms. "Sounds like harassment."

"They've been doing this lately," Shenoah said. "They camp outside our city, harassing our people and demanding gold to make them stop."

The Holy Blade stormed up to her. "Shut up, Stone Mage!" Then he said, "Go back to where you belong!"

He raised his hand, ready to hit her, but the huntress grabbed his wrist. The Holy Blades did not expect anyone would challenge them.

"Really?" Mara asked. "Racial profiling and extortion? Is Commander White aware?"

The Holy Blade wrenched his arm away. "Who the hell do you think you are?" He turned on her and grabbed her mask. Upon revealing Mara's face, the Holy Blades were stunned.

"The Cursed Herald!" The Holy Blade angrily drew his sword.

One of them asked, "Colin, what are you doing?"

Colin kept glaring at her. "If we present her head, Lord White may promote us!"

He lunged at her. Just as he brought his sword down, Mara vanished in a wisp of black smoke. She reappeared behind him. Colin tripped and fell into the snow. Mara watched as he made a fool of himself.

"Apologize for being an ass and leave," the huntress suggested. Then she noticed the other three drawing their blades. "There's no need for a fight," she said. "We can all walk away."

However, her words fell on deaf ears. The Holy Blades glowered at her with dark expressions. She looked back at Shenoah, who appeared horrified.

"Stand back," Mara told her.

Shenoah looked concerned. "Are you…?"

Mara shook her head. "I don't intend to kill them."

The huntress unclasped the sheathed blade from her belt. Not bothering to unsheathe Nightingale, Mara smacked the next Holy Blade who dared to attack her. A whack on the head sent him crumpling to the ground. The remaining two Blades attacked her at the same time. She hit one of them in the jaw and knocked out a tooth. The other took a hit to his groin, causing him to fall to a fetal position.

Once the fighting was over, Mara placed Nightingale back onto her belt. She frowned at the fallen Holy Blades.

"You have a lot of nerve attacking me," she said. "All of you are inept. If none of you could land a single hit, what chance do you have against real monsters?"

The Holy Blades scowled at her in silence.

Mara took a deep breath. "Take my advice and go home."

All of a sudden, Colin shot up to his feet. He dashed at the huntress with his sword poised to strike. Mara could hear him treading across the snow. She turned around in time to see him thrust the blade towards her head. Mara dodged, but he managed to hit her on the left shoulder. Black blood gushed from the wound, and a searing pain began to spread. The sensation of being physically attacked made her snap.

It happened so fast. The darker side, also known as the Huntress, began to manifest. Mara was given this name due to the training from Dad. And unlike the other undying, she only killed when provoked.

All reason and rationality fled Mara's mind as she gripped Nightingale. In one swift motion, she unleashed a flash of gold and silver. It went through his neck. Colin froze for a moment, and then his head toppled off. His body tried to feel for his head, but it soon collapsed to the ground. Mara stood frozen while gripping a bloody Nightingale.

The Holy Blades and Shenoah stared in shock. They could not believe their eyes.

"Look at her face," spoke one of the Blades. "She's not human!"

Mara looked back at them with glowing eyes. The blots on her face had grown dark.

A different Holy Blade stood to confront her.

Mara released a low growl. Her parted lips revealed elongated canines.

"Mara?" Shenoah called.

No longer could Mara hear her voice, as the Huntress took over. Her attention was on the Holy Blade, who sought to avenge his comrade. He released a battle cry while running at her. The Huntress closed the distance by teleporting directly in front of him. He had no time to react as she made a diagonal slice from his right shoulder to the left hip. She cut him into two pieces. Red blood splashed onto the snow.

"You bitch!" Another Holy Blade shot up to his feet and ran at her.

Mara made quick work of him. She sliced him up into several pieces. A red haze clouded her vision, yet she could still hear the pounding heart of the remaining Holy Blade. The last one lost his nerve and ran away. Through the red haze, the undying saw him dashing near the lady. He might have been planning on stealing her horse. The Huntress came after him with mindless fury.

"Mara! Stop!" Shenoah cried.

Mara ignored her once again. She only needed to deal with one more Holy Blade, and they can finally return to the workshop. Mara was on top of him within seconds. He screamed in fright. A swift swing of her blade reduced his screams to a loud gurgling sound. The little lady shrieked, but it would all be over soon. The red haze blinded her again. Bloodlust took over as she blindly hacked and slashed at her target. Despite killing the fourth Holy Blade, she continued to stab him over and over, drawing all of his blood. She wanted to make sure he was dead.

"Mara! What the hell?"

Mara suddenly stopped upon hearing Talon's voice. The Huntress went dormant as she changed back. The red haze faded away, allowing her to see clearly. The Holy Blade she killed was barely recognizable. Several gashes riddled his smashed face. Unable to stomach the sight, Mara looked at Talon and Shenoah. The old blacksmith was glaring at her in shock. Shenoah was on her knees as she sobbed into her hands.

"What the hell have you done?" Talon demanded.

Mara was confused. Why was he upset at her? She rose to her feet and wiped the sweat from her brow. The undying glanced at her left shoulder. The bleeding had stopped, and the wound was in the process of healing.

"I had no choice." Mara looked at him. "They attacked me first."

Talon frowned at her. "They were only kids!"

"They threatened to kill me!" Mara snapped. "They wanted to present my head to Commander White!"

Shenoah lifted her head and glowered at her. "Look at what you've done!"

Red blood stretched towards Mara, drawing her attention. At first, she thought it belonged to the Holy Blade, but it flowed from a downed horse. The little lady was resting on her side. Lacerations, caused by Nightingale, riddled her body. Mara's heart pounded as she began to understand Talon and Shenoah's anger. She knew the horse was near, but slaying the Holy Blade mattered above all. The stench of horse blood filled her nostrils. Mara stood frozen before the destruction she brought upon her steed. The horse's left hind leg appeared broken.

Mara fell to her knees as she kept staring at her horse. The undying's vision grew blurry. Tears were filling her eyes.

"I... I never meant to..." She looked back at Talon and Shenoah. "I didn't mean to hurt her."

Both the blacksmith and armourer remained frozen. Mara could see it in their eyes—they either feared or hated her. After a few moments, the two turned around and returned to the workshop. Mara rose to her feet and followed after them.

"Please, I'm sorry," Mara whimpered.

They stopped and looked at her, but neither one said anything. Then they walked away. Mara stood frozen as tears streamed down her face. It became clear that they no longer wanted her around, nor would she be welcomed at the workshop. Once again, Mara became homeless. She could go to Cerebell and stay with the Stone Mages. But there was a chance that Shenoah would tell everyone what Mara did. They would never welcome her.

A thought crossed Mara's mind, for there was another place she could go. She turned around and cast her eyes upon Grey Mountain.

* * *

The sun was setting as Mara travelled up the mountain path. Luckily, she had not encountered any snow beasts along the way. Within half an hour, Mara stood before the frozen fortress of Greyward Hold.

The last time Mara was here, she had her final encounter with Harold. It was also here that he revealed the truth to her. The undying looked at the ground to find nary a footprint. It seemed she was the last visitor to the abandoned fortress.

Unwilling to spend another minute in the cold, Mara pushed the large iron doors open and invited herself inside. Upon entering, the undying spotted many corpses riddling the ground. Their golden armour was familiar. The Holy Blades slain by Harold remained in the same spot. Since this was to be her home, removing the corpses was a high priority.

While removing the corpses, Mara searched the bodies for any valuables. Anything worthwhile, like gold, could be useful to her. Unfortunately, the Holy Blades' weapons had rusted, making them not as valuable.

As the huntress continued her cleaning, a skeleton rose from a sea of remains. Magic reanimated the bones of a dead Holy Blade! The living corpse began to approach with a blade, which the undying responded by unsheathing Nightingale.

The skeleton went down after a few hits, but another began to rise. After Mara took the second one down, a third rose to his feet, followed by a fourth and a fifth. The undying cut them all down, but more arose to replace the fallen. Mara became overwhelmed. In her distraction, a skeleton approached her from behind. She took notice, but it was too late to stop his attack. Mara shut her eyes and waited for the end.

The sound of metal slicing through the creature made her open her eyes again. Mara looked at the downed skeleton. She lifted her gaze to see tanned leather armour with silver plating. At first, Mara thought it was Saskia, for the woman dressed identically to her. Even her hair had a braid going down to the middle of her back. But Saskia died over two months ago. The woman had a pale face with brown eyes and dirty blonde hair.

"Don't just stand there," she began. "Help me take them out!"

Mara snapped out of it and helped the stranger. With two sword-fighters, taking out the skeletons were easier. The huntress glanced over at the Silver Thorn and noted the sword in her possession. It looked like a Silver Thorn long sword, but much thinner. Mara figured her newfound partner was using an estoc. After defeating the creatures, the two women had time for introductions.

Mara gave a friendly smile underneath her mask. "Thanks for the help." She held out her hand for a handshake. "My name's Mara."

The woman just stared at her hand. Instead of accepting Mara's gesture, she sheathed her sword. "I know who you are, undying," she said, looking at her sheathed blade. Then she gazed back at Mara. "What are you doing here?"

The huntress pulled her hand back as her smile faded. "I needed a place to stay. Thought Greyward Hold, being abandoned."

The stranger stared at her. "Been living here for the past few weeks, but haven't come around for cleaning. It's never been my forte."

Mara gave a questioning look. "I didn't see any tracks."

"I cover them up, hoping no one would find this place. But it seems I'm not the only one who still remembers Greyward Hold."

The huntress sulked. "I'm sorry." She turned towards the main entrance. "I'll just find another place."

"You can stay here," the woman piped up.

Mara stopped and looked back at her. "Are you sure?"

The female warrior shrugged. "The fortress is big enough. We can stay out of each other's way if we want." She then approached Mara and held out her hand. "My name's Jen, independent hunter. Before that, I was a Silver Thorn."

Mara returned her gesture. "I recognize the attire. Saskia wore the same thing."

Jen frowned. "Saskia was a great hunter and sword-fighter. She should have left Ozin when she had the chance."

"I don't think it would've made a difference," Mara murmured. "Commander White killed her and framed me."

Jen's jaw dropped. "That fucking prick?" The former Silver Thorn tightened her right hand into a fist. "I should've wiped that smirk off his face!"

"If it makes you feel better, I drove my sword through his gut," Mara said.

"Yet he remains alive," Jen grumbled. She placed her hands on her hips and looked around. "Well, we should clean up this place. Make it habitable again."

Mara gave a peculiar look. "Are we expecting more guests?"

Jen nodded and looked at the main entrance. "Dad, it's safe now."

Mara gazed at the main doors. A tall and pale-skinned man appeared. His wrinkled face hinted that he might be in his sixties or seventies. He had short greying hair and identical eyes to his daughter. Jen's father was not as muscular as Talon, yet he remained in good shape. For his attire, he wore a beige short-sleeved shirt, a pair of black pants, and brown knee-high boots. A black apron covered his clothes.

"This is my father, Walt," Jen introduced. "He'll be using the forge in Greyward Hold." She looked back at Mara. "And it'll be a great place for him to rekindle his business."

The undying was elated to know she would have access to another blacksmith. "That's great to hear."

Jen's father eyed Mara suspiciously. "Aren't you the one who exposed Edwin?"

Mara looked back at Walt. "Yes, Talon and I did. Edwin stole my dad's weapons and became famous off of them."

He approached her and held out his hand. "Then I have you to thank." He gave a small smile. "I'll gladly offer my services to you."

Mara returned the gesture. "Thanks," she said, shaking his hand. "Were you one of Edwin's victims?"

Jen nodded. "With Edwin gone, my dad can start again." She turned to her blade. "Dad built my weapon using silver and steel. Weighs more than an epee, but at least I can kill some monsters."

Walt eyed Nightingale. "But I've never forged a sword as elegant as that."

Mara unsheathed her sword. "My dad made this for me. It has never let me down, and it helped me defeat the Dark One and—"

"Slay the Goddess, Kallisto," Jen interrupted.

Walt looked at Mara in astonishment.

"Yes," the huntress responded, "and I also stabbed Commander White with it."

"You mean Lord White?" asked another woman.

The three turned around and saw that somebody else had joined them. Mara recognized the short black hair and steel green eyes.

"Beatrice?" Mara's eyes drifted over to her attire. No longer was Beatrice dressed in her captain's garb. She wore a plain white shirt, brown trousers, and a pair of boots. She also wore a thick cloak to protect against the cold, but she remained shivering.

Jen folded her arms. "Beatrice," she addressed. "Former Silver Thorn, and now former Captain of the Guardsmen."

Mara switched her bewildered gaze from Jen to Beatrice. "What?"

"The Guardsmen are no more," Beatrice said, lowering her travelling bag to the ground.

"What happened?" Mara asked.

"I was hoping you'd tell me," Beatrice replied. "How is he alive?"

Everyone looked at Mara. The huntress remained unsure if she should tell them the truth at this moment. Would it be worth it to reveal everything now?

"He somehow resurrected," Mara said, being partially truthful.

"Resurrected?" Beatrice questioned.

The huntress nodded. "Since then, he's caused all sorts of trouble for me."

The former captain watched her. "I've heard, yet I'm curious to see you here. Weren't you staying with Talon?"

Mara frowned. "I'm no longer on friendly terms with him."

"What did you do?" Jen inquired. "There aren't many things that would piss him off."

"Some Holy Blades drew their weapons on me. I never meant to kill them."

The others stared at her in confusion.

"That's it?" Jen asked. "He got mad at you for killing a few Holy Blades?"

Beatrice rubbed her chin. "She's right. I'd expect the opposite from Talon."

"One of them got me on the shoulder," Mara revealed. "I just snapped. Not only did I kill them, but I also slew my horse by accident. He wanted to use her for deliveries."

Jen shook her head. "Still, he can't be mad at you for that."

"Has he ever seen your undying form?" Beatrice asked.

"I've always kept my face hidden," Mara said.

"I meant if he had ever seen you fight as an undying," the former captain spoke.

Mara shook her head. "I don't think so."

"It must have been his first time," Beatrice said. "He spent twenty years of his life within these walls, while we did the hunting and gathered information on various monsters. He's likely afraid of you."

"We studied the undying," Jen explained. "We know how dangerous they can be. Saskia kept a detailed journal on them since she lived near one."

Mara nodded. "She convinced me to help her slay the White Lady. That's when I found out."

"Only an undying can kill an undying." Jen surveyed her surroundings. "I'm pretty sure the notes are still here."

Jen went to search for the notes while Walt sauntered over to the forge, leaving Mara and Beatrice alone.

The huntress gazed at the former captain. "What's happening in Mirahyll?"

"Kallikratés has gained a new leader," Beatrice said. "With the combined power of an archdeacon and a commander, Lord White is now the most powerful man in this land."

"I thought he was already powerful," Mara said.

"This is different," the former captain insisted. "The Faith learned of our attempt to reach out to Thoron. After storming the Council Hall, Lord White forced Chancellor Davis to step down. Their Holy Blades outnumbered the Guardsmen, thanks to Corlin and Loris. I heard he did the same in Hema. He annexed the Guardsmen and Hema's knights into the Holy Blades." Then, "If Thoron does respond, their envoys will be arrested upon stepping foot on Ardana."

Mara gaped at her. "The Faith is in control again?"

"More than ever. And according to the Holy Blades' decree..."

"Women have no place among their ranks. I'm sorry you lost your job."

"I'm sorry, too," Beatrice responded. "All your efforts were in vain."

Mara looked away, taking her time to absorb the new information she obtained. The imposter grew powerful within days and was likely untouchable. Her options were dwindling. "So, he's like a king? Will he take Lady Isabella's castle as his home?"

Beatrice frowned at her in silence.

Mara took notice. "What? It was only a jest."

"I wouldn't jest if I were you," said the former captain.

The huntress frowned. "If anything, he'll hopefully stay in Hema."

After a very long day, everyone decided to turn in for the night. Mara returned to her former bedchambers. She opened the door to find a layer of dust covering the furniture. Looking at the bed, the undying knew it would be less comfortable, yet it was better than nothing. Before placing Nightingale on the dresser, Mara wiped the dust away. She then grabbed the bedsheets and gave them a shake. The entire fortress was cold, so Mara decided to sleep in her armour. Before closing her eyes, the huntress figured the day she would confront the imposter would come. And when it did, she would be ready to face him.

Chapter Ten

The Trial

On the morning of January 21, Mara awoke to the knocking on her door. Before she could answer, Jen came rushing through.

"You have to get up!"

"What's going on?" Mara asked. She saw the horror in the former Silver Thorn's eyes.

"The Holy Blades are here!" Jen exclaimed. "They're looking for you."

Now wide awake, Mara pushed herself off the bed. "How do they know I'm here?"

"None of us said anything. Someone from the outside must've informed them."

Mara grabbed her sword. The former Silver Thorn led her to Harold's quarters. Once inside, Jen searched among the bookshelves.

"There's a hidden passage in this room. You'll hide until the coast is clear."

Mara helped her search. "What about you?"

"Beatrice and father are buying us some time."

"Why don't we fight them?"

"Too many," Jen said. "Besides, look at what happened the last time you challenged them."

It was then the huntress realized why the Holy Blades were searching for her. Mara looked back at the door. "I should face them."

"No," Jen argued. "You won't stand a chance."

"I've dealt with them before," Mara insisted. "I know what I'm doing."

"If you are lost, this land is doomed."

Mara looked at Jen in bewilderment. "What are you talking about?"

The former Silver Thorn gave a solemn look. "Old Master Harold believed Ardana would be free from the false gods. For that dream to come true, he needed the one who could rival them. Don't you understand? You were the key."

The huntress kept staring at her before returning to her search. A few minutes later, they found the secret passage. Jen pulled on a book that seemed out of place, producing a light clicking sound. She then slid the entire bookshelf to the side, revealing the passage.

The former Silver Thorn gestured to Mara. "Get in."

Despite some misgivings, Mara entered the hidden passage.

The former Silver Thorn closed the door. "We'll come for you once the coast is clear."

The back of the bookshelf had a sizeable crack. Mara peered through and watched as Jen walked away. Within minutes, the Holy Blades flooded the room. Leading the group was a young man dressed in the commander's attire. At first, Mara thought he was the imposter, but noticed the short black hair.

"Where are you hiding her?" asked the commander.

He walked further into the room. Mara could see several Holy Blades at the doorway, as well as Beatrice, Jen, and Walt. All three were apprehended. Despite their situation, no one spoke.

The commander gazed at them. "You do realize it is a criminal offence to hide a murderer?"

Jen glowered at him. "Like the Holy Blades are any better," she hissed.

The commander gave a baffled look. "I've no idea what you're talking about."

"Cut the bullshit!" Jen spat. "You set up fake notices to lure many Silver Thorns to their deaths, like old Theodore and my brother!"

Everyone stared at the former Silver Thorn. The commander seemed genuinely shocked.

Beatrice looked at Jen. "That's enough."

Jen looked back at her colleague. "But it's true," she murmured. "Master Harold dismantled the guild to protect the rest of us."

The commander kept watching them. "It seems we'll have to take you three to Mirahyll for further questioning."

Mara watched as the Holy Blades led them away. A pang of guilt gnawed at her. Another thought crossed her mind. Since the Holy Blades were looking for her, this might be her only chance to confront the imposter. The huntress opened up the passage. Some of the Holy Blades spotted her.

"Commander Matthews," called one of the men.

Commander Matthews turned his head and watched Mara emerge from the passageway. The huntress glanced at the two women, noting the displeased looks on their faces. But she believed she did the right thing.

"Let them go," Mara began. "I'm the one you want."

As the huntress came closer, she observed the rest of Commander Matthews' features. He appeared to be either in his late twenties or early thirties. His pale skin was flawless, hinting that he might be a highborn noble. Pale blue eyes, a small nose, and thin lips sat on an angular face. Like

Karl and the imposter, he had a tuft of dark hair under his bottom lip, yet his chin was shaven.

The commander gazed at her in a scrutinizing fashion. "The Cursed Herald."

The Holy Blades watched her with apprehension as they quickly surrounded her.

Mara stopped and glared at him. "My name is Mara Ashwood."

Commander Matthews scowled at her. "Lord White seeks your surrender. You are to come quietly."

"Fine," Mara said. She looked at Beatrice, Jen, and Walt. "Just let them go."

The commander glanced at the three. "They are accomplices."

"They did nothing wrong," Mara argued. "Besides, nothing compares to the atrocities the Holy Blades commit."

The commander gawked at her for a moment, then gestured to his Holy Blades. "Arrest her."

The Holy Blades closed in, but Mara wanted to go on her terms. She stormed past Commander Matthews.

"Where's your damn carriage?"

The commander grabbed her wrist. "Not so fast. We'll be confiscating your weapon."

As he reached for Nightingale, Mara suddenly snatched it away. The huntress glared at him with glowing yellow eyes. "Touch Nightingale and I will kill you."

The commander stared at her. "You think so?"

"My terms are simple," Mara said calmly. "Take me to your magnanimous lord, unrestrained and with Nightingale by my side, and we'll all remain alive."

He glared at her. "You think I will abide by this?"

"You don't want blood on your hands." Mara watched him. "You're not from around here, are you? In all my fifty-five years as both human and undying, I don't think I've ever seen you before."

Commander Matthews kept staring at her, then walked ahead. "The carriage is this way."

Mara followed him.

One of the Blades asked, "Sir, what about the others?"

The commander stopped, yet he never looked at his subordinate. "Let them go."

The Holy Blades obeyed and released the three. Once Mara knew they were safe, she followed Commander Matthews into the carriage. Two other Holy Blades accompanied them, to make sure Mara did not try anything. Once everyone was in their respective places, the transports began to move.

* * *

The huntress stared out the window as the carriage travelled on the snow-covered ground. Beside her was one of the Holy Blades. Commander Matthews sat opposite of her with the other Blade beside him.

The commander stared at her with folded arms. "Lord White had many colourful things to say about you."

The huntress gazed back at him. "Did he also tell you how I became cursed?"

He folded his arms and looked away. "It matters not."

Mara narrowed her eyes. "What would you know? You never had to watch loved ones die."

Commander Matthews looked back at her. "Excuse me?"

"Your goddess murdered my father," Mara said. "She triggered my curse. My mom spent thirty years in a catatonic state, blaming herself for what happened. I spent thirty years trapped in a dark hole until a few months ago. Kallisto sought to recapture me, even if it meant killing my friends. She had it coming."

He watched her in scrutiny. "I can see how you had no problem killing four innocent boys."

"Innocent?" Mara questioned. "How do you explain the Holy Blades arresting at least forty women last month? If I recall, at least fifty people lost their lives."

"I know not what you're talking about," Commander Matthews said.

"Of course," she responded. "You're just a highborn noble who seeks thrills by putting a blade to the throats of the downtrodden."

He scowled at her. "And how many throats did you put a blade to?"

"None that were innocent."

He continued to stare at her, then looked out the window. The carriage travelled by Talon's workshop.

"Stop the carriage," he ordered the driver.

The Holy Blade pulled on the reins and made the horses stop. Once the transport came to a stand-still, Commander Matthews opened the door. Mara wondered what he was doing.

Another Holy Blade followed him out of the coach. Once they reached Talon's place, the commander knocked on the door three times. Talon and Shenoah answered.

The huntress could not hear their conversation, for the workshop was far away. However, she could see what they were doing. The moment Commander Matthews handed over a large bag to Talon, Mara knew what was going on. Her insides twisted with dread as the old blacksmith accepted the bag. Talon and Shenoah briefly looked in her direction. Their eyes met for a moment, then the blacksmith and armourer went back inside.

Commander Matthews and the Holy Blade returned to the coach.

"Paid our informant," he said. "His help was invaluable."

Mara stared at the workshop, still processing what she had just witnessed. Her body trembled as she gripped Nightingale tightly. Tears began to well up in her eyes, threatening to spill over. Commander Matthews might have noticed, but remained silent. For the rest of the journey, Mara never looked at anyone.

* * *

Upon entering Mirahyll, Mara saw some Holy Blades arresting a lower-class citizen while a nobleman looked on. She reckoned they had spotted a noble being robbed and caught the perpetrator. At least the Holy Blades did their job.

The carriage stopped once they reached the Council Hall. Commander Matthews was the first to leave. Mara was next to exit the transport. Once she came out, the Holy Blades surrounded her. While being escorted, she noticed several people of various statuses and classes watching her.

"So much for being our saviour," said a lower-class citizen.

"The Faith was right," a woman murmured. "We are worst off because of her."

"Good thing they've arrested her," a nobleman grumbled. "She's not a saviour but a murderous freak."

Mara tried to ignore them, though their words stung. She stared ahead while following the commander. Upon entering the Council Hall, Mara spotted the imposter sitting in the chancellor's desk. Davis and Evan were missing, though the aldermen attended. Even Elder Ravenclaw was attending the trial. Mara glanced back at the man who called himself Lord White. He wore a garb similar to the commander's attire with some differences. His long coat was dyed black, while golden chains decorated the right shoulder pad. The Hand of Kratés, now restored, was strapped to his belt. Mara recognized the well-crafted sword by its elegant golden hilt and the fancy black sheath. Half of the grip was black while the rest was dark red, wrapped with thin gold ribbons. A ruby decorated the golden pommel, as well as the curved cross-guard. Mara assumed he had the sword retrieved from the ruins of the temple, and reforged by the new blacksmith, Raymon.

By his side were two priests dressed in gold and ivory. The imposter rose from his seat, prompting everyone else to stand.

"I, Lord Karl White of the Faith of Kallikratés, shall judge the accused. Assisting me will be Archdeacon Matthews of Corlin and Archdeacon Mendé of Loris." After taking a seat, he gazed at Commander Matthews. "Before we begin, I'd like to thank Commander Donovan Matthews, son of Archdeacon Matthews, for retrieving the prisoner."

Mara eyed Commander Matthews, who nodded in response. She knew he was not from around here, but never realized he was Archdeacon Matthews' son. Gazing at Corlin's archdeacon, she could see the resemblance, save for the wrinkled skin and the greying hair underneath his cap. Once everyone was seated, the undying looked back at Lord White to find him glaring at her.

"The prisoner stands accused of blasphemy, murdering the Goddess, and killing four Holy Blades." His eyes narrowed. "How do you plead?"

Mara glanced at the crowd. Some older nobles were glaring at her. She assumed they were the parents of the deceased. Even though the situation looked bad, something in Mara began to change. The undying looked back at the judges.

"Not guilty."

The crowd murmured among each other. Mara glanced back at the parents, to see their faces darken in anger. Deep down, she no longer cared.

Lord White leaned over and rested his chin on his hands. "Not guilty? How do you explain the recent events you were involved in?"

Mara took a deep breath. "I don't believe I committed any crime."

The judges frowned at her.

"Is that so?" Lord White asked.

Mara glowered at him. "If anyone is committing a crime, it is you."

The crowd grew puzzled as they murmured among each other. The huntress kept gazing at Lord White, who appeared very displeased. She was ready to expose him right here and now.

"I beg your pardon?" Archdeacon Matthews questioned. "What are you talking about?"

Mara kept her eyes on the imposter. "He isn't who he says he is."

The crowd gasped as their murmurings grew louder.

Lord White grew annoyed. "Silence!" The room went quiet as he glared at Mara. "Last I looked, you are the one on trial."

Mara folded her arms. "You should be the one standing here."

"You are the Cursed Herald!" Lord White declared.

"I may be your so-called Cursed Herald," Mara spat, "but at least I don't go around pretending to be a dead man!"

The other two judges looked at Lord White.

"What does she mean?" Matthews questioned.

Mendé remained silent as he watched Lord White. It seemed like he was anticipating his response.

Lord White gazed at Mara grimly. "Do not listen to her," he said. "She's telling lies."

"And you're doing such a great job yourself," Mara hissed.

His eyes narrowed. "You have derailed this trial long enough, wasting everyone's time. Are you proud of yourself, Ashwood?"

"Karl never addressed me by my last name."

His mouth opened, yet no words came out. The imposter gawked at her. She had exposed him. However, everyone else remained confused. The other archdeacons switched their attention between the huntress and the imposter.

"Karl would never be caught dead visiting a brothel." Mara gestured to his left arm. "Nor does he have tattoos."

Her comments riled up the crowd, in which they released a groan of confusion. They wanted answers. The judges remained silent, unsure of what to do.

"Silence!" Lord White roared. Silence soon followed. He rose to his feet and stepped forward. He glanced at his left arm before gazing back at her. With his right hand, he reached for the left side of his collar and gently pulled it down to show the tattoos.

"It is my understanding that there is some confusion," he told the crowd. "Therefore, I will address them now."

Mara looked puzzled. "What are you doing?"

The imposter ignored her. "I am Karl White," he said. "Upon my resurrection, Kallisto awoke the ancient power of my predecessor, the Great Lord Kratés. This tattoo is proof of my birthright."

Everyone was astounded. Mara sensed they were beginning to believe the imposter.

She shook her head. "Kallisto didn't resurrect you."

He raised an index finger while looking to the crowd. "The Goddess has shown me my path. It is my destiny to lead the Faith of Kallikratés in this land."

Mara glanced around, seeing the looks of admiration on people's faces. They had fallen for the imposter's lies. She glared back at Kratés, who gave a smug look. The huntress had lost this battle.

Lord White returned to his seat while Donovan beamed at him.

"Lord White, you are wise with a noble heart," he said.

"Thank you, Commander Matthews," Lord White spoke. He turned his attention onto Mara. "But we shall continue this trial. She must answer for her crimes."

Many of the disciples murmured in agreement.

All of a sudden, the doors swung open. A group of thirteen stormed inside. Three individuals dressed in different attire led them. The first was an older man with pale skin and a long grey beard. He wore dark brown robes with golden trimmings. On his left stood a younger and thinner man dressed in blue robes and a hat that covered his ears. On the right was a fair-skinned woman in her early to mid-thirties. She wore black robes decorated in matching feathers and a hood to obscure her face. She lowered her hood to reveal black hair and strange markings around her wolf-like eyes. The rest wore leather armour and steel plating. They brandished gleaming swords with golden hilts.

Everyone gawked at the strangers, baffled by their appearance. The Holy Blades grew apprehensive of the warriors and their brandished blades.

Lord White rose to his feet. "The Thoron Sages?" He snapped his gaze onto his Holy Blades. "I ordered their arrest as soon as they stepped foot on our shores! Why are they walking free?"

The young man adorned in blue stepped forward. "They did," he began. "Unfortunately, your men are woefully inexperienced against our battle mages and spell-swords."

"It was humiliating," said the female sage. "Like children wielding sticks."

The venerable sage retrieved a glowing blue pendant from his robes. The other two sages looked astonished, while Mara watched with curiosity.

"The soul of Aazalith is near," said the elderly man before gazing at the huntress.

Mara nodded and stepped forward. "I have it."

The sages gazed at her with a grim expression.

The older man approached her. "Oh, is that so?" He reached into his robes once more.

"Yes," Mara replied. "Thought if I give it to you, you'll help me—"

Acute pain stopped her in her tracks. Mara looked down to see a blade lodged in her torso. A moonstone mounted the hilt. She then lifted her gaze to the cold grey eyes of the old sage. Mara staggered backwards and grabbed the dagger. She managed to pull it out, even though it was painful. Then she discarded it.

The elderly sage gaped at her. "It didn't work."

Mara began to transform. Her eyes glowed while the blotches grew darker. She released a low growl as her canines elongated into sharp fangs.

The older man looked stunned, while the younger male sage stood before him.

"This is not human!" The young man glanced at the discarded dagger. "It should have released the soul, but it did not."

The female sage watched Mara with curiosity, then approached her. The other two gazed at her in bewilderment.

"Accalia?" asked the young man.

Accalia ignored them and kept her eyes on Mara. "This is a witch, but something isn't right."

The woman reached into her robes and retrieved some colourless powder. She blew it onto Mara's face, knocking her out.

Chapter Eleven

The Three Sages

Mara awoke on a bed. She assumed she was brought to a spare bedroom to sleep off the powder. Mara glanced down at her abdomen. The injury had already healed.

"You're finally awake," said an unfamiliar woman.

The huntress lifted her gaze to the one who knocked her out and grew apprehensive.

Accalia sat beside the bed, staring at her. "I won't pull any stunts as Nikolai did. Although I am curious about you."

Mara began to notice the similarities between this woman and herself.

Accalia kept watching the huntress while rising to her feet. "You're a witch, are you not? Who performed your melding ceremony?"

"A shaman from my father's home village."

Accalia looked intrigued as she came to Mara's side. "A shaman? Did they use the blood of a wolf?"

"Shadow beast," the huntress replied.

Accalia was stunned. Then her face fell to a grim expression. "How old were you?"

"Why do you ask?"

"It is important." Accalia turned around, yet she expected an answer.

"It was around the time I became very sick," Mara answered. "I was a toddler. Before I turned five."

The woman snapped her gaze onto the huntress. Her yellow eyes were full of shock, horror, and wonder. "A mere babe?"

"Is that bad?"

Accalia placed her hands on her hips as she stared at Mara in silence. Her intense gaze was intimidating, and Mara wanted to avert her gaze. The door opened to reveal the young man in blue robes. He gazed at Mara with curious blue eyes while approaching her.

"I see you are awake," he addressed Mara. "So, why is it that we were unable to retrieve the soul of Aazalith?"

"She's part shadow beast," according to Accalia. "They have remarkable healing abilities."

The young sage glanced at Accalia indifferently. "Maybe so... Yet it does not explain why the divine's soul was not released. The dagger has no defects."

"I think it's because I have the Curse of the Undying," Mara answered.

Both sages looked astonished. The young man, in particular, dropped his dismissive personality and gawked at Mara.

"Thalia?"

Mara shook her head. "I'm one of her reincarnations."

He furrowed his brow. "Impossible," he murmured, "Thalia is immortal."

"It's a long story," Mara said.

"Then do tell," Accalia responded. "I'm rather curious myself."

"Thalia used a spell called Banish on herself," Mara revealed, "and split her soul in two. And whenever a reincarnation dies, her soul is also split in two."

Accalia frowned as she shook her head.

The male sage gave a peculiar look. "Banish, you say?"

The huntress nodded.

"I have studied the lore of the immortal woman," he explained. "If I recall, a witch taught her the spell. It is very dangerous, for it can instantly kill a living being." He gazed at Mara. "Do continue."

"I went on a quest to collect the souls of the undying," Mara continued. "As far as I'm concerned, only one piece remains."

"Yet you say you are not Thalia?" he questioned.

"Kallikratés sought to prevent her return by sealing her away within me." Mara shrugged. "Regardless, I defeated Kallisto and retrieved the soul of Aazalith."

The two sages watched her, taking their time to absorb her tale.

The male sage held his hands behind his back and regained his composure. "It is safe to assume we have a common enemy." Then he said, "My name is Milo. I am a mage and a scholar at the College of Thoron." He gestured to Accalia. "This is Accalia, a witch from the Far East. The mages, witches, and priests form the three pillars of power within the Thoron Sages, the spiritual leaders of Thoron. We worship and study the Seven Divines and their mother, who are true gods."

"My name's Mara," the undying introduced. "I've heard about the Thoron Sages. When Kallisto and Kratés rose to power, they called upon your nation to abandon the Seven Divines. The sages refused and called them fake."

Accalia grinned. "They tried to conquer our land, but none of their fleets could pass Sea God Mantos."

"How did the false gods meet their end?" Milo asked.

"Kallisto slew Kratés," Mara answered. "His reincarnation, Karl White, had a small fragment of Aazalith's soul. I killed him, but an imposter has taken his place."

The mage and the witch exchanged glances.

"What of the false goddess?" Accalia questioned.

"We were both caught in a magical explosion," Mara said. "It destroyed Kallisto's soul."

Both sages looked surprised.

"You survived?" Accalia asked.

"According to legend, the magic fuelling the Curse of the Undying comes from Mother Nymera," said the mage. "This energy is stronger than the Divines. It might be the reason why you survived." Milo frowned. "In the case of the false goddess, this is why humans should never touch such power."

"You've seen this before?" Mara asked.

"Only in tomes within the archives," he answered. "And they never end well. But you are a rather curious case. You possess the soul of the Dragon Goddess, yet you do not appear to be using her power."

"I did a few times," Mara admitted. "When I first obtained the soul, it restored my human form."

"Human form?" Accalia questioned.

"The undying often appear inhuman," Milo explained. "Even Thalia was known to have zombie-like features before consuming mermaid meat."

Mara nodded. "I can also absorb magic. I was able to render Kallisto and Karl mortal temporarily by consuming their blood."

Milo looked disgusted while Accalia grinned.

"You bit the false goddess?" asked the witch. "Now that would have been a sight to see."

"Magic siphoning?" Milo inquired. "It may explain why Aazalith's powers are not manifesting at their fullest."

"Or that fake had exhausted much of her power," Accalia added.

"When the soul is complete, it is an infinite source of magic," Milo said. "I would assume the false gods never consumed the entire soul."

"Kallisto had all but a tiny fragment, and it transformed her into a monster." Then Mara said, "I don't intend to keep it. I'm willing to return it in exchange for lifting my curse."

Milo kept his eyes on her. "Trade the soul for the rose." The mage paused for a moment. "I believe we could agree on something."

Mara's eyes lit up. "You'll help me?"

"Given the circumstances, only Nymera can remove Aazalith's soul," Milo explained. "The only choice is to take you to Thoron. She might also be willing to lift your curse."

Mara shot up to her feet and gazed at him with wonder. Milo raised a hand.

"First, we must address some things." He gestured to the door. "Please, follow me."

* * *

Both Mara and Accalia followed Milo back to the Council Hall. Mara froze upon seeing Nikolai. She had not forgotten what the old geezer did. Nikolai gazed back at her with apprehension. Lord White and the two archdeacons remained in their seats, waiting for the accused to return. Lord White scowled at her in silence.

Accalia stood beside Mara, while Milo sat next to Nikolai and whispered something in his ear. Mara could not hear what he was saying but assumed they were talking about their findings. The huntress turned her attention onto the witch next to her, wondering what she was doing. The three judges were also curious.

Lord White stared at Accalia. "Have you come to defend a stranger at a trial?"

"What does she stand accused of?" Accalia asked.

"Blasphemy, murdering the Goddess, and killing four Holy Blades." Lord White glared at Mara. "All of which she has denied."

"It was self-defence," Mara claimed. "They were the first to draw their weapons."

"You slaughtered them without a moment's hesitation," Lord White argued. "You are dangerous."

Accalia placed her hands on her hips. "What about the melding ceremony performed on her long ago?"

Lord White narrowed his eyes. "What does this have to do with the trial?"

"Everything," Accalia said. "We Thoron Witches only perform the melding ceremony on girls when they come of age. Usually eighteen to twenty-one." She gestured to Mara. "Her ceremony was performed when she was a toddler."

Archdeacon Matthews looked intrigued. "Is that dangerous?"

"Psychological damage can occur," Accalia spoke. "Also, her people used shadow beast blood instead of wolf blood. Their supernatural essence will make the outcome unpredictable and dangerous."

Milo rose to his feet and joined Mara and Accalia. "And with her possessing the soul of Aazalith, her supernatural side may be more unpredictable than usual."

Lord White looked at them. "What are you getting at?"

"We're surprised she's not more fucked up in the head than she already is," Accalia spoke candidly.

Milo cleared his throat. "And having the divine's soul is no doubt causing a major strain on her mind." He gestured to Mara. "We also discovered that she is cursed. Therefore, it is impossible to remove the divine's soul with our current tools. This immense power will erode her mind unless we take her to Thoron. Only Nymera, the Mother of Gods, can safely remove the soul of Aazalith."

Nikolai rose to his feet. "Aazalith shall be reborn, returning to her rightful home in Thoron."

The judges frowned at them.

"Are you saying we should let her go?" Archdeacon Matthews inquired.

Milo nodded. "It would be best for all of us."

Archdeacon Mendé looked at Lord White. "What do you think, my lord?"

Lord White glanced at each of the Thoron Sages before finally looking at Mara. His green eyes gazed at her intensely, making the huntress uncomfortable.

Milo stepped in front of Mara. "Regardless, we Thoron Sages declare this woman to be under our protection." Then, "It is my understanding that this land remains infected by magic, caused by Aazalith. If you allow her to leave with us, Ardana will eventually be free of magic and monsters."

Everyone gazed at Lord White, who rose from his seat. Keeping his eyes on Mara, he began to approach her.

"I will not permit you to leave this land," Lord White addressed Mara. "I declare the accused guilty." He glared at her. "You will be sent to the dungeons until we find a proper sentence."

He nodded to his Holy Blades to arrest her. The Holy Blades obeyed and approached her.

However, the Thoron Sages and their retinue of warriors stood in their way. It looked like they were ready to do battle right here in this room.

The Holy Blades glanced at each other with uncertainty. They also looked to Lord White for further instruction.

Lord White gazed at the sages with disappointment. "You dare defy us?"

"We cannot let you take her," said the mage.

Lord White scowled at Milo. "How dare you? The Thoron Sages have no power in Ardana!"

"Maybe so, but any idiot knows which way the wind is blowing," Accalia said, gesturing to Mara. "She has the soul of Aazalith—a power stolen by Kallikratés. You will never let her go as long as she has it."

Lord White directed his angered gaze onto the witch. "She is guilty of several crimes and must be punished. Or perhaps you'd like to join her?"

"Are you suggesting we are prisoners as well?" Milo inquired.

"You servants of demons have no right stepping foot on our sacred land," Lord White replied. "We shall take you all prisoner. Blades!"

Mara glared at Lord White, while the latter scowled back at her. Her attention was then drawn to the Holy Blades closing in. The warriors stood their ground, unwilling to let any harm come to the sages.

Milo rummaged through his bag, retrieving a black receptacle with a blue jewel on top. It reminded Mara of one of Allen's inventions. He pressed the blue gem, and the box opened. The gemstone glowed brightly before unleashing a flash of light.

As soon as Mara's vision recovered, she saw what appeared to be a projection floating above their heads. Everyone looked up to see the projected image, showing a group of people.

"Who are they?" Mara asked.

"The High Council of Thoron," Accalia revealed. "After the fall of the Royal Valemont Family, the nation fell into disarray. The council exists to bring peace and balance, while the Thoron Sages serve as spiritual advisors."

"High Council," Milo addressed the group in the projection, "it seems we have hit a major setback."

"What happened?" asked one of the council members. "Did you find the soul of Aazalith?"

"We did," Milo replied, "but we are about to be made prisoner."

The council members exchanged glances with one another.

"This is unprecedented," said a second council member. "Where is Chancellor Davis and Interim Chancellor Evan?"

Lord White stepped forward. "They have been removed from power for choosing to side with the enemy. The people of Ardana have appointed me to take their place."

"And who might you be?" the third council member questioned.

"I am Lord Karl White of the Faith of Kallikratés," he spoke.

"The Faith of Kallikratés? You mean the church that worships false deities?"

Lord White's face darkened. "For many years, the Faith of Kallikratés have protected the people of Ardana, Corlin, and Loris. Our gods shepherded us to peace and prosperity while Thoron remains plagued by demons!"

"We know about Kallikratés and the destruction they have wrought upon those nations," said the fourth council member. "We know of the millions of lives you stole. You call our nation oppressed, while we have made great advancements in our education, medicine, and technology. Things we believe we wouldn't have reached if serving your gods." Then, "Release the Thoron Sages and their guardians. Allow them to return with the divine's soul."

"And if we don't?" Lord White questioned.

The High Council went silent for a moment.

"You have three weeks," said one of them. "Or Thoron will unleash her full might with millions of battle-mages and spell-swords."

The projection faded away as the gemstone stopped glowing. The black box closed up while everyone stared in shock.

"The Thoron Sages want that soul back," Accalia said, folding her arms. "They're willing to force the High Council's hand."

"As long as we get the soul back," Milo said, putting the device away.

Mara looked at the shocked faces of Kallikratés' disciples, who were caught off guard by the threat of war. Lord White appeared especially unnerved.

"All we seek is Aazalith's safe return," Nikolai said. "No one wants a repeat of what happened thousands of years ago."

Lord White snapped his gaze onto the Thoron Priest, but soon his eyes drifted over to Mara. He stared at her for a very long time.

"My lord," Mendé addressed Lord White, "even though they threaten us, I don't believe answering their call for war would be in our best interest. Loris suffers from poverty, and won't be of much help."

Lord White looked back at Mendé, and then Matthews. "What about Corlin?"

Archdeacon Matthews was slightly shaking. "Corlin remains strong and prosperous, but even I wouldn't condone sending our people to war. It could amount to much bloodshed."

"And Ardana is in no condition to challenge Thoron," Lord White muttered. He glared at the Thoron Sages. "How dare you threaten war upon our lands?"

Milo gave a casual look. "Long ago, Ardana declared war on Thoron to satiate their lust for power. What happened?"

"Aazalith tried to eradicate mankind after losing many of her children," Mara spoke, "starting with Ardana. The Thoron Sages saved this land by removing her soul."

Milo and Lord White looked back at her.

"Correct," Milo said. "Yet Thoron was betrayed. While the false gods rose to power, Thoron was isolated. The imposed sanctions did very little to enfeeble our land. It made her strong by being self-reliant."

Lord White kept staring at Mara. The huntress wondered why he was gawking at her like that. He eventually broke his gaze from her and looked back at the mage.

"Fine," Lord White said. "We'll release her."

The followers of Kallikratés seemed baffled and displeased.

"However, she and the sages are required to stay in Ardana for three weeks," Lord White declared. "They will not be permitted to enter any cities, towns or villages where the Faith is present. And the Holy Blades shall guard their ship in the meantime."

A Holy Blade stepped forward and bowed. "Yes, my lord."

He led a group of Holy Blades and marched out to Har' Yhan.

Mara scowled at Lord White. Getting around Ardana was going to be much more difficult. Only Désir and Cerebell were among the few places where the Faith had no presence.

Lord White approached Mara with a cold expression. "You have one hour to vacate this city before I change my mind." He returned to his desk and sat down. "The trial is adjourned."

Everyone rose to their feet and began to leave the Council Hall. Many of them murmured to each other, unsure what to think of Lord White's decisions. His behaviour drew the attention of Kallikratés' followers. Especially the parents of the deceased, who were disappointed by the outcome.

A nobleman asked, "What about our sons?"

"I've done all I can," Lord White replied.

"But Lord White," spoke one of the fathers, "she should be thrown into a dungeon!"

"She's under the Thoron Sages' protection. There's very little we can do."

Mara could see that the parents were upset at Lord White's lack of action. Then she felt a hand on her shoulder. She looked back at Milo, Accalia, and Nikolai.

"We shall take our leave," Milo said. "Before he changes his mind."

"There's a place that may accommodate all of us," Mara said.

Accalia approached her. "Lead the way."

Mara nodded. "To Greyward Hold."

As they were leaving, Mara locked gazes with one of the nobles. The eye contact drew their attention. The nobleman angrily stormed over to the huntress, stopping her from leaving.

"You should be thrown in jail!"

Another soon joined him. "Our sons did nothing wrong!"

At least eight nobles stood in their way.

Mara held her ground. "So, you think it's fine to harass and extort others?" She glanced over and spotted Ravenclaw, who was watching her. "They harassed a Stone Mage, trying to steal her armourer tools when she refused to give in to their demands."

Ravenclaw appeared very disconcerted.

Mara redirected her attention to the deceased's parents. A mother looked horrified while a father scowled at her.

"How dare you spread slander? Colin was a good lad!"

Mara scowled at him. "You're a damn liar," she said flatly. "Your son had plenty to say about Stone Mages." She pulled down her mask to reveal her face. "Once they discovered who I was, they drew their blades. Your son was the first to attack me."

The parents gawked at her with apprehension. Mara observed their faces. It became clear that the late son got his mentality from his parents.

"I'm sorry for your loss," Mara said, "but they were soldiers, and soldiers die in battle. You should have thought of that before making your sons join the Holy Blades."

Angered, the father suddenly grabbed Mara by her cloak, yanking her away from the Thoron Sages.

"How dare you?" he snarled.

Mara was about to pull away until she saw him brandishing a dagger. He raised it above his head, ready to stab her. The next thing Mara knew, she was being pushed out of the way. The dagger missed its target but acquired a new one. A whirlwind of chaos surrounded her. Milo staggered backwards into Mara's arms, and they both fell to the ground.

Accalia stormed over to the nobleman with the dagger. The witch punched him in the face, breaking his nose in the process. The impact caused a loud cracking sound, which echoed within the Council Hall. The nobleman recoiled, holding his bloody and mangled nose. A few noble-women screamed in fright as some men dared to approach. The sages' guardians stood in between them with unsheathed blades. The civilians backed off, realizing the danger.

Mara looked down at Milo. He stared up at the ceiling as dark blood oozed from his chest wound, spreading throughout his attire. She was frozen and horrified until she saw Nikolai kneeling next to the mage. The priest reached over the wound. A golden glow emanated from his hand. Milo only responded by coughing up blood. His blue eyes were beginning to glaze over.

Accalia rushed to Milo's side and looked at Nikolai. Once the priest's hand stopped glowing, he pulled it back. Nikolai shook his head. Accalia then placed her hand on Milo's chest. Mara gazed at the witch's face and noticed her veins turning black.

Accalia pulled her hand away as her veins returned to normal. "This will kill me."

Nikolai gave a worried look. "He will die soon."

"There's nothing we can do?" Mara asked.

"Wait a minute." Accalia gazed at Mara. "You can learn Healing Touch. You're also cursed; the consequences may be minimal."

Mara looked uncertain. "What are you talking about?"

Accalia grabbed her hand. "I can teach you." Then she placed Mara's hand on Milo's chest.

The huntress was unsure what the witch wanted her to do.

Even Nikolai was baffled. "What are you doing?"

"I'm teaching her Healing Touch," Accalia said, "and she'll save his life."

"This won't work," Nikolai argued.

"She's a witch!" Accalia snapped. "It doesn't take much to learn." She then looked at Mara while keeping her hand on Milo's chest. "Think about the pain he's feeling. Feel his pain."

Mara followed the witch's instructions, though she had her doubts as well. After a moment, she felt some discomfort in her hand. It grew more painful by the second.

"What the…?"

Accalia looked at her face. "It's working. Your veins are turning black."

Mara felt a sharp pain in her chest. She looked at Milo's face to see that it had grown more relaxed. Then her attention was drawn to her chest. She could feel a wound beginning to form beneath her cloak.

"Keep going," Accalia said.

The wound on Milo's chest had stopped bleeding and began to close up. The mage slowly regained consciousness as Mara drowned in her blood. Black blood ascended within her throat and seeped out of her mouth. Her strength fled from her body. She collapsed and blacked out.

Chapter Twelve

To Greyward Hold

A tingling sensation spread throughout Mara's dormant body. Her arms and legs began to twitch. Then the feeling became a burning sensation, which rushed through her veins. The huntress' eyes snapped open, her irises glowing bright yellow. She knew she had died. Mara released a pained groan while taking in a breath of air. She saw stars shimmering across the black velvet sky while lying in a moving wagon. A group of warriors surrounded the cart, all walking in the same direction.

"Ah, you're awake."

Mara heard Accalia addressing her.

The witch leaned over and stared at her with bright yellow eyes. "Stop the cart!"

The wagon stopped. Everyone gazed at the huntress, seeing her gaunt grey face riddled with black scars.

Mara slowly sat up. "What happened? Where are we?"

"Milo is alive and well, thanks to you," Accalia answered. "But that asshole threw us out of the city. We're heading to Greyward Hold."

"How do you know where to go?" Mara asked.

"They're guiding us." Accalia pointed to a group of riders.

Mara looked ahead and saw Elder Ravenclaw and his riders. He remained on his horse while looking over his shoulder.

"We should make haste," Ravenclaw said. "Greyward Hold is still a distance away."

"Give us a moment," Accalia said.

Mara reached into her satchel and retrieved a healing stone. She held the stone in her hand and watched as it shattered into a million pieces. It released the purified magic within, and it spread over her body. As soon as she regained her human form, Mara glanced up at Accalia. The witch was not the only spectator. Milo, Nikolai, and their escorts had also witnessed Mara's transformation from a raggedy undead creature to a human woman.

The mage approached the back of the wagon with an astonished look on his face. "In all of my research, no texts on the immortal woman mention this."

"Unlike Thalia, I never consumed mermaid meat," Mara said. "I use healing stones now, but they're rare."

Milo watched her in silence, then reached for his cap.

Accalia took notice. "What are you doing?"

Milo pulled his cap off. "Since you shared your true form, maybe I should do the same."

Mara's eyes widened upon seeing his long silver hair, which was tied back, and his long pointy ears. Milo frowned at the huntress, seemingly displeased by her reaction.

"Can you blame her, Milonias?" Accalia asked. "She's likely never seen an elf before."

Mara snapped out of her shock. "An elf?"

"Correct," Milo replied. "I am Milonias of the Elder Woods."

"A rare sight nowadays," Accalia added. "Elves are known to have at least ten times the lifespan of humans."

"Why haven't I seen any elves before in Ardana?" Mara asked.

"Long ago, all non-humans were hunted," according to Milo. "Some nations, including Ardana, succeeded in the complete eradication of elves, dwarves, and even halflings."

Mara shrugged. "I never knew."

"They never taught any history in your schools?" Milo questioned.

"What exactly do they teach you?" Accalia asked.

"The history of Ardana," Mara paused, "and its founding by the gods…" The huntress went silent once she realized what she had just said.

"The Faith controlled the education among many things," Ravenclaw revealed.

Milo frowned. "They used the system to indoctrinate the young."

"Not a surprise," Accalia murmured. "This land had been oppressed by false gods."

Mara cast her gaze to the ground. "I knew a friend who criticized Kallikratés for those reasons. His name was Allen."

"Doctor Allen Moen?" Milo questioned. "I met him when he visited Thoron. For an Ardanian, he had an extraordinary mind. I do not believe I have seen him since arriving here. How is he?"

"He died last month," Mara said in a sombre tone. "Kallisto killed him."

Milo frowned. "I apologize for your loss. I hear he was the advisor to the former chancellor. He could have been a beacon of hope for this land."

Accalia placed a hand on Mara's shoulder. "Once we get you to Thoron, and have Nymera remove Aazalith's soul and lift your curse, you'll be free to pursue a proper education if you wish."

Mara looked at Accalia and pondered her words.

"In the meantime, we must carry on to Greyward Hold," Milo said as he returned to the front of the wagon. They began to move again. Accalia remained by Mara's side while Milo and Nikolai sat in front. Ravenclaw and his riders moved ahead as the battle-mages and spell-swords walked beside the transport.

The elf glanced over his shoulder at Mara. "I am sorry."

"What for?" Mara questioned.

Milo looked ahead. "Thalia was said to be as powerful as the Divines, yet you have none of her powers. I will admit I was disappointed when I first met you."

Mara remained silent for a while. "I was looking forward to getting those powers, too."

"It seems I am in your debt," Milo said.

"Just get me to Thoron and help me remove my curse," Mara said.

The sages exchanged glances. They seemed uncertain, but then Milo nodded.

"Very well." Then he asked, "So, what is Greyward Hold?"

"It was the Silver Thorns' home," Mara answered. "I lived there for a while. It's up in Grey Mountain."

Accalia gave a wry smile. "It'll feel just like home."

Mara gave a puzzled look. "Home?"

Milo said, "The witches live in an ancient fortress, hidden deep in the mountains."

"It's where we undergo physical, mental, and spiritual training," Accalia explained, "as well as performing our melding ceremony."

"Training?" Mara asked.

"We deal with problem creatures."

"You hunt monsters?" Mara inquired.

"We also deal with the paranormal, and break the odd curse here and there," Accalia said. "And we study the occult and demons."

The huntress looked intrigued.

Milo looked back at Mara. "You mentioned something about Lord White being an imposter. Care to elaborate?"

The huntress gazed at the mage. "I slew the real Karl White," Mara replied. "The man you just saw is someone else."

"Do you know his true identity?" Milo asked.

"Kratés," Mara answered.

The sages looked at her in befuddlement.

"Kratés the Fornicator?" Nikolai questioned in disbelief.

Mara returned a baffled gaze. "The Fornicator?"

"We know a tale about a man who encountered Hedera, the Mother of Demons," Accalia revealed. "Once a sorceress, she used dark and profane magic to stay young and beautiful. It transformed her into a demon who seduces men."

"The demon secretes a very addictive toxin during moments of intimacy," Milo added. "It weakens the brain, causing her victims to become infatuated. They also become endowed with an insatiable urge to breed, and any future offspring are likely to succumb to evil." Then he said, "The toxin was often an ingredient in love potions."

"Kratés was one of her victims?" Mara asked.

Accalia nodded. "Long ago, people held ceremonies where they circumcised young men, believing it offered protection. However, Kratés hid to avoid his cutting, leaving him vulnerable to the demon."

"His family discovered his encounter with Hedera," Nikolai revealed. "He was to be castrated and disowned. His family believed they could regain their honour, and it was the only way to stop the spread of evil. But he ran away."

"Many tales surround him," Accalia said, "like his second encounter with Hedera, who seduced him over and over again until the effects became permanent. Or his army being destroyed because he was busy fornicating with a mermaid."

Mara gaped at the witch. "Thought mermaids went extinct."

"A few pods remain," Milo said. "They have grown fearful of humans but must breed to survive. They will only appear before the most beautiful of men." Then he asked, "Did you know Kratés was part-elf?"

Mara looked intrigued. "No, I didn't."

"His mother was allegedly half-elf," the mage said. "We elves are known to be a fair and everlasting race. Most of all, we view our blood as sacred. We frown upon individuals, like Kratés, who recklessly engages in such activities, diluting the elven blood." Then, "Still, I'm sure this is a different man from the tales we speak of."

Mara shook her head. "I'm pretty sure this is the same man. He hailed from Thoron. His family disowned him. He let his army down because he was busy having sex. And he made love to a king's mistress, in which no man was allowed to touch."

The sages gave a skeptical look.

"Impossible!" Milo exclaimed. "Even full-blooded elves cannot live to two thousand years!"

"He fled to Ardana and joined the Order of Aazalith," Mara explained. "He became Thalia's guardian, and eventually her lover before Kallisto betrayed the covenant and stole the soul of Aazalith. He ruled the western world alongside Kallisto until his death."

"But it does not explain how he is alive," Milo said.

"Thalia had preserved Kratés' body," said the huntress. "She intended to resurrect him by temporarily stopping Karl's heart. But things turned out differently."

"You killed the real Commander White," Accalia said, "and released Kratés' soul."

"Ever since he resurrected, he's been causing all sorts of trouble for me," Mara said.

Milo gave her a peculiar look. "How do you know it is him?"

"It might sound stupid, but I had a dream," Mara said.

The elven mage raised an eyebrow. "A dream?"

"I was standing before Thalia's manor, or what's left of it. Kratés was walking away. I later visited the remains of the manor. The room that housed Kratés' body is intact, but the body is missing."

The sages glanced at each other.

Milo looked back at Mara. "I believe you possess an unrefined variant of Mind Eye."

"Mind Eye?" Mara asked. "What's that?"

"A psychic ability that allows one to glimpse into the past of an individual or object. Helpful when someone is lying."

"Okay, but what do you mean it's unrefined?" Mara asked.

"Your ability only surfaced while you dream," Milo said. "It can be used at will with some training. I, too, possess Mind Eye, though it is at an advanced level."

"How did I get it?" Mara asked.

"Ordinary people are not usually granted this ability. Only those close to the gods receive such a gift, like we Thoron Sages."

"She does have the soul of Nymera's eldest daughter," Nikolai added.

"Perhaps it is Aazalith's way of thanking the one who rescued her from the imposter," Milo said. "Then again, I also know of scholars seeking to elevate their thoughts, experimenting on the brains of normal people."

"Like the Seekers?" Mara questioned.

Milo looked intrigued. "You know of them?"

"Allen mentioned them," Mara responded. "I wish he was here. He could've helped me with this new problem."

Milo said, "Maybe it is best if we keep this between us for now."

While some agreed, others were not too convinced.

"Shouldn't we at least do something?" Nikolai asked.

"The priest has a point," Accalia said. "After being exposed so many times, Kratés likely remains capable of producing those toxins."

Mara looked surprised. "You're saying he can make others…?"

"Fall in love with him," Accalia replied. "His bodily fluids carry varying amounts. He can even control others with a mere kiss."

Mara looked away. She never knew Kratés would be capable of such abilities. The huntress began to think about Thalia's relationship with Kratés, which lasted about ten years. Did she truly love him, or did these toxins cloud her judgment? What about Amara? She also encountered the former king. It was no wonder how Amara got the title of a depraved slave girl.

Mara gazed back at the sages. "Is he even aware of his ability?"

"He had it since entering adulthood," Milo answered. "I reckon he would be aware."

The huntress looked back at the city as it grew more distant.
"Then he's dangerous," she murmured.

* * *

The group finally arrived at Greyward Hold. Mara and the Thoron Sages disembarked from the wagon. The battle-mages and spell-swords gathered all of their belongings and headed for the large iron doors. Mara walked ahead of them. She wanted Beatrice, Jen, and Walt to know there was no danger. Before she could reach the entrance, however, Ravenclaw approached her with a mournful look.

"I am sorry," he told her. "I should have done more or said something."

Mara shook her head. "I don't think there's anything you could've done."

"I should have realized the consequences of performing that ritual."

Accalia directed her attention to them and approached. "So, you're from the village responsible for that botched ceremony?"

The huntress scowled at her. "Don't blame him. It happened fifty years ago."

The witch folded her arms as she stared at Mara. "You're pushing fifty?"

"Fifty-five to be exact," Mara answered. "All thanks to my curse."

Milo gave a side-long glance at Accalia. "You are in no condition to be questioning her age. You are nearly a century yourself."

Accalia snapped her gaze onto the mage. "And how old are you, Milonias? Hmm?"

Milo suddenly went silent.

After an awkward moment, Ravenclaw then said, "I understand that Greyward Hold is far from Cerebell, but we would like to invite you and your new friends for a feast."

Mara shook her head. "I don't think it's a good idea. I'm pretty sure word came out on my recent actions."

"I've heard," Ravenclaw spoke. "But Shenoah only mentioned the slaughtering of the four boys and your horse."

The huntress watched him for a moment. Deep down, she was surprised to know that Shenoah never mentioned anything about being harassed. Mara looked away. "Well, she and Talon are the reason why I ended up on trial. They saw me like that, and wanted nothing to do with me."

Ravenclaw frowned. "I will speak with Shenoah. I'm sure she never knew the gravity of the situation we placed you in."

"And I would still do it again." Mara hugged Ravenclaw. "Thank you."

Ravenclaw nodded. "Good luck with your endeavours."

Mara pulled away. Elder Ravenclaw and his riders departed for Cerebell. The huntress headed to the front doors.

"Beatrice? Jen?" Mara called. "It's me, Mara!"

After a few seconds, the large iron doors began to open. Beatrice and Jen stood on the other side. The former Silver Thorns were stunned to see Mara back but grew apprehensive of the group of strangers accompanying her.

Jen looked at Mara. "You came back!"

Mara nodded. "I did."

The former Silver Thorn approached the huntress. "I thought you'd be lost again."

Beatrice folded her arms. "So did I," she added, approaching Mara with a scowl on her face. "That was very careless of you."

The huntress gazed back at the former captain. Beatrice was now wearing an identical uniform to Jen.

Mara looked at her with determination. "I lost nearly all of my friends because they tried to help me. I wasn't going to let anyone else suffer because of me."

Beatrice frowned at her for a moment, then noticed the sages. "I assume they're the reason why you returned."

Mara looked back at the sages and their entourage. "Yes, they are." Then she introduced them. "These are the Thoron Sages. Milo, Nikolai, and Accalia."

Beatrice and Jen gazed at them with wonder.

"The Thoron Sages?" Beatrice questioned. "I thought the Holy Blades would arrest you on the spot."

"They tried," Milo responded. "However, they were woefully untrained compared to our battle-mages and spell-swords."

The former Silver Thorns gazed at the sages' guardians.

"I've heard of them," Jen spoke. "They imbue their weapons with magical spells."

Milo held his hands behind his back and nodded. "That is correct," he said. "They are simple spells, but remain very effective."

"Do you not use magic while fighting monsters?" Accalia asked.

Jen and Beatrice shook their heads in unison.

"No, we don't," Beatrice said. "Old Master Harold warned against the use of magic, for it can corrupt the hearts and minds of the living."

"Then Aazalith's rage remains," Milo said. "Her ire poisoned this land through her magic."

Mara gave him a questioning glance. "Does this happen in Thoron?"

"We normally have a good relationship with our gods," Accalia said.

"Except for one," Nikolai added.

Milo nodded. "Lonely Cenobia, who has no worshippers."

"That's the one who guards the rose," Mara murmured.

"Yes, and she may be unwilling to give it to you, let alone tolerate your presence on her mountain," Milo responded.

Nikolai walked inside. "In the meantime, this shall be our new home for now." He ignored Beatrice and Jen as he ventured towards the grand hall.

Both women looked at Mara with questioning glances. They had not expected guests at Greyward Hold.

"We needed a place to stay," Mara explained. "We'll be leaving for Thoron in three weeks."

"Three weeks?" Beatrice questioned.

"It's part of our agreement between Kallikratés and the High Council of Thoron. The Faith has three weeks to release us, or else Thoron will declare war on Ardana, Corlin, and Loris."

Jen placed her hands on her hips. "That'll give them enough time to cause more trouble. Lord White probably knows you're here."

"You mean the imposter?" Accalia asked as she walked past them.

Both Jen and Beatrice gaped at the witch before turning their attention onto Mara.

The huntress shrugged. "Yeah, about that…"

Beatrice gave a bewildered look. "You have some explaining to do."

Chapter Thirteen

The Informant

It was January 24 when Mara received a peculiar letter. A messenger had arrived earlier in the morning, braving the mountain trail to make this delivery. The huntress recognized the seal of Kallikratés, prompting her to present the letter to the Thoron Sages. At their urging, she opened it and began to read.

"To Mara," the huntress began. "I wish to speak with you regarding Lord White. Meet me at the port town of Har' Yhan. Come alone."

Mara lifted her gaze to those present in the room. Other than the sages, Beatrice and Jen were also there to listen.

Beatrice folded her arms. "Sounds like a trap."

"But whoever wrote this addressed her by her actual name," Jen argued.

Accalia looked puzzled. "Is that normal?"

Mara shook her head. "They never address me by my real name."

Milo took a step forward. "We shall accompany you."

Nikolai and Accalia looked at the elven mage.

"I beg your pardon?" Nikolai asked.

"They wanted her alone," Accalia said.

"We will let them believe." Milo reached into his bag and retrieved some silver amulets with a cloudy white gem inside.

Mara gazed at the amulets with curiosity. "What are those?"

Accalia raised both eyebrows. "Oh, stealth amulets!" She glanced at Milo. "I didn't know you carried those."

"I figured these could prove valuable," Milo said. "I have enough for all except one." He looked at Mara.

The huntress shrugged. "I guess it makes sense. I'm the one they're looking for."

Milo nodded. "We will use these to hide in plain sight. We shall be near in case things turn awry."

"Okay," Mara said. "Let's head out."

Everyone, except for Walt, headed out to Har' Yhan.

* * *

Within two days, Mara reached Har' Yhan by sunset. The sages, their guardians, and the two hunters remained close in case anything went wrong. Near the Black Smoke Inn, Mara noticed some ornate carriages. They belonged to the Holy Blades.

"Praise Kallikratés."

Hearing a deep male voice, the huntress looked over her shoulder to find a priest standing behind her. The middle-aged man wore robes of ivory and gold. A matching cap hid his white hair, while his skin possessed a lighter shade of brown. He watched her with dark brown eyes, yet he did not appear to be apprehensive of her appearance. Mara recognized the older man, for he was one of the judges at her trial.

"You," she addressed him.

The man took a few steps towards her. "Greetings," he spoke.

Mara just stared at him in silence.

He frowned. "You received my letter, did you not?"

The huntress gawked at him. "That was you?"

He nodded. "That is correct. I believe we have met before." He held out his hand. "I am Archdeacon Mendé of Loris."

Mara watched him with caution as she folded her arms. She was uncertain about shaking this man's hand. Mendé soon pulled his hand back and pointed at her.

"I can see you are without faith, but I do not blame you. Numbers of the faithless have been on the rise as of late."

"Maybe it's because you worship false gods?" Mara questioned.

Mendé gazed at her in silence for a moment. "Perhaps," he said. "There have been some unsavoury rumours regarding one of our own."

"And you think I started these rumours?"

"On the contrary, these rumours have been circulating on their own." Then, "Perhaps you'd like to accompany me to the town's church?"

She looked uncertain. "We can't talk out here?"

"It'd be unwise," Mendé replied. "Lord White, or his imposter, is here in this town."

Mara froze. It became clear what Mendé wished to discuss.

The archdeacon gestured to the nearby church. "Please, I insist."

Mara followed Mendé into the gold and ivory church. Thankfully the building was empty, and no followers were around to cast any judgmental gazes. Mendé guided her to the church's office. Upon opening the door, he gestured to a chair.

"Please, take a seat."

The huntress stared at the chair. "Will this take long?"

"I'm sure we'll finish before Lord White completes his business at the nearby inn."

Mara took the chair offered to her. Archdeacon Mendé circled the desk, taking the seat across from her.

"You called Lord White an imposter," Mara said.

Mendé nodded. "I've been thinking about your allegations," he revealed. "They coincide with the rumours surrounding Lord White. Karl had a noble heart, fiercely devoted to the Goddess. Now he has changed. He seems lost."

Mara gave a deadpanned look. "Or an imposter."

"Perhaps," Mendé answered. "It is my understanding that you assisted a surveyor group sent to Golden Mountain earlier this month."

She furrowed her brow. "I recall. Why do you ask?"

"I sent them," he confessed. "They were to investigate the ruins, where they found a commander's body pinned underneath the collapsed ceiling." He leaned forward and rested his chin on his hands. "Now, I would like to know who this imposter is."

The huntress looked down at her hands, pondering her options. Should she reveal the truth? This man was aware of the imposter. Mendé could be an ally.

Mara lifted her gaze to him. "The man pretending to be Karl White is none other than Kratés."

Mendé opened his mouth, yet no words came out. He gave her a scrutinizing look. "I beg your pardon? Did you say that he…?"

"He's Kratés."

"Lord Kratés? The one who ruled alongside Queen Kallisto?"

"Yes, but he's no longer a god," Mara claimed.

"No longer a god?"

"I said it before. Kallisto and Kratés betrayed their covenant by stealing the soul of a very powerful being named Aazalith." Mara paused upon seeing the incredulous look on his face. "Look, I don't care if you believe me or not."

Mendé sighed, "It may explain the recent actions of Lord White. This odd behaviour does match the former king's." Then he said, "You may not know this, but Lord Kratés was never one for politics."

"When it came to running the kingdom, he had very little to no say," Mara said.

"Ah, so you do know. Lord Kratés was considered to be too irresponsible and nowhere near as competent as Queen Kallisto. Therefore, he was a king only in name. But how is he alive? Didn't he sacrifice himself to save this world from the Dark One?"

"Kallisto killed him," Mara revealed. "She used a moonstone dagger to undo his immortality. He had another lover, Thalia, who preserved his body and planned to resurrect him. Karl had two souls within him. If he died,

Kratés' soul would be released and drawn back into his own body. I killed the real Karl White."

"And Kratés has been resurrected as a result," Mendé added. "So, it's true. The Legend of Kratés is false? And the gods are false as well?"

"If his true identity came out, would you follow him?" Mara inquired.

Mendé frowned. "To put him on the throne would be most unwise. Lord Kratés was better suited for war. If he ruled, he may threaten our peace and lead us to ruin."

"What will you do now?" Mara asked. "Will you stop supporting him?"

Mendé leaned back. "Right now, there is very little I can do. Archdeacon Matthews and his son still support the imposter."

"So, you have to convince them?"

"It will be difficult, especially with the son."

"Why him of all people?"

"Commander Matthews is in love with Lord White's imposter."

Mara gaped at him. "What? You're saying he's…"

"Yes, he is gay," Mendé confirmed. "Does that surprise you?"

The huntress looked away and shook her head. "Sorry, I've been living under a rock for thirty years." After getting over her shock, Mara looked back at him and asked, "So, why don't you tell them the truth?"

"Words can spread like wildfire. Should the truth be revealed from a reliable source, it could lead to chaos and even bloodshed." He rose from his desk. "In the meantime, we will keep this between just the two of us. We shall meet again." Then he bowed. "Praise Kallikratés."

Mara rose from her chair and walked out. She wandered into an alley alone. The huntress looked back to make sure no one was watching her. When she turned her head, the Thoron Sages stood before her. Soon, Beatrice, Jen, and the sages' guardians appeared around her. They had removed their stealth amulets once the coast was clear. They all watched her, waiting to learn what she had discovered.

"We might have an ally," Mara began.

"An ally?" Milo questioned.

"One of the archdeacons, Mendé of Loris, also suspects Lord White to be an imposter. And he knows the truth about Kallisto and Kratés."

"Did you tell him?" Beatrice asked.

Mara shrugged. "Didn't think it would hurt. He seemed to believe me."

"Didn't the Faith worship Lord Kratés as well?" Jen asked.

"That's just the thing," Mara said. "Mendé told me that he would never want to place him on the throne because it might lead to more ruin."

Beatrice folded her arms. "Kratés was known as a warlord."

"Right now, Mendé can't do anything unless he could persuade the other archdeacon," Mara revealed.

"So, they'll destroy themselves," Beatrice said. "The Faith could fall."

"And we might be able to depart for Thoron sooner than we thought," Milo said.

Mara nodded. It was at this moment she noticed someone was missing. "Where's Accalia?"

The remaining two sages and former Silver Thorns exchanged glances with each other. No one had noticed the witch missing until Mara piped up.

"We cannot stay here for long," Milo addressed Mara. "It would be best if you search for her alone. We will wait outside."

Mara nodded and headed out.

* * *

Upon walking out of the alley, Mara's eyes fell onto the Black Smoke Inn.

"Impossible," she muttered to herself.

Entering the inn, the huntress took notice of the Holy Blades. It was just like the other night. The Holy Blades were preoccupied with drinking and flirting. Mara spotted Lady Lorelei, who was watching over her girls and the patrons. The huntress approached her.

The inn owner spotted Mara and greeted her with open arms. "Ah, fancy meeting you here."

Mara kept her eyes on Lorelei. "I'm looking for—"

"Him?" Lorelei interrupted with a wry smile.

The huntress shook her head. "No, I'm looking for someone else."

"Are you sure?" Lorelei questioned. "He booked a room with one of my girls…"

"I'm looking for a witch," Mara said.

"Well, I'm looking at one right now," teased the inn owner.

Mara frowned. "That's not what I meant."

Lorelei grinned. "I know," she said. "Follow me."

Lady Lorelei guided her to the corridors outside of the inn.

Mara grew confused. "Where are you taking me?"

The inn owner remained silent, leading Mara deeper into the corridor. Perhaps it was a play of irony. Venturing deeper, Mara found the missing witch. Accalia stood before a peephole, peering into the room on the other side. The huntress could also hear a man and a woman rut and moan like animals.

"This is the Fornicator," the witch whispered.

Lady Lorelei approached the peephole, gesturing the witch to move aside. Accalia complied and allowed her to take a look. Lorelei peered inside, appearing very impressed by what she saw.

Mara was uncertain if she wanted a glimpse. She had all the evidence she needed. Lady Lorelei and Accalia turned their attention onto Mara, encouraging her to have a look. The huntress was hesitant, yet she walked up to the peephole. After all, she was an adult.

Looking through the hole, Mara saw the courtesan enjoying the pleasure offered by the imposter. The huntress also noticed that the woman had tanned skin and dark hair. The woman's glee-filled face was red with her mouth wide open. Mara's gaze drifted towards the imposter, who was on his knees and positioned in between the courtesan's legs. His manhood was deep inside the courtesan. Strong hands gripped her hips and thighs. He kept a simple, slow rhythm while gently squeezing her buns. The courtesan squeaked and moaned each time he pushed his hips against hers. He threw his head back and also groaned out in pleasure.

Mara was repulsed, but could not look away. Her eyes fell onto the tattoos on the left side of his torso and his left arm. It was her first time seeing those markings in their entirety since he resurrected. She should be angry because this man stole everything Mr. White left for her. And now he was blowing that money on courtesans. Yet Mara found her eyes wandering over to their hips. She watched as his hips pressed against the courtesan. He dove deeper into her body over and over, wanting to feel his length inside of her.

Accalia leaned over to Mara's ear. "He's like an incubus," she whispered. "He won't stop until he's emptied all of his tainted seed into her."

Mara looked back at the witch. "An incubus?"

Accalia nodded. "She'll likely give birth to a child susceptible to evil."

Mara turned her attention onto the imposter. "Good thing I no longer have a uterus."

"He's still very dangerous," Accalia whispered. "She's exposed to his toxins and is under his spell. She'll let him fuck her until he's finally satisfied."

All of a sudden, both the courtesan and the imposter's cries of pleasure grew louder. They were reaching their climax. After a few thrusts, Kratés slammed his hips against hers. His muscles began to twitch under drenched skin. Kratés released a low groan as he remained frozen. The three spectators figured he was in the midst of release. The courtesan remained still, her body absorbing his semen.

Mara looked away from the peephole. "We should go." She looked at Accalia. "The others are waiting for us."

The witch nodded as she held the stealth amulet up to her face.

Mara looked back at Lady Lorelei. It seemed the inn owner was oblivious to the huntress' conversation with the witch. "Thanks for your help. We need to leave before they realize we're here."

"Of course, my dear," Lorelei spoke.

Mara left the Black Smoke Inn, hoping for a swift exit before the Holy Blades discovered her. Accalia used her amulet to hide while staying close to the huntress.

Unfortunately, Mara encountered the imposter. She never expected him to recover so fast. He had just stepped outside, putting on the last of his uniform. He looked content until he spotted Mara. At first, he appeared shocked because he never expected to see her. His surprise faded away to be replaced by anger. He even perfected the late commander's glare.

He approached her with his hands behind his back. "What are you doing here, Ashwood?"

Mara ignored him while walking by. However, he stepped in front of her. The huntress stopped and glowered at him. "Now what?"

The imposter kept glaring at her. "You do not respect me."

Mara raised an eyebrow. "You get plenty of respect from the whores you fuck every week!"

She stormed past him, ignoring his scowl. Even the Holy Blades looked surprised by her comment.

"Nice," Accalia spoke lowly as she lingered close to the huntress.

They left Har' Yhan and joined the others. The group of sixteen returned to Greyward Hold.

* * *

After a couple of hours on the road, the sages, their guardians, and the former Silver Thorns dispelled their stealth amulets.

Mara looked behind and spotted some Holy Blades mounted on horses. They had been following the group for quite some time.

Accalia also saw them. "Guys," she addressed the others.

Everyone stopped and looked back at the Holy Blades.

Mara suspected that the imposter sent them. It did not take long for them to quicken their pace and catch up to the group. Mara was soon surrounded by the three sages and their warriors as if to protect her. Beatrice and Jen were on the outside. Anyone who had a sword immediately unsheathed them. The Holy Blades saw this and were none too pleased. Despite being mounted on horses, they were outnumbered by at least four to one.

Milo stepped forward. "Is there a problem?"

The Holy Blades ignored him and stared at Mara.

"You are under arrest," one of the Holy Blades addressed the huntress.

Mara folded her arms. "Let me guess—I hurt Lord White's feelings?"

"There is no need for an altercation," said the elven mage. "We can all walk away."

The Holy Blades gave a dark look. Their leader drew his blade while the others followed suit.

Milo frowned at them. "You will provoke Thoron's ire."

Accalia stood beside the elven mage. "They're not backing down."

One of the enemies dashed at the group on horseback.

"Stand back!" Accalia yelled. Black smoke began to billow from her body as her eyes glowed brightly.

Milo and Nikolai saw this and backed away. Even the warriors stood back. Mara, Jen, and Beatrice had no clue what was going on, although the black fumes looked familiar to the huntress. She watched as the black smoke engulfed Accalia from head to toe.

The wind picked up. Snow began to fall heavier while a wolf's howl echoed from the fumes. All of a sudden, a creature leapt out and snatched the first Holy Blade and his horse. Both released a cry before disappearing into the blizzard. The others took notice.

One of them dismounted from his ride. "Where is he?"

Another Blade dismounted as well, only to be abducted by the creature. His horse neighed loudly and dashed away. Only two remained.

The one who dismounted from his horse glared at Mara. "You're doing this, aren't you?"

Before he could do anything, the beast tackled him. Mara and the others finally got a good look at the creature. They saw a large grey wolf, where the shoulder height almost rivalled Mara. The Holy Blade screamed as the beast grabbed his neck. The wolf crushed his windpipe as the canines sliced through his carotid artery, reducing the man's screams to a loud gurgling sound. After slaying the Holy Blade, the beast turned to look at the group with glowing yellow eyes. The entire muzzle was red with blood. The wolf opened its mouth to reveal bloody fangs. The last Holy Blade lost his nerve and took off on his horse. The wolf growled and chased after him.

Mara was unsure about letting this creature continue the carnage. Not every young man planned on enlisting in the Holy Blades. The huntress stepped forward, only to be stopped by Milo and Nikolai.

"Do not get in her way," Milo warned.

Mara looked at him. "But—"

"Trust me on this," the elf said. "You do not want to provoke her ire when she's in this state."

The huntress had no choice but to watch the wolf chase the Holy Blade down. The beast leapt into the air and grabbed him by the back of his head. The horse faltered and hit the ground. He screamed for help, but no one came. Mara stood and watched as the grey wolf slew the last Holy Blade.

Once finished, the wolf cast her glowing gaze onto everyone before looking at Mara. Accalia began to move towards her while Mara stood paralyzed. Wolf sightings were quite rare, and the only time Mara recalled her last encounter was during the werewolf contract in November. Stopping before the huntress, the wolf began to sniff her. The witch produced a soft whine from the back of her throat. Mara gazed up at her eyes, drawn into the golden hues. Dark fumes rose out of the wolf as she changed back into a witch. Out of the plume of black smoke, Accalia emerged. Blood painted the lower half of her face. The Thoron Witch lifted her right hand and began to wipe the red liquid away.

Milo joined the two. "This is the ultimate power of the Thoron Witches."

Mara glanced at the elven mage in shock, and then looked back at Accalia.

The witch kept her eyes on her. "You do not transform?"

Mara shook her head. "Not that I know of." Her eyes drifted onto the dead Holy Blade.

"I did it to protect you," Accalia said. "You have the soul of Aazalith."

Mara's eyes wandered and found the other three Holy Blades. They were barely recognizable. "I'd imagine "Lord White" would be pissed."

"Let him be pissed," Accalia responded. "I'm sure he'll get over it once he finds another woman to fuck."

Mara sighed as she looked at the bodies. "I have to burn them."

"Why?" asked the witch.

"Magic blight," Mara replied. "You don't want them coming back to life as a monster and running amok in the countryside."

"Very well," Milo said. "We shall assist you."

The group gathered the bodies to form a pile. Milo used a spell to incinerate the corpses. After finishing, the group returned to the fortress.

Chapter Fourteen

The Confrontation

Mara had a peaceful morning until she noticed Accalia staring at her. The witch had been watching her ever since the incident a few days ago. It seemed like she wanted to say something to the huntress, but remained silent.

To Mara, it felt like a wolf was stalking her. She figured Accalia's behaviour came from the knowledge of the "botched" ceremony long ago. The huntress was indeed a curious aberration. Mara looked like a Thoron Witch, yet possessed very little to none of the abilities of one.

The morning got disrupted by four loud knocks echoing through the fortress. Mara watched as Jen and Beatrice answered the door.

All of a sudden, a swarm of Holy Blades stormed Greyward Hold. Mara and the sages shot up to their feet, anticipating a fight. The men parted to allow the imposter to pass through. Also accompanying him was Commander Matthews.

"To what do I owe to the Great Lord White?" Mara questioned.

The imposter gave a dismissive look. "Four Holy Blades were found dead. Their bodies charred." He raised an eyebrow. "Why do I have a feeling you're responsible, Ashwood?"

"We found their bodies on the way home," the huntress replied. "They were likely attacked by a creature."

He scowled at her. "Couldn't you be more specific?"

"Might've been a snow beast," Mara said. "We're in Grey Mountain."

The sages looked confused.

Donovan frowned at the huntress. "Did you see this snow beast?"

Mara shook her head. "It was long gone before we arrived. And according to custom, bodies must be burned, lest they arise as monsters. You can thank us for that."

"I don't believe you." The imposter turned his attention onto the three sages. "I've noticed a rise in monster activity since their arrival."

"It's been on the rise since Golden Mountain fell," Mara argued. "In this month alone, I've encountered a vampire and a pack of ghouls, a shadow beast that was possessed, and I recently dealt with a Labyrinth Purifier after someone disturbed her tomb."

The imposter snapped his gaze onto Mara. He remained silent for a moment. "I wish to speak with her in private," he said.

Donovan looked confused. "Are you sure?"

The imposter glanced back at him and nodded. Then he looked back at Mara. "We shall go to another room," he said as he beckoned her.

Mara gazed at the sages with uncertainty. They remained silent, knowing there was little choice. Before Mara followed him, a hand grabbed her wrist. The huntress looked down. The hand belonged to Accalia.

"Be careful," the witch whispered.

The huntress nodded, then placed her hood and mask back on. He might try to kiss her. Mara followed him into the hallway until he opened the first door on the left.

"Is this your room?" He gazed back at her, expecting an answer.

As soon as Mara nodded, he entered her room. The huntress watched as he examined her living quarters. Then he noticed Nightingale lying on the dresser.

"Why did you bring me here?" Mara questioned.

The imposter gazed at her. He tried to see her face, but the hood and mask obscured much of it. His frown began to intensify.

"Karl and I had at least one thing in common," he spoke. "We pretended to be something we're not." He held his hands behind his back. "I pretended to be a boring and stuffy noble. He was a commoner led to believe that he was special."

Mara folded her arms. "So, you finally admit you're an imposter?"

He took a step towards her. "Is that what you want to hear?" Then he said, "I woke up alone and cold. Searched for Thalia, but she was gone. So I wandered to the road where a noble family found me. They thought I was him. They clothed, cleaned and fed me. And I showed my gratitude, especially to their daughter."

Taking another step, he lifted his right hand towards her mask.

She backed off. "Don't touch me!" Mara snapped.

Kratés yanked his hand back. He appeared confused and then his face fell to a frown. "So, you killed Thalia?" He began to circle her, gazing at various parts of her body. "How is that possible?"

"Only an undying can kill an undying," Mara said. "She was in a weakened state, thanks to your reincarnation. And a creature tried to claim her soul. She urged me to end her life."

"Thalia should have killed you," Kratés said point-blank.

Mara snapped her gaze onto him and saw that he was serious.

"She should have killed all of you incomplete fragments, then none of this would've happened." He glanced at her body once more. "To think Thalia shall return in this defective vessel."

Mara froze upon hearing his cruel words.

He leaned over to her ear. "If I were you, I would have that scar looked at," he whispered.

Mara glowered at him as he headed for the door. Before leaving, Kratés looked back at Mara. He stared at her concealed face one more time, then grunted dismissively.

The huntress glared at him as he exited her room. Her right hand curled up into a fist as her fingernails dug into her skin. He was a crueller version of his reincarnation. His words stung deeply.

Mara eventually calmed down and left her room. By the time she returned to the grand hall, the Holy Blades had already left. Yet the three sages and the hunters watched her in curiosity.

"What did he say to you?" Jen questioned.

The huntress stared at the ground before lifting her gaze.

"He revealed himself to you," Accalia said. "We witches have a heightened sense of hearing. I could hear your conversation more or less."

Mara noticed their gazes on her. They could see the hurt in her eyes. She had yet to recover from the imposter's words. Instead, her anger rose again, thanks to Kratés reminding her of her deepest fear. And everyone else could sense it.

"Did he do something to you?" Milo questioned.

Mara took a deep breath. "Is it wrong of me to say that I miss Karl? Or that I regret killing him?"

The sages looked confused.

"What do you mean?" Milo asked.

"Is he just like the late commander?" Beatrice inquired.

The huntress shook her head. "No," she replied. "Karl was merely brainwashed. He was never like that."

Accalia watched her with curiosity. "The imposter called you a defective vessel."

Mara nodded. "Once the soul of Thalia is complete, I will cease to exist."

Everyone gazed at her in shock.

Milo stared at Mara. "Thalia will return?"

"She will awaken within this body," Mara said.

"And you will be gone?" Accalia asked.

No longer could Mara look at anyone. Tears began to well up in her eyes. The others had taken notice. Before anyone could say anything, the huntress headed back into her room and slammed the door behind her.

For some time, Mara never thought about her fate. The binding dagger brought her comfort, knowing she never had to fight for control. Looking at the mirror, she approached and pulled down her mask. Despite her human appearance, Mara did not see herself in the reflection. She saw Thalia gazing back at her. The huntress lifted her right hand to her face. She ran her little black claws along the right cheek. It hurt like hell, but the wounds closed promptly. Even though she had accelerated healing, it horrified Mara to see those wounds disappear. She fell to her knees and buried her face into her hands. Tears spilled out as she wept.

"It is not death you fear, but fading away into nothingness."

Mara lifted her head from her hands and looked up. Accalia invited herself inside.

"Accalia?" Mara wiped the tears from her eyes.

The witch watched her with a pair of glowing eyes. Accalia's intense gaze softened as she began to kneel.

The huntress shook her head. "I'm sorry. I must look like a fool to you."

"Milo believes the divine's soul is affecting your mind. It's amplifying your fears."

"It is?" Mara asked. "I should know better."

"There is no shame of fearing nothingness," said the witch as she helped Mara to her feet. "We live in a world where others are indifferent, making us feel irrelevant. Every Thoron Witch knows what it's like to feel worthless. And to be frank, I believe it is worse than death."

Accalia guided Mara to her bed, allowing the huntress to sit down. "Would you like to hear how the Thoron Witches came to be?"

Mara looked at her and nodded.

"Long ago, there was a small village where everyone lived in peace," Accalia revealed. "One day, a demoness came by and hypnotized every man into serving her. They built a grand city where they lived and prospered, while the women of the small village were left behind. The winters in the Far East were treacherous, and there was little food. To make matters worse, those from the city stole their food, claiming it was a tribute. They could not be bothered to have their crops, nor did they care if the villagers starved."

"Couldn't the women fight back?" Mara asked.

Accalia shook her head. "Many were hanged for attempting to steal back their food. They only wished to save their own." Then she asked, "Do you know that it is physically impossible for a woman to surpass a man?"

"Never noticed. Then again, I never had a normal upbringing."

"Helpless against the brutality, those women did not believe anyone cared until one day when one of their own entered the woods to hunt. It was there she found the Wolf Goddess Ulrika, who took pity on the girl and shared with her a gift. The girl returned to the village, looking much like you and me. She told them about Ulrika. The women travelled into the woods and swore loyalty to the Wolf Goddess. Thus the first witches were born. They became a community where none were left behind. They found their place in this cruel world."

"And they lived happily ever after?" Mara questioned.

The witch gave a wry smile. "The gift had a high price. While witches are powerful and long-lived, they are infertile. And not everyone accepted them. Even today, there's tension between us witches and that city."

"The city is still around today?"

"Their descendants are. The demon may be gone, but there has been no reconciliation. Honestly, things have grown worse."

"How so?"

"Their population is dwindling due to a lack of normal women." The witch began to brood. "These people have taken to abducting and subjecting us to experimentation, to reverse the melding ceremony."

Mara furrowed her brow. "They're trying to make your people human again?"

"So we could give birth to their children," Accalia said. "The experiments always end with the witch dying." She took a deep breath. "My younger sister was abducted. She was only eighteen years old."

"I'm sorry," Mara murmured.

"No need to apologize. I'm glad you're willing to listen." Accalia held out her hand. "Will you join me for training?"

Mara smiled as she took her hand. Both women left her room and headed outside to the training grounds.

Accalia looked at Mara. "You could use the rose."

"What?" Mara asked.

"You could make a wish to separate yourself from Thalia."

"But I need the rose to lift my curse," Mara said.

"We could find other ways," Accalia claimed. "In my experience, there has always been more than one way to break a curse."

* * *

The next day, Mara accompanied Jen and Beatrice to the workshop outside of Haranta Village. The huntress trailed behind, uncertain about the visit.

"Why are we going here exactly?"

Jen looked back at Mara. "Father needs more supplies, so his forge is unavailable. Talon's workshop is the closest."

"It may also be a good idea to reconcile with Talon," Beatrice recommended.

Mara slowed down. The two women took notice.

"Come on!" Jen spoke with a raised voice. "He can't stay mad at you forever!"

"It's not just him I'm worried about," Mara grumbled. "Shenoah saw it too."

The two women watched her, then walked ahead.

"I'm sure they'll understand," Beatrice said.

Mara sighed as she reluctantly followed. As they drew closer, the huntress could hear someone chasing after them. She looked over her shoulder and saw the witch catching up to them. In her hands was a sheathed long sword.

"Figured I tag along," Accalia spoke. "I could get my blade tempered."

Mara eyed the sword. "You have experience with a blade?"

"Yes," Accalia replied. "Knowing to wield a sword is useful, especially if I can't transform."

"Silver and steel alloy for the monsters?" Mara asked.

Accalia nodded. "Yes, it seems we have much in common."

The witch walked ahead. Mara and the others followed behind.

When they finally reached the workshop, Mara remained reluctant. As the other three entered, she stood before the doorway. It had been a while since she saw the blacksmith and the armourer. Did Talon and Shenoah even wish to see her again? Mara gathered enough courage to enter the workshop. The first thing she spotted was a broken window. It was now boarded up to keep the cold from seeping in, while shards of glass riddled the floor. Even the other women had taken notice.

"What happened to the window?" Jen asked Talon.

"Had a break-in last night," the blacksmith responded with a gruff voice.

Mara stayed behind the witch and the former Silver Thorns. She spotted Talon and Shenoah, who had yet to notice her.

"A robbery?" Beatrice asked. "Hopefully, you reported it."

"Didn't need to," Talon said. "Nothing appeared to be taken."

Beatrice looked perplexed. "But someone broke into your workshop?"

"Aye, I grabbed an axe and told them to get out! They only went as far as the forge."

It was then Talon spotted Mara and froze. Shenoah also saw her and frowned. They never expected to see her. Silence filled the workshop.

"My father needed new supplies," Jen explained, "which is why we are here."

Talon remained motionless as he stared at Mara. The look on his face seemed to imply that he did not want her around.

Accalia came forward and presented her sword. "You are decent at your craft, right?"

Talon took his eyes off Mara and gazed at the witch. The blacksmith and armourer curiously watched Accalia, taking note of the similar features she had to Mara.

"I am," Talon said. "And who might you be? I don't think I've seen you around here before."

"Accalia of the Thoron Witches." She unsheathed her blade. The witch also retrieved her coin purse. "Name your price."

Accalia opened her purse to reveal many gold coins. Even Mara was impressed.

"Talon doesn't ask for much," Jen said.

"Doesn't the cost reflect the quality?" Accalia questioned.

"That's not always the case," Beatrice said. "His services are considered to be the best, comparable to some of the more expensive ones."

"Is that so?" Accalia looked at Talon.

"Aye," Talon replied. "I offer the most reliable weapons in the whole land."

Accalia gazed back at Mara. "Come here. I'll pay for yours as well."

Mara reluctantly approached them. "Are you sure?"

"Yes," Accalia answered, holding out her hand. "Give me your sword."

Talon folded his arms and sulked at Mara. Both the huntress and the witch took notice.

"Now what?" Accalia asked.

Talon kept glowering at Mara. "I will not offer my services to her."

Mara grew discouraged while Beatrice and Jen frowned.

Accalia placed her hands on her hips. "Why?"

"Come on, Talon," Jen said. "You can't stay mad at her."

Talon kept his arms folded. "I'm surprised you're willing to stick around her."

"That's because she told us what happened," Beatrice said.

"And what happened exactly?" Accalia directed her question at Mara.

Mara took a deep breath. "He asked me to find Shenoah after she didn't show up for work." She gestured to the armourer. "Some Holy Blades were harassing her. Then they drew their weapons on me. One of them injured me. I snapped and killed them. I also killed my horse by accident. Since then, these two wanted nothing to do with me. They even ratted me out to the Holy Blades, which was why I was on trial."

Accalia shrugged. "Sounds like self-defence."

Shenoah glared at Accalia. "How could you say that?"

"They were soldiers," the witch said, "and soldiers die whether it's in training or war."

"They were kids!" Talon cried.

Accalia showed no sympathy. "Last I looked," she gestured to Mara, "she was only a baby when her father's people turned her into a living weapon."

Shenoah and Talon gawked at the witch.

Accalia focused her gaze onto Shenoah. "Do you have any idea what you've done?"

Mara stepped forward. "Accalia, it's okay. I don't expect them to understand." She gazed at Talon. "If you don't want to offer your services to me, that's fine. However…" The huntress held out her hand. "I want Dad's diagram book."

Talon gaped at her. "What?"

Shenoah stood in between the huntress and the blacksmith. She folded her arms. "That book rightfully belongs to the Stone Mages. It contains the forging techniques of our people. Talon has a right to keep it."

"It belonged to Dad, who made it," Mara argued. "Therefore, it belongs to me. I decided to lend it to Talon out of the generosity of my heart. But since neither of you wants anything to do with me, I want it back right now."

"Well, just hold on a moment," Talon spoke. "Maybe we were too quick to judge."

Shenoah looked back at him in concern. "Talon?"

Talon gazed at Mara with a sombre expression. "Ravenclaw came by and told us what you went through. It seems this melding ceremony is serious business."

Accalia nodded. "It's dangerous, especially in her case."

"We were both ignorant to your plight," Talon told Mara.

"You can say that again," Jen said. "You seemed to have forgotten the tactics the Holy Blades used to lure Silver Thorns to their deaths."

Beatrice gazed at Talon with folded arms. "Or what they did to your last forge." She gestured to Mara. "Without her, you wouldn't have been able to rebuild."

Mara looked at the two hunters. "Harold dismantled the guild to protect the remaining Silver Thorns?"

"He did," Beatrice answered. "I'm surprised he never told you. Or maybe he didn't want to expose the true nature of Kallikratés until the time was right."

"I wish he did," Mara muttered. "It could've saved me from a lot of trouble."

Talon gazed at the huntress. "How about I offer my services to you in good faith?"

Mara raised an eyebrow. "Sounds like you just want to keep the book."

"To be honest, I haven't finished studying all of the diagrams," Talon admitted. "I'd like to do that before I return it."

The huntress placed her hands on her hips. "Fine, I'll give you another week."

With that, the four women handed over their weapons to be serviced by Talon. Once they finished, they returned to Greyward Hold.

Chapter Fifteen

The Hellhound

It was the evening of January 30 when Mara was heading home from a successful hunt. Accalia had accompanied her. The witch's skills and powers had proven useful for hunting stronger creatures. The huntress wished she had those powers.

The two women were on the main road, heading towards Greyward Hold when they noticed a plume of smoke in the west. It drew both of their attention. It was way too cold to have a forest fire, and the recent snowfall would have snuffed out any flames.

Accalia suddenly froze.

Mara took notice. "What is it?"

"Listen," Accalia said.

Focusing her ears, the huntress heard the pounding of hooves. Six riders on horseback were approaching them from the western road. Mara looked to her left and spotted Elder Ravenclaw and five Stone Mage riders.

"What's going on?" Mara asked with a raised voice.

The riders stopped and looked at the two women with grim expressions.

"A powerful creature threatened Cerebell," according to Elder Ravenclaw. "We repelled the creature, but couldn't contain it."

The huntress gazed back at the large plume of smoke. "Did the monster cause that?"

"It cannot be," Accalia grumbled.

Mara looked back at her and spotted the concerned look on the witch's face.

Accalia gave a stern look at Ravenclaw. "Where is it now?"

"Near the Delta Farms and Medulla," Ravenclaw answered.

"No one has attempted to slay the monster?"

He shook his head. "We are going to Mirahyll to ask for aid."

The witch gazed at Mara. "Let's go!"

"We're going to fight it?" Mara asked.

"There's no choice!" Black fumes rose from Accalia's body. She disappeared into the smoke. A large wolf emerged. The witch's appearance spooked the horses, but the riders managed to keep them under control. Accalia gazed at Mara with glowing eyes and then crouched down.

It felt awkward mounting the witch, but the huntress had little choice. Once Mara got on, Accalia rose to her feet and took off in a sprint. Mara clutched the wolf's fur, hanging on for dear life. Accalia didn't seem to mind. Mara looked back at Ravenclaw and his riders.

"We will return with aid!" Elder Ravenclaw announced.

Mara nodded and then looked ahead. The two ventured towards the source of the smoke.

* * *

Mara held on as Accalia sprinted across the snowy field. The huntress wondered what kind of creature they would encounter. The witch was surprisingly swift on her feet, and they arrived at the village of Medulla within moments.

As soon as the witch stopped, Mara dismounted and looked around. She was stunned and horrified to see Medulla destroyed by raging fires. No one survived.

Accalia changed back and observed her surroundings. The witch looked equally disturbed. "It's a hellhound!"

Mara gazed at Accalia with a baffled look. Even Saskia's bestiary never mentioned such a creature.

Accalia looked back at Mara with a grim expression. "I assume you've never encountered such a creature."

"No, I never have."

The witch looked away. "Maybe it's for the best. I'm surprised to see one here." Accalia gestured to the destroyed village. "It's a volatile creature, capable of destroying whole cities!"

"It must've come from the Dark Labyrinth," Mara murmured. "The mountain collapsing might have drawn it out."

"Regardless, we must defeat this creature." Accalia surveyed their surroundings and pointed towards a red glow in the distance. "There!"

Mara looked in the direction the witch was pointing. By some miracle, the Delta Farms were unharmed, but the beast was heading near Haranta and Talon's workshop. Fearing the creature would claim more lives, both the huntress and the witch dashed after it. The creature's flames melted the snow with ease. Their running eventually drew the monster's attention, causing it to turn around.

Upon coming closer, Mara got a good look at the beast. It looked like a giant dog set aflame. The monster was at least twice her height. Its skull was wreathed in flames as sparse patches of fur adorned the head. Three pairs of eyes glowed like hot coals. It appeared to be a darkling of some type.

The two women drew their blades. The monster roared and dashed at them. They dodged out of the way and managed to get in a few hits. Mara teleported away when the hellhound snapped its jaws at her. As the huntress reappeared, a sulphur-like scent drew her attention onto Nightingale. A residue coated her blade.

When the creature attacked again, Mara dodged and found an opportunity to counter. She swung her blade at the beast's hide. Upon contact, Nightingale suddenly broke in two! The shattering sound of metal echoed in her mind. Mara gawked at the broken blade as the shards fell to the ground. The huntress was so stunned, she completely ignored the hellhound, which was about to lunge at her.

"Mara!" Accalia cried.

The huntress then saw a large wolf leaping over her head. Accalia clashed with the hellhound, trying to buy Mara time to escape.

However, the huntress sank to her knees. She began to pick up the shards and placed them in her sheath. Not a single piece was to be left behind. Once Mara gathered them all, she looked up. Accalia was still battling the hellhound. The creature gnashed its jaws at the wolf, forcing the witch away. Then it noticed Mara. The hellhound was about to lunge at her, but Accalia pounced on it. The witch clamped her jaws on its neck, attempting to suffocate the monster. But the hellhound was not ready to give up without a fight. The beast gathered energy and began to glow.

Mara stood frozen as she watched the bright flash of orange light. A powerful force threw them back. Mara hit her head upon landing. Her vision grew blurry while her ears rang.

* * *

Mara awoke to a pounding headache. By some miracle, she survived the explosion but was in pain. When she opened her eyes, the first thing she saw was Accalia looking down at her. The witch appeared unscathed, except for some minor burns. The huntress sat up and found herself in familiar territory. They were in the spare bedroom at Talon's workshop. Mara was a little surprised that the blacksmith allowed them to recover under his roof.

Accalia glared at Mara. "What were you thinking?"

The huntress gave a dumb stare, which seemed to annoy the witch further.

"I was distracting it, giving you a chance to run away," the witch explained. "Why were you just standing there?"

Mara began to remember what happened. Her eyes fell onto the sheathed sword leaning against a nearby wall. At first glance, Nightingale appeared fine. However, when the huntress reached for the weapon and brought it to her lap, she heard the shards sliding within the sheath. A part of her didn't want to see the damage, but she needed to. Resting her hand on the grip, Mara unsheathed a broken Nightingale. Half of the blade and several shards remained in the sheath. It looked like the sword possessed some corrosion near the break.

Mara became numb. The birthday gift, Dad once forged, was now destroyed. In the reflection of her blade, Mara noticed her glowing eyes and the dark blotches. The sad state of her sword caused this transformation. The huntress willed herself to change back, but nothing happened. She was overwhelmed by grief, yet the inability to change back seemed to be the least of her worries.

"We should return to Greyward Hold," Accalia said. "But first, I have a few choice words for Talon." The witch unsheathed her sword. Much of the steel and silver alloy had broken off near the hilt.

Mara looked at the long sword in shock. Like Nightingale, the sword possessed some corrosion at the break.

Accalia frowned at her sword before sheathing it. "I had no choice but to transform."

Mara lifted her gaze to the witch. "Beatrice and Jen also went to see him."

"I'd imagine their swords are broken by now," Accalia said.

The huntress returned her gaze onto Nightingale. How could this happen? Her face twisted in rage as she sheathed her broken sword. Mara rose out of bed and stormed out of the room with Accalia following her. While descending the stairs, Mara put her hood back on, yet her mask remained wrapped around her neck. She could care less if people gawked at her inhuman visage.

The huntress cast her glowing gaze onto the blacksmith and the armourer. Talon and Shenoah grew apprehensive upon seeing her face, yet remained silent.

Mara gave an angered look. "What the hell did you do to my sword?"

Before Talon could get a word in, Mara unsheathed the blade to reveal the damage. The blacksmith seemed horrified to see Nightingale in this state, though Mara grew skeptical of whether he was genuine.

"You have some explaining to do," Accalia said as she also unsheathed her broken sword.

Talon stared at the broken weapons with a disturbed expression.

"I… I don't know," he admitted.

Mara narrowed her eyes. Her pupils shrank. "What do you mean you don't know?"

"That's not an answer," Accalia said. "You serviced our blades. I hope Jen and Beatrice are not in the middle of a hunt like we were."

The huntress soon noticed the scent of sulphur. It came from his forge. She glanced over at his other weapons and spotted the familiar residue. "All of them have it."

Accalia also took note of the corroded weapons. "You're right." The witch snapped her gaze onto Talon. "And he's the greatest blacksmith in all of Ardana?"

Talon scowled at the witch. "My forge was tampered with!"

"It had to be from the break-in the other night," Shenoah added.

The blacksmith folded his arms. "The intruder tampered with my tools. I'll need to replace them. It'll be a while before I could forge or repair weapons."

Accalia gave a harsh stare. "And you just noticed? Even an amateur would make an effort to care for his tools!"

Mara watched him. Even though misfortune befell his forge, it did not change the fact that he was responsible for Nightingale's destruction. Accalia was right. It was a case of negligence on Talon's part. Still, there was a way to fix Nightingale.

The huntress sheathed Nightingale. "Give me Dad's diagram book."

The old blacksmith opened his mouth. "But—"

"I'm going to repair Nightingale," Mara interrupted, "and I need that book. Hand it over."

Talon sulked at her. "And who's going to reforge the blade?"

"Someone else," Mara replied.

The old blacksmith watched her for a moment, then turned to his forge. While he retrieved the book, Shenoah watched Mara with scrutiny.

"How could you be so cruel? He never intended for any of this to happen!"

Mara shifted her gaze onto Shenoah. "I'm cruel? At least I didn't rat out someone who gave a damn, and accept payment for it."

"We let you stay, and this is how you treat us?"

"Last I looked, you two drove me away." Mara tilted her head to the right. "Or maybe that was your intention? After all, our people made me into a weapon to free them from a false goddess. Maybe you were going to abandon me once I had no use."

Shenoah remained silent as she gazed at Mara. Even Accalia glanced at the huntress in concern.

Talon eventually returned with the diagram book. "Here, take this and go."

Mara reclaimed the diagram book. Instead of leaving, she opened it to search for Nightingale's diagram. Perhaps it was paranoia because all Mara could think about was how these two people could screw her over again. Being the last weapon Dad forged, Nightingale should be at the end. But Mara found the remains of a torn page.

"Where's the schematic?" Mara hissed. Her anger was coming to a boil.

Talon and Shenoah just stared at her.

"What are you talking about?" Talon questioned.

Mara glowered at him. "Nightingale's diagram is gone! Where is it?"

The old blacksmith gazed at the book and spotted the tear. It was clear that Nightingale's diagram was missing, but no one knew where it went.

Mara shook her head. "It was a mistake giving you Dad's book!"

The huntress stormed out of the workshop with a broken Nightingale and Dad's diagram book. Accalia followed her out, while Talon and Shenoah remained silent. There was nothing they could say to make the situation better.

* * *

Once Mara left the workshop, she spotted a group of Holy Blades standing before the two women. Among them were Donovan and their wonderful lord.

"What do we have here?" The imposter stepped forward, sporting Karl's classic glare on his face. "I hear you failed to slay the creature."

Mara did her best to avoid eye contact while walking by, though she sensed his eyes on her.

"What do you have to say for yourself, Ashwood?"

The huntress stopped. "At least we did something rather than sit on our asses and watch innocents burn!"

He gaped at her. Even Donovan and the Holy Blades looked displeased. After a moment of silence, the imposter stormed up to Mara and grabbed Nightingale.

"Give me that!" He snatched the weapon out of her hands.

Mara grew horrified when he took her sword away. "Give it back!"

The broken sword and all of its shards came tumbling out.

The imposter stared at its broken remains scattered on the ground. "The sword's broken," he murmured. "Now it's useless, as its owner." He lifted his boot and stepped on one of the shards, threatening to break it.

The huntress snapped. "Stop it!"

Mara wanted to push him away before he could inflict any more damage onto Nightingale. She needed every shard to reforge the blade. The imposter took notice and stepped out of the way, causing her to fall onto the shards. To Mara's fortune, none of the pieces cut her. However, she gained ridicule. The Holy Blades laughed at the spectacle. The huntress ignored them as she regathered the shards.

"This is the Huntress," the imposter said. "More like a worthless amateur." Then, "Commander Matthews and I will deal with this beast. Thanks to her ineptitude, it has vanished. We'll need to send out scouts to track it."

"Yes, Lord White," Donovan said.

Mara lifted her gaze to Nightingale's sheath, which remained in the imposter's possession. She glanced further up to see his condescending gaze.

"Here," he said, tossing the scabbard before her. "Probably the only thing worth something."

Then he walked away. Donovan and the Holy Blades followed after him. Mara glared at them with glowing eyes. She wanted to say something, but her words became lodged in her throat. Tears filled her eyes as she glanced down at the broken remains of Nightingale.

Chapter Sixteen

Firefly

Mara followed Accalia up the snowy trail of Grey Mountain, taking extra care with Nightingale's remains. Her face felt frozen from the frigid air as tears streamed down her cheeks.

The witch glanced at her. "Did your sword mean a lot to you?"

"Dad made it before he died," Mara replied.

Accalia became silent for a moment. "I'm sorry for your loss."

Mara walked ahead. "Let's get back. The last thing we need is a snow beast."

The large iron doors of Greyward Hold greeted the two women. Accalia pushed on the doors to let themselves in. Upon entering, Mara spotted Jen, Beatrice, and the other two sages. They were all waiting for their return. Accalia approached Milo and Nikolai. She whispered to them while often glancing at Mara. The huntress figured the witch was telling them about their encounter with the hellhound.

Jen and Beatrice approached Mara.

"Been looking for you two," Beatrice began. "Hope you weren't on a hunt."

"I'm afraid your warning came a little too late." Mara unsheathed Nightingale.

Both former Silver Thorns stared at the broken blade with a disturbed expression.

"Damn," Jen murmured, shaking her head. "You too."

Unable to stomach the sight, Mara sheathed Nightingale. "Talon claimed someone sabotaged his forge, but I think he did it on purpose."

Beatrice folded her arms. "I find this hard to believe. He cares about his craft."

"He had that break-in the other day," Jen added.

Mara gazed at Jen. "Can your father reforge my sword?"

Jen placed her hands on her hips and nodded. "Let's go see him. If he can't, he could at least forge a new weapon."

The huntress followed the former Silver Thorn to the forge. Walt had just finished forging some new swords.

"You have another one for me?" he asked.

Jen nodded. "She also fell victim."

Mara unsheathed Nightingale. "Can you repair it?"

Walt stared at the blade with wonder and dread. "Do you have the rest?"

Mara handed over her sheath, which contained the rest of the blade.

He took it and laid the shards on the anvil. He frowned as he studied them. "It is possible, but will require much time and money."

"But you say it's possible?" Mara inquired.

"Yes, though it may not be worth it." He gestured to the new blades. "Jen and Beatrice's swords couldn't be salvaged due to the corrosion." Walt turned his attention to Nightingale's remains. "This one doesn't appear as bad." He took a closer look. "Interesting, this possesses a siderite core. Your father was a skilled blacksmith."

Mara sulked. "And he's dead…"

He gazed at her with a sympathetic look. "I'm afraid I won't be of much help since I'm merely a journeyman. But you could ask Raymon of Corlin or Talon, for they are considered master blacksmiths." He gazed back at Nightingale. "Still, siderite is very rare to come by."

"I'd imagine the mines are tapped dry," Jen said.

"If I recall, Godstruck had a siderite core," Beatrice added.

Mara sighed, "Kallikratés destroyed that sword."

"If the shards of that sword are still around, it may be possible to reforge this blade," Walt said. "As long as you have the diagram."

Mara grew sourer. "The diagram is missing."

Walt frowned. "It's impossible." He looked at his forge. "I can forge a new weapon for you. I specialize in estocs, rapiers, and long swords."

Mara gazed at him with downcast eyes. "Thanks," she said solemnly.

The huntress returned Nightingale to its sheath. Despite the imposter's claim, she could not bring herself to throw the blade away. She could keep it as a keepsake of her father.

As Mara headed to her room, she spotted the Thoron Sages approaching her.

"Accalia had filled us in," Milo said. "We are sorry for your loss."

Mara kept looking at the ground and remained silent. When she eventually lifted her gaze to them, they had taken notice of her glowing yellow eyes. Both Nikolai and Milo seemed apprehensive, yet Accalia appeared unfazed.

"There might be a way," Accalia spoke.

The huntress stared at her. "What do you mean?"

"We can use Mind Eye."

Mara gaped at the witch. "I could glimpse into the past." She looked to the others. "I could try to replicate the diagram."

Milo frowned. "It might be difficult. Your Mind Eye seldom triggers while you sleep," the elven mage explained. "You need training and time to refine it."

Accalia stared at Milo. "Why don't we use yours? That way, you can be useful for once."

Milo looked offended, yet kept his cool. "To use my ability, her mind must be completely open to me."

"Shouldn't be a problem," Accalia said. "I could knock her out with sleeping powder. Her mind will be in a proper state."

"Very well," the mage said, then gazed at Mara. "Are you okay with this plan?"

Mara nodded. "If it means getting the diagram back, then yes! Can we do it now?"

"We must go to a place where you and your father had a strong attachment," said the witch.

"The Ashwood Workshop." Mara frowned. "But it was burned to the ground."

"It should suffice," Milo said.

Mara hoisted the book to her chest. "This can also help us since it belonged to Dad."

"Good," Accalia said. "Let's go."

* * *

Mara spent the next day leading Accalia and Milo to the ruins of the Ashwood Workshop. It had been a while since she was last here. Her parents' grave was almost invisible by the mound of snow. The huntress was the first to enter the remains of the workshop.

"I was born here," Mara began. "This was once our family home before we moved to Mirahyll."

Milo and Accalia entered the scorched ruins, venturing to where the forge once stood.

"Here," Accalia spoke, pointing at the ground. "We'll use Mind Eye here."

"Okay," Mara responded. "What do you need me to do?"

"Lay down," the witch instructed.

Lying on the snow-covered ground, Mara gazed up at Accalia and Milo. The witch reached into her robes and retrieved some sleeping powder. Then she blew it over Mara's face. The huntress grew very sleepy. Before closing her eyes, she saw the elven mage approaching her. He reached with his right hand and placed two fingers on her forehead. He pressed firmly against her skin. Mara's eyes rolled into the back of her head, and then everything went black.

Mara opened her eyes again to find herself lying on the ground. No longer was she inside the workshop but in the middle of the woods. The trees had a canopy of green, indicating late spring or summer. Songbirds sang in the distance.

Sitting up, Mara spotted a glowing bird flitting towards her. Coloured in gold, it didn't resemble a chickadee or nuthatch. The tiny creature flew past her, chirping and singing. Mara was about to follow until she recognized the workshop. The intact building stood before her as if she went back in time.

As Mara took a step, she realized she was alone.

"Milo? Accalia?"

The mage and the witch did not respond. Instead, she heard the sound of striking metal. It was Dad! Mara approached the workshop. Upon entering, the huntress found nothing but darkness. The sun had set and night had fallen. The only source of light came from the pale moon outside. Mara looked to the shelves, only to find them empty. Silence filled the workshop. She thought Dad was at his forge, working on a new creation. Now he had vanished along with his weapons.

"Dad?" Mara called. She took a step towards the forge.

"He's not here."

Mara froze. The voice did not belong to Accalia or Milo. She turned her head and saw a dark shadowy figure sitting in a chair, holding a rusted weapon. The huntress could not see a face, for the stranger had their head bowed down. And a black hood obscured any features.

She watched the shadowy person in curiosity. "Who are you?"

The figure did not respond.

While Mara kept watching her, she recognized the black hood and tattered cape. She glanced at the shirt darkened by grime. Blood discoloured the pants around the crotch. Even the gloves and the boots were filthy. The stranger shivered as black smoke billowed from underneath their cape.

"I'll wait for Dad," the stranger said, sounding more feminine.

"And he'll forge me a new weapon," both Mara and the figure spoke in unison.

The stranger lifted her head to reveal a grey, gaunt face riddled with black scars. Mara's eyes widened as she stared at her doppelgänger. The Huntress watched her with glowing yellow eyes.

All of a sudden, fire erupted around them. The workshop was burning! Realizing the danger, Mara fled to the exit. Before she left, she looked back at the undying. The Huntress remained in her seat, watching her with an eerie glow.

Upon exiting the burning workshop, Mara jolted awake. Milo withdrew his fingers from her forehead, then turned away. Before he did, the huntress spotted his disturbed expression. Even Accalia sported a similar look.

Milo gazed at the snow-covered forge. "While we glimpsed into this building's past, it was not the correct time."

Mara rose to her feet while fighting back her tears. "I remember." She gazed at the empty forge. "I was here five years ago, after escaping Kallikratés. I hid here, waiting for Dad. I wanted him to forge me a new weapon. But he was already…"

The witch gave a sombre look. "I'm sorry."

The huntress lifted her gaze to the elven mage. "Can we try again?"

Milo shook his head. "I fear it may damage your mind."

Accalia gestured to Mara. "Your nose…"

Mara could feel something warm flowing out of her left nostril. She lifted her right hand to check. Pulling her hand away, Mara saw the black blood on her fingers. "What is this?"

Milo turned to look at her face. "The first attempt has taken a toll on your mind. I suggest we return to Greyward Hold and let you rest."

Mara frowned as both sages left the workshop. She glanced at the spot where the Huntress sat. It felt as if someone or something was watching her. Mara then took off after them. The three left through the forest path and went home empty-handed.

While travelling on the main road, Mara heard a horse neighing. She looked behind but saw no horse or rider in the distance.

* * *

On the way home, Mara and the sages encountered Raymon on the road just outside of Mirahyll. They kept to themselves as they walked on by, yet the Corlin blacksmith chose to engage them.

"Ah, we meet again," Raymon addressed Mara.

The three stopped and looked at him.

"What do you want?" Mara demanded.

Raymon's gaze wandered to her belt, only to notice Nightingale was missing. "I've heard about the incident at Talon's workshop."

Mara gave a questioning glance. "How do you know?"

"Unless he was the one responsible for destroying our blades," Accalia said.

Raymon looked shocked. "What?"

The huntress tilted her head to the left. "You knew about the break-in."

"Of course," he said. "News spreads quickly."

The huntress folded her arms. "It must be convenient to have less competition."

Raymon gazed at her in disbelief. "You truly think I'm responsible? I'm very disappointed that you'd accuse me of such a thing. I am an artist, and a true artist respects the work of others, especially if they put in a lot of effort."

Milo watched him. "He seems genuinely honest."

The Corlin blacksmith shook his head. "I do apologize for your loss. Your sword was a piece of high-quality art. Whoever did this is permeated in envy, and has a lot of hatred."

He then walked away.

Accalia gazed at Milo. "You believe him?"

Milo held his hands behind his back and walked ahead. "He did not do it."

"How do you know?" asked the witch. "Did you use Mind Eye?"

"On the week of the break-in, he had a massive backlog of requests. He is very well off." He glanced at Mara. "Perhaps you should ask him to reforge your blade."

Mara gave the elf a peculiar look as she pondered his words.

* * *

The three arrived at Greyward Hold. Everyone watched them, wondering what the results were.

Mara shook her head. "We failed."

Walt sighed and turned to his forge. "I'm sorry." He retrieved a long sword. "Here, I'd imagine you'd be needing this. It may not be your Nightingale, but Jen seems to like them."

Mara accepted the sword. "Thanks," she said while unsheathing the sword. She inspected the blade. "Looks much like the one Talon once forged for me."

"I'll take that as a compliment," Walt responded, returning to his forge.

While the huntress sheathed her blade, she noticed the two hunters and the Thoron Sages talking among each other. Even Accalia had joined.

Mara approached them with curiosity. "What's going on?"

The five looked back at her.

"I'm working on a new bestiary," Jen said, holding the large leather book in her hands.

The huntress gazed at the book. "It looks much like the one Saskia had."

"Yes, you could say I'm continuing her work." With that, she handed over the book. "Here, take a look."

Mara took the book and began to flip through the pages. "Yes, it's just like Saskia's," Mara said. "I had it for a while before being captured in early December." The huntress reached a page and stopped. "What's this?"

The illustration depicted a horse with a horn protruding from its forehead. The horn looked like a double-pronged fork with the upper prong longer than the other. The lower prong had a gemstone attached to it. Four glowing eyes adorned the creature's face. The mane and tail were white while the entire body was black.

Jen gazed at the page as well. "I've seen this creature roaming the fields at night. It moves very fast. None have been able to capture it, and some got injured trying."

Milo took a glimpse of the page. "I believe this is a godling—a unicorn-type."

"A deceased horse resurrected by magic," Accalia explained. "They're pretty common in Thoron."

Mara snapped her gaze onto the witch, the wheels turning in her head. "Any creature infected by magic can return to life as a supernatural." She turned her attention back onto Jen. "When did you start seeing this creature?"

"About two weeks ago," Jen answered.

The huntress recalled another event that also happened two weeks ago. "The incident with the Holy Blades," she mumbled.

The others watched her in concern.

"Is something wrong?" Accalia asked.

Mara looked back at everyone, noticing their gaze on her. "No, it's okay."

The others shrugged and continued with their business. Many thoughts raced through Mara's mind. She grabbed some food to eat and then turned in for the day.

* * *

Hours passed while the huntress remained awake. Gazing out the window, she saw a clear dark sky where the stars shone brightly. Even the pale moon was present, giving light to the land below. Looking out to the vast snow-covered fields, Mara noticed a flash of green light. A horse appeared. Although from a distance, Mara could see the white mane and black body. It matched the description of the new entry in Jen's bestiary. Wanting a closer look, Mara snuck out of Greyward Hold without waking anyone up.

The huntress swiftly made her way down the frozen mountain. The night air was frigid. Still, Mara wanted to find this creature. Her eyes scanned the vast snowy field.

Sparks of green converged in one spot within the frozen air behind her. The huntress turned around to see a dark creature emerging from the light. Mara saw the double-pronged golden horn with a green gemstone mounted on the lower prong. Then she spotted the four glowing red eyes gazing back at her. A few red spots glowed on its black body. The bright moonlight made its white mane and tail glow while the black coat shone in various greens and blues.

She stood frozen, her eyes transfixed on the creature.

"It's you," Mara murmured.

The resurrected mare snorted, behaving the same as before. Mara began to approach her. How did this happen? She recalled the little lady bleeding to death in the snow, caused by her blade. Now here she was, resurrected as a darkling or godling.

Once Mara came within five feet, the darkling neighed and reared up. As soon as her front hooves hit the ground, the horse dashed towards Mara. The huntress had no time to react. Once the creature reached her, the darkling vanished in a flash of green light. Mara stood in awe while surrounded by floating particles of green. They looked like tiny fireflies. The huntress glanced around, trying to look for the darkling again. Another bright green flash drew her attention. The former steed stood behind her, watching cautiously.

Mara was surprised. The darkling could teleport. She approached the creature again, hoping to get close enough to mount her, but the resurrected mare dashed away. Like before, she ran circles around Mara. The huntress became frustrated but was not surprised if the little lady remembered what happened. The darkling neighed once more and dashed away. The huntress gave chase in the moonlit night.

"Wait!" Mara cried out, her voice echoing through the fields. The mare ran away. The distance between them grew wider. "I'm sorry!"

The darkling suddenly stopped and gazed back at her. The huntress attempted to get closer, but the mare moved away. Realizing the darkling's fear, Mara stopped and slowly raised her right hand.

"I'm so sorry." Tears filled Mara's eyes. "I never meant to hurt you."

The darkling watched her for a moment. Then she began to approach the huntress. Mara remained still. Once the darkling came within distance, she began to sniff Mara's face. Her inhuman appearance no longer fazed the creature. The mare spotted the tears falling from Mara's eyes.

The creature began to nuzzle the huntress before lowering her body. Mara mounted her carefully, knowing there was no saddle. Once she was on, the darkling stood back up and took off in a dash. Mara was taken by surprise at the creature's speed. She noticed green sparks coming from the darkling's hooves as she dashed through the snow.

* * *

By the next morning, everyone was at the stables, staring at the darkling. They were unaware of the huntress wandering out last night, nor did they expect her to return on the back of the mysterious creature.

Jen stood in awe of the majestic beast. "You managed to catch it?"

Accalia slowly approached the creature. "How did you get it under control?"

"I know who she is," Mara said. "The incident where the Holy Blades tried to kill me."

"The one you went to trial for?" Beatrice questioned.

Mara nodded. "This was my horse."

"Well, she seems to forgive you," Jen chimed.

Milo watched the creature with wonder. "Godlings are intelligent creatures. They are capable of understanding others, including humans." He looked at Mara. "Did you give her a name?"

"The guardsmen used to call her the little lady," Mara revealed.

Milo raised an eyebrow. "How creative," he said sarcastically.

"What should I call her?" Mara asked.

"How about Firefly?" Jen suggested.

"Firefly?" Mara looked back at the resurrected mare, who seemed to like the name. The huntress smiled. "Like me, she can also teleport. Whenever she does, she leaves behind green sparks that look like fireflies."

"It is a much more suitable name," Milo said. "I can see she is very loyal to you. Take care of her."

Mara nodded in agreement.

Jen retrieved her bestiary from her belt and opened it. "I know I already added her, but you don't mind?"

"Not at all," Mara said.

As Jen worked on Firefly's entry, Mara noticed the frowns on the sages' faces. Nikolai looked unnerved, while Accalia and Milo appeared less fazed. The huntress wondered what their problem was.

Chapter Seventeen

Theo's Request

It was past midnight on February 4. Not a single soul stirred within the stone walls of Greyward Hold. Mara was sleeping peacefully until a hand clamped over her mouth. The huntress jolted awake and saw a familiar pair of amber eyes.

"Don't yell," Theo ordered. "Meet me outside."

He took his hand off her mouth. Mara watched as he left her bedchambers. She was disturbed to know he somehow entered Greyward Hold without anyone noticing. After getting out of bed, she grabbed her long sword just in case. Mara left the fortress without awakening everyone.

Upon passing through the iron doors, the huntress found herself surrounded by Blackthorns. They all watched her warily with weapons drawn. Mara responded by unsheathing her blade.

"Easy," Theo said as he emerged again. "There's no need for a fight."

Mara hesitantly sheathed her blade. "What do you want?"

The Blackthorns' leader approached her with a smile on his face. "I've heard about the incident at the workshop below. I'd reckon he suffered a significant hit to his business."

The huntress glowered at him. "That's what you want to talk about?"

"I know you were most affected by this."

"How do you know? Through one of your spies?"

"As I've said before, we have much in common," Theo explained. "Do you know Edwin?"

Mara furrowed her eyebrows. "If I recall, he was one of your business partners."

"Only to keep his secret," he admitted. "I've been aware of his dishonesty for a long time."

"You blackmailed him."

"I'm a businessman," Theo claimed calmly. "When Edwin fled Ardana, he still owed me much gold. Fortunately, he has returned. And he targeted that workshop."

Mara looked baffled. "What?"

"You and the blacksmith exposed him. So Edwin colluded with the Holy Blades to get revenge. He's currently under Lord White's protection."

Mara placed her hands on her hips. She was not surprised that Edwin sought revenge. But why was the imposter protecting him? She glanced up at Theo. "You want my help finding Edwin? What makes you think I want to help you?"

"I believe I have something of yours." He reached into his pocket and retrieved a piece of paper. Theo unfolded it, revealing a schematic of a familiar sabre. It was Nightingale!

Mara stood frozen. "How?"

Theo folded the diagram and placed it back into his pocket. "We obtained this after clashing with some Holy Blades. It seems Lord White has become less tolerant of our presence."

"Probably because you're a liability." Mara glanced away. "I never thought he'd conspire with Edwin. He must've ordered his Holy Blades to break in and sabotage the workshop, but why steal the diagram?"

"I'd imagine it has much value. It's the only other Lord Slayer."

The huntress folded her arms. "So, why come to me? You could've traded it for Edwin."

"True," Theo admitted, "I could meet Lord White during the upcoming banquet at Bartharoy Castle. But he may have me arrested on sight."

"That's why you've come to me?" Mara frowned at him. "I'm not allowed to enter any place where the Faith is present."

"It's an open invitation," Theo revealed. "Regarding this prohibition, I'm sure he'll make an exception for one night. Either way, I have a guarantee."

"You expect me to rescue you when things turn ugly?"

"Yes, especially if you want the diagram back."

Mara gazed at him. "What do I have to do?"

"Accompany me to the banquet." Theo gazed at her attire. "Oh, and I recommend you have something suitable to wear. You do have something suitable?"

Mara glanced down at her attire, then shook her head. "Not really," she admitted. "And I have another issue." She removed her mask and hood, revealing her inhuman visage.

The Blackthorns looked apprehensive, for this was the face of the Black Smoke without the undead appearance. Yet the guild's leader did not appear fazed in the slightest.

Theo sighed, "I'll provide proper attire, as well as transportation to the banquet." Then he pointed at her face. "However, I can do nothing about that. You are on your own."

With that, he walked away. His men sheathed their weapons and followed suit. Mara watched as they all left.

* * *

The huntress returned to her chambers and laid on her bed until the sun rose. She spent much of her time awake, wondering if she should tell the others of her encounter. Then again, Accalia, Jen, and Beatrice had a right to know because they were also affected. When she heard the others stirring, Mara made her move. The huntress entered the grand hall. Everyone was already seated, ready to begin another day.

Mara's eyes drifted over to the sages. The witch and the mage were speaking to each other, while Nikolai watched her warily. He had been like this since yesterday. Mara wondered what his problem was. Milo and Accalia took notice and watched her as well. Mara gazed at them for a brief moment before joining Beatrice and Jen for breakfast. Some bread, dried fruit, and cheese were on the menu this morning.

While the huntress ate her share, she found the silence overwhelming. Mara glanced over at the sages and saw Accalia approaching her.

"Where did you go this morning?" asked the witch.

Mara gawked at her, astonished that Accalia could hear her leaving the fortress. So much for being secretive.

"With your sense of hearing, you should consider being a spy," Mara said dryly. Then she noticed everyone's eyes on her.

"What is she talking about?" Jen asked.

"Out with it," Beatrice said. "You might as well tell us."

Mara took a deep breath. "I know what happened to Talon's forge."

Everyone gathered around her.

"Is that so?" Milo asked.

Accalia's stare intensified. "Well, don't keep us in suspense! What did you find out?"

"Edwin did it," Mara answered.

The sages looked confused, for they never knew the culprit. Beatrice and Jen, however, knew the so-called blacksmith. Their eyes went wide, and their mouths dropped open. Soon, the shock faded from their faces, only to be replaced by anger.

"Him?" Beatrice hissed. "He returned?"

Mara nodded. "He collaborated with the Holy Blades to sabotage Talon, and is under that imposter's protection."

"Who's Edwin?" Accalia asked.

Mara and the former Silver Thorns gazed at her.

"He was a master blacksmith until he got exposed," Jen explained.

"Exposed?" Milo inquired.

"Edwin stole weapons from other blacksmiths and passed them off as his own, including my father's," Mara revealed.

"And mine," Jen added.

"But he was unaware of Nightingale and the diagram book, which could identify Dad's weapons," Mara continued. "He destroyed the Ashwood Workshop before fleeing. And now he's returned."

Beatrice gave Mara a puzzling look. "How did you get this information?"

"Theo," Mara answered. "He has Nightingale's diagram."

Beatrice gaped at her. "What?"

"He got it after an altercation with some Holy Blades. He'll return it in exchange for my help."

"Which is?" Accalia asked.

"I help him find Edwin," Mara said.

Beatrice frowned at her. "So, you're working with the most wanted man in Ardana?"

"If I can get the diagram back, I'll be one step closer to getting Nightingale repaired."

Jen shrugged. "I guess you don't have much choice."

Accalia folded her arms. "Why do you need to help? Couldn't he do this on his own?"

Mara shook her head. "If the imposter sees Theo, he'll have him arrested on sight."

"And I guess there's no point handing Edwin over to any authorities," Beatrice said.

"At least it means Talon is innocent," Jen pointed out.

Mara looked at Jen and frowned. Both former Silver Thorns took notice.

"Come on, Mara," Beatrice said. "He never meant to destroy our blades."

The huntress put her hands on her hips and looked down.

"Maybe you should give Edwin to Talon," Jen suggested. "I'm sure he'll be thrilled to come face-to-face with the one who ruined his forge again."

Mara lifted her gaze. "I'll think about it." Then, "Theo should be arriving soon, but I need to do something about my face." She gazed at Accalia. "No offence, but where I'm going, I'll stick out like a sore thumb."

Milo placed his hands behind his back. "Perhaps I could be of assistance."

Mara looked intrigued. "How so?"

"Excuse me for a moment."

The elven mage disappeared into his room. Within a few moments, he returned with a black and gold choker decorated with white pearls. A sizeable smooth stone dangled from the centre via a gold chain. It sparkled in a variety of colours, drawing Mara's attention. The necklace looked very expensive. Even the other two sages eyed the stone suspiciously.

"That stone…" Nikolai began.

"Wait a minute!" Accalia snapped her gaze onto Milo. "Isn't that one of the ancient treasures stolen a while back?"

"I purchased this from a jeweller a few years ago," the mage claimed. "I simply had it fashioned to look like the real thing."

Mara kept her gaze on the necklace. "What is it? And what do you mean by ancient treasure?"

"This is Thalia's Stone," Milo said. "According to ancient tales, Thalia struggled to control her inhumanity after consuming mermaid meat. She used a magical stone to hide her true form until she learned to change at will. The stone is an ancient treasure associated with the immortal woman, but there are replicas with the same ability." He held the necklace out before him. "Since you are Thalia's reincarnation, I believe you have a right to own it."

After taking the necklace, Mara returned to her room to find a mirror. Looking at her reflection, she noticed the remains of Dad's gift. Despite never finding a replacement moonstone, she could not bring herself to throw the necklace away. Mara took it off and placed it on the dresser. Then she replaced it with Milo's gift.

Once the new choker went on, the gemstone began to glow in a pale light. Within seconds, Mara's inhuman form faded away. Her yellow eyes became light brown. Her fangs shrank down, though she did not feel it. Even the dark spots around her eyes disappeared! Mara was shocked. It had been a while since she had seen this face. The huntress lifted her right hand to feel her face. Not only did she look human, but her skin felt normal as well. The stone was pretty powerful; it was not some mere illusory magic.

Mara stared at her reflection for at least a moment before leaving her room. Everyone stood frozen with mouths agape when she emerged.

"She looks exactly like Thalia," Nikolai mumbled.

The mage kept his composure. "I trust it is to your liking?"

Mara nodded. It was more than what she had expected. Then they heard a knock on the door. Jen and Beatrice went to answer. Mara suspected it would be Theo. When the doors opened, Mara's suspicions were correct.

"Ah, there you are," Theo began as he entered Greyward Hold. The Blackthorns' leader was already dressed for the banquet tonight. Like the funeral, he had groomed himself to look presentable. He even wore a clean black suit. Theo kept gazing at Mara. "I see you've resolved your inhuman issue."

Everyone watched him with apprehension. Mara was also cautious until she spotted a box in his possession.

Theo took notice. "Yes, I have your dress as promised." He handed the box over to Mara.

She opened the box to reveal a red satin dress.

"My apologies if I didn't get your measurements completely accurate," Theo said.

Mara stared at the dress. "I'll go upstairs and change."

She returned to her room and changed into the dress.

"Red…" Mara murmured. It was not her favourite colour, but the bustle dress did look nice. For a bandit, Theo had a decent fashion sense. Mara then put her armour and sword into a travelling bag. After slinging the strap over her left shoulder, she exited her room. As she returned to the grand hall, Mara drew everyone's attention.

"Don't you look ravishing." Theo noticed the travelling bag in her possession.

Mara noted his curiosity. "I'm taking my armour and sword in case things go awry."

"Good. It seems we both have the same idea." Theo reached for the bag. "I'll take it for you. It's the gentleman thing to do."

The Blackthorns' leader left Greyward Hold. Mara glanced outside to get a glimpse of a carriage. Theo had everything planned. As she took one step forward, Mara felt a hand grabbing her wrist. The huntress gazed back at Accalia.

"You shouldn't be doing this alone," the witch warned her.

"It'll be fine," Mara said. "I'm only going after Edwin."

"Who is protected by the Faith," Accalia argued. "What if they come after you? You do have the soul of Aazalith."

"I won't be alone," the huntress replied.

"True, but I wouldn't trust Theo," Beatrice said. "He's the most wanted man for a reason."

"I know," Mara responded.

"I hope so," Milo said. "Be careful out there."

The huntress nodded, then left Greyward Hold. She followed Theo into the carriage. As soon as everyone settled in, the coach began to move towards Hema.

* * *

Hours had passed by the time they reached the city of Hemal. Mara gazed out the window, watching the setting sun. Then her eyes fell upon Bartharoy Castle. She had not been here since Lady Isabella's death.

"So, what's the plan?" Mara asked. "How are we going to find Edwin?"

"Lord White's office is within the castle," Theo explained. "It'll offer a clue to Edwin's whereabouts."

"What do I have to do?"

"You will draw Lord White's attention while I sneak into his office."

"Excuse me? Are you telling me that I'm just a distraction?"

Theo smiled. "Don't forget—you are the backup plan in case things go awry."

Mara sighed, "How do I draw his attention away?"

"Your mere presence will be more than enough." He glanced at her dress. "This attire will turn heads."

She gazed down at her dress with skepticism. "Really?"

"Don't believe me? I'll show you."

Once the carriage stopped, Theo exited the transport. He left behind the bags containing their belongings. The Blackthorns' leader turned and gazed at her.

"If you don't mind." He held out his hand to her.

The huntress glanced at her belongings before looking back at him.

"Don't worry," Theo said. "Your possessions will be safe in this carriage."

"I hope so." Mara took his hand.

Theo led her out of the carriage and into the castle, where several others were attending the banquet. They passed through the frozen gardens, as servants removed many dead plants. The foyer was much brighter, with more candles illuminating the dark. The guests wore fancy and colourful attire. Very few seemed to notice Theo, yet many were watching Mara. Her red dress, in particular, seemed to draw their scrutinizing gazes. Mara sighed while looking away. She had yet to see the imposter.

"Seems my suspicions were correct," Theo said. "He's watching you."

Mara looked back and saw the imposter. He stood with some nobles while staring at her. His gaze appeared to be more focused on her face rather than her dress. Still, Kratés kept his distance.

Theo held her close to his body. "I sense that he's jealous."

"Jealous of what?" Mara glanced back at the imposter, who remained glaring at the two. Not even the young noblewoman next to him could draw his attention away.

"He wants you," Theo said.

"What are you talking about?" Mara questioned. "He hates me."

"You believe him?" Theo questioned. "His body language tells a different story."

"Well, I'm surprised he hasn't thrown me out yet." Mara looked back at Theo. "Are we going to do this?"

"Of course." Theo leaned in towards her face. The Blackthorns' leader was close enough to kiss Mara on the lips. "Keep his attention on you. I'll find a way to get into his office."

Theo pulled away and disappeared into the crowd. Mara glanced back at the imposter to find him still staring at her. She turned away, doing her best to ignore him. Approaching a table with some food and drinks, Mara took a glass of white wine. She sipped while glancing around. The wine was very dry and bitter, but it was the only drink available. With her back turned, Mara listened as a group of nobles engaged the imposter in a conversation.

"Lord White, I know you likely heard this question before, but why is it that women are not allowed to join the Holy Blades?" asked a nobleman.

"If I recall, women are generally weaker and unsuitable for combat," another spoke.

"That is false," the imposter argued. "It has always been my belief that men were placed on this earth to serve the Goddess and protect women."

Mara looked back and watched as the imposter approached the nobles with a stoic look.

"All women are important, for they give birth and raise our children," he continued. "Lord Kratés bestowed those teachings at first, but the obligation to serve the Goddess and the vow of celibacy shadowed them."

The imposter turned his gaze onto a young noblewoman. The noblewoman blushed as he reached for her blond hair and caressed her face. After a moment, the imposter looked at Mara. His eyes stared into her own. Then he gazed at the young noblewoman.

"May we speak in private?"

He took her by the hand and vanished into the crowd. Mara reckoned he was taking the woman to his office to have intercourse. But Theo had yet to return. Mara put down her wineglass and followed them. For a few moments, her eyes scanned the crowd. She wandered past many groups while looking for a way out. Unfortunately, she spotted Donovan approaching her. The commander from Corlin looked sour upon seeing her here. He stopped before her and held his hands behind his back.

"If I recalled, you were forbidden from entering any place where the Faith is present."

Mara's eyes searched for the imposter. But Kratés, or the woman he was with, was nowhere to be seen. The undying gazed back at the black-haired commander, who demanded an explanation.

"I received an invite," Mara answered.

Donovan stared at her. "By Lord White?"

"No," Mara replied.

His face darkened. "Then you have no right being here. Off to the dungeons you go."

Mara glared at him. The plan was unravelling. Now she wished she had not left her belongings behind. Before Donovan could do anything, Mara spotted two Holy Blades coming her way.

"Lord White wishes to see you in his office," one of them addressed her. "If you would come with us."

The commander from Corlin looked concerned. "What is the meaning of this?"

One of the Holy Blades looked at him. "Lord White made the request."

Donovan began to sulk. "Then, I shall accompany her."

The Holy Blades frowned at him. "With all due respect, he asked us to escort her."

The black-haired commander's face darkened. "And with all due respect, I possess a higher rank than both of you. Or did Lord White neglect to tell you this?"

The Holy Blades watched him in silence.

"Fine," said one of them. "This way."

The two Holy Blades led them to Lord White's office. Mara grew uncertain. What was going to happen to her? Where was Theo?

Mara stared ahead while being escorted by Donovan and the Holy Blades. She could sense the rage radiating from the commander from Corlin. As they drew closer, she spotted the young noblewoman from earlier. The red gracing her cheeks hinted at what transpired. The noblewoman avoided eye contact with the four as she walked past them. Donovan watched her in confusion, but he appeared to have caught on.

One of the Holy Blades knocked on the door. "She's here, Lord White."

"Send her in," the imposter called.

The Holy Blades opened the door, allowing both Donovan and Mara entry. The huntress found the imposter sitting at his desk. He looked confused to see the commander from Corlin standing with her.

"Commander Matthews, I didn't expect you to accompany her."

Donovan kept his composure. "She defied your request. I intended to arrest her before your men arrived."

The imposter gazed at him. "Very well." He turned his attention back onto Mara. "I wish to speak with her alone."

Donovan gazed at him in befuddlement. "Why do you wish to see her alone?"

The imposter grew annoyed. "It's none of your concern."

The black-haired commander frowned at him before reluctantly walking out. The other two Holy Blades also followed suit.

Mara looked back at Kratés, who rose from his seat. His eyes remained fixated on her as he circled his desk.

"I never imagined Commander Matthews could hate you so," he told her.

"Of course he does," she said. "He's a Holy Blade and a disciple of the Faith."

"It's much more personal than that." He approached her. "I can see it in his eyes—the desperation of wanting to be loved. Yet the one he desires will never love him back."

The huntress then recalled Mendé's words about the commander from Corlin. "He's in love with you. But what does this have to do with hating me?"

Kratés raised an eyebrow. "I'm not that kind of person, and he knows it." He walked around Mara to take in her image. His eyes roamed up and down her body. "You have something he can never possess."

Mara grew uncomfortable. It seemed the noblewoman was not enough. Gazing at the desk, the huntress could not see a single piece of paper. She reckoned they made love on it. "What do I have that he lacks?"

"You're a woman, although I'm unsure if you even fit the description of one. I heard some interesting things about you, like how you lack a uterus. I hope you saw a doctor regarding your deformity."

She stared at him. "Why do you care?"

"When Thalia returns, I will shower her with gifts and my love. The least you could do is make sure her vessel is in the best condition."

The huntress' right hand tightened into a fist. She wanted to hit Kratés for saying those words. Once again, he was belittling her very existence.

He switched his attention onto her dress. "Red," he said. "Never thought the colour would suit you. Theo has great taste."

Mara tried to keep calm. "And where is Theo?"

"Arrested," he replied. "He currently resides in the dungeon awaiting judgment. I'm sure he won't have a good outcome since he's the most wanted in all of Ardana. But I never imagined you'd associate with such a man."

The huntress glared back at him. "Are you going to ask why I was with him?"

Kratés returned to his desk. "Theo is searching for Edwin, who owes him money and asked for your help. In exchange…" He opened a drawer and retrieved a piece of paper. Returning to Mara, he held out the paper before him. "He offered this to you."

It was Nightingale's diagram. Dread washed over Mara, knowing the schematic was now in Kratés' hands. The huntress was more relieved when Theo had it.

Kratés gazed at her. "I believe this is yours. Go ahead. Take it."

She gazed at the diagram for a few seconds before snatching it out of his hands. Mara studied the schematic, making sure there was no damage to it. It appeared okay. She looked up at the imposter. "Why are you giving me this? I know you plotted with Edwin to sabotage Talon's forge."

Kratés held his hands behind his back. "True," he said. "Some are willing to pay a lot of gold for it, but I decided to return it to you. In exchange, I want you to leave within the hour. You will cease your search for Edwin."

Mara furrowed her brow. "You do realize you're protecting a crook?"

Kratés grew agitated. "That is none of your concern. Now, get out!"

Mara stared at him for a while before turning around. Before walking out the door, the huntress stopped. "You claim men are supposed to protect women. If so, where were your ideologies during the mass arrests two months ago?"

With that, she left him alone in his office.

The huntress stared at Nightingale's diagram. She should have been happy to know she retrieved it. But should she leave Theo behind? What about Edwin? The huntress kept staring at the schematic while walking through the crowd. Lifting her head, Mara saw Donovan watching her. Kratés might have been right about the commander from Corlin. She could see envy in his eyes. Yet he never approached her.

The huntress put the schematic away as she approached the foyer of Bartharoy Castle.

Chapter Eighteen

Bittersweet Revenge

Mara walked out of the castle. At least the carriage containing all of her belongings remained. However, some Blackthorns stood near another coach. She reckoned they were reinforcements. They approached her with frowns on their faces.

One of the bandits asked, "What the hell happened? You were supposed to protect him!"

"This was a risk," said the huntress. "We were all aware of this."

Mara walked towards the carriage, but the Blackthorns stood in her way.

Another brigand scowled at her. "Where the fuck do you think you're going?"

His hand grabbed her necklace and ripped the stone off. Within seconds, Mara's eyes began to glow. Dark blots appeared on her face. She parted her lips, revealing elongating canines. The Blackthorn froze as the huntress snatched the stone out of his hand. The necklace was now useless. She had to make sure to return every piece to Milo. The bandits backed off in fright, knowing she was responsible for the near decimation of their guild.

"Do you want me to help rescue your boss?" Mara growled. "Then get out of my way."

The bandits backed away, allowing her entry into the carriage. She changed into her Silver Thorn armour. After a few moments, Mara exited the carriage equipped in her usual gear and weapons. She gazed back at the group who kept watching her in apprehension.

"Has anyone ever broken into the castle dungeons?" Mara inquired.

The Blackthorns gawked at her.

The huntress took notice. "Well? Are we not going to save him?"

One of the bandits approached her. "It'll be dangerous. The place will be crawling with Holy Blades." He gave a stern look while retrieving Theo's possessions from the coach. "If you want to help us, then follow us. Follow my instructions, and we all walk away happy."

Mara was unsure about working with criminals. She had the diagram for Nightingale, but she wanted something more, and Theo was the key.

The huntress followed the thugs into the sewer systems underneath the castle. The bandits seemed to know their way around. Mara assumed they had broken into this dungeon before. They soon encountered Holy Blades. Members of the faith militant drew their weapons in response. Within seconds, it became a bloodbath with most of the casualties being Holy Blades. Despite being outnumbered, the bandits were more skilled. Even Mara claimed a few Blades.

They eventually reached the cells and found Theo bound in chains. The Blackthorns' leader wore only his trousers. Many scars riddled his muscled torso. Some were faded while others looked fresh. Theo looked up and smiled at his men. He seemed relieved to see his rescuers. Then he noticed Mara, and the smile faded away. His eyes remained on the huntress while some of the bandits undid his shackles.

"I never expected to see you here," Theo began. Once freed, the Blackthorns' leader lowered his hands and rubbed his wrists. He inspected them for a moment before lifting his gaze to Mara. "You have the diagram, do you not?"

Mara nodded. "I do."

"So, why are you here?"

"It's not just the diagram," Mara said. "I want to find Edwin." The huntress gripped her sword. "I trust you found his whereabouts?"

Theo looked intrigued. "He's located in a house in Mirahyll."

Mara gave a questioning look. "That's not very specific."

"It's guarded by Holy Blades. We'll know it when we see it."

One of the bandits approached him with his gear.

"Thank you." Theo took his shirt and put it on. "We'll take the carriages back."

The huntress folded her arms.

"I'll wait outside," she said, walking out.

Theo smiled as he got dressed. Once he was ready, the Blackthorns' leader and his group went outside to greet the huntress.

"I suppose we are ready to go," Theo said.

They took the carriages to Mirahyll.

* * *

Mara and the Blackthorns arrived within a few hours. Once they entered the city, the carriages stopped. Theo was the first to leave. He led the way to Edwin's hideout, located near the noble quarters. Two Holy Blades stood before the front entrance of a home, just as Theo had claimed. The guards spotted them and drew their weapons. Mara, Theo, and the Blackthorns responded similarly. They made quick work of the two Holy Blades. Theo searched their pockets, finding a key to the residence. He went to the front door and opened it. Upon entering the home, more Holy Blades came rushing towards them. Mara and the Blackthorns defeated them with relative ease.

"Split up and search the rooms," Theo ordered.

Mara headed upstairs. Perhaps it was dumb luck because upon searching the first room, she found an older man standing in the corner. She recognized the miserable old geezer by the glasses adorning his face and the balding top of his head. Looking at his face, Mara could tell he never expected to see her, nor did he wish to see her.

One of the Blackthorns entered the room and spotted Edwin as well. "Here! He's in here!"

Within seconds, Theo and his men arrived. The Blackthorns' leader smiled at the older man.

"Ah, Edwin," Theo began, approaching the crook. "I've been looking for you for quite some time. You owe me a lot of gold."

Edwin gazed at them like a cornered animal. All of a sudden, he dashed to a weapon leaning against the wall.

"Stay back!" Edwin yelled, unsheathing the sword.

Mara and the Blackthorns watched him warily, while others began to draw their weapons.

Theo, however, seemed unfazed and raised a hand. "No need for a confrontation. We're only here for the gold."

"Why is she here?" Edwin pointed at Mara. "Don't you know who she is?"

Mara glared at him. "You mean the daughter of Bear Ashwood?"

Theo gazed at Mara with intrigue. "I see," he addressed her. "So, this is why you agreed to help me find him."

"This man stole my father's work!"

"Your father was an inferior man!" Edwin shouted.

Mara released a low growl as she scowled at him with glowing eyes. She wanted to kill Edwin for insulting Dad, but Theo held her back.

"Check this room," Theo instructed his henchmen.

The Blackthorns complied and searched the room for gold.

Edwin lost his composure. "No, the gold is mine!"

He lunged at Theo, but the Blackthorns' leader anticipated his movement. Theo grabbed the wrist holding the sword, then slammed him against the wall. Edwin cried out in pain as he crumpled to the ground.

"That was not a wise move," Theo said. He glanced back at Mara. "Although I am curious as to why you think her father was inferior. Could it be the fact that he, a Stone Mage, surpassed you as a blacksmith?"

Mara gazed at Theo in confusion. "What?"

"I'm well aware of the discrimination towards Stone Mages. The Faith of Kallikratés spread lies and hate towards a group they deemed dangerous. Yet people's hatred was unfounded." Then, "Mara, your father was descended from the one who forged Godstruck, am I correct?"

Mara nodded. "Yes, he was. How did you know?"

"Father used to speak favourably about Bear Ashwood. If he were alive today, his name would've gone down in history as the best blacksmith in all of Ardana. Not that many would admit it. How did he die?"

"Kallisto murdered him, then made my mother drag his body to Mirahyll."

Theo sighed, "And this man stole your father's work."

One of the Blackthorns approached Theo. "Boss, we found at least one hundred thousand gold!"

The guild leader was stunned. "Well, that certainly covers the amount owed to me." He looked at Edwin. "Thank you, Edwin. That is all." Before leaving, Theo gazed at Mara. "I'd imagine you have unfinished business with him."

Once the Blackthorns left, Mara returned her attention to Edwin. She gazed at the miserable old fart, taking note of the scowl on his face.

"You have a lot of nerve," the huntress hissed. "How dare you destroy my father's work?"

The expression on his face never changed. Edwin showed no remorse for what he did.

Mara gripped the hilt of her sword. "Without the Guardsmen, I know I'll have no justice. Guess I'll have to take matters into my own hands."

Pulling down her mask, Mara bared her fangs on purpose. She wanted to scare him. Edwin's eyes widened in horror while his jaw dropped. He looked astonished to see her supernatural form. A weak whimper escaped his lips as his breathing became hitched.

"Get away from me," he whispered.

Mara took another step. "I'll never forgive you."

Edwin tried to move away, but his legs became useless. "Stay away from me!"

"Or what?" Mara asked, taking another step towards him.

All of a sudden, he flew into complete hysterics and screamed, "Get away from me! Stay away! You're supposed to be dead! You're supposed to be dead! You're supposed to be dead!"

Mara grew confused. Then she noticed his gaze past her right shoulder. She glanced to her right, but no one was there. Looking back at him, Mara noticed his shortness of breath. He was unable to breathe, clutching his chest. By the time Mara realized what was happening, it was too late. Edwin was gone.

* * *

After a few moments, Mara left the residence. Much to her surprise, Theo and his men were waiting outside.

"Is it done?" Theo asked.

Mara nodded. "Yes, he's dead."

Theo looked intrigued. "Oh, he is? Did you…?"

The huntress shook her head. "He died of a heart attack before I could even touch him."

Theo smiled. "I guess he gave you the slip once more."

"I suppose," Mara responded.

"Guess it ended well for both of us." He reached for a bag of gold. "Here's your reward—five thousand gold."

Mara stared at the bag. "I'm not sure if I should take it."

"Well, I originally planned on giving you only the diagram, but you came through for me in ways I'd never expect. Just take the gold, and we'll call it even."

"Fine," Mara said, taking the bag.

Theo watched her. "Why were you willing to help me find Edwin?"

She looked away. "You already know the answer."

"You care deeply for your father, don't you?"

"My father spent much of his life dedicated to his craft," Mara answered. Then she looked back at him. "This was the least I could do for him."

"So justice has been served," Theo said. "I, too, loved and admired my father."

"Heard what happened to your father. I'm sorry."

"Don't be," Theo told her. "I'm a firm believer in karma."

Mara folded her arms. "You mean you got back at those who killed your father?"

"Not just them…"

Hearing a feminine scream, Mara turned to see two thugs mugging a middle-aged woman.

"Help me!"

No one came to her rescue. As Mara watched the robbery unfold, she recognized the victim. Once, she tried to help this noblewoman. Theo stood next to the huntress. He smiled while the woman had her jewellery and coin purse stolen once more.

"Hello, Mother," Theo said underneath his breath.

Mara heard his words and looked at him in astonishment.

Theo looked back at the huntress. "As I said, karma can be a blessing."

Then the Blackthorns walked away. Mara watched as they disappeared from her sight. She gazed back at the middle-aged woman, who looked distraught at being robbed again. But the huntress knew better.

Mara headed for the western gate. As she drew closer, she noticed a green flash of light and a horse-like creature appeared before her. Firefly had arrived to take Mara home. The huntress was surprised at first. Then she recalled Milo mentioning how these creatures were intelligent. Mara mounted her steed and soon felt the discomfort of riding on the creature's back.

"I need to get you a saddle," Mara addressed Firefly. The darkling snorted in response. They left the City of Mirahyll.

* * *

Mara spotted Talon's workshop while travelling on the road. She stopped and stared at the building for a moment, wondering if it was worth talking to Talon. The huntress had realized that the old blacksmith was never at fault, and she could not stay mad at him forever. Mara doubted Talon was aware of the saboteur. She could spare a few moments. The sun was rising by the time she approached the workshop.

The door was already open, so Mara let herself in. Upon entering the workshop, she found the old blacksmith at his forge. Talon sat before his anvil, making sure it was ready for use again. Though he was not forging any weapons, and Mara could not see any tools.

A creak from the door drew his attention. "Ah, Shenoah," Talon began. "You're here early."

He turned to look. Instead of Shenoah, he saw Mara. Talon froze as he stared at the huntress.

"Hello, Talon," Mara began. "How is your business?"

Talon kept staring at her for a moment before turning away. "What are you doing here?"

The huntress frowned. "I just wanted to talk."

The blacksmith tended to his forge without looking at her. "There's nothing to talk about."

Mara watched him. It became clear that he wanted nothing to do with her. "Fine," she said, heading for the door. "Guess I don't need to tell you who ruined your forge."

"Wait!" Talon shouted.

She stopped, then looked back at him.

Talon watched her warily. "You know who did it?"

Mara nodded. "Edwin did it."

His eyes went wide while his mouth dropped open. Soon, anger replaced his shock. "That bastard!" Talon growled. "He returned?"

"He colluded with the Holy Blades to sabotage your forge. They also stole Nightingale's diagram." The huntress reached into her pocket and retrieved the diagram. "Got it back." She put it away. "At least I'll be one step closer to repairing Nightingale."

Talon appeared relieved. "I'm glad you got it back. But what about Edwin?"

"You don't need to worry about him anymore."

Talon's eyes widened. "Really? Did you…?"

"He died of a heart attack before I could touch him."

Talon gawked at her for a moment. Then he erupted into a bout of laughter. It was as if he heard something hilarious. "Damn, the weasel slipped away again," he said. "Well, good riddance to that bastard."

Mara nodded in agreement, then turned to the door.

"Wait a minute," said the blacksmith.

The huntress looked at him. "What is it?"

Talon scratched the back of his head. "I'm sorry for everything. I never intended to sell you out to the Holy Blades." He turned to his forge. "My new tools have yet to arrive. When they do, I'd like to help reforge Nightingale."

Mara watched him for a moment, and then she nodded. "Or we could use the forge in Greyward Hold. We have tools there, and I'm sure Jen's father wouldn't mind."

"Damn, you're going to make me walk up there?" Talon asked in a mocking tone. "Fine, it'll be like old times. Just let me know when you're ready, and I'll head up there."

"We just need the ore," Mara said. "It might take a while."

"Very well," Talon said. "I'll see you then."

With that, Mara headed out. While the huntress mounted Firefly, she spotted Shenoah coming towards the workshop. The armourer was starting her day. As Mara rode out, they crossed paths. The huntress raised a hand to give a light wave. But Shenoah never responded. Mara was not too surprised and figured more time was needed to settle things with her.

However, Shenoah did notice Firefly. The armourer stared at the darkling, stunned by her appearance. Then she glanced up at Mara and frowned. The huntress had no idea what her problem was and continued to ride to Greyward Hold.

Chapter Nineteen

The Haunting

On the morning of February 6, Mara was heading to the grand hall when she heard a knock on the door. Being the closest, she went to answer. The huntress walked by Milo on the way. His frown was persistent as he made repairs to her necklace.

Opening one of the iron doors, Mara greeted an unexpected visitor. On the other side was a man in his forties wearing a black suit. His black hair with grey strands and green eyes were familiar.

"Greetings, Miss Ashwood," André began, holding his hands behind his back.

Mara slammed the door in his face and walked away. Upon turning around, she saw Jen and Beatrice. Both women gave weird looks, while Jen walked over to the door. She opened it to reveal a very shocked André. The butler stood frozen with his mouth agape.

"My goodness!" André cried. "Have you forgotten the proper etiquette of inviting others?"

Mara gave a sour expression. "After what you've done, yes."

André furrowed his brow. "What have I done?"

The huntress folded her arms. "Your master accused me of killing Mr. White, which I didn't. Neither you nor the servants came to my defence."

The butler grew silent for a moment. "Well, that is what I wish to speak to you about," he said. "Paranormal forces have gripped the manor!"

Mara looked puzzled. She never expected those words to come out of the butler's mouth. "What are you talking about?"

"I regret saying this, but I believed you were the cause of it, and your removal would stop it."

Accalia, who happened to be nearby, overheard the conversation and approached them.

"You have a ghost?" Accalia addressed the butler.

Mara glanced at her while André gave a grim expression.

"It is affecting everyone," he continued. "Ten workers have quit in the last two weeks, putting a strain on the remaining staff. I have reason to believe the spirit is Mr. Arthur White."

"It's possible." The witch looked at the huntress. "Did he die in the manor?"

"Yes, he did." Mara soon realized the reason behind André's visit. "Wait a minute. You expect me to deal with this?"

"Please, I insist," he said.

"You couldn't ask a priest from Kallikratés to perform a cleansing?"

"We did invite one to remove the spirit, but it has proven ineffective," André admitted. "Honestly, the activity seems to have increased."

The huntress shook her head. "I'm forbidden from entering Mirahyll."

"Lord White stays in Hema," the butler responded. "I will give you permission to enter the White Manor since it's under my care."

"You can't expect me to do this for free," Mara said flatly.

"I shall pay you, as well as offer an item from the manor."

"And I will help," Accalia added. "I've dealt with ghosts before."

Mara gazed at her, sensing this task would be more trouble than it was worth.

* * *

André offered them a ride in the carriage. Firefly followed from a distance, insisting on being close to the huntress. Mara did not want to draw any attention, but it was nice to have her steed around. The darkling could be useful on the return trip.

"You used to live there?" Accalia questioned.

"Until my eviction." Mara looked out the window. "I had strange dreams when I lived in the manor."

"Strange dreams?"

"I'd see Commander White—the real one," Mara answered. "Ever since I left, I stopped having them."

Accalia gave a stern look. "It's often a sign of a spirit attaching itself to you."

Mara looked concerned. "Really?"

"If you stopped having those unsettling dreams, then the spirit is no longer attached to you."

Within a couple of hours, they arrived in the city. Firefly vanished in a green flash to hide until Mara returned. The two women exited the carriage and followed the butler into the manor. Soon, Mara noticed the scrutinizing gazes of nobles passing by.

"What are they doing here?"

"Is Lord White aware?"

"Someone should let the Holy Blades know!"

Mara ignored them as she accompanied Accalia and André into the manor. Upon entering, the huntress immediately sensed a dark atmosphere within the home. The familiar air had grown more intense. Accalia frowned while observing her surroundings.

"I sense something sinister." Looking to the stairs, Accalia ascended them while Mara and André followed. Once they entered the hallway, the witch's gaze locked with the door to the right. "What room is this?"

"This is where Lord White resided," André explained.

The witch placed her hand on the doorknob. She was about to open the door, but stopped and pulled her hand away.

"It's gone," she murmured.

"What do you mean?" Mara asked.

"It went somewhere else. However…" Accalia turned her attention onto the door at the end of the hall. "The other one is near."

Mara looked baffled. "There are two ghosts?"

André's face grew pale. "Oh my…"

The witch approached the door at the end of the hall. She placed her hand on the doorknob. "It's behind this door."

Mara and the butler braced themselves. Accalia opened the door to reveal an empty bedroom.

"We keep this room closed at all times," André explained. "Ever since Mr. White's passing, no one ever comes here."

Accalia stared at the bed. "He's here."

"What?" Mara asked.

The witch turned her attention onto Mara. "He's looking right at you!"

Mara looked around the room. "I don't see him."

"Look out!" Accalia shouted.

An unknown force rushed towards Mara. Before she could react, it hit her, causing her to lose her footing. She fell onto the floor and slipped into an unconscious state.

When Mara opened her eyes again, she found herself alone in the hallway. She rose to her feet while glancing around cautiously.

"Accalia?" Mara called.

A man's stifled wailing came from the end of the hall. While Mara approached the door, the pained cries grew louder. It was Mr. White. Entering the room, she saw him in bed, as well as a shadowy figure towering over him. The creature sank its hand into his chest. A dark bruise appeared while the veins turned black. Mr. White turned pale as he made a feeble attempt to grab its arm, but his heart could take no more. Once his body went still, the shadow figure pulled its hand out of his chest. Mara stared in shock and horror. The shadowy figure stood up straight, then gazed at her. An image flashed in her mind, revealing the portrait in the living room.

Mara's eyes snapped open to see Accalia and André looking down at her. Without saying a word, she shot up to her feet and dashed down to the living room.

"Show yourself!" Mara shouted. "I know you killed him!"

Gazing upon the portrait of Commander White, she noticed a shadowy figure peering over his shoulder with glowing red eyes.

"Mara," Accalia called.

The huntress saw the witch and the butler approaching her. Mara looked back at the painting.

"He's in the painting," Mara said.

The butler studied the portrait and grew horrified. "It was never like that before!"

"I see him as well." Accalia gazed at the painting. "This thing has trapped the former owner's spirit in the manor."

Mara looked back at the witch. "Trapped?"

"We must remove this evil spirit." Accalia retrieved a book from her robes and flipped through the pages. "I'm going to perform a cleansing. Be on your guard."

Mara nodded as she began to unsheathe her sword.

"By the power of the Seven Divines, I command you to show yourself!" Accalia chanted.

Black ooze seeped over the image of Commander White, ruining the portrait. He emerged from the puddle before them, making a series of disturbing sounds as if in pain.

"In the name of Ulrika, I command you to tell me your name!"

The creature released an unsettling groan, yet refused to reveal a name.

"Tell me your name!" Accalia yelled.

All of a sudden, a knock on the door drew their attention.

André looked confused. "Who could it be at this moment?"

Mara also took notice. "Can you send them away? Now's not a good time."

The butler nodded and headed to the front door. While Mara watched Accalia perform the cleansing, she also heard an argument at the foyer.

"What are you doing?" André demanded.

Mara looked behind to see two Holy Blades and a priest of Kallikratés storming into the manor.

The priest scowled at them. "What is this devilry?"

"We're in the middle of a cleansing!" Mara exclaimed.

"This is witchcraft!" The priest pointed at Mara and Accalia. "Stop this ritual at once," he ordered the Holy Blades.

Before Mara could do anything, a Holy Blade stormed up to Accalia and grabbed her.

The witch was displeased. "The cleansing ritual must not be disturbed!"

Before anyone could say something, the ghostly creature stood up and dashed towards a Holy Blade, knocking him down. The impact created a cloud of black dust as it circled him. The Holy Blade began to convulse violently. Everyone looked stunned.

The priest scowled at Mara and Accalia. "What kind of dark magic have you performed?"

"We were performing a cleansing ritual, you idiot!" Accalia snapped.

The huntress looked back at the fallen Holy Blade. He rose to his feet, yet it looked like an unseen force was pulling him up. He looked at his fellow Blade and approached him from behind. He reached for his sword.

"Look out!" Mara cried, but it was too late.

The Holy Blade grabbed the sword and stabbed his comrade in the back without a second thought. The other crumpled to the ground where he bled to death. The priest saw this and grew horrified. The Holy Blade gazed at the priest and stepped towards him with a bloody blade.

The priest questioned, "What are you doing?"

The Holy Blade said nothing as he approached the older man.

Mara noticed black ooze seeping from his ears and nostrils. "What is that?"

"Ectoplasm," Accalia answered. "It's the most obvious sign of a ghost's presence. When someone is possessed, they often exude ectoplasm. We need to perform an exorcism before he kills anyone else. Distract him."

Mara dashed at the Holy Blade with her long sword. The Holy Blade turned on her. While the huntress fought with him, she saw his face transform, taking on a familiar appearance. Mara recognized his semi-long hair and the tuft under his bottom lip. Thin eyebrows sat above glowing red eyes. However, his face was gaunt and grey.

"Karl…"

"You will pay!" the entity shouted through the Holy Blade.

Mara recognized his voice. "All this time, you were here. The nightmares I had—you caused them!"

The possessed Holy Blade glared at her as more ectoplasm seeped from his eyes. He lunged at her again, but the huntress blocked his attack with little effort.

"I will avenge Kallisto!" Karl screamed at her. The Holy Blade's face became distorted as his mouth opened to reveal a blackened maw. His eyes glowed like burning coals.

Mara was stunned by this transformation. The pure hatred and rage radiating from the possessed Holy Blade reminded her of the time Karl nearly beat her to death. The lights began to flicker as a gust of wind came rushing through the living room.

"By the power of the Seven Divines and Mother Nymera, I banish you to the underworld!" Accalia boomed. "Begone, evil spirit!"

"No!" Karl screamed.

The Holy Blade he possessed began to shake. He threw his head back and spewed out a black substance. Dark fumes rose from him, revealing Karl's ghostly image one last time. The Holy Blade collapsed and reverted to normal.

André stood frozen with a slack jaw, while the priest sat dumbstruck by what transpired.

Accalia closed the book, then turned her attention onto the unconscious Holy Blade. "We need to make sure he's okay."

The butler snapped out of his shock and offered to help.

Mara stood and watched. She, too, was numb after encountering the real Karl White. While watching them tend to the Holy Blade, she sensed a presence behind her. The huntress looked back to see a plump and short nobleman standing before her. His pure white hair with a matching moustache and beard was familiar.

"Mr. White?" Mara asked.

Mr. White smiled at her with sorrowful eyes. "I'm sorry," he said. "I tried to warn the others, but my words couldn't get through."

Mara reached out to touch him, but her hand went through. A frown formed on her face. "If only I knew he followed us home. If only I talked about the nightmares…"

"It's not your fault," he said. "None of us knew."

Mara shook her head. "You didn't deserve to die like that."

"I am thankful that you removed Karl, although I'm concerned." Mr. White sighed, "I never thought he could become this dark entity."

The door opened to reveal a blinding light.

Mr. White smiled. "I think it's time for me to go." Before walking out the front door, he gazed back at Mara. "Ask for a black box. It should be in the safe within my room."

Mara watched as he departed into the light. The door closed.

André heard the door closing and approached the foyer. He looked at Mara in confusion. "Did someone leave?"

"Mr. White left the manor," the huntress answered.

The butler appeared surprised. "You saw him?"

"Yes, I did."

André watched her while holding his hands behind his back. "Miss Ashwood, there's something I wish to speak to you about."

"What is it?"

"The ghost you and your friend banished—why did it look like Lord White?"

Mara wondered if it was a good idea to tell André the truth. Then again, doing the right thing was not always easy.

"That is Karl White," said the huntress. "The man you're serving is an imposter."

André gawked at her for a moment before looking away. "Well, that may explain the changes within Lord White's behaviour."

"Like what?"

"He had an affair with one of the maids. I voiced my concerns, seeing how unprofessional it was. Ultimately, I had to dismiss the maid. But it created tensions between him and I. Also, he refused to see any doctors."

"Not surprising," Mara said. "I've seen him at the brothels."

André looked disturbed. "Oh my… What should I do?"

"I'm figuring out a way to expose him," Mara answered. "Don't worry about it."

The butler looked uncertain. "I see," he said. "As for your reward, I will pay you five thousand gold. As promised, you are also welcome to claim one item within this manor."

He handed her a large bag of gold, which the huntress accepted without hesitation.

"Okay," Mara responded, recalling her conversation with Mr. White. "I'm interested in a black box. It should be in a safe in Mr. White's room."

"Are you sure this is what you want?"

Mara nodded. "Yes, this is what I want."

"Very well," the butler said. "Follow me."

He led her to Mr. White's former room. André knew the safe combination. Once he opened it, Mara saw the black box. André reached inside and took it.

"I hope there is something of value in here," he said while handing the box over to her.

Mara took the box, which no key was needed. The huntress grew curious about what was inside. She lifted the lid and took a peek. Anyone would think this was a joke, for the broken remains of a sword filled the box. Even Mara was baffled by such a sight until she got a glimpse of the black and gold hilt. The empty socket used to house a moonstone. Despite being broken in several places, the blade shards still gleamed in the light.

Mara could not believe her eyes. "Godstruck!"

At first, she was uncertain if it was the real blade since there were two versions. But with the moonstone missing, it was safe to assume this was the real Godstruck.

André appeared confused. "Are you sure you want this?"

"Yes, this is perfect." Now Mara had the metal needed to reforge Nightingale's blade.

The huntress closed the box and gazed at André. "I guess that's it. We'll be on our way."

The butler held his hands behind his back and nodded. "Very well. Oh, and one more thing…"

"What?"

"I'm sorry. I should have caught on sooner that Lord White was an imposter."

"It's okay."

"This fiend stole what was rightfully yours. Maybe I should contact the barrister?"

Mara shook her head. "He probably spent most of the gold on courtesans. I wouldn't be surprised if I got less than a quarter of the money back. Take care."

The huntress approached Accalia with the box. "Are you done here?"

Mara glanced down at the remaining Holy Blade. He was awake yet shaken up by the ordeal. The witch nodded and looked back at her.

"Yes, he is fine." Accalia's eyes drifted over to the dead Holy Blade. "Unfortunately, I cannot say the same for him." She glanced back at Mara. "The cleansing was a success, but I am concerned."

Mara frowned. "About what?"

"I've heard of spirits possessing the living and making them kill others, but I have never known of one who could kill on their own. Unless…"

"Unless what?"

Accalia looked back at the formerly possessed Holy Blade. "He told me of the pure darkness and rage he felt while being possessed." She gazed at Mara. "I believe this was a demon."

Mara gaped at her. "Karl is a demon?" She looked away in disbelief. "Did Kallisto do this?"

"The false goddess might have triggered his transformation, but Hedera was responsible." Then Accalia reminded her, "Any man seduced by Hedera is likely to have his offspring succumb to evil. Kratés encountered the demon long ago. And Karl was his descendant. He likely had this darkness within him since birth."

The huntress looked back at the witch. "I suppose we should go." She reached for the reward from André. "You deserve half of the gold since you removed him."

Accalia shook her head. "No, you keep it. You might need it more than I."

Mara put the gold away. "I guess we should leave before Lord White finds out."

With that, the two women left the manor.

While walking down the street, Accalia took notice of the black box in Mara's possession. "What's that?"

Mara opened the box. "The remains of Godstruck. I can use them to reforge Nightingale."

Accalia looked stunned.

Mara closed the box. "I have everything I need. Talon said he was willing to help. I told him he could use the forge at Greyward Hold. I need to let him know when he can come."

"Very well," Accalia said. "We can go to the workshop on the way back."

As the two women approached the western gate, Firefly reappeared to greet them. Mara mounted the horse while Accalia watched.

"You should get a saddle," Accalia said.

"I'm planning on it." Mara looked back at her. "Aren't you getting on?"

The witch placed her hands on her hips. "Not enough room. I have a better idea."

Black fumes rose out of the witch's body. Accalia smirked. "How about I race you to the workshop?" She transformed, then took off in a dash.

Mara smiled as she shook her head. She looked down at Firefly and shouted, "Yah!"

The darkling neighed as she took off after the witch. The two raced across the snowy field.

Chapter Twenty

Skeletons in the Closet

Mara and Accalia arrived at the workshop the next morning. Both Talon and Shenoah were present. The old blacksmith looked up and approached them.

"What brings you here?" he greeted. Then he spotted the black box in Mara's possession.

The huntress placed the box before him and opened the lid. Talon peered inside and froze upon seeing the broken remains of Godstruck.

"I have everything I need to reforge Nightingale's blade," Mara said.

Talon lifted his astonished gaze to her. "Where did you get this?"

"Mr. White had it." Mara gazed down at the shards. "I think this is the original. It's missing the moonstone."

Talon nodded. "Very well. I'll head to Greyward Hold as soon as I can."

Once finished, Mara and Accalia headed out of the workshop. On the way out, Mara noticed the apprehensive look on Shenoah's face. Not only did she appear cautious of Mara, but the armourer seemed surprised to know Talon was helping in Nightingale's repair. Once the huntress was outside and mounted Firefly, she looked back at the workshop. Shenoah was staring at her through the window. The armourer's gaze was fixated on Firefly once again. Mara wondered if Shenoah recognized the little lady. She looked away and saw Accalia transform. Then the two returned to Greyward Hold.

* * *

By the afternoon, the two women approached the frozen fortress. Accalia changed back and pushed open the iron doors. Mara followed after her and spotted the other two sages and the former Silver Thorns. They were waiting for them. Even Walt was waiting. Their attention fell onto the black box in Mara's possession. They grew curious as to what the box contained. The huntress opened it to reveal the broken sword.

"Lord Slayer Godstruck," Jen murmured.

"The blade Kallikratés sought to destroy," Beatrice said, "and the Silver Thorns swore to protect."

Nikolai folded his arms. "These weapons could be easily forged in Thoron."

Milo gazed at Mara. "Did you find a blacksmith willing to reforge Nightingale?"

"Talon is willing to help," Mara said. "He'll arrive within a day or two."

The mage glanced back at Godstruck's remains. "You have everything you need?"

"Yes, that's correct," Mara responded.

"I have a proposal." Milo gazed back at Mara. "You have a bond with your father, correct?"

Mara nodded.

"Then we wish to help you reforge that bond," he said.

"And make sure this sword never breaks," Accalia added.

Mara looked intrigued. "What do you have in mind?"

"I have studied the undying for some time," Milo revealed. "They have immense power within them. I believe we can harness that power and imbue it into Nightingale."

Mara looked at the mage and the witch with a questioning glint in her eyes. "How?"

"It's a technique of the magesmiths," Accalia explained. "They can add magical properties to a weapon."

"You mean creating unique weapons like Lord Slayers?" Mara asked.

"More than that," Milo said. "It is my theory that combining the undying's essence into your sword will make it unbreakable."

Walt folded his arms. "I've never heard of this."

"Same here," Mara added. "How do we do this?"

"You can start by collecting the bone fragments of the undying," Milo replied. "You will need four pieces."

"The four undying, buried within this land," Mara murmured. "There's one near Talon's workshop."

"We can start there," Milo said.

Mara folded her arms. "I'd imagine Talon won't be pleased. He buried her."

"We will tread carefully," Milo assured her.

Accalia nodded in agreement. "And he'll be none the wiser. Let's go."

* * *

Mara led Milo and Accalia down the mountain and headed west to Madeline's grave. Mara rode on Firefly while Milo used the horse that previously pulled their wagon. Accalia was in her wolf form. It did not take long to reach the border of Lupine Woods. They never encountered Talon, assuming he had yet to leave his workshop. The three found the grave underneath a blanket of snow. Mara and Milo dismounted while Accalia changed back.

"Madeline's grave," Mara said, spotting a nearby shovel. She took the shovel and began to unearth the grave. Accalia and Milo looked on.

"Did you know her?" Milo questioned.

"A little," Mara answered. "Harold mentioned her before sending me to kill her. At the time, I believed it would help lift my curse."

Once she reached the coffin, the huntress opened the lid. A ghastly sight greeted them. Both Accalia and Milo were taken aback by Madeline's charred appearance. Mara remained unfazed.

"By the Divines, what happened to her?" Milo asked.

"She was a herbalist who lived in this area," Mara explained. "Karl, who was immortal, claimed she was a witch. Haranta Village killed her. A plague wiped out the village, but everyone claimed it was the witch's curse."

Milo and Accalia exchanged glances. The two sages were still for a while before helping Mara with the body. The elven mage reached for a finger bone and gently snapped it off.

"This should suffice," Milo said, handing the bone fragment to Mara.

The huntress glanced down at the tiny piece before looking up at him. The elf and the witch looked back at the body.

"We should rebury her," Milo said as he took the shovel and reburied Madeline. Accalia helped by using her hands. Once they finished, the two looked at Mara.

"Where to next?" Accalia asked.

"The closest one is in Misty Valley," Mara replied. "It's to the south."

Milo and Accalia approached her, awaiting her guidance.

"Lead the way," Accalia said.

* * *

The next day, Mara led them to Misty Valley.

"Haven't been here in a while," the huntress murmured. "Not since slaying the White Lady."

Looking around, Mara found Misty Valley different from the last time she was here. The old rickety shacks no longer housed any Forgotten Ones. Mara reckoned they were killed off by the winter, or perhaps other hunters came by. She led Milo and Accalia to the waterfall, where Evelyn's resting place was. Once they reached the bottom, Mara grew uneasy about seeing the body. Her eyes scanned the area until she spotted a dark patch in the bog.

"Over here." The huntress dashed ahead and began to unearth Evelyn's body. Mara's eyes drifted to the rotted torso, where the unborn child used to be. The parasitic roots remained alive, drawing nutrients from the undying's body. The left side of her face remained destroyed, thanks to the effort to save Saskia. Mara found it difficult to gaze upon Evelyn's peaceful face after learning the truth about Karl.

Milo and Accalia eventually helped the huntress. Mara found a suitable place to harvest a bone fragment by snapping off a rib. After obtaining the item, the three began to bury Evelyn.

"What is this?"

Mara looked up and saw the Holy Blades standing before the three. Among them was Lord White and Donovan.

The huntress frowned. "What are you doing here?"

The imposter scowled at her while approaching them with his hands behind his back.

"I've been looking for you, Ashwood. First, you defied my request by entering Hemal. Then, you allowed Ardana's most wanted to escape! And now I hear you entered my home in Mirahyll without my consent!"

"André invited us," Mara claimed, "to deal with a spirit after one of your priests failed to remove it."

"I've heard," said the imposter. "And I fired André for allowing it."

Mara narrowed her eyes. "Are you sure you didn't fire him for another reason?"

Donovan noticed Evelyn's body. "What is this?"

Kratés stepped forward. "They must be performing witchcraft or necromancy, which is illegal!" He gestured to Accalia. "They do have a witch among them."

Accalia scowled at them.

Milo stepped in. "We are only here to harvest bone fragments. We mean no harm or disrespect."

The imposter shook his head. "I've heard enough," he hissed. "You three are under arrest!" He briefly glanced at his Holy Blades. "Dispose of the body."

The Holy Blades obeyed and approached Evelyn's body.

"No, leave her alone!" Mara tried to stop them, only to be held back by another two Holy Blades.

Both Milo and Accalia were also apprehended. They could only watch as the Blades doused the body with a flammable liquid, then set it ablaze.

Mara glared at Kratés. "How could you do that to her body?"

The imposter gave a smug look. "We'll take them to the city to be judged."

Just as the Holy Blades were about to haul the three away, they heard a gurgling sound. Everyone turned and spotted a creature emerging from the swamp. It appeared to be a hunched-over man with long arms and sharp claws. He resembled a Forgotten One, but less thin. The rotten flesh looked bloated. The undead beast growled at them, baring razor-sharp teeth.

"What is that thing?" Donovan questioned.

Accalia gave a peculiar look. "A myling—the result of unwanted fetuses tossed away. But this one seems very unusual."

"How so?" Mara asked.

"This one is cursed and corrupted by powerful dark magic," Accalia explained. "Its energy feels similar to the demonic spirit we confronted in the manor."

The monster's gaze fell onto the imposter. All of a sudden, the creature dashed on all fours towards him.

"Lord White, look out!"

A Holy Blade stepped in front and drew his weapon. He wished to protect his lord. The myling turned his aggression onto the Holy Blade and lunged at him with an open maw. The beast grabbed his neck and bit through his carotid artery. Blood sprayed out, and the Blade was dead within seconds. Another Holy Blade tried to challenge the creature, but the monster latched onto his arm and ripped it off at the elbow. The Blade fell backwards, screaming as he held onto whatever remained of his arm. The myling lunged at the fallen soldier and bit at his neck, shaking him violently. The other Holy Blades lost their nerve and ran. Even Kratés didn't want to linger. Once the beast finished off the Holy Blade, he turned his attention onto the fleeing imposter. He roared with glowing eyes filled with anger and hatred.

"Lord White!" Donovan lunged at the creature, but the monster appeared annoyed by the commander from Corlin. He slashed at him, making him back away. Then he turned his attention onto the imposter.

Mara watched in shock. "Why is he going after him?"

"I've seen this before," Accalia said. "If a myling crosses paths with the parents who abandoned it, it will kill them. I've also read that they're very protective of their parents' corpses, especially pregnant women who die before giving birth."

The huntress looked at her in confusion. "Wait, this thing thinks he's the father?"

Accalia nodded. "Either that or he's pissed." She gazed at Evelyn's burnt corpse. "I reckon she was his mother, and destroying her body enraged him."

Mara looked back at the creature. "It can't be, can it?"

She approached the myling. Milo and Accalia took notice and were none too pleased by her actions.

"What are you doing?" Milo demanded.

Mara ignored them and kept approaching the monster. The creature eventually took notice and did not hesitate to attack her. The huntress held her own in battle, but the myling overwhelmed her with gnashing jaws and a flurry of swipes. Mara backed away, but the creature's claws snagged her mask. He managed to knock her down and rip off her mask.

"Mara!" Accalia tried to rush to the huntress' side. Then she noticed how the creature looked at Mara's face.

The myling froze and then began to cry. Everyone was confused by the creature's actions. A sense of dread washed over Mara, for the sounds the monster emitted was heartbreaking.

"He thinks you're his mother," Accalia said.

Mara shook her head. "This is Karl and Evelyn's unborn child."

Donovan looked stunned. "This cannot be!" He stared back at the imposter. "You were never married. You told me yourself."

The imposter frowned.

"He lied," Mara continued. "He murdered his pregnant wife while under Kallisto's control."

Everyone stared at her, then the imposter. The huntress saw how furious he became, but no longer cared. If he wanted to pretend to be Karl White, then he should be ready to live with the baggage left behind by his reincarnation.

Donovan shook his head. "No, you are wrong!"

"It matters not." Accalia pointed at Kratés. "He should suffice."

"How?" Mara asked.

"By giving it a name," Milo explained. "It is an ancient rite, but it should prove effective even today. To be given a name is an act of respect and love. One of the greatest gifts a parent could give to a child."

"I know the incantation." Accalia gazed at the imposter. "Come, name your child."

Kratés grimaced upon noticing all their eyes on him. He rose to his feet and walked away, leaving them with the myling. "I'm not naming it."

Donovan ran after him. "Lord White!"

Accalia placed her hands on her hips and sighed. She looked at Mara. "You'll do it."

"I'm not Evelyn," Mara said.

"You share the same soul," Milo responded.

"Look at the child," Accalia instructed. Then she chanted, "Through the power of the Seven Divines. Through the grace of Mother Nymera. Forgive me—say his name."

The huntress glanced over at Accalia. "What do I name him?" Mara asked.

"Just think of one," the witch replied.

"Put yourself in Evelyn's place," Milo suggested. "What would she call him?"

Mara looked back at the monster, taking in the sages' advice. The huntress recalled the time when Evelyn took over to say goodbye to Karl. She remembered feeling all of the wife's emotions and seeing her memories. Evelyn had planned for a life with Karl while raising his son. The huntress reckoned that the former wife had a name in mind.

Then a name surfaced in Mara's mind. "I'm sorry, Jason."

The myling looked at Mara in shock and began to shake.

Accalia nodded as she reached over to touch Mara's shoulder. "Repeat after me," said the witch. "I embrace thee as my son."

Mara gazed into the glowing eyes of the myling. "I embrace thee as my son."

Upon collapsing, the monster's body became warped while his limbs shrank. His low guttural cries became high-pitched. Black fumes rose from the creature, obscuring their view. Once the smoke lifted, Mara saw an infant crying for his mother. As if by instinct, she took the child into her arms and comforted the tiny one. The baby calmed down before crumbling away into dust. Mara grew numb.

Once again, Accalia rested her hand on the huntress' shoulder. "You did well." She gazed at the charred remains of Evelyn. "I'm sure his mother is resting easier, knowing that her son found peace."

Mara looked back at the body and nodded. Evelyn was barely recognizable, but they buried her regardless.

The three left Misty Valley.

* * *

The next body to harvest was Thalia. The journey to Désir was quiet. Accalia rode with Milo this time. Mara remained numb from the incident in Misty Valley.

"I'm not surprised he refused to put the child to rest," the witch began.

"Really?" Mara asked.

"According to ancient tales, Kratés always abandoned the women he impregnated," Milo revealed. "He had no intention to become a father despite being driven to plant his seed."

"That's Kratés the Fornicator for you," Accalia said.

Mara looked ahead and gave a light sigh. What did Thalia see in him? Why did she want to resurrect him?

As the three arrived in town, Mara then said, "We should let Kai know."

"Kai?" Accalia asked.

"He served Thalia," Mara answered. "And he cared for her. I think he should at least know what we're doing."

"Very well," Milo said.

However, Mara needed to know where the former butler was staying. He used to live in Thalia's manor. The huntress spotted a middle-aged man on the other side of the street.

"Excuse me," Mara called out to him. "Do you know Kai?"

The middle-aged man gave a strange look. "Kai?"

"Morgan's former butler?" Mara inquired. She made sure to use Thalia's alias, for not everyone knew the real name of the original undying.

"Oh, Kai," the man said. "I remember him. His house is a few blocks yonder. I hear he's got a new mistress to serve."

Mara looked mystified. "A new mistress?"

"Yes, her name is Miss Alraune," the man explained.

The huntress was quite amused to hear Kai found a new mistress to serve. Mara smiled. "Okay," she said. "Thank you."

The three approached a townhouse. The huntress knocked three times. The door opened to reveal a young man with pale skin, black hair, and blue eyes. He even sported the goatee on his chin.

Kai frowned at her. "What do you want?"

Mara was slightly taken aback by his greeting. Kai seemed very annoyed, making her wonder if she was intruding upon something.

"Sorry if I disturbed you, but I wanted to let you know about our plan."

"What plan?"

Milo stepped forward. "We intend to unearth the body of your former mistress and harvest a bone fragment. Is that all right with you?"

Kai stared at him, then to Mara. "Yes, yes, this is fine," he said quickly. With that, he closed the door in their faces.

All three stared at the closed door.

"Well, I guess that's it," Accalia said, walking away.

Milo followed suit. "What a strange fellow…"

Mara could not help but agree. Kai was probably busy, so she brushed it off.

The three ventured to the charred remains of the manor. Mara led them to the grave since she knew where it was. They unearthed the mummified corpse. Both Accalia and Milo were speechless, while Mara harvested a bone fragment. After obtaining the piece, she gazed up at the mummified face.

"I'm sorry, Thalia."

Accalia remained in awe of the body.

Milo stepped forward. "This is Thalia?"

Mara looked at him and nodded. She turned her attention back onto Thalia's corpse. "I know. I was surprised to see her become this."

Milo took a closer look. "Could it be because of her age?"

"I don't know," Mara said. "A creature tried to claim her soul." Both Accalia and Milo looked confused. The huntress took note of their reactions and said, "I couldn't see it, but I believe it might've been the Grim Reaper."

Milo gave a strange look. "That is impossible. While the reaper exists and is invisible to most, those who are undying are immune to it. It must have been another creature."

The huntress looked back at the original undying. She began to rebury the body, while Milo and Accalia assisted her.

The three went to Har' Yhan.

* * *

As soon as the three entered the town, they encountered Lady Lorelei. The woman of pleasure took notice of them.

"Fancy meeting you here," Lorelei began.

"Likewise," Mara said. "We're here to run some errands, and we need Aria's body."

Lorelei raised an eyebrow. "For what reason do you need her body?"

"I just need a bone fragment," Mara said.

"You didn't answer the question," Lorelei responded.

"It is for her sword," Milo interjected. "To make sure it will never break."

Lorelei gazed at Milo. She appeared aware of who he was. "Oh, so you're a magesmith?"

"We're just using a technique," Mara explained. "If done right, the sword will never break."

The inn owner gazed back at Mara with a questioning glance. "And you're okay with this?"

Mara nodded.

"I see," Lorelei spoke. "I had some men retrieve her body. I couldn't leave the poor thing in the cove. We buried her in the graveyard, just outside the town."

"Thank you," Mara said.

The three went to the graveyard located northwest of the town. It did not take long to find Aria's grave, which sat in the far corner with a single frozen flower. Mara figured Lady Lorelei placed it there. They dug into the partially frozen ground and unearthed the body. Aria remained in her white dress, now dirtied by the soil.

"How did this one meet her end?" Accalia asked.

Mara looked over the whole body before focusing her gaze on a frozen finger. "She was driven to suicide after losing her voice." The huntress reached over and snapped the finger off.

"Was Karl responsible?" Milo asked.

Mara gazed at the bone fragment. "Yes, he was."

The three reburied Aria and returned whence they came.

On the way back, the huntress and the two sages witnessed a squadron of Holy Blades marching through the streets of Har' Yhan. Mara watched as they left the town, then noticed Lady Lorelei standing nearby.

"What's going on?" Mara asked.

"They're going to slay the hellhound," Lorelei revealed. "The creature has been sighted in Hema."

"At least they'll be out of our hair," Accalia said.

"Yes," Milo added. "Come, let us return to Greyward Hold."

Now that they had everything they needed, the three returned to Grey Mountain.

Chapter Twenty-One

The Undying Blade

It was late in the evening on February 13 by the time the three returned. Mara, Milo and Accalia found two carts posted before the iron doors. Mara suspected one of them belonged to Talon but was unsure about the other one. After dismounting from the horses at the stables, Mara and the two sages entered Greyward Hold. Upon entering, they discovered the usual inhabitants, as well as new visitors. Talon had arrived earlier, yet Shenoah's presence was unexpected. However, the armourer's appearance did not surprise Mara as much as a certain Corlin blacksmith.

"What's he doing here?" Mara asked, pointing at Raymon.

A hint of surprise decorated Talon's sour face. "You didn't invite him?"

Raymon held his hands behind his back. "No, she did not. However, I did overhear her conversation in Mirahyll." He gazed at Mara. "I hear you have everything needed to repair your blade."

Mara folded her arms. "I do, but why are you here?"

"I've decided to brave the journey to this mountain fortress, and offer my services to you." Raymon gazed at the forge. "While waiting, I saw the forge and tools. While the forge is adequate, I'm afraid these tools are unacceptable." He gazed back at Mara. "Which is why I am willing to lend my tools," he said, gesturing to his own, which were out on display.

Talon scowled at Raymon, while Mara raised an eyebrow. The Corlin blacksmith was so full of himself. Walt, on the other hand, compared his tools to Raymon's.

"He has a point," Walt said. "His tools are nothing to scoff at."

"Of course," Raymon added. "When one's tools improve, so should their standards. I'll even offer to repair the blade for free. In exchange, only I can reforge Nightingale."

Talon looked furious. "What the hell? She asked me to repair her sword!"

Raymon looked at Talon dismissively. "I understand you care deeply for this craft, which is something I respect," he said. "But her blade will also need a full restoration, in which only a certified master blacksmith can offer."

Walt shrugged. "He is right."

Talon snapped his glare onto Greyward Hold's blacksmith. "Whose side are you even on?"

The huntress switched her gaze between the two blacksmiths. Even though Mara initially asked Talon, Walt made a good point. Nightingale's repair should be flawless if she wished to have her sword back. Mara then noticed Milo approaching the three blacksmiths.

"We appreciate the trouble the two of you went through to come here," said the mage. "Whoever we choose, I would also like to point out that we are not using any of your methods to restore the blade."

Both Talon and Raymon looked back at the elven mage.

"What?" Talon questioned.

"I beg your pardon?" Raymon asked.

Accalia stepped forward. "We're using the techniques of the magesmiths from Thoron."

"That is correct," Milo said. "We will be restoring the blade using magic, as well as adding a specific property to it."

Raymon gave a peculiar look. "Which is…?"

"It'll become an undying blade," Accalia said. "If done right, the blade will become unbreakable." She gazed at Mara. "It'll be immortal, like its owner."

The three blacksmiths looked stunned.

"Surely, you have some magic items?" Talon asked.

"We have everything we need to make this happen." Milo gave a stern look. "You are more than welcome to assist in the blade's restoration, but you must follow our instructions accordingly." He turned his attention onto Mara. "Now then, I believe the final decision is yours. Who do you want involved?"

"Me?" Mara asked.

"It is your sword," Milo said.

Mara gazed at the three blacksmiths. Talon and Raymon made it very clear they wanted to be involved in Nightingale's restoration. Walt had already stated the repair might be beyond him, though he appeared interested in playing a small role at least.

The huntress looked at Talon. "Remember the fake Godstruck?"

"Aye, what about it?" Talon asked.

"You forged that blade, didn't you?"

Talon nodded. "I did. Exactly as the real blade forged thousands of years ago."

Mara placed her hands on her hips. "Fine," she said. "I want you to reforge the blade."

While Talon seemed elated, Raymon looked very displeased.

"How is he going to reforge the blade?" Raymon questioned. "By merely combining the shards of two different weapons? That won't work!"

"He's right," Walt added. "You'll also need to extract the siderite, which means the loss of the outer layers. But since your sword's outer layer is a silver and steel alloy, we can easily replace it."

"Is that something you can do?" Mara asked Walt.

"We can all do it," Walt said.

Raymon frowned. "Where does this leave me?"

Mara gazed at him. "Well, since you claim to be such a great blacksmith, you can do the refinement and much of the restoration." She handed over Nightingale's schematic. "I can lend you the diagram to study. I trust you have the proper solution to give the blade its dark gold colour."

The Corlin blacksmith studied the diagram. "Yes, I have plenty. I can do the etchings as well."

"Good," Mara said. "I want the blade to look as it did before it broke."

Raymon scowled at her. "I am a master blacksmith! I forge each weapon as if my reputation depends on it!"

Mara stared at him with glowing eyes. "Then, I demand perfection." She took a step towards him. "If I find a single flaw, I will hunt you down."

Raymon held his ground, though a hint a fear was present on his face.

Talon smirked. "Ooh, I've seen that look before, and that was when Nightingale first broke."

The Corlin blacksmith kept his eyes on Mara. "Very well." Then he broke his gaze with her.

"Then let us begin," Milo said, gesturing the three blacksmiths to the forge. Mara followed after them, but the elven mage gazed back at her. "You must wait."

"Okay," Mara said. "How long do I have to wait?"

"It shall take two days at most," the elven mage replied.

"Two days?" Mara questioned in disbelief. "What am I supposed to do for two days?"

Accalia shrugged. "Do some monster contracts. Maybe help Jen work on her bestiary."

The huntress looked at her. "You're helping them?"

"Accalia could be of some help," Milo said. "We are not dealing with normal fire for the blade's reforging."

Mara sighed, "Fine."

The huntress watched as they took away the remains of Nightingale and Godstruck. As Walt prepared the fire for the forging, Milo threw the bone fragments into the flames, turning them blue. Mara would love to stay and watch, but it became clear they had all the help they needed. She moved away from the forge.

Heading into the grand hall, Mara spotted the others. Beatrice was work-ing with Jen on her bestiary, so Mara's help was not needed. Nikolai kept to himself, writing in a journal. He looked as if he did not want to be disturbed. It was then Mara realized someone was missing. Her eyes scanned the grand hall again. Then she approached Jen and Beatrice.

"Excuse me, but have you seen Shenoah?"

The two women gazed at her in confusion.

"Shenoah?" Beatrice questioned.

"A Stone Mage, like me," Mara explained. "She accompanied Talon."

"I saw her heading outside," Jen revealed.

Mara looked baffled. "Isn't that dangerous? There could be snow beasts on the prowl."

"Perhaps," Beatrice said, "but not many snow beasts come around here."

"She might've gone home," Jen suggested.

Mara hoped Shenoah returned home on horseback. Leaving Greyward Hold had its risks, regardless if one encountered snow beasts or not.

"I'm heading out as well." Mara was going to follow Accalia's advice and find herself a monster contract. With Firefly, fulfilling some hunts would be quicker.

Once the huntress was outside, she spotted hoof prints in the snow. It seemed Shenoah did head home. She could have stayed the night since they had plenty of room. Or maybe she was just uncomfortable being around Mara?

Mara ventured over to the stables, only to discover Firefly was missing. She gawked at the empty stall where she left her steed. At first, she sus-pected that Firefly had teleported somewhere.

"Firefly?" The huntress looked around. "Firefly?"

She carefully scanned her surroundings. The darkling might appear behind her as she always did. Mara looked behind. She saw no sign of the creature. The huntress grew more concerned. Firefly was missing, and Shenoah was gone. Mara began to realize what had happened.

* * *

The huntress dashed along the mountain trail. To her luck, she never encoun-tered any snow beasts. Mara teleported from one spot to another, moving swiftly like the wind, although it drained her stamina. Mara needed to catch her breath once she reached the foot of the mountain. She lifted her gaze and scanned the field before her. Shenoah and Firefly were nowhere in sight. However, upon looking at Lupine Woods, Mara spotted the white mane of her steed. It had to be Firefly. Shenoah was guiding her through the woods to avoid detection. As soon as Mara caught her breath, she dashed after them.

"Hey!" Mara shouted as she caught up with them. She managed to reach them at a clearing.

At first, Shenoah ignored her while taking Firefly to Cerebell. They only stopped when Mara ran in front of them.

"What are you doing?" Mara asked. "Why did you take Firefly?"

Shenoah glared at the huntress. "She is not your horse!"

Mara looked baffled. "What are you talking about?"

The huntress then saw the blinders adorning the darkling's face. The green gemstone in the middle glowed ominously. Firefly's eyes were also glowing green instead of their usual red colour. The steed seemed calmer than usual.

The huntress looked disturbed. "What is that thing on her face?"

Shenoah remained silent, yet continued to glare at her.

Mara shifted her attention onto the armourer. "Why are you stealing my—"

"She is not your horse!" Shenoah shouted.

The huntress watched her. "Are you still mad at me?"

"We Stone Mages have a strong bond with horses," Shenoah explained. "We would never dare produce a blade upon such an innocent creature! You don't deserve her at all!"

Mara looked perplexed. "Wait, you know who she is?"

"Of course," Shenoah admitted. "For some time, I've sought this creature to no avail. And then you come along, riding on her back."

"She forgave me," Mara claimed. "She knows I never meant to bring her harm."

"You expect me to believe that?" Shenoah demanded.

Mara began to sulk. "No," she answered. "Then again, I don't think you care." She folded her arms. "I'm like this because of our people."

"You mean my people?"

"I'm also a Stone Mage."

"No, you are not!"

Mara froze for a moment. "I thought you were kind. Or was it all a lie?" She shook her head. "You're just as bad as Kallikratés."

"Shut up!" Shenoah yelled.

Not wanting to put up with any more of this nonsense, Mara approached Firefly. "I'm taking back my ride!"

"No, she's mine!" The armourer lunged at Mara and pushed her away.

The huntress was stunned for a moment, and then she recovered. She approached Shenoah and gave a swift slap across the face. Mara hit her hard enough to knock her down.

"You stupid girl!" Mara raged.

All of a sudden, Firefly released a loud neigh and reared up on her hind legs. Mara saw this and dodged out of the way before the darkling could stomp on her. After witnessing this attack, the huntress began to realize something was wrong with Firefly.

"Firefly," Mara called.

The darkling began to stomp her front left hoof. She lowered her head, pointing her horn at Mara.

"Firefly, please stop," Mara pleaded. "This isn't you."

The creature charged at her. Mara evaded the attack. As the huntress recovered, she noticed Shenoah standing at a distance. It became clear that the darkling was under the armourer's control. No one else had placed those strange blinders on Firefly.

"Tell her to stop!" Mara shouted at Shenoah.

Shenoah remained silent. Mara looked into her eyes and knew the armourer had no intention of stopping Firefly. The darkling charged at her again. Mara dodged, only to see the creature rear up and attempt to stomp on her. The huntress evaded her again. Firefly swung her head, hoping to skewer the huntress on her horn. Then the darkling distanced herself for another charge. Mara realized she could not hold this up forever and reached for her long sword.

Shenoah took notice. "No, leave her alone!"

Mara scowled at the armourer. That was easy for Shenoah to say, though the huntress would also feel guilty about killing her steed again. She pulled her hand away while coming up with another solution. The huntress then noticed the blinders. If Mara could take them off, she could end this madness. The darkling stomped her hoof again, indicating that she was ready to charge at her.

As the darkling charged, Mara managed to grab Firefly's horn. The darkling reared up and neighed, causing Mara to swing around. Fortunately, she ended up on the creature's back. The darkling was none too pleased and tried to buck the huntress off. Mara held on. She reached over with her other hand and unfastened the blinders. Once it came loose, the huntress grabbed it. Firefly threw her off of her back before collapsing. Mara landed on her bottom but survived the fall. It hurt like hell. Looking at her right hand, the huntress spotted the blinders that she removed from the darkling's face. She then gazed at Firefly, who remained stunned.

The darkling opened her eyes to reveal the ruby hues. Firefly gazed at Mara while rising to her feet. She approached the huntress and nuzzled her.

"It's okay," Mara spoke in a soft tone.

The huntress noticed Shenoah approaching them. Mara grew uneasy, seeing the armourer's eyes fixated on Firefly. Even the darkling took notice and was gazing at Shenoah with apprehension.

"Please, come to me," Shenoah pleaded. "I can take better care of you. I would never hurt you."

Mara shook her head and then noticed Firefly turning towards Shenoah. It seemed the darkling was going to choose her, and Mara would lose her steed. However, Firefly suddenly stopped and began stomping her hoof. The huntress realized what was going on.

"She's going to charge," Mara warned.

Shenoah scowled at her. "No, she's not."

Mara shook her head. For someone who claimed to know a lot about horses, Shenoah seemed so oblivious to the danger before her. The darkling took an aggressive stance, snorting several times. She lowered her head and pointed her horn at Shenoah.

Shenoah froze once she realized what was going on. "What's wrong? I promise to treat you better."

The huntress could sense the aggression radiating from the darkling, and it was not lifting. With the target within sight, Firefly charged at the armourer.

What was Mara thinking? She teleported in front of Shenoah and pushed her out of the way. The huntress only wanted Firefly back. No one was supposed to die. Yet here she was, skewered on the golden horn. Time stood still as the huntress watched the pointy end pierce the right side of her chest. It missed her heart, but she could feel her right lung collapsing. Black blood surged up and flowed out of her mouth. By some miracle, Mara managed to push herself off of the horn. She could not feel herself hitting the ground. Mara saw Shenoah running away as her vision grew blurry. A black pool formed around her body. She could hear Firefly neighing, although it sounded like a scream of dread and sorrow. The darkling seemed distraught at what she just did. But it was okay because no one else had to die.

The huntress gazed up at the blackened sky. It was difficult to see any stars with blurred vision. As her heart slowed to a halt, Mara wondered what it meant to gain redemption. The distraught cries of Firefly grew more and more silent.

* * *

When Mara awoke, the first thing she saw was Milo towering over her. The elven mage had two fingers pressed to her forehead. Mara was confused. Did she die? She felt no pain upon awakening. No searing heat in her veins or the sensation of being set ablaze from the inside.

"What's going on?" Mara asked. Checking her surroundings, the huntress found herself back in Greyward Hold. They were in her bedchambers.

Milo withdrew his fingers. "The memory is true and complete."

Accalia approached her with a healing stone. "Here, this should help you."

Mara took the healing stone, though she remained confused.

"We had you sedated as soon as you returned to life," the witch explained. "Milo used Mind Eye to recover that memory and show everyone."

"I don't remember coming back to life," Mara said.

"There's not much to remember," Accalia told her. "Only what happened beforehand is all that matters."

The huntress used the healing stone to restore herself. Mara then saw Elder Ravenclaw and his riders. Shenoah was also present, which made Mara apprehensive. But upon careful observation, she noticed the armourer had her hands tied behind her back. The elder's riders surrounded Shenoah. Even Talon was present with a frown decorating his face. Mara looked back at the elder, who was facing away. He appeared to be holding something.

"How could you use this forbidden item?" Ravenclaw sounded very upset. He turned to reveal the blinders in his hands.

Shenoah remained silent. She stared at the ground with a sour look on her face.

The huntress looked at everyone else. "How did I get here?"

"You were missing for three days," Accalia said.

Mara grew baffled.

"We have completed your sword's restoration," Milo said. "The black-smiths have done an outstanding job, despite lacking the skills of a magesmith. We intended to give you the sword, but could not find you anywhere."

"I…" Mara began.

"You don't have to say anything," Accalia interrupted. "We all know what happened."

"How did you know where to find me?" Mara asked.

"Firefly led us to you," Milo said. "She arrived at the gates alone, appearing very distressed." He gestured to the Stone Mages. "By the time we found you, they were also at the scene."

Elder Ravenclaw looked at Mara. "Shenoah came to us, claiming you attacked her."

The huntress scowled back at the armourer. "If you call a slap to the face an attack, then yes."

"Yes, Alkina had sensed Shenoah was not being truthful and asked that we search for you." Ravenclaw looked down at the blinders. "You were holding onto this when we found you."

Mara gazed at the item. "What is that thing?"

"Enchanted blinders," Ravenclaw explained. "When placed on an animal—a horse in particular—it makes them obedient to the one who placed it on."

"It's a mind-control device?" Mara questioned.

"That is correct," Ravenclaw admitted. "However, if removed, it can sow mistrust. We consider this to be a forbidden object, knowing what it is capable of."

Milo stepped forward. "Firefly is a creature of higher intelligence." He glanced at Shenoah. "I would imagine the godling was furious with her."

"We planned on destroying the blinders, but it disappeared over a month ago," Ravenclaw said. "Now we know what became of it."

Mara gave a deadpanned look. "So, that's how she's good with horses?"

Talon looked at Shenoah in disappointment. "How could you?"

Shenoah lifted her gaze. Rage was present in her eyes. "How could you take her side after everything she did?"

"You mean the Holy Blades I saved you from?" Mara asked. "Talon sent me to find you, but maybe I shouldn't have. Your opinion of me wouldn't have changed much anyway."

"We are enemies of the Faith," Ravenclaw added. "For many years, they have oppressed us." He gestured to Mara. "She defeated the false goddess. She's the reason why our people are in a better place. How could you do those things to her?"

"You always preferred her over me," Shenoah hissed. "No matter what I did, it was never good enough."

Mara looked confused. "What is she talking about?"

Ravenclaw gave a stern look. "We can talk about this later. Just you and I."

Shenoah's face twisted in rage as she pointed at Mara. "You wished the half-breed was your daughter instead of me!"

Everyone was dumbstruck.

Mara gaped at Shenoah. "Half-breed?"

The huntress heard the word before. Some have called her this, thanks to having two different parents. But never did she expect to hear it from a Stone Mage.

Ravenclaw gazed back at his daughter. His face was void of all emotion.

"You committed a grave crime by stealing a forbidden item, then using it to commit theft." Ravenclaw closed his eyes. "You are banished from our community. No longer will you be welcomed in Cerebell."

Shenoah looked numb as tears began to flow. Ravenclaw remained stoic, though Mara sensed he was not proud of what he did. The huntress only wanted Firefly back. Yet she never expected this to happen. Mara glanced over at Talon, wondering what he might do since Shenoah did work with him.

The old blacksmith folded his arms and shook his head. "No longer will she be working with me," Talon said, "nor is she welcomed at my workshop."

The armourer looked back at the old blacksmith with rage-filled teary eyes.

Mara gazed back at Ravenclaw, who nodded to his riders. They escorted Shenoah out of Greyward Hold.

The huntress approached Ravenclaw. "How did she reach such a conclusion? We only helped each other out."

"Her mother raised her alone until she died. I was rarely in her life."

"But what does this have to do with me?"

"It was your destiny to stop the false goddess, and you did," Ravenclaw said. "You are a hero among the Stone Mages, but it seems your reputation made my daughter envious of you."

Mara shook her head. "Why would she envy me? I have this damn curse."

Ravenclaw gave a sorrowful look. Even he didn't have an answer to her question. Instead, he said, "Take care, Mara."

As the elder followed his riders out, Mara could tell he was hurting deeply. The huntress also realized how fortunate she was to have parents like Mom and Dad. She then spotted Talon approaching her.

"I overheard your conversation with the elder," Talon said.

"I don't like how this ended," Mara spoke solemnly. "I only wanted Firefly back."

"Regardless of whether he decides to forgive his daughter, I'm not changing my stance. What she did to you was beyond cruel."

"I've had worse," Mara said. "Kallisto sought to kill me simply because I was Thalia's reincarnation."

"Now I see why you're so willing to forgive her."

"I didn't forgive her," Mara argued. "I just think the punishment is too severe."

Talon placed a hand on her shoulder. "You're way too good to a fault." Then, "There is something else you should know."

"What is it?" Mara asked.

"Shenoah persuaded me to rat you out," Talon admitted. "I knew the way to Greyward Hold."

Mara gaped at him.

Talon sighed, "I know I did something stupid. I wanted to say nothing, but she instigated it."

The huntress frowned and shook her head.

"I'm sorry," Talon said.

"You already apologized." Then she switched the subject. "I hear my sword is ready."

Talon's eyes lit up. "Aye, it is. Follow me."

He led Mara to the forge where Nightingale was waiting. Walt was there, yet Raymon was missing. Mara suspected that the Corlin blacksmith wanted to get far enough away in case she found a single flaw on her sword. At least he did not take anything with him. Nightingale's diagram sat near the weapon. Oddly enough, Raymon's tools remained here. The huntress gazed at the tools curiously, drawing the attention of Jen's father.

"Raymon was kind enough to give us his weapons," Walt explained. "He had plenty of tools."

"He even gave me some," Talon said. "He's not so bad."

Mara gazed at Nightingale.

"Go right ahead," Talon said. "It's your sword."

While Mara reclaimed Nightingale, Milo and Accalia approached her.

"When your sword was forged within the flames, fuelled by the bones of the undying, it absorbed their very essence," Milo said. "According to my calculations, the blade is immortal, like yourself. It will never break, making it one of a kind."

Mara unsheathed Nightingale. It looked the same as before. While gazing in the reflection of her restored blade, Mara could see her face reverting to normal. Her eyes stopped glowing while the markings on her face began to fade. She could feel her fangs shrinking down. Upon further inspection, she noticed that the hollow opening in the pommel seemed different.

"I made a small modification there," Walt said. "Aside from moonstones, you can also mount a smaller weapon, like this one." He retrieved a fairly sizeable dagger in a sheath. The pommel of the dagger looked oddly shaped as if it could fit into Nightingale. "We had some leftover material. Raymon thought it was a good idea to forge a paired weapon."

Accalia inspected the dagger. "Ah, like the parrying daggers I've seen sword-fighters use."

Mara took the dagger and equipped it to her belt. She then glanced at everyone. "Thank you. If not for you, I don't think this would be possible." The huntress gazed at the sages. "I realize three weeks had passed since the trial."

Milo nodded. "Yes, it would appear so."

"Then the Faith can no longer hold us," Mara said. "We're free to travel to Thoron."

"As agreed between the High Council and Kallikratés," Accalia said.

"We will stay here tonight," Milo said. "At first light, we will head to Har' Yhan and board our ship."

Talon gazed at Mara. "I guess this is it," he told her. "Best of luck on lifting your curse."

Mara nodded. "Thank you."

The old blacksmith left Greyward Hold, while the rest ate their dinner together.

"I hear you're leaving tomorrow," Jen told Mara.

"Yes, I am," the huntress replied.

The former Silver Thorn handed her the bestiary. "Here, take this."

Mara reluctantly accepted the book. "Are you sure?"

"It's a copy," Jen told her. "I'm still working on my own, but it'll be interesting to see what you may encounter in Thoron."

"Sure," Mara said, flipping through the book. She noticed many blank pages. "Looks like you're already putting me to the task."

After the dinner, Mara headed outside and went to the stables. Firefly spotted Mara and greeted her with whinnies. She seemed happy to see the huntress. Most importantly, Firefly was back to normal. Mara gazed into her red eyes while approaching her.

"It's good to see you're okay," said the huntress. "I don't know what I would do if something bad happened to you."

Mara petted the darkling for a few moments before heading back inside the frozen fortress. Everyone else had retired for the night, leaving Mara the only one still awake. She returned to her bedchambers and turned in for the night. While sleeping, Mara kept a sheathed Nightingale by her side, refusing to part with it.

Chapter Twenty-Two

The Divine Flame

It was early in the morning when several loud knocks echoed throughout the fortress. Mara opened her eyes and gazed out the window. It was still dark. She had no desire to get up, but the knocking grew more insistent. Accalia opened the door and peered into her room.

"We should check it out," the witch recommended.

Mara groaned as she dragged herself out of bed. The huntress held onto Nightingale and followed Accalia to the large iron doors. By the time they reached the grand hall, the others had joined. Walt and Beatrice opened the main entrance, and two men tumbled through. Mara immediately recognized the young black-haired commander and the imposter. Blood and ashes stained their uniforms.

"What are they doing here?" Mara wondered out loud.

Donovan looked up, revealing a face covered by ashes. He had a gash above his left eye, blood staining the side of his face. "Please, we need help…" he pleaded. "The hellhound… It wiped out our entire squad!"

Everyone watched in astonishment.

Walt folded his arms. "Damn…"

Mara switched her attention onto the imposter, who remained unconscious. Blood soaked through his white pants, and a massive bite wound was visible on his upper left leg. The area around the bite wound was charred.

"The hellhound bit him," Accalia stated, also looking at the imposter's injury.

The commander from Corlin nodded. "It attacked him… He hit his head. He hasn't regained consciousness."

"He may have a concussion," Accalia observed. "The creature's teeth went all the way down to the bone, burning him in the process. He's probably in shock."

Mara's eyes drifted over to Kratés' face. Blood seeped from a wound hidden under his hairline. Like Donovan, smoke and ash darkened his face. She looked back at the commander from Corlin. "Why did you come up here?"

"He kept calling for Thalia," Donovan said. "You are Thalia, are you not?"

"I'm her reincarnation," Mara said, shaking her head.

"But you're also the Cursed Herald. You slew the Goddess. Surely you can stop this beast."

"That was different," Mara argued. "Besides, Kallisto had Thalia sealed away. It's not like I could wave my hands and destroy this creature for you."

"Maybe not," Accalia said, "but you do have your sword back."

The huntress gave the witch a questioning glance. "Are you saying we should deal with this creature?"

"I won't," said the witch. "I have to tend to these injuries."

"But what about—"

"Thoron can wait," Milo interrupted. He gazed at Nikolai. "We will let the High Council know that our journey will be delayed by a day or two."

The priest nodded in agreement, although he seemed a little cross about the delay.

"Jen and I will go," Beatrice offered.

"And I will lend my assistance," Milo added. "We will also employ our battle-mages and spell-swords." The mage gazed at Donovan. "Where is the creature?"

"It's heading towards Mirahyll," Donovan told them.

Mara gripped her newly reforged Nightingale. "Guess we don't have a choice."

"Come on, let's go!" Jen said as she grabbed her sword.

Mara accompanied the two former Silver Thorns and the mage. The sages' guardians also followed behind. They went to the stables. The others quickly set up the wagon for transport, while Mara mounted Firefly. The darkling neighed as she galloped ahead, while the cart followed behind.

* * *

Riding towards Mirahyll, Mara and the others spotted a red glow and black smoke billowing into the air.

"Look!" Jen cried.

Charred corpses of Holy Blades littered the ground before the busted gate. They were only recognizable by the remains of their golden armour.

"Burned to a crisp," Beatrice murmured.

Passing through, the group of fourteen searched their surroundings.

"Not many people on the streets," Mara said.

"Hopefully, the citizens have evacuated to safety," Milo told her.

While riding through the streets, the group reached the Grand Cathedral. A large crowd had gathered outside the gold and ivory building, banging on doors sealed shut.

A male civilian shouted, "Please, let us in!"

"We're at full capacity," a man called from the other side. "We can't take any more!"

Mara dismounted from Firefly as the others disembarked from the wagon. The people took notice and watched them cautiously. The huntress walked through. Upon reaching the door, she knocked three times.

"What's going on?" Mara asked. "You have a crowd outside your doors."

"Are you deaf?" the man responded condescendingly. "We cannot take any more!"

The huntress grew skeptical. "How can you be at full capacity?" Mara demanded. "The cathedral can take half of the city!"

"Well…" He paused for a moment, trying to find an excuse. "We're at full capacity! Go away!"

Mara sighed. The huntress looked behind to see several desperate eyes on her. Among the crowd, she saw terrified mothers clutching crying babes to their breast. The children were also crying, knowing they would die. The men kept a strong face, but there was no hiding the desperation in their eyes.

"Go back to your homes if you still have them," Beatrice ordered the crowd. "If you don't feel safe there, head to the Council Hall or the hospital."

"Beatrice and I will escort them," Jen said. "We'll make sure they get to safety."

"Take some of our warriors with you," Milo said. "The rest of us will find the creature."

The crowd dispersed. Beatrice and Jen made sure they got to safety, and not a moment too soon. Mara and Milo never needed to find the hellhound, for the creature emerged from behind a building. The intense heat and embers set a home ablaze. People screamed as they began to flee, drawing the creature's attention.

"The battle-mages and I shall provide magical support," Milo said, lifting an ornate dagger. "We must draw it away from civilians."

The battle-mages followed suit and raised their weapons. They began shooting at the creature with orbs of blue light. The hellhound turned on them and began to growl. Mara unsheathed Nightingale and dashed towards it. She landed a few hits on the creature, drawing its attention onto her. The fiery beast moved away and circled the huntress. It watched her while growling. Then the hellhound began to charge. Mara dodged out of the way, causing the monster to slam against the Grand Cathedral's entrance.

With the doors busted open, Mara saw several people inside, but the building was nowhere near full capacity. The inhabitants fled once they realized the danger. Unfortunately, they also attracted the hellhound's attention. Mara attacked the creature to draw it to her. The spell-swords also assisted her in the fight. With silver blades glowing in blue hues, they inflicted significant damage. Mara glanced down at Nightingale to make sure it did not show any signs of breaking. Thankfully, it appeared fine.

The hellhound hit a pillar, knocking it down. Mara and the spell-swords managed to dodge falling debris while attacking the beast.

"You must leave!" Milo shouted. "The building has grown unstable!"

The spell-swords looked at the mage and nodded. They fled the building before it could collapse. The huntress followed after them, but then she froze. She looked at her hand to see it engulfed in blue flames. The flames spread up her arms and consumed her whole body.

"Mara!" Milo shouted. "Look out!"

Mara lifted her gaze and turned around. The hellhound towered over her. The beast opened its jaws, ready to clamp down on the upper half of her body.

All of a sudden, the blue flames around Mara began to intensify. It was like an explosion bursting out of her. The huntress had no idea if she was screaming, nor could she feel any pain. Mara had no time to respond as she slipped away into blackness.

* * *

"Mara, can you hear me?"

Mara's eyes fluttered open to see the elven mage and the spell-swords looking down at her. The grogginess faded away, allowing her to sit up. The first thing the huntress noticed was the blackened sky and the snow falling around her. The battle took a toll on the cathedral. All the pillars had fallen, causing the ceiling to collapse. Mara rose to her feet as she stared at the cathedral's remains with wonder.

"Do you know what you have done?" Milo questioned.

Mara looked back at him with a dumbfounded look. She glanced back at the ruins. "Where's the hellhound?"

Her eyes fell onto a charred skeleton beneath the fallen pillars and debris. Mara approached the body with wonder and caution. She lightly kicked the corpse to make sure it was dead. Then she raised Nightingale and hacked the creature's head off. The charred skull fell to her feet. Mara leaned over and picked it up. While claiming her prize, she also discovered a healing stone gently rolling out of the head. She took the gemstone and carefully placed it inside her satchel.

The huntress emerged with the beast's severed head. Milo followed behind, unnerved by what transpired. As Mara walked out into the streets of Mirahyll, a large crowd gathered before her. Even Beatrice and Jen stood among them. Mara stopped and threw the monster's head at the civilians' feet. Everyone was mystified.

"She killed the hellhound by herself?" asked a male civilian.

Some of the disciples approached the destroyed cathedral.

A priest of Kallikratés gawked at the ruins before turning his aggression onto Mara. "What have you done?"

Milo stepped forward. "She saved this city."

Another follower shouted, "She destroyed another place of worship!"

The priest pointed at Mara. "She should be arrested!"

The huntress glared at him. "How many lives did you save tonight?"

The priest scowled at her. "That has nothing to do with—"

"Answer the question," Mara interrupted. "I saw the large crowd gathered at your door."

"Well, that's because we couldn't take anymore," the priest claimed.

"Unless you have trouble counting," the huntress retorted, "the cathedral was nowhere near full capacity."

"You led the hellhound to us!" yelled another follower.

The huntress sulked. "You caused a large crowd to gather in one place… large enough to lure the creature." Mara looked to the lower-class citizens. "This is why Kallikratés should never exist! They care for no one but themselves!"

A lower-class man stepped forward. "She's right! The Faith has abandoned us once again."

"Where is Lord White?" asked a woman. "He claimed he would stop the hellhound!"

Even a nobleman approached the priest. "My son was in that squadron meant to take down the beast. What became of him?"

Other nobles began to approach, searching for answers. The priest stood there in silence, unable to answer the question.

Mara shook her head. "Only Commander Matthews and Lord White survived the encounter."

The nobleman looked at her in astonishment, while the priest glared at her.

"She is lying!" the priest claimed.

The two former Silver Thorns came forward.

"Then trust our word," Beatrice announced. "They came to us, begging for our assistance. It was the reason why we came tonight."

"And it was Commander Matthews who revealed their entire unit to be wiped out," Jen added.

The nobles gazed at the two women. A mother broke down in tears as the father gaped at them.

"Twenty of our sons were lost?" asked the nobleman. He glared at the priest. "Where is Lord White?"

"He should step down!" shouted another.

Mara looked around. She could see the fire in the eyes of the middle, lower, and even the upper classes. Whatever spell or honeyed words the imposter used on them had begun to wear off.

Beatrice approached the huntress and leaned into her ear. "It seems the Faith will fall."

Milo placed a hand on Mara's shoulder. "We should take our leave," he told her. "We must prepare for our journey to Thoron. I think the people of Ardana will be fine."

Mara mounted Firefly while the others returned to their cart.

* * *

Mara rode on Firefly while heading back to Greyward Hold. The wagon was near as it travelled in the same direction. Milo sat in the driver's seat. Beside him was one of the spell-swords holding the reins. Mara glanced over at the mage, noting the concerned frown on his face. She turned her gaze back onto the road.

"Do you honestly not remember anything from the battle?" Milo inquired.

"No," Mara answered. "What happened?"

"Aazalith's power had fully manifested, unleashing the Divine Flame."

The huntress looked at him in confusion. "What's that?"

"I have only read about it. It is an immense power only possessed by two of the Seven Divines. Flame God Pharos and Dragon Goddess Aazalith." Then, "Did Kallisto ever use it?"

Mara shook her head. "She only used it to show off."

Milo looked ahead. "I see."

The huntress watched him. "Is it something I should be concerned about?"

"I have never seen a Divine willing to offer their power to a lower being." He glanced at Firefly. "And it seems it was not the only power she granted you."

"What do you mean?"

"You were present when your horse died. A few days later, Firefly appeared in the fields."

"Are you saying I resurrected her?"

"Is it not true that all things who die resurrect as a supernatural?"

Mara looked back at her steed. It was true. The magic permeating the land came from Aazalith and her soul, which was now inside of Mara. The thought never crossed her mind until now.

* * *

The group returned to Greyward Hold the next evening. The iron doors opened upon their approach. Accalia and Nikolai were the first to greet them. As soon as the wagon stopped, the elven mage disembarked and approached his fellow sages.

"May I speak with you both in private?" Milo asked.

Mara dropped Firefly off at the stables, while Jen and Beatrice freed the other two horses from the wagon. Even the spell-swords and battle-mages helped them with putting the transport away.

The huntress walked ahead of the group as she entered Greyward Hold. She suspected the elven mage was talking with Accalia and Nikolai about her using the Divine Flame. However, Mara noticed a familiar black-haired commander, who stood next to Accalia. Donovan appeared to have made a full recovery. But the imposter was nowhere to be seen. Mara stopped and watched them from a distance.

"His injuries are far too great," Nikolai spoke. "He won't survive the night." The witch shook her head. "Healing Touch is out of the question."

Mara ventured into the hallway. The door to her right was wide open. Peering inside the bedchamber, she saw Kratés lying in bed. He looked as if he had already died with his skin so pale. But careful observation revealed that he was still breathing.

"Thalia," Kratés choked out. "Help me…"

Mara approached his side and looked at him. She knew Healing Touch, for Accalia taught her the ability. The huntress could help him, though it would end with her dying.

"Thalia, please," he pleaded. "Help…"

Mara placed her hand on his chest and closed her eyes. She tried to visualize his pain. A burning sensation flowed into her arm. Her heart pounded as she hissed in pain. The scorching heat seared her veins. Mara wanted to remove her hand. What was she thinking? This man caused her nothing but pain. He had said words meant to undermine her purpose in life. A part of her believed he deserved to die. But she thought about the consequences. Some of Kallikratés' followers might hunt her down, accusing her of killing him. And she might never go to Thoron. So Mara decided she was not saving him, but herself. She blacked out from the intense pain.

* * *

The huntress woke up in pain, thinking it was the lingering effects of Healing Touch. But the mirror revealed a raggedy undead with scars riddling her face. She sat there, staring into her glowing eyes. Mara used to be ashamed of her undying form. Now, she had no desire to pull her mask up. The hood remained on her head. Mara took her eyes off the mirror and found herself back in her room.

Accalia appeared in the doorway. "Ah, you're awake."

The huntress gazed at her, and then rose out of bed. Mara searched her surroundings and discovered Nightingale was missing. "Where's my sword?"

"Milo and Walt are checking it," Accalia spoke, "to make sure the reforging was correct."

Mara gazed at the witch for a moment. Then she exited her bedchambers. The witch looked at Mara in concern.

"What about…?"

The huntress looked back and saw Accalia pointing to her face.

"Don't you have any healing stones?" asked the witch.

"Yes," Mara answered. "There's something I need to do first."

The huntress entered the grand hall. Everyone who saw her was taken aback by her undead appearance.

"What is that creature?"

Mara heard the commander from Corlin. She saw him standing next to the imposter, who was now awake. Both disciples grimaced upon seeing her face. The huntress ignored their reactions and spotted a silver walking cane in Kratés' possession. Walt probably used some ore at his forge to make it. At the moment, the imposter could not shift all of his weight on his injured leg. She gazed at him for a while before turning her attention onto Walt, who held onto Nightingale.

"You have my sword?" Mara questioned.

Jen's father watched her apprehensively before handing it over. "Checked it out while you were recovering." He glanced down at the blade. "It's durability has not changed at all!"

Mara unsheathed the blade to inspect it herself. While focusing on the sword, she could sense the imposter's gaze on her.

Milo held his hands behind his back. "I believe a small amount of gratitude is in order."

Agreeing with the elven mage, Mara lifted her gaze and waited for Kratés' response. However, the imposter remained silent. He had no intention to thank her. Even Donovan stood speechless yet befuddled, for an enemy of the Faith had chosen to rescue their precious lord.

Kratés limped away. "Ready my horse."

Donovan obeyed his orders nonetheless. As the two men walked out into the cold, Mara chased after them. She stood before them, stopping them from going any further.

"What now?" Kratés demanded.

Mara gave a stern look while reaching into her satchel. She retrieved a healing stone, which she used to restore her humanity.

Kratés raised an eyebrow. "Not much improvement," came his snide remark.

The huntress continued to glare at him as she removed her hood. "It's been at least three weeks."

"So?" asked the imposter.

"As agreed between Kallikratés and Thoron's High Council, you cannot keep us here for any longer," Milo said, "lest you incite Thoron's wrath."

Kratés looked over his shoulder and sulked at the elven mage.

Mara placed her hands on her hips. "I'm going to board that ship. I am going to Thoron, and I will lift my curse."

The imposter looked back at her. "Are you? What then?"

"I have no intention of returning to Ardana!" Mara took a step forward. "It must be a relief for you as it will be for me."

Kratés continued to glare at her, and then he stormed past her. "Fine," he snarled, "board your ship. I never want to see you again!"

Mara watched as they mounted their horses and went down the mountain trail. She could sense that Kratés was upset, for he would never see Thalia again.

As the large iron doors closed before her, Mara looked back to the others.

"So, what do we do?" Mara asked. "Should we depart for Har' Yhan right now?"

Milo shook his head. "We will leave tomorrow morning. In the meantime, we shall let the High Council know that we are okay."

Mara nodded. "Sounds like a plan."

With that, everyone dispersed. Jen headed to the archives to continue her work, while Beatrice went to the training grounds to practice. Walt returned to his forge to smith new weapons. And the sages went to another room for a private discussion.

Mara decided to return to her room to pack her things. Luckily, she had very few possessions, being a couple of healing stones, the new bestiary, and the keepsakes of the undying. Mara had considered throwing the relics away. The withered flower and the faded letter had seen better days. Yet when Mara looked at the comb, she could never bring herself to do it. After packing everything, Mara went to lay on her bed, clutching Nightingale to her chest.

Chapter Twenty-Three

The Prowling Beast

Mara opened her eyes to see the first of the morning light. It was time to go. She rose out of bed and gathered her things. The sages had to be awake by now.

The huntress left her bedchambers and headed for the grand hall. Everyone else was now wide awake, including Jen and Beatrice.

"Didn't expect to see you both awake," Mara addressed both Beatrice and Jen.

"I figured we see you off," Beatrice responded.

Mara smiled and hugged them both goodbye.

"Work on that bestiary," Jen said.

"I will," Mara responded. She turned her attention onto the three sages. They appeared to be ready to leave.

"I reckon you're ready to go," Accalia said.

Mara nodded. "I've been waiting for this moment."

Milo stepped forward with his hands behind his back. "I would imagine so." Then he suggested, "We could give you some time to say goodbye to the rest of your friends."

Nikolai gazed at the elven mage with a scrutinizing look on his face. "I beg your pardon?"

"Sounds like a great idea," the witch said. "If what you say is true, then this will be your last chance of seeing them."

"That's true," Mara agreed. "Talon already wished me well, but I'd like to say goodbye to Elder Ravenclaw and Alkina."

"We can accommodate this," Milo said.

Taking her travelling bag, Mara followed the sages and their guardians out of Greyward Hold. Snow began to fall within the frigid air. It was not the ideal weather for travelling, but they had no choice. Mara looked back at Beatrice and Jen one last time. The two former Silver Thorns waved goodbye as the large iron doors closed before the huntress.

Mara headed into the stables to fetch Firefly. Some of the battle-mages were equipping the horses, while the spell-swords placed the luggage onto the wagon. Mara approached Firefly and began to prepare her for the journey. At least the huntress remembered to buy a saddle for the darkling. Walt had one lying around, which she purchased for a thousand gold. She glanced back at the three sages.

"Is it okay if I take her with me?" Mara asked.

Accalia and Milo nodded.

"Of course," said the witch. "We have plenty of space on the ship."

"It would be ideal," Milo added. "Thoron is a much larger place."

The huntress turned to her steed and mounted her while the three sages boarded their transport. It was time to go. As they left, Mara looked back at Greyward Hold one last time as the fortress vanished in the distance.

* * *

It took a couple of hours to reach the foot of the mountain, where the snowfall had lessened. Mara was relieved, for it seemed the snow would never cease. Cerebell might have been out of the way, but the sages accommodated Mara's request. While travelling on the road, the huntress saw Talon's place. It would be her last time looking upon the workshop, Haranta Village, and Lupine Woods.

The wagon nearly got stuck at least once, and the roads became a little more treacherous. But the group had to carry on. Mara looked ahead while riding with the sages.

While venturing through the burnt remains of Medulla, the huntress doubted it was worth rebuilding. While riding through the former village, Mara felt uneasy. The stillness and the silence unnerved her.

"What is that?" Accalia asked as she suddenly leapt out of the wagon.

Mara stopped as she watched the witch approaching the woods. Even she grew curious and dismounted from her ride.

Milo stopped the wagon. "Mara? Accalia?"

Nikolai looked cross. "We are wasting our time!"

The huntress ignored them as she followed Accalia. The witch stopped before a large dark mass. Coming closer, Mara recognized the brown fur, razor-sharp claws, and muzzle. It was a dead grizzly bear. A pool of blood stained the frozen ground. Accalia got on one knee and began her observation.

"A large male," the witch said, "yet he's out of hibernation."

"What does it mean?" Mara asked.

"Something disturbed his slumber," Accalia suspected. "Came out of his den to investigate." She took a closer look. "Several deep gashes. He died of blood loss." Accalia moved away.

Mara looked at the bear and noticed large footprints leading into the woods. "It went into Lupine Woods."

Milo and Nikolai soon joined them.

"Is there a problem?" Milo asked.

Accalia raised her right hand as she gazed towards the woods. "Do you hear that?"

Mara shook her head. "Hear what?"

"Exactly," the witch said. "I don't hear any animals. This creature has taken over."

"This close to Cerebell?" Mara asked. "Maybe Elder Ravenclaw knows about it?"

"We are wasting our time," Nikolai said.

A rustling sound in the woods drew their attention. It grew louder as if it were coming closer. Firefly and the other horses became nervous. The spell-swords and the battle-mages immediately surrounded Mara and the sages. Firefly neighed loudly, luring whatever hid in the woods.

Accalia unsheathed her blade. "It's coming!"

The sages' guards also drew their blades. Within seconds, a great beast rushed out of the woods. The grey blur reminded Mara of her encounter with the wendigo.

"Is that...?" Mara's thoughts were cut short upon seeing the beast pursuing Firefly. It swiped at the darkling with large claws. Firefly barely dodged the attack and ran. The creature chased after her.

"Firefly!" The huntress soon gave chase after the monster, hoping to stop it from harming her ride. She could not lose Firefly. She ran after the creature and shouted, "Hey!"

The monster stopped pursuing Firefly and looked back at the huntress with glowing red eyes. It resembled a wendigo, except for the rabbit-like head. The light grey creature possessed healthier fur which covered the whole body. A pair of deer antlers sat atop the head. Its body was quite thin with its ribs sticking out. Attached to the body were long arms and legs ending in sharp claws. Upon further observation, Mara noticed a pair of breasts, hinting that the creature was female. Another thing she noticed was the rope around the monster's neck.

Mara unsheathed Nightingale while staring down the female beast. The creature released a roar while lunging at the huntress. The sound coming out of the monster's mouth sounded feminine. Mara dodged and countered. She managed to land a few hits on the beast. The creature was none too pleased and took a swipe at her. Mara tried to dodge backwards, but the beast's long arms had greater reach. The huntress received four cuts to her abdomen.

"Mara!" shouted the elven mage.

Mara turned and saw Milo and Nikolai running towards her.

The mage asked, "Are you okay?"

Before Mara could respond, a giant wolf lunged at the beast. Accalia had transformed. The witch sank her fangs into the beast's neck, attempting to crush her windpipe. The monster slashed at Accalia, forcing her to let go.

Mara continued the fight once her wounds healed. While Accalia distracted the monster, the huntress landed a few hits on the right arm. Blood splashed out from the appendage while the creature cradled her arm. Then the huntress targeted the left leg, slashing at it several times. The monster lost her balance and lowered her head. Mara stabbed Nightingale through the left eye. The creature released a pained roar as she threw her head back, almost taking Nightingale along with her. Mara held on, and the sword slid out. Blood drenched Nightingale's blade, for it tore through vital parts.

However, the female beast was not going down without a fight. She lifted her head and roared while her body glowed in a pale blue light. Within seconds, her wounds vanished.

Mara and the sages gaped at the creature.

Milo looked surprised. "This creature used magic to heal?"

Once the creature's health fully restored, she looked at Mara and gave another roar. The huntress gripped Nightingale tightly, realizing this was going to be a difficult fight.

The elven mage reached into his travelling bag. "I have something that may help." He retrieved a round bottle filled with an unknown liquid and mist.

Milo threw the bottle at the monster. It shattered upon contact, releasing its contents. The creature roared in anger as fumes rose from her body.

"That should stop her from healing," Milo said.

Mara dashed at the beast with Nightingale in hand. Accalia joined in and fought by her side. While fighting the creature, Mara made sure not to hit the witch. She found an open spot, landing some hits on the monster's right leg. The beast lost her balance yet again and lowered her head. Mara approached the beast's face and stabbed Nightingale through the forehead. Before the monster could throw her head back, Accalia pounced and clamped her jaws on the creature's neck. Unable to do anything, the beast died from blood loss and suffocation. The light faded from her eyes before she closed them forever.

"Father…" came a weak whisper.

Mara stared in confusion as black fumes rose from the monster. The huntress withdrew her blade and took a few steps back. At first, she thought Accalia was changing back. But the wolf released her hold on the creature and jumped away. The witch began growling at the black mist rising from the beast. While the huntress watched, she spotted the familiar face of a deceased commander.

"Karl!" Mara cried, taking a step forward.

Accalia, who changed back, stood beside her. "He was inside this creature!"

The demon gave a smug look as he dissipated into the air.

Mara gazed at her. "Why did he possess this monster?"

Upon looking away, the huntress saw Elder Ravenclaw standing before her. A mournful look decorated his face. Mara blinked, only to see him vanish.

"Elder Ravenclaw?" Mara called. She then saw the elder wandering into the woods. Mara took off and chased after him.

"Mara!" Milo and Accalia called in unison, but Mara ignored them.

Mara followed the elder into the woods, but soon lost sight of him. She stopped and looked around. Toppled trees and claw marks revealed that the monster came through here. They formed a trail, leading her to a tall and broken tree. Approaching the twisted tree, Mara found a branch with a rope tied around it. It was similar to the one around the beast's neck. A crumpled note sat near the tree. She walked over and picked it up.

'I have lost everything, thanks to the half-breed. My spirit guide, who appears in my dreams, has shown me how to regain my father's love.'

Mara lowered the letter, then fell to her knees.

The mage and the witch were near. Once they spotted Mara, they drew closer.

"Mara?" Milo called. "Why did you run off like that?"

Both sages froze when Mara cast her sombre gaze upon them. She rose to her feet while holding the note in her hands.

* * *

The journey to Cerebell was silent. At least everyone, including the horses, survived the ordeal. Firefly never went too far, and Mara was able to get back on her steed.

The huntress had already filled the sages in. It was unfortunate she would have to tell the people of Cerebell about their discovery, but they had to know.

Entering the city, Mara spotted six bodies wrapped in white sheets, awaiting a funeral pyre. One of them was placed on top while the other five were resting at the sides. The Stone Mages gathered around to say their farewells while others spotted Mara and the sages. The huntress scanned the crowd, but neither Alkina or Elder Ravenclaw were among them. They were likely at home.

"This is a funeral," Milo said.

"They likely encountered the creature," Accalia added.

Mara looked ahead. "Let's find Elder Ravenclaw and Alkina. They need to know what happened."

While heading to the elder's house, Mara noticed the lack of Elder Ravenclaw's presence. He often greeted her with open arms. Yet things had changed since the incident with his daughter. Still, she could not stop thinking about the encounter in Lupine Woods. Mara was positive that she saw the elder.

Mara and the sages approached the front door. The huntress knocked three times.

"Come in," called a frail and elderly voice.

Mara recognized Alkina on the other side.

Upon inviting themselves inside, Mara and the sages found many people surrounding Alkina. Some were crying while others tried to console them, though everyone was overwhelmed by grief.

The huntress approached the shaman.

"I came to say goodbye," Mara began, "but…"

Alkina gave a sombre look. "I wish we could've met under better circumstances."

"I assume they fell victim to the monster prowling the woods?" Milo asked.

Alkina nodded. "They were Elder Ravenclaw's riders. While on patrol, a foul creature emerged from Lupine Woods and attacked them last night."

Accalia folded her arms. "We also encountered such a creature," she said. "We killed the monster, so the woods should be safer."

The Stone Mages glanced at each other. News of the monster's death helped lighten the solemn occasion.

Mara glanced down at the crumpled note in her hands. "Where's Elder Ravenclaw? I need to speak to him."

The shaman remained silent, though her facial expression was very telling. She began to shake as tears filled her eyes. The older woman slowly shook her head.

The huntress stood frozen. "But I saw him."

A man approached them, resembling Elder Ravenclaw but younger with shorter black hair. "That is impossible. Elder Ravenclaw was with his riders when the attack happened. He did not survive."

Mara looked back at him. She remained numb from the revelation. Deep down, she knew all along, yet did not want to admit that she had encountered Ravenclaw's spirit.

Spotting the letter in Mara's hands, the shaman reached over and took the note. Mara did not protest. After all, these people had a right to know.

"The monster was Shenoah," Mara said.

Alkina took her eyes off the note and stared into Mara's soul. The other Stone Mages watched her cautiously, anticipating her to elaborate.

"She hanged herself in the woods," the huntress revealed, "and came back as a monster."

Alkina and the Stone Mages looked both surprised and horrified.

The shaman asked, "Do you think she sought revenge?"

Milo shook his head. "Her actions might have been influenced."

"A demon attached himself to her," Accalia added, looking at Mara.

Alkina gave Mara a questioning look.

The huntress took notice. "Karl White is seeking revenge against me. I believe he was using her."

The shaman gave a small smile. "It seems we're in your debt yet again, only we don't have much."

"I'm not looking for money, but do you know how to deal with the demon?" Mara glanced at Accalia. "We tried to banish him before."

"I do," Alkina said.

The huntress snapped her gaze onto the shaman. "You do?"

Alkina gave a stern look. "How willing are you to stop this foul spirit?"

"I'll do anything," Mara replied. "If only I realized he was capable of such things, then Mr. White and Shenoah…"

"That wasn't your fault," Accalia spoke. "None of us knew until it was too late."

Milo folded his arms while gazing at Alkina. "I assume your method involves sealing the demon away."

Alkina nodded. "It does." She beckoned a younger man to her.

He came closer, allowing her to whisper in his ear. The man stood up straight and gave the shaman a concerned look. He disappeared into another room.

"I have something that may be of use," said the shaman.

The man returned with a small scroll and a black candle. The other Stone Mages saw these items and grew horrified.

One of them asked, "The shaman is giving her a forbidden item?"

Mara gazed at the others in confusion. The young man approached the huntress and handed over the candle and scroll.

"What is this?" Mara asked while looking at the candle in her hand.

"It is a summoning candle," Alkina explained. "Use it to draw his spirit to you." She glanced at the scroll. "This contains the instructions for casting the spell."

Mara opened the scroll and began to read. "To summon a spirit, light the summoning candle. Burn an item of significance to draw the spirit to you." She looked up at Alkina. "A significant item?"

"In the past, we used hair for it was most effective," Alkina spoke. "But something that once belonged to him, something he touched, could work."

Mara placed a hand over one of her satchels. "Like the tarnished comb, the faded letter, or the withered flower. If I burn any of those, he'll come to me?" Mara looked down at the scroll. "What's this? Prepare to engage the spirit in battle?"

"You must subdue the demon by force," Alkina said. "Only then can he be sealed away."

Milo looked concerned. "Is she to be used as a host?"

Mara lifted her gaze to the elf, then glanced at Alkina for confirmation. The shaman gave a solemn look and nodded.

The mage turned his astonished gaze onto Mara. "You must not go through with this."

"Why?" Mara asked.

"He's right," Accalia said. "There are too many factors to consider. The demon could become a parasite, feeding on your physical and mental well-being. You have the soul of Aazalith within you. We don't know what will happen if you seal him away within your body."

"Oh, okay…" Mara turned to Alkina, ready to hand the candle back to her.

Milo nodded, then headed out of the house. "We should take our leave."

"Come on," Accalia added. "Let's get to Har' Yhan before the Faith changes their minds." Then the witch followed the mage outside.

Now alone with the Stone Mages, Mara looked back at Alkina and held up the candle. "I guess I'll return this."

Alkina stared at the candle, then to the huntress. "Keep it."

Mara looked perplexed. "What?"

"Since when did you listen to strangers?" The shaman released a small laugh. "I know you quite well. You will seal the spirit away, and you will have an opportunity to do so." Her smile faded away. "But be aware," Alkina warned. "This demon will never stop until you're dead."

"I will," Mara said.

Before leaving the shaman's house, the huntress stuffed the items into her travelling bag. Regardless of what others might think, this was between Mara and Karl.

On the way out of the city, Mara watched as the funeral pyre went ablaze, burning all six bodies. As Mara watched the fire, she saw Ravenclaw on the other side. He gave a mournful smile before disappearing.

Chapter Twenty-Four

A Delayed Departure

Mara and the sages travelled on the road to Har' Yhan. It would take two days to reach the port town. All the huntress could think about was performing the spell.

The witch glanced over at Mara. "You must be excited. You'll finally leave this land."

The huntress nodded. "As I said before, I've been waiting for this day." Then she asked, "As soon as we reach Har' Yhan, we immediately board the ship?"

"Correct," Milo said, "before the Faith changes their minds."

"Of course," Mara murmured. A frown formed on her face as she thought about her plan. She just needed some time to cast the spell.

Accalia looked ahead. "There are people on the road."

Mara lifted her gaze and recognized the golden armour. "Holy Blades!"

Milo pulled on the reins to slow the horses down. "This cannot be good."

The Holy Blades spotted them as they drew closer. Mara and the sages were unsure what to do. It was then the huntress recognized a man in gold and ivory robes.

"Wait," Mara said. "That's Mendé, the archdeacon of Loris."

The sages looked at her.

"Isn't he the guy who wished to speak with you a while back?" Accalia questioned.

Mara nodded. "He believed me when I said Lord White was an imposter, and Kallisto and Kratés weren't gods." She suggested, "Maybe we should talk to him."

Nikolai looked uncertain. "It could be a trap."

Milo stopped the wagon. "You will not speak to him alone," he addressed Mara. "We will accompany you."

Mara dismounted from her ride. The sages accompanied her as she approached the archdeacon. Coming closer, she saw the worried look on Mendé's face.

"Thank the gods I found you," Mendé began.

"What's going on?" Mara asked.

"You must stay away from Har' Yhan!" Mendé exclaimed.

The huntress and the sages exchanged glances.

"Why?" Mara asked. "What has happened?"

"It seems you have caused an upset once again. The people have deemed Lord White to be inept after that incident in Mirahyll."

"You mean with the hellhound?" Mara asked.

Mendé nodded. "Many lives have been lost since he became a lord. Many nobles have begun to pull support after losing their sons. He is losing power. In desperation, he has declared you an enemy of Kallikratés."

"That's nothing new," Mara responded with a deadpanned look.

"He is plotting to capture you as soon as you enter Har' Yhan," Mendé insisted. "He plans to reclaim the soul of Aazalith."

Mara gaped at him, while the sages watched him with scrutiny. Accalia placed her hands on her hips while Milo folded his arms. Nikolai stood in the back as he stared at the archdeacon.

Milo stepped forward. "It is impossible! Only Nymera can remove Aazalith's soul."

"There is another way," Mendé claimed. "An incantation once transcribed by the ancient ones—the Call of Nymera."

The sages froze upon hearing those words.

"The… the Call of Nymera?" Nikolai questioned.

Mara looked at the sages and saw the looks of dread on their faces. "What is it?"

"Long ago, the Thoron Sages used the Call of Nymera, extracting Aazalith's soul to stop her rampage," Milo explained. "They used a moonstone as a medium."

"The incantation was lost!" Accalia exclaimed.

Mendé shook his head. "We have the incantation, translated for the modern tongue. It is one of the ancient treasures stolen from its progenitor, the Order of Aazalith."

"But you require a proper moonstone to contain that power," Milo told Mendé.

"We have such a medium," said the archdeacon.

Mara furrowed her brow. "Why are you telling us this?"

"As I said before, he intends to take the soul for himself," Mendé explained. "And if he is truly Kratés, then we are all in danger. He could kill us all."

The huntress looked at the sages. "What do we do?"

"We could take the risk," Milo said.

"What if the Holy Blades are blocking our way to the ship?" Accalia asked.

"We can assist you," Mendé told them.

The sages looked back at the archdeacon.

"You're willing to turn against your own?" Nikolai questioned.

Mendé gave a determined look. "There are those within the Faith who have been aware of the truth from the start. If we have to turn on the ones who remain blindly devoted, then we will."

Milo nodded. "Blind devotion can be very dangerous."

"While we distract them, you will board your ship and escape," Mendé said.

"What about you?" Mara asked.

"Should anything happen to me, then the truth shall be unleashed. The Faith will fall."

Accalia shrugged. "Sounds like a plan. Let's go."

With that, everyone returned to their transports. Mara mounted Firefly and rode with the sages and the rogue followers to Har' Yhan.

* * *

Time seemed to pass quickly as Mara and the Thoron Sages drew closer to Har' Yhan. In the distance, she could see the large ship at the port. They slowed down to a stop and disembarked from their rides.

"There it is," Milo said. "Our ship is here."

Accalia looked around. "So far, so good."

Mara kept her gaze on the port. While excited about reaching her goal, the huntress could not help but feel they could be running into a trap. After dismounting from Firefly, Mara scanned the streets of Har' Yhan. She could not see any Holy Blades. But they might be stationed in front of their ship. Hopefully, they were no match for the huntress, the three sages and their guardians, and those who defected from Kallikratés.

Milo walked ahead of them. "We must make haste to the ship."

Mara nodded in agreement. She guided Firefly while following the sages. She looked behind to see Mendé and his entourage of Holy Blades. They were to provide support should anything go awry. As they drew closer to the port, Mara's fears came to life. A large group of Holy Blades stood before the ship. Commander Matthews was among them.

Mara and the sages stopped. The spell-swords and the battle-mages drew their weapons as they watched the Holy Blades with caution.

Donovan gave a casual look as the Holy Blades unsheathed their swords. "We shall not allow you to take the Cursed Herald. Lord White has issued an arrest warrant for her."

Milo stepped forward. "This was not our agreement," he scolded. "The High Council had given the Faith three weeks to release us and let us return with Aazalith's soul."

Accalia glared at him. "Unless your magnanimous lord wants the soul back?"

Donovan looked past their shoulders and saw Archdeacon Mendé. "Your Grace," he addressed the archdeacon. "Thank you for bringing the prisoner to us. I am sure Lord White expresses his gratitude."

Baffled, Mara looked back at Mendé, who gazed back at her with a cold expression. His men began to unsheathe their swords.

"What is he talking about?" the huntress questioned.

"It's a trap!" Accalia exclaimed.

Mara was stunned as she stared back at Mendé. The look on his face was very telling. He never had any intentions of helping the huntress. Mara scowled at the archdeacon while reaching for Nightingale. Accalia also drew her blade, while Milo retrieved his ornate dagger.

"Don't make this difficult," Donovan said. "We can take you all peacefully."

"We only need the Cursed Herald," Mendé addressed the commander.

"Not if we kill you all!" Accalia snarled.

Donovan frowned. "Then you leave me no choice. Blades!"

A whirlwind of chaos surrounded Mara. She saw four Holy Blades stabbing a spell-sword to death. Turning around, she witnessed them cutting down a battle-mage. Blood gushed from the throat of another. The Holy Blades greatly outnumbered the sages' guardians. Before Mara could attack, she felt a blunt hit to the back of her head, knocking her out cold.

* * *

When Mara came to, she found herself chained up and behind bars. Nightingale was no longer on her person. The huntress reckoned it was taken away while being arrested. Even her travelling bag and the paired dagger was missing. She recognized the dungeon from before when helping to free Theo. The huntress was now in Hema, below Bartharoy Castle.

"You are awake," Milo called.

Mara turned to see the other sages in the cell with her. They were awake yet worse for wear. They possessed bruises around their eyes or forehead. Another thing she noticed was the lack of spell-swords and battle-mages.

"What's going on?" Mara asked.

"It is just as Accalia suspected," Milo answered solemnly. "They killed all of our guardians." He shook his head. "They intend to reclaim the soul of Aazalith."

Mara took a step towards them. "What do we do?"

"I'll tell you what we're going to do," Accalia hissed as her eyes glowed. Black fumes billowed from her body.

"Accalia," Nikolai warned. "Now's not the time."

"They will steal back the soul and then kill us!" Accalia snapped under her breath. "I'm not going down without a fight!"

"We can do little," Milo said. "They claim to know the Call of Nymera."

Mara gave a questioning glance. "So, it's real?"

"It is no coincidence," Milo admitted. "Mendé mentioned the ancient ones, or the Ascended."

"Who are the Ascended?" Mara asked.

"Ancient beings who have existed since the beginning," Milo said. "They are the only ones who know the most about Mother Nymera and the Divines. However, they tend to keep to themselves, barely sharing their knowledge with other races."

"But aren't they a myth?" Accalia argued. "No living person has ever seen such a being."

Mara's ears perked up to the sound of the door opening. Looking through the bars, she saw Donovan and two Holy Blades coming her way. The commander from Corlin stopped before the cell and stared at her.

Mara gazed at him for a brief moment. "Where's my sword?"

Donovan held his hands behind his back. "We took it away," he told her. "I'm sure it'll make a fine trophy for Lord White, to remind him of his triumph."

The huntress looked down. "Karl once said the same thing before I killed him."

Donovan scowled at her. "You will speak no more," he said. "You are to be presented to Lord White, and answer for your crimes."

Mara gazed up at his eyes. "Do you hate me?"

"Of course!" Donovan snapped. "You are the Cursed Herald!"

"No," Mara said. "That's not the reason. You're jealous because I'm the very thing you could never be."

Donovan's face darkened. "How dare you mock me?"

"I'm simply repeating the words spoken by Lord White himself. I know you love him, but he'll never love you back, nor will he ever love me. We've something in common, yet I have come to realize how important my family and friends are. Do you?"

Donovan grew red in the face. He tried to avert his gaze. "What are you talking about?"

"Take my advice and leave," Mara advised. "And if you care for your father, bring him with you."

The commander from Corlin scowled at the huntress. "Blades, take her."

After opening the cell, the Holy Blades walked in and grabbed her arms. They forced her to her feet. Mara did not attempt to resist. She sensed Donovan's hateful gaze on her, but she chose to ignore him.

Chapter Twenty-Five

The Call of Nymera

The Holy Blades escorted Mara to the throne room on the evening of February 23, where Kallikratés' disciples were waiting. The huntress glanced around at the dark blue and golden walls. Even though she had been to Bartharoy Castle before, never once did she step foot in the throne room. The golden throne, encrusted with jewels, sat atop a few steps. It was also where the imposter sat, watching his subjects drag Mara along.

Donovan approached the imposter. "My lord," he began while giving a bow. "I present the Cursed Herald."

Kratés glanced at him for a brief moment. "Thank you, Commander Matthews," he said, waving him away.

Mara watched as Donovan returned to his father while donning a look of melancholy. Her eyes wandered over to the others. Both archdeacons sat at the side. The huntress saw Mendé and scowled at him, yet he did not seem fazed in the slightest.

Upon being pushed forward, Mara looked ahead to see the restraining contraption. She hadn't seen another one of these since her capture in late December. The Holy Blades grabbed her and forced her into the device. They secured the straps over her neck, wrists, waist, and ankles.

Despite being made to face the imposter, Mara had no desire to look at him.

"I suppose you want the soul back?" asked the huntress.

Kratés glared at her as he rose from his throne. His loyal subjects followed suit.

"You've stolen what is rightfully ours," the imposter said.

Mara kept her gaze on the floor. "The reason why you delayed my journey to Thoron—was it because you needed time to remove the divine's soul?"

Mendé gave her a hard look. "The power rightfully belongs to us. We could not allow you to leave this land."

Kratés glanced at Mendé. "Mendé has been very resourceful." He looked back at Mara. "But we should be thanking you. If not for you, none of this would be possible."

Mara looked back at him in confusion. "What are you talking about?"

Mendé took a step forward. "Do you remember the surveyor team? The ones you saved from a shadow beast?"

Mara furrowed her brow. "They were sent to—"

"Retrieve ancient artifacts believed to be lost when the mountain collapsed," Kratés interrupted, "in which you caused. Thankfully, we retrieved them."

Mara scowled back at him. "So, you're finally going to admit the truth?"

Kratés gave a casual look. "There's no need." He waved to the followers. "Many of us knew all along."

The huntress turned her attention onto the other two archdeacons. The malicious look on Mendé's face confirmed her suspicions. However, both Archdeacon Matthews and his son appeared oblivious.

Kratés also noticed the looks on their faces. "Well, not all of us," he admitted.

Archdeacon Matthews approached them with a scrutinizing gaze. "What are you saying?"

"I'm telling you the truth," the imposter spoke. "Kallisto and Kratés were never gods."

Both the father and son stared at him in shock.

"What?" Archdeacon Matthews began to shake. "After all those years, we worshipped. We followed. We believed."

Corlin's archdeacon looked at Mara. He had just awoken to the fact that the huntress' claims were right all along.

Three priests entered the room, each holding a shining round stone. The smooth gemstones were as large as a human head.

Upon seeing them, Mara's eyes widened. "Moonstones?"

Then she noticed Mendé retrieving a parchment from his robes.

The imposter also gazed at the scroll. He reached for the paper, which Mendé willingly offered to him. Kratés opened the scroll and studied it.

"The Call of Nymera," said the imposter. "Never imagined I'd see this again." Kratés looked back at the blue moonstones. "But three moonstones?"

"To split the power between us three," Mendé admitted. "We shall become gods! We can reshape this world as we see fit. We can even bring back the Golden Age."

Both Archdeacon Matthews and Kratés stared back at Mendé. While Matthews grew horrified, Kratés appeared more displeased.

Mendé took notice. "We will rule equally."

Matthews shook his head. "I… I want no part in this."

Both Mendé and Kratés looked back at him.

Donovan gazed at his father in concern. "Father?"

"This is blasphemy!" Archdeacon Matthews lifted a quivering finger at the two. "To think we worshipped false gods!" He grabbed his cap and threw it off. "Kallikratés should have never existed!" Matthews looked at Mara. "And the Cursed Herald—is that false as well?"

Mara nodded. "It is," she answered. "They made it up, so they could murder innocent girls. I've seen their victims. Many were children, and one had yet to be born. They even tried to kill me when I was a child."

Matthews looked horrified. "This is madness!" He approached Mara and reached for her restraints.

Kratés, Mendé, and Donovan looked surprised to see Corlin's archdeacon helping her.

"What are you doing?" Mendé demanded.

"For once, I'm doing the right thing!" Matthews shouted. "I am letting her go." He looked to his son. "Have your Holy Blades release the sages. They are free to go."

Mara gazed back at him. "At least there's one decent person in this room. Haven't seen anyone like that since Mr. White."

The archdeacon gave a small smile. "I will fix this. We'll share the truth, and then—"

All of a sudden, Archdeacon Matthews froze. Mara grew concerned, wondering what was wrong. His face grew pale while his veins turned black. The transformation of his flesh was familiar to Mara. Archdeacon Matthews fell to the ground before her feet. He remained unmoving. Staring down at him, she spotted a wound on his back. A mix of red and black began to spread.

Mara lifted her gaze to the culprit. Mendé stood before her with a familiar green blade. She recognized the basilisk blade, yet it seemed different than before. It had a moonstone mounted in its pommel.

"Father!" Donovan cried.

The black-haired commander stared at his dead father for a moment before turning his aggression onto Mendé.

"How dare you?" Donovan reached for his sword.

Mendé looked back at the son. The look on his face was devoid of any guilt for what he had done. "Blades!"

Without warning, a Holy Blade attacked Donovan. The commander from Corlin managed to turn around and blocked the hit.

"What are you doing?" Donovan demanded.

The Holy Blade remained silent and continued to attack. The others joined in, outnumbering Donovan. A different Holy Blade stabbed him in the leg, causing Donovan to recoil. Another ran his blade through his back. Within seconds, the commander from Corlin fell. Soaked in blood, Donovan crawled to his father.

"Father…"

The Holy Blades swarmed him, stabbing their weapons into his body over and over again. Blood sputtered from Donovan's mouth as he went still. His glassy eyes stared at his dead father.

The brutal display shocked Mara to her core. The death of the father and son brought back those memories of when she lost Dad.

"That was a little extreme," Kratés said nonchalantly.

Mendé glared down at the bodies. "Their faith wasn't strong. They were bound to betray us." He then gazed at the blade in his hands. "We strengthened this basilisk blade with a moonstone," he explained. "It'll weaken her flesh, so removing the soul should be easier. Then we will lock her away. She'll never see the light of day, nor will she interfere with our plans ever again."

"I see," Kratés said, "although I have better ideas."

"Whatever you say, my lord," Mendé said, handing the blade over to Kratés. "I believe you should have the honour."

Kratés reached for the blade and studied it. He looked up at Mendé. "Thanks." He turned to look at Mara, who remained gawking at the father and son. Kratés gazed at their bodies momentarily. "Do you feel sorry for them?"

Mara looked back at him, yet remained silent.

He gave a smug look while holding the dagger in his hands. "To be honest, I'm relieved," Kratés spoke in a low voice. He reached over and tore her cape off, exposing the open "V" shape on her shirt. "If only you saw the way his son looked at me. I could see it in his eyes, how he craved my body." Kratés stared at her chest. "But he wasn't my type."

Mara's skin crawled upon seeing the lustful look in his eyes.

"A shame," the imposter said, raising the dagger. "You would've been perfect." He lowered the blade towards her chest. "Perhaps I will haul you out for entertainment, and throw you back into your cell when I get bored."

"Like Amara?" Mara snapped.

Kratés froze for a moment. His face twisted in confusion. "What did you say?"

Mara glowered at him. "Let me guess…" she hissed. "You said the same thing to Amara. And Thalia as well!"

All of a sudden, he stabbed the blade into her chest. He used a significant amount of force, making her body jolt in pain. Mara was unable to stifle a cry of pain. She looked down to see her skin beginning to decay. Kratés glared at her while keeping the blade buried within her chest. He made sure enough poison was spreading through her veins. He pulled the dagger out, and her wound began to heal. The poison seeped out of the gash before closing up. Within seconds, the decayed skin returned to life.

Kratés looked intrigued. "Interesting," he said. "So, the dagger is only effective as long as it's inside you?" He buried the dagger into her chest once more.

Mara screamed as her skin began to decay around the new wound he created. Severe pain surged through her veins.

The imposter looked back at Mendé. "Start the incantation."

"Yes, my lord." Mendé opened the scroll. "In the name of Mother Nymera," he read out loud, "I order you to leave your vessel!"

Mara looked up at the three moonstones. They began to glow as magic flowed into them.

"In the name of Mother Nymera," Mendé repeated, "I order you to leave your vessel!"

The huntress felt awful. It was like something deep within was being ripped away. Each moonstone pulled on the divine's soul—her one ticket to removing her curse.

"Simple yet powerful words," Kratés murmured. "Yet not as elegant as the way the ancient Thoron Sages spoke them. A pity I barely remember my native tongue."

The huntress looked at him as he kept the dagger within her.

"All he needs to do is repeat those words one more time, and Aazalith will leave you," the imposter spoke.

As this was happening, a Holy Blade approached Kratés and Mendé.

"My lord," he addressed Kratés.

The imposter looked back at him. "What is it?"

"The Thoron Sages have escaped! They're on their way to the throne room!"

Kratés glared back at Mara. "So, your friends managed to escape?" He glanced back at the Holy Blade. "Gather some Blades and hunt them down. Kill them on sight!"

"Yes, my lord!" The Holy Blade bowed and then left the throne room.

Kratés stared back at Mara. "Don't worry. It'll be over soon."

Mara looked at the dagger embedded in her chest. The physical pain was terrible, but not compared to the thoughts running through her mind. The quest to lift her curse was ending. Her heart was crumbling. The sensation reminded her of the day she first died. The feeling of being betrayed, and then watching Dad die drove her over the edge. Tears leaked from her eyes as she breathed heavily.

"No," Mara spoke barely above a whisper. "Stop…"

She looked up at him, but no longer did she see the imposter. Commander White stood before her, torturing her in the name of his so-called goddess. Mara gazed at the followers. All of their evil eyes were on her, waiting for her to die. Every atrocity these people and their false goddess committed filled her mind. She lost everything because of Kallisto and her followers. They were to blame! A fire began to build within Mara's heart. Rage overwhelmed her. She wanted to kill them all.

Mara began to hyperventilate. "You never cared…"

An intense blue flame ignited within Mara's chest.

Kratés took notice. "The soul of Aazalith is nearly out," he announced. "One more time!"

Mendé obeyed. "In the name of Mother Nymera," he repeated once more, "I order you to leave your vessel!"

The magic flowing into the moonstones began to intensify, as did the flame within the huntress' bosom. Mara's anger boiled over, and no longer could she contain her rage.

"You're all fucking monsters!" Mara screamed into Kratés' face.

The imposter seemed unfazed by her outburst. Instead, his attention fell to the glowing flame in her chest. A powerful force knocked Kratés away. He grunted while sliding across the ground. The extraction caused a magical explosion that shook the walls of Bartharoy Castle, frightening most of the disciples. Kratés recovered and looked at the orbs. The moonstones had ceased absorbing any more magic. Mendé lifted his gaze from the scroll as he stopped reading.

"We have it," said Loris' archdeacon.

The burst of energy from the extraction had also weakened Mara's restraints. The straps came loose, causing the huntress to fall to the ground. Now on her knees, Mara reached for the blade. With rage fuelling her strength, the huntress ripped the basilisk blade out. The small traces of magic reversed the effects of the dagger. Her tanned skin returned to normal as her veins became less visible. She held onto the blade, for it was the only weapon she possessed. Mara looked up at the three orbs while slowly rising to her feet.

A Holy Blade spotted her. "Sir!"

Kratés and Mendé looked back at Mara. She had recovered from the poison but felt significantly weaker from losing the divine's soul. Ignoring everyone, she focused her gaze on the three moonstones.

"Give it back," Mara hissed, raising her left arm.

It became clear to the followers that she was after the divine's soul.

Mendé glared at the huntress. "Kill her!"

A Holy Blade unsheathed his sword and dashed at Mara. She did not seem to notice him until the final moment. As he raised his sword, Mara gripped the basilisk blade tightly. In one swift motion, she slashed him across the neck. He staggered backwards, holding the ugly gash. Within seconds, his skin turned pale while his veins blackened. He fell to the ground, making loud gurgling sounds, then he went silent. His gruesome fate shocked the other Holy Blades.

Kratés looked very displeased. "Blades! Stop her at all costs!"

The Holy Blades gathered their courage and ran at Mara. Dark markings formed on her face while her eyes glowed yellow. She bared her elongating canines as black smoke billowed out of her body. The darker side, also known as the Huntress, began to surface. She immediately teleported and reappeared in front of a Holy Blade. She made a swift horizontal slash across his neck, killing him instantly. Then she turned her attention onto another and plunged the dagger into his skull.

Some of the Holy Blades lost their nerve and ran away. Mara saw one of them fleeing with Nightingale and the bag containing her belongings. Unwilling to let him escape with her things, Mara chased him down and stabbed him in the back. She yanked her belongings from his dead fingers. After equipping her weapons, the Huntress drew both Nightingale and the paring dagger. Then she continued the battle against the remaining Holy Blades, who remained courageous. Mara cut them down without a second thought.

Many disciples grew frightened and began to vacate the throne room. In the chaos, the undying saw Archdeacon Mendé and Kratés running towards the moonstones.

"We must take the soul!" Mendé shouted.

Before the archdeacon could get his hands on one of the orbs, Mendé froze at the sight of a dark gold and silver blade protruding out the front of his torso. Mara had teleported behind the man and stabbed him in the back. Mendé released a pained cry while falling to his knees. The Huntress gave a frozen expression as she kicked him off of her blade.

After hitting the ground, Mendé lifted his gaze to Kratés. "Help me, my lord!"

Kratés looked at Mendé, but then he saw Mara. The Huntress had already set her sights on him. Rather than fighting an unhinged creature, the imposter turned and ran with the crowd.

"Kratés!" Mendé shouted.

There was little surprise that the imposter abandoned his loyal subjects. Mara knew he never cared for anyone but himself. He was a perfect match for Kallisto. Kratés was blending into the crowd to avoid the undying. He planned to use them as shields. Mara would cut them down without a moment's hesitation.

"Mara!" called a familiar elven mage.

Mara looked to the doorway and saw the Thoron Sages, who arrived in the throne room just as the survivors were fleeing. Mara began to calm down as the Huntress went dormant. Even though her attention was on them, the sages' gaze fell upon the three shimmering moonstones. The three stared in awe and wonder.

"The soul of Aazalith," Nikolai murmured.

Even Milo looked surprised. "They used the Call of Nymera."

Accalia spotted the discarded scroll on the ground. She picked it up and studied the text. "It's real."

Nikolai approached the three orbs. "We shall take the moonstones and depart for the ship."

Upon hearing the Thoron priest's plan, Mara sheathed her weapons and began to approach the sages. "What about my curse?"

Nikolai gave a strange look. Deep down, Mara knew he had no intention of helping her. But when she looked at Milo and Accalia, she saw a similar look on their faces.

"It has always been our task to retrieve the soul of Aazalith," Milo said sombrely.

Mara's face twisted in horror while her body began to tremble. "After all the things I've done for you." She snapped her gaze onto Milo. "I saved your life!" Tears began to well up in Mara's eyes as she looked at Accalia. "I defended you."

Milo and Accalia gazed at her. Neither one said anything.

Nikolai shook his head. "We're wasting our time." He looked at the other two sages. "We have the soul. Let's head for the ship, and make our pilgrimage to Thoron."

Mara stood defeated. She felt like a fool because she believed they were her friends. Then again, kindness was not always rewarded. She watched with downcast eyes as the sages approached the three orbs. "You never wanted to help me!"

The three sages continued to ignore her. Just as Nikolai reached for the nearest orb, the fallen archdeacon from Loris began to stir. Mendé remained alive by some miracle.

"No!" Mendé shouted as he shot up to his feet. He shoved Nikolai to the side and grabbed the orbs. "The soul is mine!"

The sages watched the archdeacon with a dismissive air.

"What a bother," Milo murmured.

Accalia unsheathed her blade. "I'll take care of this."

Mara watched as the sages moved in to deal with Mendé.

"The soul is mine!" Mendé cried again.

The orbs suddenly shattered, releasing the soul of Aazalith. The sages were astonished.

"The moonstones were not strong enough!" Milo shouted.

Accalia gazed at a shard. "They're probably defective."

The soul rose into the air, burning with intense fury. Mara stood in awe until she saw Mendé standing below the divine's power.

"Come to me!" Mendé shouted. "Bestow your power unto me!" The soul flowed into the archdeacon. "Yes, I can feel the power of the gods!"

Nikolai stepped forward. "No! We have to stop him!"

"Nikolai, look out!" Milo shouted as he and Accalia grabbed the priest. They pulled him back while Milo stepped forward. The elven mage raised both of his hands, creating a barrier.

An intense light emanated from the archdeacon. Mendé yelled while engulfed in blue flames, unable to contain the divine's essence. Milo's magic shield offered safety for his fellow sages, but Mara was on her own to find a hiding place. The huntress dashed out of the throne room to duck for cover. Despite her curse, Mara didn't want to stick around to see if she could withstand the Divine Flame.

As soon as she ran into the hall, something snagged her right arm. Mara ended up in a small space between the walls, offering protection as the flames surged past her. However, her attention was pulled from the blue flames and onto her saviour. Mara froze as she stared back at Kratés. Their hiding place grew even smaller. They were mere inches apart. Mara never expected him to rescue her. Some of the flames came in and licked at his left shoulder. Kratés flinched in pain as he pushed himself further in, taking Mara with him.

Mara wanted to say something, but the roaring fire drowned out her voice. He suddenly grabbed her and held her close to protect her from the divine's wrath. Mara stood frozen in his embrace. Her discomfort and confusion continued to grow.

Once the flames subsided, Mara wriggled out of his arms. Confusion lingered within her mind as she tried to figure out what was happening. Kratés only looked back at her while holding his left shoulder. The gold plating was now warped and deformed. The huntress and the imposter continued to stare at each other, unsure of what to say.

A booming roar echoed from the throne room, drawing Mara's attention away from Kratés. The huntress went to investigate. The Thoron Sages remained alive, although Milo was exhausted from using his energy to protect them. The ashes and smoke made them cough. The entire throne room was scorched.

Mara looked at Mendé, only to see that the archdeacon from Loris was no longer human. At first, he appeared charred from being burned by the divine's power. Yet upon careful observation, the huntress saw large leathery wings instead of arms. Dark blue scales and spines covered his flesh. A tail emerged from the smoke.

Each of the sages sported a look of dread on their faces.

"No, it can't be!" Nikolai cried.

The former archdeacon raised his head to unveil a reptilian-like face. Curved horns adorned the top of his head, as spikes ran along his spine. He sported a long neck. Yet he was nowhere near as massive as Aazalith, nor did he possess front legs or arms.

"He became a wyvern!" Accalia exclaimed. The witch stepped forward while clutching her blade. "This creature must not be allowed to live!"

Nikolai frowned at the broken moonstones. "But we have no way of storing the soul."

Milo looked back at him. "We must use a vessel—something that could constantly drain her magic." Then he spotted Mara near the hallway.

Both Accalia and Nikolai also took notice of her. Mara knew why the sages were staring at her, but why should she help them?

"Mara," Milo called.

Mara looked uncertain. The lingering question burned in her mind.

"You must help us!" Nikolai shouted.

The huntress scowled at him. "Why should I?"

"Don't be an idiot!" Accalia scolded.

The huntress shook her head. "Kindness is not always—"

Mara was interrupted by the wyvern's roar. Everyone watched as the giant lizard leapt up to a higher part of the wall. Mendé looked to each of the sages before focusing his glowing blue gaze on Mara. After watching her for a moment, the wyvern released another roar. He opened his mouth to reveal a burning blue flame in the back of his throat. Mara grew pale. She sensed the wyvern was targeting her. The creature leapt from the wall and lunged at her. Mara escaped into the hallway. While running into the foyer, she saw Kratés sauntering through the main entrance. He turned and saw her fleeing the blue flames.

Upon seeing the large wyvern, the imposter began to close the doors. Mara saw this and was none too pleased.

"Don't close the door!" Mara yelled.

However, he sealed the doors shut. The huntress tried to pry the large doors open, but they would not budge.

"You piece of shit!" Mara screamed, slamming her fists on the doors.

The huntress turned around to see the wyvern hanging from the ceiling. Mendé watched her for a moment before giving another roar. Mara saw the flames in his throat growing brighter. Realizing the imminent danger, the huntress dodged the flames Mendé spewed at her. Mara returned to the hallway, where she found a stairwell. The huntress ascended to a familiar room. The abandoned room remained the same, except for the boarded window. Approaching the window, she began to pry the boards off. The huntress needed an escape route.

Once Mara removed all of the boards, she looked out the window. She could land on the roof below, but it was quite a drop.

"Hope I don't break my legs," Mara muttered to herself.

After gathering enough courage, the huntress leapt out onto the roof. The fall was painful, but not enough to kill her. Snow blanketed the castle with a few spots covered in a sheet of ice. One wrong move could cause her to fall.

Mara began to tread along the roof while searching for a way down. She heard distant voices, though she could not understand them. Mara looked down and saw a massive crowd of people gathered before the castle. Some had spotted Mara and began pointing at her. She ignored them as she continued to search for the exit.

Walking along the roof, Mara heard another crash. The large wyvern flew above her as his roars echoed in the night. The spectators below screamed in fright, yet it was not enough to draw the beast's attention.

Mendé landed before her and gave another roar. The huntress shook her head as she unsheathed her sword. She had no choice but to engage him in battle.

The wyvern leapt into the air and lunged at her with his massive sharp claws. Mara evaded his attack. She then ran up to him and slashed at his back. The scales were like stone, making Nightingale bounce off. If anything, her attacks seemed to annoy Mendé. He whipped his tail at the huntress, knocking her off of her feet. Mara grunted in pain as she hit the ground. One of her satchels came undone, causing an item to fall out. While Mara got back up, she spotted a familiar blue gemstone in the snow. It was a moonstone! How did it end up in her pocket? Despite her surprise and confusion, now was not the time for such questions. Defeating this monstrosity was now possible.

The huntress grabbed the moonstone while rising to her feet. Facing the wyvern, she inserted the gem into the pommel. The etchings on her blade began to glow bright blue. Gripping her sword tightly, Mara ran at the wyvern. Mendé gnashed his jaws, trying to bite the huntress. Mara teleported behind him and attacked. Nightingale slashed through his scales, creating deep gashes.

Mendé howled in agony, growing furious. He spread his wings and flew into the air. He circled the huntress before spitting out a fireball at her. Mara jumped out of the way. The wyvern swooped in and breathed a large stream of flames at her. Mara teleported to safety, leaving behind a plume of black smoke. The monster landed several feet away and became immobile for a moment, allowing the huntress to attack him. Nightingale sliced through vertebrae, causing his tail to fall off. Mendé screeched, then turned to bite her once more. Mara stepped to the side. Looking at his neck, the huntress raised her sword above her head.

In one quick motion, she brought her blade down onto his neck. Nightingale cut through the scales with ease and even slashed through muscle and bone. The wyvern's body shuddered as the head fell to the ground. Mara stared at the body while holding a bloody Nightingale. For some reason, it would not release the soul. Her eyes drifted to a pulsing light within the chest. Mara recognized the core, which contained the divine's soul.

Mara positioned the tip of Nightingale over the beast's glowing chest. After she plunged the blade into the core, the headless corpse shuddered once more before going still. Black fumes rose from the rotting corpse. A pungent smell invaded Mara's nostrils, making her cringe.

The decaying flesh unveiled the damaged core, which released a bright flash of light. Mara stood transfixed as the blinding light consumed her.

Chapter Twenty-Six

The Aftermath

Upon opening her eyes, Mara found herself standing on a hill with a lone tree. A sea of wildflowers bloomed, indicating spring or summer. The sun was setting. Looking back at the tree, Mara saw Kratés standing with a woman. She initially suspected the woman to be Kallisto judging by the gold and ivory dress. But the false goddess never sported a thick head of dark hair. Locks of wavy dark brown fell past the lower back and partially braided. The fabric of her dress was thin in the light of the setting sun, leaving very little to the imagination. Mara's eyes widened, for she knew who the woman was.

"I want to be with you," Kratés began as he got on one knee. "Be my wife, Amara."

Amara stood frozen, appearing genuinely shocked at his proposal. Even Mara saw the ring he held up.

"I can't lose you again," he continued. "I waited so long."

"What about…?" Amara asked, but Kratés shook his head.

"I am no husband to Kallisto."

"And father…"

"He refused to see us together. Even though I tried to explain, he threatened to take you away. I couldn't let him."

Amara gazed at the ring. "I'd love to, but… I'm only human, and you're a god."

Kratés gave a small smile. "There is something that can make me mortal."

Mara watched in confusion.

"A sword—a non-fatal stab is all it takes," he continued.

"What?" Mara questioned out loud, although none could hear her.

"I've ordered its creation," Kratés revealed. "It is called Lord Slayer Godstruck."

Mara gawked at Nightingale, which had the remains of Godstruck, the same sword Kallikratés sought to destroy. She looked back at the two. Kratés held Amara in his embrace as he kissed her on the lips.

Kratés pulled away and said, "I love you."

Mara remained confused, but when she saw Amara, the huntress could see how happy the first reincarnation appeared to be. Amara seemed to be genuinely in love with him.

* * *

Mara's eyes fluttered open to a sea of stars. Looking around, the huntress found herself in a moving wagon. She felt for Nightingale, which thankfully remained by her side, as well as the paired dagger. Even her bag, containing the summoning candle and the scroll, was in her possession.

"Took you long enough," spoke a familiar male voice.

Mara lifted her head and gazed at the driver of the wagon.

Instead of fancy attire, Kratés wore a plain white shirt, black baggy pants, and brown knee-high boots. A black hood hid his face. By his side was a sizeable bag containing the last of his belongings.

Mara grew confused. "What's going on? Where am I?" She spotted a collapsed mountain in the distance. It looked like Golden Mountain Ruins. "Where are you taking me?"

Kratés stared ahead as the horse pulled the lone cart. "The Faith of Kallikratés is no more. You must be pleased with yourself."

"What are you talking about?"

"Mendé knew I was an imposter. The group of surveyors he sent earlier found more than those artifacts." Then, "He, among many, knew the truth, that the soul of Aazalith could make anyone into a god. He gave me an ultimatum—help him steal back the soul, or he would expose me. We were to split the power between us three, but you saw what happened."

Mara watched him cautiously. "What are you going to do now?"

"With Mendé dead, his confidants shall expose the truth." Kratés sulked at her. "At least you retrieved the soul of Aazalith. The sages are looking for you, but I got to you before they could. I left them a note to meet us in Har' Yhan. For trading you, they'll let me board their ship. They get the soul back, and I'll start a new life in Thoron."

Mara glowered at him. "What makes you think I want to go to Thoron?"

Kratés raised an eyebrow. "Isn't that what you want?"

"They never wanted to help me," Mara said solemnly.

Kratés stared at her, then looked ahead. "Somehow I'm not surprised. They also refused to help Thalia."

They drew closer to Golden Mountain Ruins. Once they reached the path to where the Temple of Kallisto stood, the wagon stopped.

"Why are we stopping?" Mara asked.

Kratés stared up at the pathway. "Something I need to do."

Getting off the wagon, Kratés headed up the trail. After taking a few steps, he looked back at her. "Are you staying here?"

Mara watched him with scrutiny before leaving the wagon.

Kratés nodded. "Perhaps it's best. At least you won't steal my wagon."

Mara had her reasons for accompanying him. It was the best opportunity to obtain a lock of Karl's hair, which would increase her chances of summoning him.

She glanced down at Nightingale before looking at the back of his head. "You gave me a moonstone."

"I did it while shielding you from the flames," Kratés admitted. "It was the only way to stop such a creature."

"Why did you do it?"

"You saw it yourself. The power is dangerous in the hands of mere mortals."

As Mara followed him, she gazed up at the ruins. A large gaping hole stood in place of the original entrance to the temple. Before she could enter, a lingering thought stopped Mara in her tracks.

Kratés stopped and looked over his right shoulder. "What is it?"

Mara remained silent, which seemed to annoy him.

"Fine," Kratés said, turning his head. "You can wait out here."

"You're the reason why Godstruck existed," Mara said.

Kratés froze. "What did you say?"

Mara approached him. "You ordered my ancestors to forge the sword. You wanted to use it so you could be with Amara."

He gazed at Mara with a baffled expression. "How did you know? Very few knew about my plan."

"I saw it in a vision," she hesitated. "Milo called it Mind Eye."

"The ability to glimpse into one's past?" Kratés asked.

"You know about it?"

He nodded. "Very useful if you want to determine if someone's lying." Then he asked, "So, you saw me with Amara?"

"You proposed to her despite being already married."

"Kallisto was never my wife." He walked ahead.

Entering the hallway, the huntress stopped to see the temple ruins. Some pillars had collapsed in the hall before the throne room, though traversing over them was not a challenge. The ceiling had given away, allowing the pale moonlight to creep in.

Mara then looked back at Kratés. "You separated her from her father, and then raped her."

Kratés stopped for a brief moment. "Yes," he admitted, "until I saw her tears. I couldn't understand why she was crying. Thought I had hurt her, so I left her alone for three days."

"And then Kallisto found her?"

"I eventually apologized to her. I told her about Thalia, how I believed she was her reincarnation. At the time, I thought Thalia was dead. Amara had no feelings for me, so I let her go."

Mara's eyes widened. "You're lying!"

"The palace wasn't safe," he argued. "She couldn't find her father. To make matters worse, she injured her ankle. I carried her back to the palace and tended to her injuries. Kallisto remained unaware. I helped Amara search for her father, yet we couldn't find him."

The huntress folded her arms. "What did you do?"

"We fell in love. At first, she was hesitant because I was already married, but I made myself clear. Kallisto never considered me as her husband, let alone a king or a god. It made me realize how much I loved Thalia. I wanted to make things right. So I begged Amara, as Thalia's reincarnation, to forgive me and become my wife."

"And she agreed."

"I carried her home where we consummated our marriage. I had planned to cast aside my immortality and become her husband." Then he stopped. "But Kallisto found out about the sword and Amara."

Mara walked up to him. "Amara was taken prisoner, while you did nothing."

Kratés gave a sorrowful look, which caught the huntress off guard. "If I tried to save Amara, it would've ended with my death."

Mara looked confused. "What are you talking about?"

"Kallisto didn't just capture Amara because she was Thalia's reincarnation," he revealed. "Kallisto thought I was going to use the sword on her. She made me choose between Godstruck or Amara. I refused. If I gave Kallisto the sword, she would slay me with it, and keep Amara prisoner."

"You didn't trust her?" Mara questioned.

"I knew Kallisto too well, especially after what she did in Hema. She'd never keep her promise. Godstruck went to the Silver Thorns to be protected, and I paid the ultimate price."

"Then what?" Mara questioned. "Once you discovered Thalia was alive, you forgot Amara? Did you see her as another incomplete fragment?"

Kratés glared back at her. "What was I to do? How could I love someone who would cease to exist one day?"

He turned around and entered the throne room.

Upon entering, Mara spotted the corpse of a guardsman as well as a few Holy Blades. The decaying bodies were in terrible condition. It had been months since the disaster at Golden Mountain. Mara turned away and saw the dilapidated interior of the throne room. Like the hallway, the ceiling had given away, allowing the pale moonlight to shine into the ruins. The fallen pillars had crushed some of the bodies. The stench of decay wafted into her nostrils as she searched her surroundings. She eventually found Kratés crouching down.

"What are you doing?" Mara asked, coming closer to investigate.

Kratés was inspecting a corpse pinned beneath the rubble.

Mara's gaze drifted onto the body, recognizing the commander's garb. She froze. "Karl..."

The late Commander White had seen better days. His decaying skin had turned grey. His lips turned black, and his eyes were white and sunken. The fallen ceiling crushed the lower half of his body.

Kratés took his sword and made a clean slice across the corpse's neck.

"When Kallikratés falls, heads will roll. People will seek mine on a silver platter." Once the head was severed, Kratés rose to his feet. "But not if I give them this."

He had difficulty gripping the hair, as the decayed scalp threatened to break off. Despite holding such a grotesque object, Kratés casually walked past Mara.

"Come on," Kratés said. "We're not done."

* * *

Mara followed Kratés out of the Temple of Kallisto and down the mountain path. Once they reached the foot of the mountain, he stopped and dropped the head.

"We'll make a camp here," he said. "You can keep Commander White company."

He entered the nearby forest to gather some wood.

Mara sat on a tree stump as she stared at Karl White's remains. She grew numb at the disturbing sight. She picked up the head and stared into his dead eyes.

"The Great Commander White," she murmured. "Who would've thought we'd meet again?"

The severed head was only an empty shell, though it reminded her of the last time she saw him alive.

Kratés returned with some wood. He laid them down into a pile and took some flint. Realizing what he was planning, Mara pulled out a lock of Karl's hair. It took little effort thanks to the advanced decay. She quickly put the hair away.

He looked at Mara briefly while attempting to start a fire. "Must be strange coming face to face with the source of your pain."

Mara kept her eyes on the severed head. "He wasn't the only source."

"Are you still mad at me?"

Mara looked at Kratés to find him scowling at her.

Kratés rolled his eyes. "Get over it."

"You nearly took everything from me!" Mara snapped.

"I did it to survive," he admitted flatly. "I doubt you know anything about survival."

"Survival?" She narrowed her eyes. "I spent thirty years trapped in the Dark Labyrinth because of your former wife!"

Kratés gazed at her momentarily before tending to the fire. He remained silent.

The huntress could sense that he was indifferent. She looked back at Karl's severed head.

"You don't care. After all, I'm nothing more than an incomplete fragment." Then Mara asked, "What about the others? Did their lives mean nothing?"

"It doesn't matter anymore. Once Thalia returns, you'll be gone." He gazed at the rising embers. "I've heard that my reincarnation was married to one of them."

"Her name was Evelyn," Mara said.

"I could care less what her name was," he responded, approaching Mara. Kratés looked at the head and took it. He turned around and faced the fire. "I'd imagine he also knew the truth."

"He loved her," Mara argued.

"He was a fool."

"No, he wasn't. Karl loved her for who she was. Evelyn existed." Mara gazed at the fire. "I had family and friends. They loved me."

"And where are they?" Kratés asked as he looked back at her.

The huntress frowned. "Dead," Mara murmured.

Kratés kept watching her before looking back at the severed head in his hands. "They would've been better off abandoning you." Then he dropped Karl's head into the fire.

Mara saw this and shot up to her feet. "What are you doing?"

"Faking my death," Kratés said. "They'll think the Divine Flame killed me."

The flames ate the putrid flesh, revealing the skull underneath. Mara stared at the flaming skull, mesmerized by the sight of seeing Karl burn away. The fire eventually dissipated, leaving behind charred remains. Kratés reached over and grabbed it.

"Now to deliver it," he said.

"Where is it going?" Mara asked.

"Mirahyll," he answered, putting out the fire.

Mara followed him to the wagon, and they departed for the city.

* * *

The two entered Mirahyll by midnight. The streets were empty. Mara and Kratés wandered into the noble quarters until they reached a familiar mansion.

"The White Manor," Mara muttered.

Kratés looked at the manor and began to approach it. "Tonight is a night of new beginnings." He placed the skull at the front door. "Once they find "my" head, they'll report it." Kratés stood up and knocked on the door three times. Then he ran away from the manor.

Mara followed after him. "What makes you think they'll fall for it?"

"They will," Kratés said. "My plan is perfect."

They hid around the corner and watched as someone answered the door. A servant, who remained awake, glanced around before turning his attention onto the grim discovery before him. The servant backed away in fright and alerted the others within the manor.

"Come morning, news of my death will spread." Kratés moved away. "We'll be heading to Har' Yhan."

The two returned to their wagon and left the city.

Chapter Twenty-Seven

The Trade

The sun had risen on February 26 by the time they reached Har' Yhan. As the two entered the town, people did not seem to pay them any heed. The hood hid Kratés' face, making everyone around him oblivious.

"We'll stay at the Black Smoke Inn," he said, walking ahead. "You will arrange a room for us and find out where the sages are."

Mara gave a strange look. "Why don't you do it?"

"I'm supposed to be dead," he reminded her. "Now, chop-chop!" He clapped his hands twice.

Mara rolled her eyes as she ventured towards the Black Smoke Inn, where she soon found the inn owner.

"Well, fancy meeting you again," Lady Lorelei greeted.

Mara nodded. "I was nearby."

Lorelei looked intrigued. "Is that so? I heard the Faith captured you."

"It's a long story."

"I'm sure it is. Maybe we can talk about it over breakfast?"

"Great idea," Mara said. "By the way, have you seen the sages? I'm afraid we got separated."

"I believe I saw them earlier," Lorelei revealed. "They were staying at the hotel across from here."

"Well, that's good to hear," Mara murmured.

"I suppose you're going to meet them?"

"Yes, but I came here to rent a room."

Lorelei shrugged. "We can arrange that." She looked at Mara from head to toe. "And you could use a bath." Lady Lorelei flagged down an innkeeper. "Have the deluxe suite available."

The innkeeper nodded and went to make the arrangements.

Lorelei looked back at Mara. "Perhaps I'll treat you to breakfast. It'll be a while before the room is ready."

Mara nodded. "Sure, why not."

Lorelei led her to a table.

"Have some eggs and toast ready," the hostess told another passing innkeeper. "Bring some juice, fruit, and cheese as well."

"Yes, ma'am," the innkeeper replied as she smiled.

After the two took a seat, some servers arrived with breakfast. The huntress saw a plate of eggs and toast placed before her. At the side were some slices of fruit and cheese. Mara lifted her gaze to Lorelei while the innkeeper poured a glass of juice. After serving breakfast, the innkeeper walked away, allowing the two women privacy.

Lorelei gazed back at her. "How are you?"

Mara reached for the glass. "I slew a dragon last night."

Lady Lorelei's eyes widened in disbelief. "Did you?"

"Kallikratés nearly succeeded in reclaiming Aazalith's soul. Archdeacon Mendé used it to become a dragon. Pretty much destroyed the interior of Bartharoy Castle."

Lorelei stared at her. "I heard there were many victims, like Archdeacon Matthews and his son. Even Lord White didn't survive. They found his charred remains this morning in Mirahyll, or what's left of them. I guess this is the end of the Faith."

"How so?" Mara asked, despite knowing the truth.

"Didn't you hear, my dear?" Lorelei questioned. "Several followers revealed the truth. Kallisto and Kratés were never gods. And the Faith was built on a foundation of lies."

"I told them that months ago," Mara grumbled.

"But not many believed it until they heard it from the horse's mouth," Lorelei spoke. "I'd imagine many nobles will withdraw their support. Without their money, the Faith will fall."

Mara turned her attention onto her plate. "At least they won't be a problem anymore."

"Like stopping you from travelling to Thoron?"

The huntress looked up at the hostess. "I'm not sure if I'm going."

Lorelei gave a questioning look. "Wasn't this your goal?"

"Ran into some issues," Mara murmured. "I don't know if the sages will help me lift this curse."

Lorelei shrugged. "Once, the Thoron Sages refused to help Thalia. They may refuse to help you, too."

"Because I'm her reincarnation?" Mara asked.

Lorelei nodded. "As a Thoron native, let me give you some advice—be aware of the Witch Hunters."

"The Witch Hunters?"

"They are a band of executioners who hunt those allegedly using dark magic. Long ago, Saint Kallius founded the guild. He is a hero to many, while others view him as a mass murderer. Kallius had personally hunted Thalia, who he deemed to be a witch."

"This Kallius… He's no longer around?" Mara questioned.

"No, but his guild remains," Lorelei replied. "If you go there, you may draw their attention. So, be careful."

The huntress stared at her before looking down at her plate. She reached for the glass and took another drink while thinking about Lady Lorelei's words. As soon as Mara finished her breakfast, the innkeeper came by with the key to her suite.

* * *

Mara headed out of the inn, where Kratés was waiting beside his rickety wagon.

"Oh, hello," he began, folding his arms. "Have a nice breakfast? Or did you forget what you came here for?"

Mara rolled her eyes. "I got a room for us at the Black Smoke Inn. And the Thoron Sages are staying at the hotel across from here."

Kratés stared at her for a moment and then turned to his wagon. "Finally," he muttered, grabbing his travelling bag. "Give me the key to the suite."

"Why should I?"

"I'm the one paying." Kratés lifted a large bag full of coins. "I have the gold for it."

"You mean my gold?"

"Get over it." He snatched the key out of Mara's hand. Kratés looked at the number on the key. "Ah, I know this room."

With that, he walked ahead.

Mara followed him to the suite.

Upon opening the door, Kratés walked inside. "Just like home," he murmured.

Mara recognized the room she once shared with Commander White. She glanced at a table and spotted a fruit basket before looking at Kratés.

"So, now what? Do we find the sages?"

Kratés lowered his hood and raised an eyebrow. "Get me breakfast," he ordered.

The huntress grew baffled. "What?"

"Are you dense?" Kratés questioned. "I had to wait while you gorged yourself. I spied an all-you-can-eat buffet."

Mara glared at him. "I'm not your damn servant!"

"And I don't think you realize the gravity of the situation," he said. "If I go out there, someone will recognize me."

"How is this my problem?" Mara asked. "I don't have anything to lose, unlike you."

Kratés scowled at her. "You are incredibly ungrateful. I'm the one paying for our stay." He gestured to the room around them. "I am the reason you'll be sleeping in the lap of luxury tonight."

Mara placed her hands on her hips and frowned at him. Then she glanced over at the basket again. "Why don't you have some fruit?"

Kratés looked at the basket and cringed. "I doubt these are fresh."

Mara took an apple and bit into it. "This is fine."

He grimaced. "Of course you think it's fine. What would a peasant know?"

The huntress glanced down at the apple, then tossed it at him. "Here," she said.

Kratés caught the apple, though reluctantly. He stared down at it. "You expect me to eat this?" He placed it back on the table. "I made myself clear—get me breakfast."

The huntress rolled her eyes. "Fine," she muttered.

Mara headed out to the tavern within the inn. She sauntered over to the large table where various food was available. She gathered some things without looking too conspicuous.

By the time she returned, Mara had witnessed Kratés stripping himself before her. He had removed his cloak and his hood and was now in the process of taking off his shirt.

Mara began to blush. "What are you doing?"

Kratés looked back at her indifferently while removing his shirt. "Oh, you're back," he said. "Thought it'd take you longer; I was going to have a bath." He approached her, seemingly unfazed by her discomfort. His attention was on the tray of food. "This is my breakfast?" He reached for a grape and ate it. After chewing it, he shrugged. "I guess it'll have to suffice." Then he ordered, "Place it on the table. I'll eat when I finish my bath."

Mara rolled her eyes as she placed the food on the table. Upon completing this task, she turned to see him completely naked. Kratés just casually walked beside her with his exposed genitals on full display. His penis was nearly halfway down his thigh. And his testicles were large enough to suit a bull. Now she understood what Milo meant when he mentioned Hedera's victims being endowed with an insatiable urge to breed. Her eyes were stuck on his obscene display until he stopped. She lifted her gaze to see his bitter scowl.

"What are you looking at?" Kratés demanded.

"Well, I…" Mara began, but the words became lodged in her throat. In truth, she had never looked upon a naked man before, and it showed.

Kratés turned to face her, placing his left hand on his hip. "You are such a child."

Mara looked away. "Sorry…"

Kratés grunted as he headed into the washing area.

While he turned away, Mara glanced at him and saw his bare buttocks. Kratés was like a perfectly sculpted statue. As he entered the tub, the warm water rose to his chest. He tilted his head back while resting his arms on the tub's edge. Mara figured he was going to be there for quite some time, so she decided to head into her room and wait.

* * *

After waiting an hour, Mara emerged from her room to see Kratés leaving the washing area. He was in the process of putting his pants on when he noticed her.

He frowned. "I assume you're going to have your bath now?"

Mara ignored him. Once inside the washing room, the huntress undid her cloak. The tattered cape fell behind her. Mara proceeded to remove her clothes. She loosened her braid, allowing her dark hair to flow free. Once Mara was reduced to her white tunic and underwear, she picked up her clothing and placed them in the other tub. The huntress began to clean her clothes. The black shirt went first, although it was the least stained. Then the pants came next. While Mara washed her clothes, she could sense Kratés standing nearby. He was trying her patience.

Mara stopped and glared at him. "What do you want?"

Kratés returned a similar look. "You're not having a bath."

"My clothes are dirty. I'm cleaning them first." Mara looked back at her clothes and continued to wash them.

However, Kratés refused to leave. His eyes roamed over her entire body.

"Did you ever get that scar looked at?" Kratés asked. "The one on your lower abdomen."

Mara paused. "Why do you care?"

"Did you inflict that on yourself?"

The huntress glanced back at him. "It happened after my first death," she revealed. "A monster ripped me open and tore out my uterus."

Kratés' eyes widened as his mouth opened. Yet he remained silent. Judging by the look on his face, Mara figured he would not expect such an answer.

"The monster was Amara's father," she continued. "Khan mistook me for her. He couldn't stand the idea of a certain king defiling his daughter."

He eventually closed his mouth. "Interesting," he said. "I'd imagine it must be frustrating."

Mara shook her head. "What?"

"You're unable to experience pleasure," he told her. "I still remember my first time. Her name was Hedera. And she pleasured me in ways that I could not imagine. That woman awoke something deep within me—an insatiable hunger. I recall every kiss she planted upon my flesh. The spongy texture of her tongue. Her lips around my cock."

Mara stared at him before tending to her clothing. "I heard she's a demon who seduces men. Is that why your family disowned you?"

"I was never a perfect son. My mother, father, and even brothers and sisters would look for ways to cut ties with me. After what happened that night, they found the perfect excuse." Kratés walked away. "We shall meet the Thoron Sages this evening and discuss the trade."

Mara looked at him as he disappeared, then continued to clean her clothes. After completing the task, the huntress focused on cleaning herself. After stripping the last of her clothing, she entered the tub. The water remained warm and even looked clean. She glanced out the doorway and saw Kratés approaching the food on the table. He had yet to place a shirt back on. Kratés sat down and helped himself to breakfast. He took a few bites before stopping. It seemed he was not pleased with the food she brought him. His breakfast likely turned cold. He turned his attention onto the fruit basket and reached for another apple. Mara rolled her eyes as she continued to clean herself.

Once Mara finished cleaning herself, she rose from the tub. The white tunic and underwear went back on. Then she took the rest of her clothing and left. While emerging from the washing area, the huntress could see Kratés eating his food. He glanced back at her as he took another bite out of the apple. She gazed at him for a moment before going to her room.

* * *

The evening hours had arrived. Her clothes had dried, allowing her to place them back on. As Mara emerged from her room, she saw Kratés standing before her. He was also fully dressed and ready to meet with the three sages. He briefly gazed at her while putting his cloak on.

"Are you ready?" Kratés asked.

Mara nodded as she held onto her travelling bag.

He took note of her bag. "Leave it here," he told her.

"Why?" Mara asked.

He folded his arms. "I doubt they'll let us board the ship immediately."

The huntress sighed, "Fine." She returned to her room and put the bag down. Mara could only hope she would come back for her things.

The two left the Black Smoke Inn, heading over to the hotel across the street. Entering the lobby, they found Milo, Accalia, and Nikolai. The sages remained silent as Mara and Kratés approached them.

"There you are," Milo began while holding his hands behind his back. He looked at Mara in particular. "It has been some time since we last saw you."

Mara shifted her gaze onto Nikolai, who had retrieved his pendant. The blue gemstone shone through his fingers. Even Kratés, Milo, and Accalia took notice.

"You have the soul of Aazalith once again," Milo added.

Accalia turned her attention onto Kratés. "And you're with him of all people," she said. "The same man who's supposed to be dead."

Kratés gazed at them from under his hood. "I'm willing to return her to you. In exchange, you'll let me board your ship."

The three looked at him, appearing unfazed by his request.

"What makes you think we will agree?" Milo questioned.

Kratés frowned at them. "Fine," he said, "I guess it has come to this."

Mara looked confused. "What are you talking about?"

Kratés turned towards Mara. He lifted his hands and reached for her head. The huntress was alarmed, and then she saw the lustful glint in his eyes. Kratés remained silent as he pulled her face close to his own. Before anyone could react, Kratés pulled down Mara's mask and pressed his lips to hers. The huntress' first reaction was to push him away, but he held onto her tightly, refusing to let her go. A tingling sensation began to spread over her face, down to her chest, and finally her legs. Every nerve flared with excitement. Kratés relaxed his grip on her head and slowly moved his hands down her body. They finally rested on her waist. He held her close to his body as he deepened in the kiss.

Eventually, he pulled away, leaving Mara confused. The tingling sensation faded away, only to be replaced by disgust. What was this man trying to do?

"Hedera's toxins are now inside of her," Kratés claimed. "She's now mine to control."

Upon looking at Kratés, Mara's face twisted in rage. Lifting her right hand, she delivered a swift slap across his face. The huntress hit him hard enough to knock him down.

"How dare you?" Mara snarled, her eyes glowing brightly.

Kratés sat frozen on the ground, stunned by what transpired. He lifted his gaze to the huntress, revealing a red mark on his face. He was confused. Accalia burst into laughter, while Milo and Nikolai looked rather displeased.

"I reckon he was unaware that witches are immune to Hedera's toxins," Milo spoke.

"Our metabolisms can break them down," Accalia explained. "We only experience a brief tingling sensation."

Mara gazed down at Kratés, who remained stunned. His plan blew up in his face. He sat on the ground, appearing defeated.

"Now, I trust you have everything you need for the journey," Milo addressed Mara.

The huntress began to sulk at the three sages. "What makes you think I'm going with you?"

The three sages frowned at her.

"We have an agreement," said the elven mage.

"We had an agreement," Mara corrected him. "When Kallikratés removed the soul, you took back your word. You never wanted to help me."

Accalia gave a sombre look and approached her. "We intended to take the soul back, given the circumstances. But things have changed. We still want to help you."

Mara gave a skeptical look. "Why should I believe you?"

The elven mage stepped forward. "I shall be honest," Milo told her. "When Aazalith's power had fully manifested, it became our concern. At the time, we believed that the Divine's magic was beyond your siphoning abilities. We needed to take you to Thoron as soon as possible or have the Faith remove the soul from you. It was the only way to make sure no harm came to you or those around you. Thankfully, that power has diminished due to the battle at the castle, but only for a time."

The huntress was astounded by the elf's confession. She never realized that Milo and Accalia wished to protect her.

"We never forgot what you did for us," Accalia said softly. She gestured to the mage. "If not for you, Milo would not be here. And you protected me."

"We apologize for betraying your trust," Milo spoke. "Please come with us, and we promise to help you lift the Curse of the Undying."

Mara placed her hands on her hips as she looked to each of the three sages. Milo and Accalia seemed genuine and showed remorse for what they did. Nikolai, on the other hand, appeared less than thrilled. She sensed that the old priest would never help her. Mara shifted her gaze back onto Milo and Accalia.

"Fine, I'll go." Mara looked at Nikolai once more. "But don't you dare do that again."

Nikolai appeared apprehensive, yet Milo and Accalia seemed less fazed.

"You have our word," Milo said. "We will know better than to break your trust."

"Yes," Accalia agreed. She gave Nikolai a sidelong glance. "Isn't that right, old man?"

Everyone looked at Nikolai, expecting an answer from him.

The old priest sighed in defeat. "Yes, I'll agree to this."

Mara watched the Thoron priest. Sensing his dishonesty, she needed to watch him. He could cause trouble in the future.

"Now, what about him?" Milo questioned.

Mara looked back at the elven mage and then noticed Kratés rising to his feet. The huntress and the sages watched him with curiosity, wondering why he was still here.

Kratés frowned. "Please," he spoke softly, "I'm a mere mortal with nowhere else to go."

"You may be mortal," Nikolai said, "but you're still a danger to mankind."

"He's right," Accalia added. "You remain infected. There's a chance you could produce offspring like that reincarnation of yours."

Kratés appeared baffled.

Mara watched him. "Karl is a demon," she revealed. "He haunted the White Manor."

Kratés looked back at Mara. He kept his mouth shut.

"Ever since your resurrection, you never spent much time in the mansion." Mara shook her head. "You probably knew all along Karl was haunting the mansion and killed Mr. White. Yet you accused me instead."

Kratés kept frowning at her. "Then I need help," he claimed, looking at the sages. "Thoron holds the key to my salvation."

"What are you talking about?" Mara asked.

"The Lunar Sanctum," Kratés said.

Nikolai gaped at him. Milo and Accalia also appeared astonished.

Milo gave a hard stare. "How do you know about the Lunar Sanctum?"

"I was born in Thoron," Kratés claimed. "Of course, I know of one of the most sacred places in the world! It is where Mother Nymera's roots descend to."

Nikolai looked horrified. "Out of the question!" He gestured to Mara. "The sacred spring shall only be used to remove the soul of Aazalith from her and have the Divine reborn."

Accalia shrugged. "Its water could purify him, and any future offspring he has will be free of Hedera's curse."

"It is true," Milo said, "yet it will not undo everything."

Kratés gave a humbled look. "I'll do anything to gain your approval."

Accalia folded her arms and looked at Mara. "I believe she should have the final say."

Mara glanced back at the witch.

Milo nodded in agreement. Then he asked Mara, "Should he be allowed to travel with us?"

The huntress looked back at Kratés, who seemed unhappy to know his fate was in her hands. After watching him for a while, Mara finally reached an answer.

"No," Mara said, then looked at the sages. No longer did she have any desire to look at that man. "I trust we're leaving soon?"

"We shall leave in the morning," Milo said. "Much of our belongings are stored on the ship."

"What about Firefly? What happened to her?"

"I believe she escaped when we got captured," the mage replied. "Upon our arrival, we did see her wandering just outside the town. Since you have returned safely, she shall come to you. You can call her later."

"Fair enough." Mara nodded. "I'm pretty much ready to go. Rented a room at the Black Smoke Inn. I'll join you at the docks tomorrow morning."

"Very well," Accalia said.

Once everything was said and done, Mara and the sages parted ways. The huntress continued to ignore Kratés, who was glaring at her.

"You've found yet another way to screw me over!" Kratés hissed.

Mara kept walking. "And you have a lot of nerve pulling that stunt."

"You want to keep Thalia and me apart!"

Mara stopped. "I wonder if Thalia loved you." She looked back at him to see his astonished face. "And what about Amara?"

Kratés scowled at her. "How dare you entertain such an idea?"

The huntress shook her head, then approached the Black Smoke Inn. "Just as I thought."

"What?"

"I'm sure without that toxin, you are nothing."

Mara returned to her suite with Kratés following after her. She checked to make sure she had everything she needed for her departure tomorrow morning. The huntress did her best to ignore Kratés, who was staring at her.

"What do you want from me?" Kratés questioned. "What must I do to persuade you to let me board that ship?"

She paused and thought about his question. "Nothing," Mara replied.

"Nothing?" Kratés asked. "Not even the money I stole from you?"

"How much of my gold do you even have left?" Mara inquired. "Less than half? Maybe a quarter?"

"I never spent any of it."

Mara gave a skeptical look. "I think you're lying!"

"It's true," he claimed, "I amassed a large fortune. Many nobles from both Ardana and Corlin threw their support behind me. Not only did they have their sons join the Holy Blades, but they also offered generous donations. The coffers were overflowing, which I took for my expenses."

Mara stared at him. "You mean you also stole from others?"

"I'll show you."

The huntress decided to take a look. He led her into his room. Opening the bag, he revealed several large sacks of gold. The travelling bag looked very heavy, yet Kratés managed without much issue.

"How much is this?" Mara questioned.

"Five million," Kratés said.

Mara snapped her bewildered gaze onto him. "You've been carrying that much on you?"

Kratés closed the bag while looking at Mara. "I have more than enough to start over comfortably. I'll even give you a million if you let me board the ship tomorrow morning."

Mara looked back at the gold. A million gold was a lot of money, but there was a problem. She looked back at Kratés and said, "I have a better idea. How about you return the money you stole, and maybe, just maybe, they won't hang you for theft!"

With that, Mara turned around. She was about to leave the room when something grabbed her left arm. Before the huntress could realize what was happening, Kratés crashed his lips upon her own. He was trying to expose her to the toxins again, despite knowing the fact that she was part-witch. Perhaps he was trying to seduce her, but it was nothing more than a poor attempt.

Mara was having none of it. She placed her hands on his chest and pushed as hard as she could. The huntress broke free, only to fall backwards. A sharp pain hit her in the base of her skull. As soon as she hit the ground, Mara found herself unable to move. A pool of blood formed around her head. She could also feel it pooling in her skull, putting pressure on her brain. Mara gazed up at Kratés, who looked back at her with a horrified expression. As she slipped away into the darkness, she could see him gathering his things and rushing out the door.

Chapter Twenty-Eight

The Cage

A tingling sensation flowed through Mara's body. Her muscles began to twitch as every nerve returned to life. Soon, it became a burning sensation, jolting her awake. The huntress realized that she had died. The first thing she saw was a pair of glowing yellow eyes. A familiar witch sat by the bed, awaiting Mara's resurrection.

"Accalia?" Mara asked, rising from her bed.

The witch watched her in silence.

Mara looked to her side to find Nightingale nearby. She was relieved to see it, for a certain someone would've stolen it. The huntress glanced at the doorway, noticing the silence.

"Where's Kratés?" Mara asked the witch.

"Gone," Accalia replied. "I came to see you and make sure he caused you no trouble." She gestured to the floor. "I found you lying on the floor. You hit the back of your head against the sharp corner of a dresser."

Mara frowned at her. "That bastard forced himself onto me. I managed to push him away but lost my footing. He took his things and left."

Accalia turned her attention onto Mara's travelling bag. "That explains some things." She reached inside and pulled out the black candle and the small scroll. "Now, would you like to explain why you have these?"

Mara froze upon seeing the summoning candle and the scroll, both of which she received from Alkina. "I…"

The witch shot up to her feet while keeping her intense gaze on Mara. "We agreed that you would never summon the demon!"

Mara glared back at her. She stormed up to Accalia and snatched the candle and the scroll out of her hand. The huntress turned away.

"We don't know what the spell will do!" Accalia exclaimed.

The huntress snapped her gaze onto the witch. Her eyes began to glow in a similar hue. "I'm the only one who can stop him!"

Accalia stared at Mara. The witch seemed genuinely shocked by the huntress' words.

"Don't you see?" Mara asked. "Karl will continue to haunt me as long as I'm alive. You've seen him yourself. He'll even harm those close to me."

"There are other ways," Accalia spoke.

The huntress glared at her. "This is not up for discussion. I'm going to summon him tonight. I will seal him away. Then Karl will never hurt me or anyone ever again."

Accalia watched her. "So, what do you have to do?"

Mara placed the summoning tools on the table. The huntress reached into her pocket to retrieve a piece of Karl's hair.

Mara looked at the candle. "I need to light this."

Searching the suite, she found a small box of matches in one of the drawers. Mara returned to her room. Accalia watched as the huntress retrieved a match stick. Using the matchbox, she produced a tiny flame. The huntress reached over and placed the lit match over the wick. The fire carried over, and the candle began to glow.

Accalia gazed down at the scroll. "Prepare to engage the spirit in battle," she read out loud.

"I think I'm supposed to fight him," Mara said, looking at Nightingale.

"Could be dangerous." The witch unsheathed her sword. "I'll help you."

Mara nodded as she strapped Nightingale to her belt. Then she turned her attention onto the clump of hair. The huntress picked it up and held it over the flame. Once the hair caught fire, Mara dropped it onto the candle. The huntress and the witch watched as the hair burned. It released dark fumes and a notable stench of death.

The candle went out as if by a gust of wind. But all of the doors and windows were closed. Both women looked up and noticed the room growing darker. It became so dark, neither one could see anything. A raspy breathing sound came from behind. Mara turned around, only to confront the demon she summoned. Karl lunged at her with a blackened maw. The last thing Mara saw before being enveloped in darkness was his burning eyes.

* * *

Mara groaned in pain as she woke up. Her head pounded while she tried to figure out what just happened. Opening her eyes, the huntress found herself in the familiar corridors of the Dark Labyrinth.

"This place," she began, rising to her feet. "What am I doing here?"

Soon, Mara realized she was alone.

"Accalia?" Mara called, her voice echoing through the halls.

The witch never responded.

Mara heard the raspy breathing again. She spun around and saw a shadowy man rising to his feet. The dark mist lifted, revealing the commander's blackened garb.

Karl opened his eyes to unveil a pair of burning coals. A dark haze exuded from him, while pure rage and hatred decorated his face. He took a step towards Mara, then unsheathed his sword.

"You will pay," Karl hissed.

Mara reached for Nightingale, but only grabbed air. Baffled, the huntress looked down and realized her sword was missing! Where was it? She looked up at him. Karl gripped his sword as he drew near. The sound of his boots grew louder with each step. Mara had only one option, and it was to run.

She fled in the opposite direction to get away from him. Mara looked behind to see Karl still following her. He kept a steady pace, never running or sprinting. Mara dreaded the thought of him catching her. So she kept running through the labyrinth, unsure if she would hit a dead end.

While running like a rat in a maze, Mara collided with something that just emerged from a corner. She was thrown back upon collision, hitting the ground with a thud. Although stunned, the huntress scrambled to her feet. She had to go, or Karl would catch her.

"Mara?" asked a familiar male voice.

Realizing she collided into someone, Mara looked at the man and froze. She recognized his long greying hair and dark skin.

Elder Ravenclaw stood before her, looking both confused and upset. "What have you done?"

Mara shook her head. "How can this be? You're supposed to be dead." She looked behind. "I have to get out of here. He'll be here at any moment."

As she stormed past him, Ravenclaw gave a mournful look. "You cannot leave."

Mara stopped. "What?" She gazed back at him.

"This is a Demon's Cage," Ravenclaw explained.

"A Demon's Cage?"

The former elder nodded. "It was created upon casting the spell."

Mara was baffled. "You know about it?"

"I saw you cast it to lure that foul demon." Then he asked, "Why are you doing something so reckless and dangerous?"

"I have to stop him," Mara claimed. "He'll keep destroying lives!"

"What do you mean?" Ravenclaw inquired softly.

"He was influencing Shenoah," she explained. "He made her commit suicide. He's the reason why she became the monster that killed you."

The former elder stared at her with a frozen expression. He then closed his eyes. "To contain him and escape this prison, you must defeat the demon. However, if he defeats you, he could escape or take over your body."

"I'll stop him," Mara said. "As long as I live, he'll never harm another."

A chirping sound echoed through the dark corridors. Mara peered into the darkness and saw a golden bird flying towards her. The tiny creature hovered before her face chirping constantly, as if it tried to talk.

"Ah, a golden nightingale," Ravenclaw said with a smile.

Mara looked confused. "A golden nightingale?" Seeing the animal reminded her of the golden bird chiselled onto her sword. "A golden nightingale." Her mind drifted back to the first time she laid eyes upon her father's gift. "Nightingale."

The huntress reckoned the bird was a clue to her sword's location. Mara looked back at Ravenclaw. "I'm sorry," she said. "I have to find my sword."

The former elder raised his hand as if to say farewell. "I pray for your success."

Mara gave chase after the little bird. The tiny creature flitted along the dark halls. The huntress was uncertain where it was taking her, but hoped it would lead her to Nightingale.

The little bird led Mara into a large circular room where a black and gold coffin sat at the centre. The bird vanished, but its help was no longer needed. The huntress was certain Nightingale was inside the coffin.

As Mara approached, the grave reminded the huntress of being sealed in one of these. She gathered her strength and pushed on the lid. The lid slid over to reveal a familiar sheathed sabre. Elated to see her sword again, Mara reclaimed Nightingale.

"A coffin. How appropriate..."

Mara spun around upon hearing Karl's voice. He stood at the doorway, gripping his sword.

"I'll gladly put you inside of it once I'm through with you!" Karl declared as he lunged at her.

Mara stepped back, avoiding his swing. The huntress glared at him while drawing Nightingale. She got into a fighting stance while gripping her blade with both hands. Karl lunged at her and took another swing at her. She dodged and countered. Mara managed to cut him in his side.

Karl was none too pleased. "You think your little attacks will stop me?"

The demon went on the offensive, growing fast and aggressive. Mara was unable to land as many hits, for Karl had very little to no reaction. He swung at her again. The huntress could barely get out of the way as his weapon narrowly missed her neck.

Without warning, his fist collided with her face. Mara went flying as black blood gushed out of her nostrils. The impact of hitting the ground stunned her. She could see his shadow looming over her.

"I can finally have my revenge!" Karl threw his head back. "Kallisto, look upon me and watch as I slay our enemy!"

Mara coughed up some blood. "She can't hear you."

"What did you say?" Karl demanded.

Mara looked behind to gaze upon Karl's enraged face. "Her soul was destroyed. She no longer exists."

"Shut up!" Karl kicked Mara in the stomach.

Mara was stunned as she flew a few feet into the air. She cried out in pain as she hit the ground with a thud.

Karl stormed over towards Mara. His face twisted in pure rage. His eyes burned brighter like fire as the darkness spewed from his mouth. "For what you did to the Goddess, you will pay!"

Mara had to think quickly. She then spotted Nightingale by her side. She grabbed the hilt and looked back at Karl, who raised his sword above his head. It was now or never.

Gathering the last of her strength, Mara drove Nightingale into Karl's chest.

The demon froze before looking down at the blade in his chest. His body began to tremble as blood seeped out of his mouth. He descended to his knees before falling backwards onto the cold ground.

Mara rose to her feet while looking back at the fallen commander. The darkness exuding from him was fading. The burning coals in his eyes dwindled. Her eyes drifted to the spot where she stabbed him. Nightingale had gone through his heart, sealing his fate. Yet Karl struggled to survive. He gasped for air as blood began to spread from his stab wound.

"You will pay," he spoke barely above a whisper. "You will pay."

His fallen form reminded her of the day she took his life. Even though he was already dead, he still fought a losing battle to survive. He stared at Mara and attempted to lift his right arm to her. No longer could he speak without coughing up more blood.

"I'm sorry for your loss," Mara murmured, settling Nightingale over his forehead. The huntress gazed at Karl once more, understanding that this was the right solution. As she drove the sword through the demon's head, everything went black.

Chapter Twenty-Nine

Journey to Thoron

Mara awoke to the morning light. Her room seemed brighter, considering what happened last night. The battle in her mind left her exhausted, yet she was relieved to know that Karl would no longer be able to harm another innocent.

The huntress lifted her head from the pillow and looked to the table. Accalia remained asleep, resting her head on her hand. The witch eventually opened her eyes and gazed at Mara.

"Did it work?"

Mara nodded as she rose from the bed. "I think so." Nightingale remained strapped to her side. Rising from the bed, Mara spotted the black candle on the table. The flame had already died.

"You think so?" Accalia asked. "What happened?"

Mara approached the candle. "The spell created a prison for Karl." The huntress gazed at Accalia. "I had to defeat him, so he'll be trapped there."

"And did you?"

"Yes," Mara answered, picking up the candle and putting it away. She planned to dispose of it later, in case someone else found it. "He'll never hurt anyone ever again."

"But you were his main target," Accalia argued. The witch rose from her chair and took a closer look at Mara. "Hmm…"

Mara gave a strange look. "What are you doing?"

The witch placed her hands on her hips as she carefully observed the huntress. "I was trained to sense demons. But I cannot sense him. Either this is a strong spell, or…" Then she asked, "Are you sure you trapped him?"

"Yes, I'm sure." Mara approached her travelling bag, making sure she had everything.

The witch watched her. "And what are we going to tell the others?"

The huntress stared back at Accalia. "We're not going to tell them anything."

Mara reached into her pocket and pulled out a healing stone. She used it to restore herself.

Accalia gave her a firm look. "Mara…"

"If they find out, I'll never hear the end of it!" Mara exclaimed. "They could try to remove him, undoing all of my efforts."

The witch's face softened. "Look, we don't know what containing him within your body will do to you or the soul of Aazalith."

"I'm fine," Mara claimed. A small smile appeared on her face. "I haven't felt this much better in months. Sealing Karl away brings more peace to my mind." She looked at the witch with pleading eyes. "So, please," the huntress begged, "don't tell them."

"Fine, I won't tell the others." The witch turned around. "But I must warn you—trapping a demon within your body would be most unwise. He could grow more powerful using Aazalith's soul, which is why we must leave today. The sooner we remove that soul from you, the better off you'll be."

Accalia walked out of the room. "Come, they're waiting for us."

Mara nodded as she followed after Accalia. Before leaving, the huntress looked back at the room once more. The events of last night remained in her mind.

* * *

Mara followed Accalia to the port, where the other two sages were waiting.

"Ah, there they are," Accalia spoke as she walked ahead.

The huntress watched as the witch approached Milo and Nikolai. Mara's eyes drifted to the large ship. The huntress reckoned she would become the first Ardanian to step foot on Thoron since her friend, Allen. If only he and James were here to see her leave. Looking away from the ship, Mara saw Accalia speaking to Milo and Nikolai. The other two sages gazed at the huntress with dread. Mara grew suspicious. Did Accalia reveal what happened last night?

As Mara drew near, Milo was the first to approach her.

"Accalia has told us what happened last night," the elven mage began.

Mara frowned. "Did she?"

Milo held his hands behind his back. "Yes," he said. "To think that depraved man would force himself upon you. And he never helped you when you got injured."

The huntress sighed in relief. The other events of last night remained a secret.

"No, he never did," Mara said. "He just left me there. I hope I never have to see him again."

Nikolai cleared his throat. "Well, without any further delay…"

"Of course," Milo spoke. "Let us board this ship. The sooner we arrive in Thoron, the better."

With that, everyone boarded the vessel. Milo and Nikolai were the first to get on. Mara followed after Accalia. The witch slowed down and looked back at the huntress.

"Did you think I told them?" Accalia asked.

Mara gave a wry smile underneath her mask. At least the elven mage and the old priest did not sense Karl. Before boarding the ship, the huntress almost forgot one more thing.

Mara turned around and shouted, "Firefly!"

In a green flash of light, Firefly appeared before her. The huntress was relieved to see her steed unharmed. The darkling also drew the sages' attention.

"I will help you with your steed," Milo said.

Mara took the reins and guided Firefly onto the ship. She followed Milo to the lower decks.

"We can place her here," Milo said.

Mara looked at the row of stables. Some other horses were present, though they never seemed to mind Firefly's unusual appearance. The huntress guided her to an empty stall, and the darkling seemed very content.

The mage gazed at Mara. "Now would be the time to say goodbye to Ardana."

"Good idea," Mara agreed.

The ship was already departing by the time she reached the upper deck. Approaching the rails, Mara spotted some people waving goodbye to her.

"So long and good luck!" Talon called. "I hope you write to us!"

Mara was shocked to see the blacksmith waving goodbye. Even Jen and Beatrice came to say goodbye. Lady Lorelei left the Black Smoke Inn to see her off. The huntress also spotted Alkina and some Stone Mages who accompanied her. The shaman waved goodbye. Before Mara responded, she saw Elder Ravenclaw standing next to the shaman. He smiled as he waved farewell. Mara blinked, only to see the former elder vanish. Mara then looked to those who remained and waved goodbye one last time. She moved away from the rail and returned below deck.

* * *

"This will be your room for now," Milo said, guiding Mara to her quarters.

As Mara walked beside him, she spotted Accalia in her room. The witch was cleaning her blade.

Once Milo opened the door, Mara entered and inspected her room. It looked very decent. Once Mara got settled in, she looked back at the elven mage.

"We shall have lunch at noon," he said. "Will you join us?"

Mara nodded.

"Very well," Milo said, holding his hands behind his back. "I will see you then."

Before the elven mage left, he reached into his bag. "Oh, I guess I should return this to you," he said, retrieving Thalia's Stone.

"I already have a few healing stones," said the huntress. "And I doubt there's anything that will kill me at the moment."

He handed it over to her. "As I have said before, it rightfully belongs to you."

Mara accepted the necklace and placed it on. The illusory magic caused the faded markings to disappear. At least the huntress had another alternative.

Milo nodded. "Please do not break it again."

"I'll try not to," Mara responded. "Thanks."

The mage left the huntress alone to inspect her temporary home. Mara began by testing her bed. Not as comfy as the one from the inn, but it was a first for sleeping out on the sea. She got up and began to unpack whatever few items she had.

While placing Nightingale at the side, Mara began to wonder what became of Kratés. The huntress doubted he would remain in Ardana since faking his death. Yet she had her doubts that he would go to Corlin or Loris. Kratés loved Thalia and wanted to be near when she returned. But no one knew when that would happen. It could take years before another reincarnation was born. Another thought had crossed Mara's mind. What if Kratés stowed away on this ship? As far as she was concerned, this was the only vessel heading to Thoron. With Kallikratés fated to fall, more ships would be able to venture out to the eastern land. Though Kratés was determined to be with Thalia once more.

So Mara decided to explore the ship. She left her quarters, thinking of all the possible hiding places. She began at the stables.

Firefly greeted her with snorts and whinnies. She always seemed pleased to see the huntress. Mara approached her and petted the darkling between the ears. While doing this, she glanced around at every corner. There was nary a sign of anyone living here.

The next place she thought of was the crew's quarters. The crew members kept to themselves for the most part. Nothing seemed to be out of the ordinary. Should a stowaway be found here, everyone would know.

The ship had a few vacant rooms. If anyone was to hide away, they could hide in any one of them. Mara checked the empty rooms but found no evidence of anyone living in them. It seemed like Kratés was not on this ship.

The huntress gave up on her search for today. She would have another two weeks of exploring the ship. Returning to her room, Mara soon realized her goal was almost within reach. She was one step closer to removing this curse and one fragment away from completing Thalia's soul. Deep down, Mara did not want to think about her fate.

She might have either a few years left or another three decades. Her fears returned as tears filled her eyes. The huntress went to lay on her bed. She wanted to be alone for the time being.

Chapter Thirty

A Proper Name

Later that night, Mara had difficulty falling asleep. The creaking from the ship was a constant problem, and the churning sea offered no comfort. Mara was not used to travelling, being her first time on a vessel. No one else had any issues due to having more experience with sea travel.

"Mara," a male voice called.

Mara opened her eyes to see someone standing before her bed. The pale moon offered very little light, but she saw the commander's garb.

The huntress shot up to a seated position, stunned to see him standing before her. "Karl!"

Karl stepped into the moonlight to reveal a greyish face. The area around his eyes was black while his lips were dark grey. His eyes burned like hot coals as he smiled wickedly.

"You will pay…" he hissed as black fumes and embers billowed from his body. The demon suddenly lunged at her and grabbed her neck.

"You will pay!" Karl shouted as he began to strangle her.

Awakened by her terrified screams, the huntress shot up to a seated position and looked around. Mara was unnerved by the dream. Soon, she felt a burning sensation around her neck. The huntress found a mirror and approached it. Gazing at her reflection, she removed the choker. The faint blotches returned, but the red mark stretching around her neck left her shaken.

"It can't be," Mara mumbled to herself. She looked at her necklace and noticed the width of the choker. It was the same as the red mark around her neck. "It must be the necklace." The necklace was quite tight. She tried to readjust it to no avail. Mara figured she would need to see Milo about it.

* * *

After getting dressed, Mara headed to the upper deck. The sun rose into the sky. Today was a new day, as this ship brought her closer to Thoron.

"Ah, so you are awake as well?"

Mara looked behind and saw the elven mage approaching her.

She nodded. "Yeah, I was looking for you."

"You were?" Milo questioned as he stood beside her. Then he spotted the red mark on her neck. "Your neck…"

"That's what I wanted to see you about." Mara handed over the necklace. "It's a little tight. I tried readjusting it."

"I see," Milo said, taking the necklace. "I will readjust it for you."

"Thanks," the huntress said. Mara looked over the elven mage's shoulder and spotted Accalia. The witch saw them and began to approach.

"You two are awake as well?" Accalia asked them. As the witch drew closer, she looked at Mara and noticed the red mark around her neck.

The huntress saw the look on the witch's face. "It's the necklace," Mara claimed. "It was a little too tight."

Accalia gave her a skeptical look.

A loud splash drew their attention. Mara was startled, though Milo and Accalia seemed unfazed.

"What was that?" Mara looked over the rail and saw a massive creature breaching the water's surface. Thick bony plates and large dorsal fins covered its back. Shimmering scales of blue and green decorated the body, as well as glowing blue spots. Mara thought it was a dragon, but it had large triangular fins and a very long tail. It looked more like a manta ray. The creature almost rivalled Aazalith in size. It released a low bellowing growl as it swam past them.

The captain yelled, "Brace for impact! We're going against the wake."

After seeing everyone grabbing the rails, Mara followed suit. The whole vessel began to rock and sway upon impact. It was much more violent than anticipated. The huntress feared the ship would sink. Thankfully it passed, but Mara remained curious.

"What was that creature?"

"Sea God Mantos," Milo revealed, "of the Seven Divines."

Mara was stunned, for she got to see a real living divine. She looked back at Mantos.

"So, that's the one who crushed Kallikratés' army?"

Accalia tilted her head to the right. "It's odd to see him this far out. Don't we still have two weeks at sea?"

Milo nodded. "He must have sensed Aazalith's soul." He gazed at Mara.

Mara gave a strange look. "Is that something to worry about?"

"No," Milo replied. "I believe he is elated to see his fellow Divine return after so many years." Then he walked away. "We shall have breakfast in the decks below. Would you like to join us?"

"Sure," Mara said.

Accalia reached for the huntress' arm. "There's something we need to talk about." The witch looked back at the elven mage. "We'll meet you at the decks below."

Once Milo was out of sight, Accalia frowned at Mara. The huntress figured it was about the mark.

"Did your necklace truly cause that mark?" Accalia questioned sharply.

Mara looked away. "Yes, it did."

"Don't lie to me," the witch warned.

The huntress eventually gazed back at Accalia.

"You didn't sleep well last night," Accalia continued.

"Never slept in a ship," Mara admitted.

The witch took a step towards the huntress while folding her arms. "I'm beginning to think it was a mistake letting you cast that spell."

"I had no choice."

Accalia stared at her. "You loved him, didn't you?"

"I did until I learned the truth," Mara answered. "It changed the way I looked at him."

"Yet you still loved him."

Mara looked back at her. "If only you saw the real Karl White. He was nothing like Kratés."

"And he's also a demon," Accalia said flatly.

The huntress gazed out to sea. "Isn't there a way to help him? Maybe the Lunar Sanctum can purify his spirit?"

Accalia gave Mara a solemn look. "His fate was sealed from the very moment Hedera seduced Kratés." She placed a hand on Mara's shoulder. "I'm sorry, but you should consider removing him after lifting your curse."

Mara looked uncertain. "But what about—"

"He could become a parasite," Accalia interrupted. "It's not a way to live. When you lift your curse, you'll at least have many more years to live should you remain as a witch."

"What should I do?"

"We need to remove the divine's soul first," Accalia said. "The purified water should also weaken the demon for the time being."

"Then what?"

"Find a home," said the witch. "You said you're going to live in Thoron. You'll have to learn our customs."

"Can't be that hard," Mara said. "But where will I live?"

"Home is often a place you travel far to find."

The huntress looked back at her. "It'll be my first time owning a house."

"One thing at a time." Then the witch moved away from her. "We've talked long enough. I'm sure the others are waiting for us."

Mara nodded as she followed Accalia to the decks below.

* * *

After a long day, Mara finally retired to her room. She removed her Silver Thorn armour and was ready for bed. Checking herself in the mirror, the huntress could see the red mark fading away. She also saw him in the reflection. Karl sat in the chair next to the bed, giving her his classic scowl. Mara turned around to look at the chair, only to find it empty. She walked by the chair before climbing into bed. The air around it felt as cold as ice. According to the bestiary Jen gave to Mara, cold spots indicated a spectral entity. Speaking of which, she needed to do some work in the bestiary. Several blank pages were for monsters never seen before. Earlier in the day, she had begun her first entry within the bestiary. While grabbing the book, Mara could sense Karl's glare on her. He rose from the chair and walked around the bed. Mara ignored him as she opened the book. Turning the pages, she found the entry she was previously working on. Taking a pen, she continued her work.

"You think you can ignore me?" Karl questioned in a dark tone.

He took two fingers and pressed his nails against her leg. He created two long gashes. Mara flinched in pain, but her accelerated healing made the injury fade. Karl grew angrier.

"How dare you ignore me?" Karl stormed to her left. The demon was ready to attack her again until he spotted the book. He saw the entry and froze. It was an image of himself. His eyes wandered over to the title next to his picture: the Dark One.

Mara lifted her gaze to him. Her eyes remained on the demon, trying to gauge his reaction to his new name.

Karl kept looking at the entry of himself. "How appropriate."

Mara closed the book.

About the Author

Born and raised in Edmonton, Alberta, Canada, Rina S. Mamoon got into writing at the age of fifteen. Her favourite stories include Hans Christian Andersen's *The Snow Queen* and H. Rider Haggard's *She*. A fan of fantasy movies like *The Lord of the Rings*, *The Hobbit*, and *The Mummy*. She's also a lover of video games such as *Demon's Souls*, *Baten Kaitos*, *Bloodborne*, *Dark Souls*, *BioShock*, *The Witcher 3*, and *Fatal Frame*. In addition to writing, she's also a digital artist and a photographer as a side-gig and hobby.

On August 5, 2013, she embarked on a personal project using a first-generation iPod Touch. It was from there *The Dark One* was born. The original story and the first remake, which became *The Lost & Cursed* and *The Cursed Herald*, were written almost exclusively on that device.

www.ingramcontent.com/pod-product-compliance
Lightning Source LLC
Chambersburg PA
CBHW071500170626
46811CB00007B/2658